Stir Until Thoroughly Confused

Heather Wardell

Acknowledgements

My fifth book! It's hard to believe. But I think I'm just getting started.

The cover illustration uses a photo by www.istockphoto.com/LdF, and the wooden spoon picture on the title page was created by www.istockphoto.com/samgrandy.

Thanks to Holly MacLeod and Tanya Sweeney for your quick and kind response to my "what am I going to *call* this book?" email. I appreciate your not rolling your eyes where I could see you.

Holly MacLeod, Tanya Sweeney, and Jess Wilkinson again read and gave feedback on this book in various drafts and I'm so grateful.

I'm running out of ways to thank my incredibly supportive husband, so I'll have to go with what's both a cliché and completely true: I could not do any of what I do without you.

And as always, major thanks to every last person who's read my other books. I love getting feedback from you, and I also love knowing that people are reading and will never give me feedback. That's great too. Either way, happy reading!

Prologue

After everything I've learned and all the ways I've changed over this last year, how can I possibly be here again, trapped between a man and work?

This time is different, though. It is. Charles didn't want me to have a career. Kegan does. But he wants our relationship too, and we've more than proven we simply can't work together *and* be together.

My shaking legs carry me away from Steel and I wonder what will happen when I return tomorrow. I love working here, and I love Magma even more. I've dreamed of being a chef forever, and now that dream's come true twice over.

But I've also found Kegan, of whom I *didn't* dream because I'd never have been able to imagine someone so right for me. Why does he have to be my boss? But if he weren't, would I have fallen for him? Without his amazing work with his restaurants, without his focus and attention and drive, would I have fallen hard enough to consider leaving the kitchens I adore?

After the emotions of last night I knew something had to give, but I didn't expect him to say, "We can't go on like this, Mary. I want you, and I want full control of my restaurants, but I can't have both. I can't decide which I want more, which I'll resent less for making me lose the other. I need you to decide for me, for us."

His words ring in my head and the shock mixed with fury I felt as he spoke tenses my body again. The shock makes sense but I don't know why it made me so angry. I understood. He's lost too many girlfriends to his control issues to risk letting it happen again. He has to leave the decision to me.

But understanding doesn't make deciding any easier.

I need to find something that will, so I call the spa where Tanisha sent me to relax post-Christmas and book myself an overnight visit and a long massage. It's not cheap, and it's a good hour's train ride from

1

Toronto, but I need a quiet and peaceful place to think and I've never felt more peaceful anywhere else.

Except maybe in Kegan's arms after the first time we made love.

I take a deep shuddering breath and make myself push the memories away. I have to be strong, stand on my own two feet, and choose: stay as the chef of Kegan's two restaurants and end our relationship, or stay with him and try to find a job that's even close to as perfect for me.

I know for many women there'd be no question: career comes first. And a huge part of me *wants* to make that choice. But I also know Kegan himself has been amazingly good for me and I don't want to lose him either.

I turn off my phone so I won't have to talk to anyone. I need to listen to myself. After a quick stop at home for overnight gear, I take a taxi to the train station and am soon on my way.

I don't get any closer to resolving my dilemma on the train, and once I've checked into the spa and am resting in my room before heading down for a late lunch I wonder if replaying everything that's happened between Kegan and me from the day we met will help. It might, but it'll hurt too.

But I need to find the answer for us, so I give in, close my eyes, and relive the last four months of my life.

Chapter One

My hands shook so hard I could barely open the front door of the restaurant I'd seen praised in so many reviews. My potential new boss, the rising star of Toronto's food scene, was a class act. Why would he consider hiring me, especially with how I'd left my last job?

Once I made it inside, the sharp hint of smoke in the air stung my eyes and made me even more uncomfortable. I looked around at the chaos, trying to guess where I should go.

A tall dark-haired man, the classy and good-looking one I'd seen pictured in the reviews, appeared at the back of the dining area and beckoned to me.

Taking a few deep breaths as I went to calm my nerves, I picked my way through the ash and dirt and muddy boot prints marring the gorgeous golden hardwood floor, making sure not to interfere with the people wielding brooms and studying clipboards while also carefully avoiding a vacuum cleaner cord being dragged across the floor.

As I neared the man, the woman lugging the huge industrial-looking vacuum turned it on, creating an incredible racket. The man grimaced and pointed down a hallway, so I followed him past piles of half-burnt dish towels and scorched kitchenware into a glassed-in office, walking carefully on the hallway's warped and lumpy hardwood floor. The water damage back here had clearly been extensive.

He pushed the office door open and held it for me. "I'm Kegan Underwood, by the way," he said loudly over his shoulder. "And you're Mary, I hope."

I stepped past him into the office and waited until he shut the door, dulling the vacuum's roar, before I said, "Right. Mary Ralston." I hoped my voice hadn't sounded weird. It felt weird. I'd been Mary Welland for six years, technically still was. Using my maiden name added yet another twist of confusion and complication to my already tangled emotions. I needed this job so badly, and I was so afraid, and now even my name didn't feel right.

But then Kegan and I shook hands and looked directly at each other for the first time, and everything changed.

His dark blue eyes, bloodshot and full of pain, swept away my doubts and desperation, swept away everything but him. Those poor eyes made it clear he'd been in that smoky air as much as he could since the weekend's fire, like you'd stay, struggling to accept and understand your loss, by the corpse of someone you loved.

The restaurant reviews had shown me how hard he'd worked to make Steel a success, and now it was in pieces and he needed to figure out how to rebuild his career and life. Knowing we had that in common, and being all too aware of how hard it was, made my heart ache for him even before he said, "Sorry you're seeing the place like this. Things used to be a little...cleaner. And quieter."

My throat tightened but I managed to say, "I know. I'm so sorry."

I'd never felt such strong sympathy, and I saw him recognize it. "Thank you. I've never wanted any career but this, and now... Well, it's hard to be on the brink of getting everything you want and then see it fall apart."

I nodded slowly, unable to look away from those tired but so mesmerizing eyes. "Yes, it is."

He studied me, probably wondering what had fallen apart for me, but he didn't ask. Instead, he gestured me to a guest chair, and as we both settled into our seats he said, "I should tell you I still want to open Magma even though Steel obviously needs a lot of attention. I don't like changing my plans, and I think I can make it work. No, I'm sure I can."

He didn't sound sure, but I said, "I'm sure you can too", giving my words all the sincerity I could muster, hoping our wishes would make it so. I *had* wondered whether he'd decide to postpone Magma, which would be disastrous for me, so his statement was a relief.

"I hope you're right. So. What do you have for me? Thanks for using your own kitchen, and for letting me change the rules at the last moment."

The original plan had been for me to cook for him on the spot with ingredients he provided, but since Steel's kitchen was out of commission he'd asked me to bring food instead. I'd actually quite enjoyed the "cook for me" interview I'd done to win my last job, coming up with new and interesting dishes to use an unexpected array of ingredients, but cooking at home was definitely more relaxing. "You're welcome. And you gave me two days' notice, which was great. I was just glad you still wanted to see me."

I opened my insulated bag and pulled out the various containers, then set out plates and cutlery. As I arranged the food on his desk, he said, "I so love people who are organized. You even brought your own dishes."

I looked up and smiled. "What kind of chef would expect you to eat right off the table?"

He smiled back, and my heart skipped a beat. The energy suddenly snapping in his eyes as he focused on moving forward instead of on Steel's condition made him even more attractive. When he wasn't exhausted, those eyes would be truly breathtaking. And the rest of the package wasn't bad either. Tall, dark, and handsome indeed.

Fine, your boss is hot. But he'll never be *your boss if you don't focus.* I made myself look away and finished setting out the food that would make up the better part of my job interview.

Kegan ran his eyes over the dishes. "Nice preparation." He pulled the appetizer plate toward himself. "Tell me about this one."

I started to explain the ingredients I'd used and my reasons for doing so, but he cut in with, "Oh, and don't be worried when I don't eat much. I've interviewed four other chefs today. Hardly any room left." He patted his flat stomach.

"Good to know."

He bit into the minced chicken on toast and chewed thoughtfully as I talked about the ingredients. Once I'd finished I waited as calmly as I could while he took another bite, and couldn't help noticing he wore no wedding ring. Of course, I didn't either, so it didn't necessarily mean anything.

"That's great." He set down the rest of the toast. "It's spicy all right, but it doesn't just burn. The first guy I saw today should have had a fire truck following him around."

Delighted he knew the difference, I said, "There's a big difference between spicy and hot. I like finding ways to give dishes a real kick without..."

"Without requiring emergency services?"

He smiled at me and I returned it. "Exactly."

He moved on to the bean soup, and then to the steak strips I'd laced with lime and garlic and a hint of cinnamon. The accompanying citrus-flavored rice didn't have quite enough kick for him, but he did say it was close, and I redeemed myself with my spinach salad topped with shreds of peppery cheese and a spicy dressing.

As he ate, he asked me casual questions about the food and the ingredients, and he kept his eyes on me while I answered, clearly taking in my appearance as well as my responses.

I knew what he saw: shoulder-length brown hair caught back in a neat braid, neutral pink lip gloss and a touch of mascara with green eye liner to perk up my brown eyes, a simple interview-appropriate navy sweater and black skirt. But what did he *think*? Did I look like, sound like, act like, what he wanted for his restaurant?

I wasn't sure. His image, from the sleek haircut to his elegant dark suit, was of style and class. Even his slightly silvering hair just made him look more distinguished. But I wasn't entirely classless myself, and his reaction to my food gave me hope.

Once he'd tried everything I'd set out I said, "One more," and pulled out the dessert I'd kept in my bag so it wouldn't melt. I'd spent hours since his call working to perfect the cinnamon caramel peaches that topped my homemade chai ice cream, and I held my breath as he dipped his spoon.

He ate what he'd taken, then looked me in the eye and slowly shook his head, a smile growing on his face. "Why the hell are you available? This is amazing."

Relief filled me. I needed this job so badly, and now that I'd met him I wanted to work for him for his own sake too. We so clearly agreed on how spicy food should be made. "Thank you."

The relief didn't last, though; he said, "I'm serious. Why don't you have a job already?"

I'd hoped this wouldn't come up, but I'd known it would. "I was at Aspire, down the street, for about three months. But that ended two weeks ago, and—"

"Why?" Those deep blue eyes caught mine, and held hard.

For a split second I wanted to get up and slink out the door, but I pulled myself upright instead. He might as well know my beliefs up front. No point pretending to be someone I wasn't. Not any more. "I didn't see eye-to-eye with Alan."

Kegan pulled the soup bowl closer and took another spoonful. "I'd overlook a lot of differing opinions for food like this. It has to be more than that."

I looked at him and realized he already knew. I'd listed Aspire on my resume, not wanting to leave out the biggest and highest-quality place I'd ever worked, and no doubt he'd called Alan and knew the truth. So I might as well tell him. "I don't believe in making exactly the same meal over and over. I like to change things up a bit, make sure the patrons can still get what they like but make a few tweaks so they don't get bored. Alan didn't want any surprises. He was worried about his bottom line--"

"Which he has to be, or his restaurant goes under."

Not making this any easier, are you? "True. I think if the food's not catching people's attention your bottom line will suffer anyhow. I knew what I wanted to make and how I wanted to make it, and he did like my food but not the way I modified it. He wanted me to stick exactly to the written menu, even when I offered to update it daily myself."

"Then what happened?"

I looked into his eyes and didn't want to tell him. Having met him, I wanted this job. More, I *needed* it. In the ten months since I'd left Charles and moved to Toronto, I'd had three jobs, two at small diners and then Aspire, interspersed with four months of unemployment during which I lived off the money from selling my car. When I finally landed the job at Aspire I'd thought I'd found my golden goose but it had been a rotten egg instead, and if Kegan didn't hire me I'd soon have to admit my mother was right and I couldn't survive on my own.

I nearly begged Kegan to give me the job but I could already tell he wasn't the type to respond to groveling. Instead, I raised my chin and laid it all on the line, hoping he'd appreciate my honesty. "Then I told him I would never agree with him, and I walked out two seconds before he fired me."

Kegan tipped his head to one side and studied me. "Interesting."

Watching me commit career suicide was interesting? I didn't know what to say.

"Why couldn't you compromise with him? Change up one recipe a month or something?"

I shook my head. "He wouldn't have let me, and it wouldn't have been good enough anyhow. If I get an idea for how to improve a dish, I want to go for it. Otherwise I'll know it's not the best I could do, and I think the patrons deserve the best."

He nodded, then picked up my resume and gave it a quick scan. "Excuse me one second."

Feeling a bit deflated at his lack of response to my honesty, I said, "Of course."

He picked up his cell phone. "Tess, hi, it's Kegan. You and Jen went to Aspire for me, right? I could look up the date, but do you happen to remember it?" He waited for a response, then said, "Thanks. That's what I thought. Got to go. Say hi to Forrest for me."

He set down the phone and smiled at me. "The last time I had Aspire checked out, my friend raved over the food. I was almost afraid she'd never come back to Steel again. You were working there then."

I blushed. "I'm so glad she liked it."

"She has good taste. And you're so right about what patrons deserve. Alan's always been an idiot. He should never have let you go."

My blush became uncomfortable. "Thank you."

"Don't mention it. But *do* mention this: what other dishes do you think would suit Magma?"

I nodded, glad we were moving past my work history. "I know Steel is known for top-quality food, and you want Magma to be the same only spicier."

He nodded, and I said, "I'm not sure how closely you want their menus to match, but I was thinking you could duplicate Steel's menu except with the kick turned way up."

He got up and left the office, calling back, "I was thinking that way too." He returned with a menu and pulled his chair over beside mine. "I do want to redo Steel's menu as well, but for now, here's what we've got. Walk me through it."

He chose various dishes at random, and I came up with ways to spice them up. After a few, he said, "You know your seasonings, don't you? How'd you learn all that?"

"When I was thirteen, my mother had to go back to work because my dad lost his job. I ended up doing the cooking since my brothers couldn't handle it. Our budget was pretty low and using the same base ingredients every day got boring, so I tried out different herbs and spices to make my meals more interesting. Nobody else liked hot food, but they'd eat spicier stuff if it didn't burn. So I learned how to do that."

He nodded and glanced at my resume. "Formal training?"

"Just a one-year college program."

I didn't want to tell him anything else, but as I heard how cold and dead I sounded I knew I'd have to, and sure enough he said, "By choice, or..."

I took a deep breath. "No. I wanted to go to the culinary academy in Ottawa. They did a presentation for my high school graduating class. I hadn't known what I wanted for a career but I decided during their talk to become a chef. I did the college program so I could get kitchen jobs and start saving for my year's tuition for the academy."

"A few thousand bucks, I assume?"

"Try closer to fifty thousand."

Kegan sat back in his chair. "For a year?"

I nodded. "Plus living expenses."

"No wonder you needed to save. So what happened?"

I pressed my lips together, trying to find the right words. "I wanted to go by the time I was thirty, but I got married when I was twenty-eight and we needed money so he could get his business degree, and..." I shrugged.

He frowned. "But after he had the degree? Why didn't you go then?"

Why indeed? That was precisely the question I'd tried, with no success, to get Charles to answer. *Why can't I go now?*

First, he'd said I needed to take care of his aging parents. Once they passed away a few months apart it was my parents that Charles claimed needed my support, although I'd eventually realized he liked having a full-time maid and cook and didn't want that to change.

I'd berated myself daily since I left him for letting him take control of my life and dissuade me from following my dreams, but my whole marriage had been like that story of a frog in steadily warming water: at first it had been comfortable letting someone else guide me, and familiar since my mother had always told me what to do, and by the time I realized I was boiling I'd been in too deep to get out.

I couldn't tell Kegan any of that, so I said, "Money, mostly. But I have a new plan. I'm going to start saving again, and I hope to get to the academy before I turn forty-five." At my current rate of savings I wouldn't get there much before I turned forty-five hundred, but I kept that to myself. I didn't want to discuss it any more, so I made my voice bright and said, "And I have all but one of their cookbooks and I read them all the time for tips and inspiration, so I'm getting at least part of the experience now."

"All but one?"

My voice might have been bright, but apparently I wasn't. "Um, yeah. I don't have the newest one."

"Don't like the topic?"

I could have agreed, but I found myself not wanting to tell this man anything but the truth. "It's only been out a few weeks, and I kind of can't afford it right now. But I have lots of other cookbooks to read, so it's all right. I'll get it some day."

Kegan opened his mouth, then closed it again. He rubbed his forehead, then said, "Good for you."

Before I could speak, although I had no idea what to say in the face of his strange reaction, he frowned. He looked down at my resume, then back up at me, his eyes narrowed. "How old are you?"

Technically an illegal question, but I had a feeling I knew where he was going with it. "Thirty-four."

He picked up my resume again. "I'm thirty-six," he said absently. "So you graduated from high school fifteen years ago or so, right?"

When I admitted this was so, he said, "And got married six years ago. But you have no work history from your marriage until the last ten months. What were you doing?"

"I did cook throughout, for friends' weddings and parties and that sort of thing. But otherwise, I was married."

He looked up. "And that's a full-time job?"

"Not always. But it was for me." I couldn't quite keep the bitterness from my voice.

"Are you still married?"

I shook my head, then qualified it with, "Separated since I moved here in January. We'll be divorced next January."

"So you quit him, and you quit Aspire. Are you a quitter, Mary?"

I heard a chuckle in his voice but I didn't see anything funny. "I quit whatever's holding me back and making my life unbearable. Otherwise, I'll work until I drop."

Kegan blinked twice. "I apologize. Stupid thing to say. I'd have quit Aspire too if I'd been unlucky enough to work for Alan, and your ex-husband doesn't sound much better. I was trying to make a joke but I should know by now I'm no comedian. Can you forgive me?"

As I took a breath to accept his apology his eye twitched and I realized again how exhausted he was. "Of course I forgive you. Have you had any rest since the fire?"

He leaned back in his chair. "As little as I can manage. I need to get Steel running again. I've promoted someone to replace the... idiot chef who let the fire happen in the first place, but the building itself is in bad shape. They haven't told me yet when it'll be ready to open again, but it sounds like weeks. Still, I want to be here in case there's anything I can do."

"Thank you so much for meeting with me with everything else going on."

"The pleasure was all mine. Now, you're my last interview for Magma, so I'll figure out what I'm doing and give you a call tonight. All right?"

I nodded.

"Let me help you pack up the rest—" He broke off. "Did I eat all that?"

I grinned. I'd noticed him picking away at the food while we discussed Steel's menu but I hadn't said a word, not wanting to make him stop. "All except the last bit of the peaches."

He picked up the dessert dish and made short work of the remains. "There," he said, slipping the bowl into my insulated bag. "I do love how everything's got spice and flavor and yet I don't need to drink Lake Ontario to quench the flames."

I pushed myself carefully to my feet and began gathering my containers. My right leg had for some reason been getting sore and tight whenever I sat for too long, and I wanted to give it a chance to recover before I had to walk. "Thank you. I'm so glad."

Once I'd packed up Kegan gestured for me to leave the office ahead of him. On my way out I glanced into an arched doorway across the hall and gasped.

"Yeah. It's messed up."

I stood frozen. "Messed up" didn't come close to describing the kitchen. The stainless steel countertops bore mounds of ash and tangles of burned wires, and the cabinets were blistered from the fire's heat and blackened by soot. The equally blackened ceiling over the stove hung in strips of paint and plaster, except where it had given way completely to reveal charred pipes and wiring dangling between ruined support beams. Even the appliances were scorched, some looking beyond repair, and I had no idea what color the floor was beneath its layer of filth.

My eyes filled with tears and I turned away, unable to bear looking at the devastation another second. Realizing it must be a million times worse for him, I murmured, "I'm so incredibly sorry."

He looked at me, his eyes again flooded with pain, then moved toward the front door.

I followed, wishing I could hug him.

When we were a step or two from the door, he turned to face me. "I have to tell you I really enjoyed this. Your food, obviously, but also talking with you. My favorite interview ever."

Delight bubbled through me, and I looked up into his eyes and yet again told him the truth. "Mine too."

The interview left me so happy I almost didn't mind walking eight long blocks back to my apartment. My insulated bag's handle cut painfully into my fingers after only one block but I had to walk: I couldn't afford a streetcar ride.

I'd been doing all right financially, not getting ahead but not falling too far behind either, until last month. Why my cousin chose to get married in England when she and her groom were from Toronto I didn't know, but my mother had insisted I go since my brothers couldn't make it. I suspected those two weasels had fabricated business trips to give themselves an excuse. Sadly, I hadn't been quick enough on my feet.

Alan had graciously given me ten days off, naturally without pay, and since my job seemed secure I'd been fairly comfortable paying for the flight and hotel and the wildly extravagant wedding present Mom had sent in my name.

But Alan had a friend's son fresh out of culinary school fill in for me and the kid's "whatever you say, oh brilliant leader" attitude had clearly resonated too well with him; our arguments had increased on my return until my frustration spilled over and I quit.

Of course, when I cooled off I'd realized I had nothing but the paycheck Alan had given me minutes before that last blow-up. I had managed to pay November's rent, but if Kegan didn't hire me I'd have to find a job before December or crawl back to my parents. Back to the same town as Charles.

I'd rather eat cat food.

I unlocked my building's rickety front door and climbed the four flights to my apartment. After dropping the bag in the kitchen, I pulled a can from the cupboard. When I popped it open, I wrinkled my nose at the offensively fishy smell, but before I could stick a spoon into the can the scent woke the furry beast on my battered couch and he rushed over to dance around my feet.

"C'mon, Saff." I gently pushed him away. "Let me get a bowl."

I scooped out half the can and stood watching him devour his food. The day I moved in I had seen the big orange cat lurking by the front door, shivering in the snow and terrifyingly skinny, and fallen for him at once. I'd always wanted a cat but Charles hated them. Finding one that day had felt like fate.

I scratched Saffron behind the ears then set to washing my food containers while daydreaming about working for Kegan. As I dried the last one, I heard the knock I'd been expecting and dreading. I checked the peephole then opened the door. "Hey, Brian."

He leaned against the door frame, still a good few inches taller than me even on an angle. "Hey. How'd the interview go?"

Happiness filled me again but I held it back, not wanting to jinx it. "Pretty good, I think."

Saffron, done with his food, came over to let Brian pat him. Bent over the cat, Brian said, "Great. Look, any way I could borrow a twenty?"

I had seventeen dollars in cash and sixty-eight dollars and thirty-seven cents in my bank account. Though every fiber of my being felt guilty, I said, "I really can't. I'm sorry."

"Hell. I have that interview tomorrow and I'm out of gas. I thought maybe, since I took care of Saffron while you were in England..."

I sighed. If he didn't go to his job interview I'd feel terrible. And he *had* been great with Saff. "I can do ten."

He brightened. "That's awesome. Thanks. And I'll come over tomorrow night and tell you about the interview."

I'd almost give up my remaining cash to prevent that. Brian expected me to listen and give him advice, but he'd never once returned the favor. Making a mental note to be out tomorrow night, I pulled the bill from my wallet, careful not to let him see the rest of my money.

He took the cash and tried to give me a hug, which I deflected by pretending I'd stepped on Saffron's tail while moving forward. I couldn't hug Brian. We'd hugged while hanging out together drunk and miserable on Valentine's Day, and it had escalated into something that should never have happened. Unless I wanted another meaningless and unmemorable sexual encounter, I wouldn't hug him again. He hinted frequently about a repeat, but the fact he obviously thought we'd had a great night and didn't realize he'd left me utterly unsatisfied made ignoring those hints pretty easy.

Even if I did want to sleep with him again, I wouldn't have. Charles and I were still married, and hadn't even started the divorce process. Our handful of phone calls and one meeting since I left had made it clear we wouldn't be getting back together, but I still didn't feel right about being with another man. Charles would be livid if he knew; he'd been upset enough I hadn't also been a virgin when we met.

Brian left, clutching my money, and I vowed for at least the tenth time this would be the last time. He owed me easily three hundred dollars, money I could sorely use, money I knew I'd never see again. But he only asked for a little each time so I'd felt I had to give it to him.

"But no more," I told Saffron, trying to sound convincing.

I put away my containers and set to work on the beef stir-fry with ginger and paprika I'd discussed with Kegan. I had the cheapest beef I could find, but once I got the seasoning right I'd know the taste would be even better with good meat.

The flavor was just approaching perfection when my cell phone rang. I glanced at the screen and excitement flooded me at my soon-to-be-boss's name on the call display.

Hours later I still lay on the couch where I'd dropped after ending the phone call, unable to summon the motivation to move.

Of course Kegan could do whatever he wanted with his businesses, but why didn't he decide *before* interviewing me not to open Magma? I wouldn't have had my hopes raised that way, raised then crushed like a grape underfoot.

Now what? I'd have to find a job; I couldn't keep Saffron in cat food without one. But I didn't want to work anywhere that wouldn't further my career. I'd already had one job in Toronto that was nothing more than glorified dish-washing and I didn't want to take another. I *would*, to avoid moving home, but I hated the idea.

Kegan had probably meant to ease the blow by saying, "If you don't have a job in three months, although I'm sure you will, come see me and we'll open Magma." But his words had made my pain even worse. I was three months too early for my dream to come true. I pulled in a deep breath and let it shudder back out. My dream career waited in January for me. Three months. Such a short time. An eternity.

Saffron wandered over and meowed, and I put out a hand to keep him from jumping up. I didn't want to be sat on. He ducked my hand and made it halfway up before I pushed him gently back down. "I said no, buddy. It's not a good time."

Clearly unconcerned, he stalked to the end of the couch, jumped up there, and walked back along between my legs until he could climb onto my stomach.

I shook my head and scratched him behind the ears. "You don't listen, do you? You just keep trying and eventually I give in."

14

My fingers stilled on the now-purring cat as I realized what I'd said. Could that work on Kegan?

He'd clearly been regretful, but he'd also given no sign he'd change his mind. I ran through our conversation in my head anyhow, wondering if there might be a loophole.

"Mary, I hate this, but I can't open Magma right now. I've been agonizing since your interview but I have to face it: the timing's all wrong. I'm truly sorry."

I hadn't been able to say a word, too shocked, so he'd gone on. "If you need me to rave about you to another restaurant, it's done, although I have no doubt you'll be able to find a job on your own with how wonderful your food is."

This had stirred me enough to say, "I won't. None of the top restaurants are hiring right now."

Kegan's turn not to speak and mine to carry on. "You won't consider... I think I'm perfect for Magma, and—"

"You are perfect. No doubt. This isn't about your ability, please don't think that." He'd then said the whole "I'll hire you in three months" bit, apologized again, and ended the call.

He'd have called the other chefs he'd interviewed too. Did he tell them they were perfect for Magma? Suggest they come back in three months? Offer to rave about them? Maybe not.

Probably not. Though I could hear my mother's voice in my head saying, "Don't be so braggy, Mary," I had to be honest with myself. He had definitely liked my food, and I'd felt we saw the restaurant business the same way. I probably had been his top choice.

Could I somehow convince him to open Magma?

If I acted like Saffron, could I work my way into Kegan's lap? His career lap, of course.

15

Chapter Two

I changed my mind about the wisdom of my plan easily a dozen times, but seven in the morning found me sitting on the edge of a concrete flower box outside Steel armed with a notebook, several pens, and my favorite cookbooks and reference manuals. I spent a few minutes planning what I'd say to convince Kegan and then settled into creating new and innovative recipe ideas for Magma. When Kegan showed up, I wanted him to see me hard at work and focused, just like I'd be *when* he hired me.

After I'd made notes for a handful of dishes, I heard a foot scuff against Steel's walkway and I looked up to see Kegan approaching, his face inscrutable.

My heart shifted into a too-high gear and terror wiped my speech from my mind, but I put down my stuff and stood, drawing my shoulders back and trying to approximate Saffron's "you will do what I want, you just don't know it yet" attitude.

He stopped and said neutrally, "Good morning," his eyes searching my face.

"Hello," I managed. Not liking my shaking voice, I took a quick breath and pushed my shoulders back even further. "I'm here to talk to you about Magma."

"Didn't we talk yesterday?"

I held his gaze. I had to be strong. "We did. And I can't accept it."

Kegan's eyebrows went up. "You can't accept *my* decision about *my* business? Not sure that matters."

Panic swept me. "I don't mean it like that. It's just... I need this. Please."

Nice. Groveling. Good job.

"Mary, as I said yesterday, I can't. I'm sorry you wasted a trip down here, but I won't be changing my mind."

He walked past me, toward the restaurant's front door, and I knew all hope would be gone once he went inside. I went after him, words falling from me. "I'm doing this wrong and I'm sorry. But answer me one question."

He took hold of the door handle but didn't turn it.

"Please. One question."

He turned to face me.

Through my relief, I planned what to ask and realized one wouldn't be enough. "Two questions."

The corner of his mouth quirked into a smile but he straightened it out quickly. "Two."

I looked into those deep blue eyes. "Do you *want* to open Magma now?"

"I just told you I can't."

"That's not the question."

He looked to the side, then back at me, and I saw the answer on his face before he spoke. I'd known it before I asked, but I'd wanted him to say it. "The only thing I want more is fixing Steel. So I can't. But yes, I do want to. Very much."

I'd thought we'd connected during my interview, thought he would be honest with me, and I was glad to be right. His words had set an idea growing in my mind, a way I might be able to convince him, but I needed more information first. "Second question."

He waited.

I took a breath but couldn't bring myself to speak. I probably *did* have it wrong. He couldn't have meant it the way I heard it, and asking him would leave me humiliated. I took one step back, still looking at him, then started to turn away.

He started to speak but I turned back before he could get the words out. Humiliation be damned, I couldn't give up until I'd done absolutely everything possible. "You said if I didn't have a job in three months I should call you. You said you'd rave about me. You said you were sorry, and that I'm perfect for Magma."

"I did. None of that is a question."

I raised my chin, took another deep breath, and made myself ask, "Did you say that to everyone you interviewed?"

He studied me, and I struggled to keep my face calm. Then he said, "No. And since you don't have a third question, I'll give you a free answer. I didn't say that to anyone but you, and I meant it."

I shut my eyes, overwhelmed, and couldn't hold back the smile trying to spread over my face. He'd really wanted to hire me. I'd impressed a top restaurateur that much. I opened my eyes again and looked up at him. "Then—"

"Then nothing changes. And while we're at it, I have a question for you. Why don't you find another job for three months?"

"Because it's my dream to work for you."

"You met me yesterday. Short dream."

I shook my head, struggling to find the words to express how I felt. "I want to work at a restaurant that cares about customers, that's passionate about them and won't give them anything less than the best. That's all I've ever wanted. I didn't know I was dreaming about Steel and Magma, and you, but I was."

His eyes softened, and I seized my advantage and laid out my idea. "You want to open Magma, and I want you to. I know how to make this work. I'll spend every day at Magma, make sure it's set up exactly how you want, and you can supervise Steel's repairs. Then you'll have both places running and your dreams will come true. Mine too."

Kegan stood frozen, and I dared to hope. Then he said, "Come back in three months," pulled open the door, and locked it behind himself before disappearing into the darkened restaurant.

I stood staring at the closed door as if I could somehow bring him back out, then sank onto the flower box filled with nothing but dirt and dropped my head into my hands. Tears and hopelessness swirled in me but I held back the first and tried hard to shake off the second. I couldn't give up yet.

Once I was sure I wouldn't cry, I sat up straighter and took deep breaths, looking for a solution. He'd said no, but I knew he'd wanted to say yes. Maybe if I went home and—

As I thought of leaving, even to search for a new strategy, I realized it would be disastrous. If Kegan didn't see me, he wouldn't have to think about me and my offer. If I stayed, though, camped out on his very doorstep, I would prove my sincerity and be a constant reminder that he could open Magma but had chosen not to.

I turned the plan, such as it was, around in my mind. I might well annoy him enough to keep him from hiring me, but I could also end up impressing him with my determination. Since I didn't have any other ideas, I decided to go for it. I would stay at Steel until Kegan hired me.

The hours perched uncomfortably on the narrow flower box should have passed more slowly than they did, but I lost myself in the task of finding interesting possibilities for both restaurants' menus and almost managed to forget where I was and how much it mattered.

At around noon, Kegan walked past me without a word. I watched him go, willing him to turn around and hire me. He didn't, so I took the opportunity to grab a sandwich and tea with my remaining cash at the café two doors down from Steel since he'd gone off in the other direction. I ate the unexpectedly tasty meal on the flower box then got right back to work, not wanting him to catch me slacking off.

I was mentally debating the right ratio of cumin and cinnamon for a chicken recipe when I sensed someone standing nearby watching me. A quick glance, without raising my head from my work, confirmed it was him. Nervousness filled me but I didn't look up. If he wanted my attention, he'd have to talk to me.

He stayed for a few seconds, without a word, then walked away into Steel.

I sat staring at my notes without seeing them, again hoping I was doing the right thing. If he wouldn't speak to me, he'd never hire me.

And he didn't seem inclined to speak. He went out a few times in the afternoon, always passing me in silence, and none of his employees, some clearly construction workers and some probably his regular staff, acknowledged me either whenever they walked by. Their neglect did nothing for my hopes of success.

People began to leave Steel at around five. A bleached-blonde woman, rail-thin and heavily made up, opened the front door as I was taking a brief break from reading the tiny print in my cookbook. Our eyes met, and she pulled her over-lipsticked mouth into a puckered frown and walked away without a word. The short round woman with white hair who left a few minutes later didn't say anything either, but she cleared her throat and when I glanced up she gave me a furtive thumbs-up with her hand at her side. She hurried away before I could respond, but the warm glow of knowing someone supported me made all the difference, let me believe for the first time that I might actually change Kegan's mind.

The glow vanished, though, an hour later when my battered cell phone began to sing, "Ding dong, the witch is dead". As always, I felt guilty for having downloaded that ring tone for my mother, but I'd done it after a particularly annoying call and the flicker of satisfaction it gave me was too enjoyable to resist. I considered not answering, but

I knew from past experience she'd keep calling until I talked to her, so I gave her as cheerful a greeting as I could.

"Mary, don't you think this has gone on long enough?"

I first thought she meant my hours on Kegan's flower box, but of course not. She was still obsessing over something even less likely to end. "No, I don't. I told you last week, and the week before—"

"I saw poor Charles today. He looks exhausted, and he's lost weight. I'm sure he'd forgive you for all this."

Poor Charles. She'd been calling him that since I'd left. Never once had I heard "poor Mary". She'd never even wanted to hear why I'd left him, why I hadn't felt our marriage could be saved. I had tried to tell her but I'd have had better results telling the flower box how to cook crepes. "I don't want him to forgive me. Not that he has anything to forgive me—"

"Nothing to forgive! When you walked out on him and—" She gave a deep and clearly fake sigh. "Well, I didn't call to rehash this with you."

"Good, because I'm not going back to him."

She ignored me. "It's his birthday Thursday, you know, and you should come home to help me with his party."

While I struggled to find a response that didn't include any four-letter words, my heart skipped a beat as Kegan opened the restaurant's front door and stood looking at me. "Mom, I have to go."

He shook his head and held up a hand in a "carry on" gesture. Sweet of him, but I so didn't want to carry on.

My mother did, though. "So you'll be here then. Six o'clock."

I'd probably still be holding my vigil outside Steel. "No, I can't."

"Can't or won't?"

Both. "He doesn't want me there. And even if he does—"

"Mary, he's still your husband. And I know you'll work this out and he'll forgive you."

"If there's any forgiving to be done, it goes the other—"

"Mary Welland, you stop that right now. Charles is a good man and he didn't do anything wrong."

How would she know? "I'm Mary Ralston now, Mom. I really have to go, so—"

"Bring a chocolate cake on Thursday."

"I will not be there on Thursday."

I only got the full sentence out because she'd already hung up.

I put the phone away, realizing too late I should have faked an "Okay, bye, love you" ending to the call so Kegan wouldn't know my mother had hung up on me. With everything he'd heard, though, that probably didn't matter. I took a deep breath, trying to push away the frustration my mother and her "poor Charles" attitude always caused, and turned to him. "Sorry."

His eyes held unexpected sympathy. "No problem. Everything okay?"

I shrugged, too tired to hide the truth. "Everything's typical. Is that the same thing?"

He grimaced. "Parents, eh?"

"Don't get me started."

"Me either."

Silence for a moment, while I wondered what his parents could possibly dislike about his successful life, then he straightened his back and said, "Look. It's not going to work, Mary. You're not going to change my mind."

I didn't answer. Saying "Yes, I will" seemed inappropriate, and admitting I also thought it wouldn't work could hardly help my cause.

He shook his head and walked away, and I began to pack up my books.

"Hey."

I turned toward him.

"I'll be here tomorrow at five-thirty in the morning."

His voice challenged, and I accepted. "See you then."

He shook his head again, with a bit of a smile this time, and left for real.

Chapter Three

When I reached Steel at five-twenty the next morning, Kegan sat in my spot on the flower box. He stood as I approached, his face expressionless, then walked into the restaurant and locked the door behind him.

Trying not to read too much into his total lack of response, when I'd been hoping he'd be impressed I'd arrived so early, I took up my place and set to work, willing myself not to yawn.

As threatened, Brian had come over to talk at me about his job interview, and had stayed until nearly midnight, complaining about everything from the receptionist's disapproving look when he spent 'only a few minutes' on his cell phone in the waiting room to how he thought the courier uniform he'd have to wear should be redesigned to make him look better, moving from one minuscule issue to another without giving me a chance to get a word in.

At eleven I'd tried to discuss my job woes, but he'd been so clearly uninterested I'd given up. I'd finally told him I had to be up early enough times that he deigned to leave, and then I was so annoyed I'd had trouble falling asleep. But I would fight through the fatigue. I had to.

When the construction workers arrived at nine, all but one walked past me without a word. The one, though, stopped and said, "What are you doing out here?"

I looked up, my eyes skimming over filthy jeans and a torn sweatshirt covering an overstuffed belly before they reached his faintly sneering face. "Reading cookbooks."

"Why?"

"Because I like reading them."

"No, why here? And all day yesterday too."

I looked around. "Why not? It's nice enough. Good to get some fresh air."

"It's going to rain later."

Ack, I hoped not. I didn't have an umbrella. "Then I might stop reading them."

He shot a glance at Steel. "Are you trying to work for him? Don't. He's a nightmare."

For this guy, Kegan probably *was* a nightmare. For me... "He's only a nightmare if you sleep on the job."

The guy's face crumpled into confusion, an expression it seemed to wear often, and he took a breath to speak but instead jumped as Kegan opened the door behind him.

"Jimmy, get in here and quit talking to her."

"I just wondered why she was outside."

His whining tone grated on me, and clearly on Kegan too because he said, "You don't need to know. Go work on the kitchen floor."

Jimmy wandered into the restaurant, clearly in no hurry, and Kegan looked at me. "Mary, go home. Seriously. I can't have Steel delayed. Go. Now."

His cold tone and set face made my stomach twist, but I shook my head. "I won't talk to him again, but I'm staying until you accept my proposal."

He shut the door without a word.

I cuddled myself against the crisp fall air and my sick nervousness. If I antagonized him too much, he wouldn't even hire me in January.

But I couldn't wait that long anyhow.

As I pondered, Kegan reappeared. He dropped onto the flower box next to me and said, "Take another job. Mildred's hiring at the café. Three months, and then come back here. Why does it have to be now?"

"I came to Toronto to be a chef. A real one. I don't want to work at a coffee shop. I want this." I gestured to Steel. "I want the big time. I'm ready for it."

"And you'll get it. Just not right now."

I shook my head. "It has to be now."

"Why?"

Anger and fear and frustration tore through me and dragged the truth from my mouth. "Because I'm so close to what I've wanted forever and if I don't get it then leaving everyone I know and coming here was a mistake and I can't handle that!"

His expression changed, moved from brisk impatience to understanding and sympathy, and I thought I had him, but then he stood up and said, "Maybe it *was* a mistake."

Yeah, maybe. But I wouldn't admit that out loud, not even to him.

When I didn't speak, he said again, gently this time, "Mary, go home."

I didn't know whether he meant home as in Toronto or home as in back to my parents, but it didn't matter. My whole life, I'd let people bend me, dissuade me from what I wanted. I wouldn't let it happen even once more. I was finally standing on my own two feet, and those feet weren't leaving Steel until I had a job.

I went back to my cookbook, pretending he wasn't there. I felt him watching me, his eyes burning into my bent head, for several seconds, then he went inside.

Ten minutes later, rain began to fall, cold and hard, and I hurried to get my books safely stored in my plastic bags then sat huddled in my jacket. Unable to work, I had far too much time to think awful thoughts about what I was doing and what I'd do if it failed and how desperately I wanted to get up and go home.

Eventually, when I couldn't sit another second, I decided hot tea might help me keep going. I pushed myself to my feet but nearly fell as my right leg cramped. I stomped my feet to get the blood moving then went to the café.

As I paid for my tea with the twenty dollar bill I'd reluctantly withdrawn from my bank account, nearly a third of the money I had left, the cashier said, "Honey, what *are* you doing out there?"

Unexpected tears filled my eyes. "I don't know. Nothing, from the looks of it."

"All day yesterday, and now today too?" She shook her head, her round age-creased face full of concern. "You're not trying to get Kegan to do something he doesn't want to do, are you? You might as well try to move Steel an inch to the left."

I blinked away my emotions and managed to smile. She obviously knew him well. "Yeah, that might be easier."

She reached out her hand, its black skin turned gray by flour, and patted my arm. "He's a good egg, but good luck cracking the shell to get in there."

I sighed. "I'm starting to see that."

She gave me my change, then stuffed a chocolate croissant into a paper bag and handed me that too, brushing off my protests with, "If you're going to sit in the rain, you should at least have something good to eat."

My throat tightened. "Thank you."

She chuckled. "Just don't give him any until he does what you want. He loves these."

I smiled and headed back to my flower box, feeling comforted by her kindness and by the paper cup's warmth against my hands. I sat, trying to ignore the cold wetness of the concrete seeping into the seat of my jeans, and drank tea and nibbled at the surprisingly delicious croissant for an hour or so.

When Steel's door opened, my heart jumped but it wasn't Kegan. The blonde woman who'd frowned at me yesterday, now clutching an umbrella over her head, stopped in front of me and didn't share her umbrella's shelter. "Kegan says go home."

I raised my eyebrows. "He sent you to say that?"

She shrugged. "More or less."

I wouldn't have expected him to do such a thing. "He's said it himself and it didn't make any difference. Why does he think sending you would work better?"

She didn't bother answering. "I've worked for Kegan since he opened Steel, longer than anyone else here. So listen up. What you're doing is pointless. He'll never hire you. He said as much yesterday when we asked why you were out here."

My stomach twisted at this revelation. He really didn't plan to hire me if he'd told his staff. But she'd probably pass along whatever response I gave, so I made myself smile and say, "We'll see."

She rolled her eyes. "If you think he's going to feel bad because you look so pathetic—"

"I don't think that."

"Well, good, because he won't. He's especially cranky now because of the fire but he's always a hard-ass and you'll never change his mind. He just wants what he wants and right now he wants Steel fixed. That's all that matters to him. He does not want you."

But it wasn't all that mattered. He longed to open Magma, and it seemed this woman—

"What's your name?"

She blinked. "Crystal."

She didn't know how much Kegan wanted Magma to open. I did. I was the doorway to his dreams, and he was the doorway to mine. "Crystal, you can tell him I'm here until he changes his mind."

She stood up, shaking her head. "God, you're just as stubborn as he is."

A tiny bit more, I hoped.

I again lingered at Steel until Kegan left, this time without speaking to me or even turning to look at me, before dragging my sad soggy self home. After a long hot bath I spent the evening reading on the couch with Saffron and trying not to think, then woke the next morning to the sound of rain smacking against my bedroom window.

Marvelous. Another day, another numb butt from sitting on the flower box.

Kegan arrived at five-fifteen, and actually laughed. "How early did you get here?"

"Earlier than you," I said, smiling and trying not to show I was panting. I'd seen him in the café and rushed to take my seat before he finished buying his coffee.

He squatted in front of me, holding his umbrella over us both. "I admire this. I do. But it won't change my decision. I can't open Magma now and that's that."

No, it wasn't. I'd researched him the night before, in the bath trying to get warm with my ancient laptop balanced on the edge of the tub, spent ages reading all about him. "That doesn't go with your reputation."

His eyebrows went up. "Really. What reputation is that?"

"You opened Steel in six weeks. Nobody thought it was possible, or even reasonable, but you did it. And two months later it was already the hottest restaurant in Toronto, and it's stayed that way for two years."

His jaw tightened. "True. But finish the story. What happened next?"

I swallowed. "The kitchen caught fire last weekend."

"Exactly. Do you know why?"

I shook my head.

"Because I wasn't here. My moronic chef showed up drunk, and I didn't know because I was off looking at locations for Magma. The guy spent his whole shift drinking, and then he apparently left a dish towel on a lit burner when he left."

I sat silent, taking this in. Horrible, to be sure. But... "It could still have happened if you were here."

He shook his head sharply. "I'd have known he was drunk, and I always check the place before I leave. If I'd been where I belong, Steel wouldn't have burned."

"So, what, you have to be here every second?"

"Ideally, yes." Before I could protest, he went on. "But I can't. But I *can*, and will, avoid taking on another full-time responsibility. When Steel's back together and running properly, I'll be ready for Magma. But for now, and with a new chef—"

"Crystal?"

He blinked. "How do you know Crystal?"

Ignoring this, I said, "Is she your new chef?"

"No. I promoted someone else. Isaac. How do you know Crystal?"

I sat up straighter. "Nice try. You know how I know her."

He frowned. "I might be able to follow this at six in the evening, but not now. What are you trying to say?"

I said it slowly, almost insultingly. "You sent her out yesterday to tell me to leave."

He leaned back and his eyes searched my face. "Describe her."

"Blonde, skinny, mid-forties, wearing probably half her body weight in makeup."

He nodded. "You did see her. But I didn't tell her to talk to you."

"She said you did."

He looked deep into my eyes. "Mary. Do I give you the impression I have other people do my dirty work for me?"

I had a flash of wishing I'd met him socially instead of at work. The early morning light made his eyes unbelievably blue, and him unbelievably attractive. I pushed that aside, though. He was right. "No, you don't."

"I did not send her to talk to you."

"I believe you." And I did. I'd doubted it at the time, I remembered, had known he wasn't that way. I considered asking if she'd also made up the part about him telling the staff he wouldn't hire me, but was too afraid of the answer.

He shook his head. "Sometimes she acts like *she* owns the place, not me."

"She said she's worked for you longer than anyone."

"True."

"So why isn't she the chef instead of Isaac?"

"For... a variety of reasons, none of which I'll be sharing right now."

Had they maybe been together and now weren't? Lucky bitch. "I see."

We sat in silence for a few moments, then he said, "Anyhow. As I was saying, I *will* get back to Magma. I know how it'll work, how it'll look... it's so real in my mind I can almost touch it. Trust me, I will not be holding back forever. Just for now."

Every time he said he wouldn't go ahead with Magma my spirits dropped a little lower, and after three days of it they'd lodged in the soles of my wet running shoes. My desperation and frustration spoke before I could stop them. "It's too bad you pick now to be a coward."

Fire flashed in his eyes, and he pushed to his feet and went inside without a word.

Brilliant. Why didn't I kick him in the balls while I was at it?

The rain poured down all morning. I couldn't read my cookbooks for fear of ruining them, so I just sat huddled in my jacket and grew wetter and colder and angrier at myself for what I'd said to Kegan. His decision not to open Magma made perfect sense. I hated it, but it did make sense. And even if it didn't, where did I get off criticizing him for being afraid to move forward? How long had I stayed stuck with Charles?

A bit before noon, I couldn't stand sitting and sulking any longer, so I got up and dragged myself to the café.

The cashier from the day before shook her head when she saw me. "You look like a drowned rat, honey."

A woman standing at the counter said, "Mildred! That's no way to talk to the poor girl."

Kegan had mentioned Mildred was hiring. I hadn't realized I'd been talking to her yesterday.

Mildred laughed. "Well, she does. And I think she knows it." She pulled folded dish towels from under the counter and handed them to me. "Go to the bathroom and get dried off, honey. Then come back for your tea."

Alone in the tiny but spotless bathroom, I scrubbed my hair and did my best to smooth it back into a fresh ponytail then squeezed water from my clothes. As my poor chilled body began to warm, I started to shiver, and I found myself crying before I knew it. If a textbook existed on how to piss off a potential boss, I'd have been the prime case study.

Unable to stop and knowing I needed the release, I let myself cry quietly, working on my clothes at the same time. When I calmed down, I was also nearly presentable. I swiped the last of my mascara from my face with my remaining tears, slicked on a bit of pink lip gloss, and headed back out.

The customer at the counter had left, and the only other patrons were engrossed in their laptop computers or newspapers. Mildred smiled at me. "Good girl."

"Thank you." I passed her the wad of wet towels, and to my shock she hung one up on an empty wall hook.

She burst out laughing and pulled it back down. "Just wanted to see your face."

I laughed. I couldn't help it. She was crazy but hilarious.

"Now. Tea?"

"Yes, please."

I sat at an empty table and watched her putting together my tea, exactly how I liked it. "You remembered," I said when she brought it over.

She sat across from me. "It's my business, honey. It impresses people when I know their order. Of course, it means I have to be here nearly all the time, but what else have I got to do?"

The older black female version of Kegan. "I suppose."

"Now, I'm old." Over my protest, she said, "Oh, come on. You're not blind, honey. I'm old and boring." She jerked her head toward Steel. "That one, though, is too young, and too cute, to be there all the time. I keep telling him, but he won't listen to me. Maybe he'll listen to you?"

I sighed. "He hasn't yet."

"Well, I think you'd be adorable together, so keep trying."

I blushed. "I'm trying to get him to hire me, not... anything else."

"Ah." She leaned back in her chair. "And he's said no, has he?"

"Many times."

"But you're still there."

She sounded proud of me, which made me smile despite everything. "I really want to work for him."

"If there's one thing I know, he'll like your persistence."

I rolled my eyes. "He doesn't seem to so far."

She patted my hand. "Don't give up, honey. We'll change his mind."

I blinked. "We?"

"Two heads are better than one, you know." She grinned at me. "What's your name?"

I couldn't imagine how she'd help me convince Kegan, but I'd take any help I could get at this point. I gave her my name, and she gave me another chocolate croissant and patted me on the head as I slipped back into my wet jacket. "Go get him, Mary."

With the rain still cascading down, I was afraid to wreck my cookbooks, but I could keep a notebook dry by hunching over it, so I did. I wanted to make notes and plans. I was tired of doing nothing.

I'd filled three pages when the weather took a turn for the worse, with a bitter wind whipping the raindrops at me. I put the notebook away before it blew away then clutched myself tightly in a desperate search for warmth while letting my mind wander to a happier place.

Kegan has opened Magma, and I'm the chef. Steel is in perfect shape, and we've created two amazing places together, and I'm blissfully happy and fulfilled, and I never ever even consider stepping outside when it rains.

As if my thoughts had called him up, Kegan left Steel and walked down the sidewalk. He didn't pause, or even slow, as he passed, and I didn't bother trying to speak to him. What else could I say?

After a few minutes, he returned and squatted before me, holding out a cardboard tray with two paper cups on it. "Mildred says you've been buying tea. Thought you might like one."

My eyes filled with tears but I forced them back. The warmth of the cup sinking into my flesh helped calm me. "Thank you."

He leaned a little closer and I caught a hint of deep sexy cologne. "This must be so terrible for you. Really, go home."

I shook my head. "I want to be here when you change your mind."

He leaned away again. "Why would you want to work for a coward?"

I swallowed, again wishing I hadn't said that. Then the perfect response hit me. "I don't want to work for a coward. And I won't be."

Our eyes met, and I saw him recognize what I meant. A faint smile touched his face, then he pushed to his feet. "Enjoy your tea."

I needed all my willpower to get out of bed on Friday. My fourth day camped outside the impregnable fortress trying to convince the unmovable Kegan to change his mind. Might as well have tried to teach Saffron to bark.

Once I'd managed to get myself out from under the covers, I couldn't do anything else. I sat on the edge of the bed, trying to ignore my poor leg which still hurt after the days spent cramped up on the flower box, and struggled to gather the energy to return to Steel.

Had Kegan's gift of tea been a sign? Or was it like how people flip a quarter to a beggar? Either way, I had to go back. If I gave up now, he'd certainly never hire me.

I finally hauled myself to Steel and took up my all-too-familiar spot. I should have been there earlier to make sure I beat Kegan but I'd been lucky to get there at all. Fortunately, he showed up an hour after I did. He walked by, carrying a paper cup from the café, without a word or a glance. If Mildred planned to do anything to help me, she clearly hadn't started yet.

When the construction crew arrived, Jimmy hunkered down in front of me. "What are you doing here? Seriously. Four days? What's the point?"

I'd promised Kegan I wouldn't talk to Jimmy so I didn't speak. Not that I wanted to.

"I want to know." His whiny-kid impression was spot on.

My phone began singing about dead witches. Ordinarily this would have been a perfect way to get out of talking to Jimmy, but getting myself *into* talking to my mother about my absence from Charles' party the night before wasn't much better. I silenced the phone and stared down at my cookbook.

"You either want to work for him or you want to bone him." Jimmy snickered. "Or both."

Anger flared through me but I kept my head down and my mouth shut.

"Probably better to bone him," he went on as if I'd replied. "He might not be as picky in bed as he is as a boss."

"Or I might be worse."

We both jumped, and Kegan said, "Jimmy, get the hell inside and leave her alone."

Jimmy sputtered for a moment then stomped into Steel.

"I didn't talk to him," I said. "I keep my promises." Spotting a potential chance to help myself, I added, "Like I will *when* you hire me."

"I'm sure you do." Kegan looked down at me, his eyes narrowed and his face expressionless, then went back inside.

His blank look confused and worried me, and I couldn't focus on my work for the next hour or so. I'd just managed to get myself into a recipe when a piercing call of "Yoo hoo!" made me look up to see Mildred, wearing a puffy red coat over her apron, trotting up the path.

I stood up as she neared me, and she said, "Listen, honey. This is nuts." She pointed toward Steel, shaking her head. "He's not going to hire you."

I stared at her in surprise. She'd seemed so certain yesterday that he would.

She shook her head again, then her hands swung, both of them, to point toward her café. "Come work for me instead. I need another good cashier, and it's pretty obvious you're reliable." She pointed at me, then herself. "You, come work for me."

What was with the hand gestures? "Mildred, I appreciate it, really. But I know I'm meant to work here and I can't give up on that. The only job I want is with Kegan."

"You've got it."

Shock sending tingly heat through me, I spun around to see him behind me. Did the guy walk on air? "I didn't know you were—"

"Mildred, get your interfering butt back over there." He pointed toward the café. "And leave her—" Both hands pointed at me. "Alone."

She grinned. "Whatever you say, honey. Bye, Mary." She walked away, danced really, leaving Kegan and me by ourselves.

I had no idea what to say. Had I heard him right? Had he offered me the job?

He shook his head. "That woman is a meddler. And you, you're incredible. If I wanted a statue outside Steel, I'd buy one. I assumed after yesterday you wouldn't be back but now I know you're never going to give up. And I do admire that. So I give in, Mary."

Unbelievably, I felt guilt instead of delight. "I didn't mean to pressure you."

He laughed. "The hell you didn't. Were you sitting on that wet concrete for fun? Of course you meant to pressure me."

I winced, but before I could find anything to say he added, "And you were right, I *was* being a coward. But you have to understand that I love Steel. Love it like I assume parents love their kids. The mess it's in right now, it's killing me."

"I understand."

"I know you do. You were nearly crying looking at the kitchen on Monday, right?"

I nodded, surprised I wasn't embarrassed that he'd noticed, and he said, "I have to fix it. I'm taking you up on your offer to handle Magma while I focus on Steel. Don't assume my giving in here means I'm a pushover, though. Jimmy's right, jerk that he is. I am not an easy boss. And I won't be changing for you."

"I don't want you to. That's a huge part of why I want to work for you."

32

He smiled. "Then let's get started. You'll set up Magma's kitchen how you want to, and supervise the renovations to the restaurant itself. I make the decisions there, of course."

"Of course," I echoed.

"But you'll be there to make sure it all happens properly. Once it opens, I'll take over the day-to-day stuff so you can focus on the food."

"Sounds like a plan." It was starting to sink in. I'd won. I had my dream job. Excitement began pulsing through me and I longed to laugh and cry and jump up and down all at once.

"Yup." He smiled at me. "*We* will make this work."

I smiled back. "Absolutely."

He sobered. "I wanted to open Magma, you know, the whole time. I just couldn't let myself risk Steel."

The emotion in his voice made my throat tighten but I got out, "I know."

He looked into my eyes. "Thank you for making it possible."

To my embarrassment I dissolved into tears. "I'm sorry," I managed to gasp out. "I'm just so happy. I've wanted this forever. And I need it. A lot."

He put his hand on my shoulder. "Trust me, I understand proving yourself to family. Now, I have an awkward question so quit crying so I can ask it."

I had to laugh. "That's not much of an incentive."

"True, but it worked." He smiled, and gave my shoulder a squeeze then released it. "Am I right that you could use an advance on your salary?"

I blushed. I could use it desperately, but felt awkward admitting it. "You don't have to do that."

"Listen, Mary, I hate all that crap. If I offer something, it's because I'm willing to do it. You don't have to dance around, just say yes or no."

I looked him in the eye, though I was trembling. "I have forty dollars to my name. So yes, it would help. Thank you."

He smiled. "Good job. Now, let me buy you another tea, and then we can get inside and I'll put you to work."

I smiled back. "Sounds good."

Chapter Four

Sitting across from Kegan in his hardwood-and-glass office, I struggled with renewed doubts and fears. Everything about him and his business screamed class and quality. No, actually, it didn't scream; it spoke in a cool, refined, and elegant tone, clearly aware it didn't need to shout to get attention. Could I really elevate myself and my cooking to such a level? Charles hadn't thought I could and neither had my mother. If the people who knew me better than anyone didn't believe in me...

"You do know what she was doing, right?"

I blinked, forcing away my awful thoughts. "Who?"

He swung both arms to point in the general direction of Mildred's café. "She knows me pretty well. Offering to hire you right off my curb? I saw her and got mad, so I knew I did want you." He shook his head. "She planned the whole thing."

I thought about denying it in case he didn't approve, but I didn't want to start our business relationship on a lie so I nodded. "She asked why I was camped out then said she'd try to help. She's sweet."

"She's insane. But yes, also sweet."

I grinned. "True to both."

"Well, you're mine, not hers. So what did you come up out there?"

I fumbled for my notebook, and he said, "Talk at me while I do this," and pulled a check book and calculator from his desk drawer.

Trying to sound calm and professional instead of like a terrified child, I explained my favorite idea, that we divide the menu by spice so people could find appetizers and entrées and desserts and even drinks all flavored with the same spice, then gave him some suggestions for seasoning combinations.

He nodded and made the occasional comment while also writing a check and pay stub. "I like it," he said when I'd finished.

Relief turned my fingertips tingly and my shoulders released tension I hadn't realized they were holding. He'd hired me under duress and I desperately wanted to make him glad he had. "Thanks."

He passed me the check and the stub.

I skimmed both then took another look. "Thirty-six hundred? This isn't right."

"Too low?"

"You know it's not." I pointed at the stub. "You paid me for four full days this week. Plus two weeks ahead."

"That's what an advance means. Paying ahead."

I shook my head. "You know what I mean. Why on earth did you pay me for this week?"

"You were working."

"I was sitting on your flower box."

"If I'm too stupid to let you work inside, that's my problem, not yours."

I tried to protest again but I couldn't find the words, and then I remembered what he'd said about not liking that sort of thing. I *did* need the money, and I had in fact worked hard, except when the rain became unbearable. I looked up at him. "I buy coffee next time. Once I've deposited this, I mean."

He smiled. "I accept your condition. Oh, and here." He rifled through a desk drawer and gave me several official-looking forms. "Can you fill all this out for tomorrow? My accountant will want to get you in the system right away." He gave me another smile. "If you're sure you want to work for me, that is."

I smiled back, feeling my shoulders relax even more. In the system. Employed. Here. "Oh, I'm pretty sure."

"Good. Me too. For the record, Mildred didn't change a thing. I was finishing up a conversation with the contractor and then I was going to come out and offer you the job. She just made it even more clear I did want to."

Really? "But you looked mad after Jimmy talked to me."

"That was about him, not you. That guy makes me nuts." He smiled. "I can be a beast sometimes. I hope you know what you're getting into."

I gave him a mock frown, then smiled back, so glad I hadn't got my job purely on Mildred's interference. "I'll take my chances."

"Good stuff. So, I still want to open Magma on Valentine's Day."

"Today's November sixth, so..."

He went to his wall calendar and flipped its pages. "We have about fifteen weeks. But Christmas and New Year's are in there so let's say thirteen."

"Lucky thirteen."

He returned to his desk and nodded. "Our big tasks are getting the place set up, and letting people know it exists."

If I'd been in any more over my head, I'd have needed a snorkel. I knew how to cook. That was it. But I had agreed to help with everything and I'd do my best. "Do they just need to know the restaurant's opening, or should they get to try out the kinds of food we'll serve?"

Kegan raised his eyebrows. "Nice. I thought of that too, and was planning to make one of Magma's dishes be a weekly special at Steel until Magma opened." He grimaced.

"Any word on when Steel will reopen?"

"December fifteenth. It'll be tight but Danny the contractor assures me it's doable."

"So five weeks. A little more."

He nodded.

"It's too bad we have to wait that long to show off the Magma dishes. There's no way of partially opening Steel or something, is there?"

He shook his head. "The only option would be to cook elsewhere and then bring the food here, and that's tough logistically."

For sure. Keeping such large quantities of food at the right temperature in transit would be incredibly difficult. I drummed my fingers on the table. "So we need a way to let people try Magma's food but we can't do it here or at Magma." I realized I hadn't confirmed this. "You haven't picked the location for Magma, right?"

"Not yet, but I've got it down to two places, so let's go check them out today."

I nodded, and he picked up his cell phone and arranged with the realtor for us to see both sites at four o'clock.

While he talked, I thought. When he put down the phone, I said, "Is there anywhere else we could do a taste testing for Magma?"

He frowned. "Like where, your kitchen?"

"Only if you don't want more than two people at a time. My place is tiny. I just thought maybe we could use another location."

He leaned back in his chair and looked up at the ceiling. "The other restaurant owners around here are hugely sympathetic over the fire, but

I doubt that'd extend to letting me use their facilities to push my own food."

"No, probably not."

We sat in silence then both said "Banquet hall" at once.

We chuckled, and he said, "That could work. Rent a facility with a kitchen, then have people come for dinner."

"Who would come?"

"All our friends and relatives."

"If you count my cat, I can bring two. If I count."

"No friends?"

Brian? Would I want to bring him and let him say who knows what to Kegan's guests? "Nope." I added, "Not here, anyhow," so he wouldn't think I was pathetic.

"Well, I've got some contacts and I know a few people. We could get a little crowd together, I'm sure."

"So when do you want to do it?"

He started to answer then narrowed his eyes. "How long would it take you to be ready?"

I thought frantically. "If all the ingredients are reasonably available..." I bit my lip.

"A week? Two? One hour?"

"I could have it planned in an hour, but I couldn't possibly have food ready. If the menu wasn't too complicated, I..." I swallowed, knowing whatever I said would be taken as a commitment. "I could be ready in two days. *If* I had staff to help."

"You do. We should go meet them." His eyes had gone far-away. "Two days. Sounds good."

"So, when?"

He stared at me, but I could tell he wasn't seeing me. "Do you have plans any weekend between now and December fifteenth?"

Did hanging out with Saffron count? "None. I'm available whenever you need me."

His eyes focused. "Good stuff. Okay. Let's meet the staff, and then you can go have lunch, and could you bring me back a sandwich and coffee? Mildred knows what I like."

He pulled some money from his wallet and offered it to me.

I took it, since I could barely buy lunch for myself with my own money never mind for him. "You're going to stay here?"

He nodded. "I have some phone calls to make."

I didn't exactly have a relaxing lunch. Mildred was so proud of herself for convincing Kegan to hire me that she wouldn't stop discussing it. She'd have been devastated to learn she'd had nothing to do with it, so I let her enjoy her moment. I did wish she'd kept it to *one* moment, though, instead of coming over whenever she had a second between customers to crow yet again about his expression when he'd come out and how she'd known she'd make him change his mind.

In between her braggings, I ate a delicious sandwich, worked on a possible menu for the Magma tasting, and tried not to worry about Kegan's staff. They were, to be sure, a mixed bag.

Isaac, the newly promoted chef of Steel, had barely been able to look at me. He shouldn't have felt threatened by me, since I was only there for Magma, but he seemed to and I didn't know why. Kegan had suggested we have lunch together on Monday to discuss recipes, and while Isaac had agreed he'd looked even more stressed and sick. But then I'd noticed he also seemed uncomfortable talking to the other staff members, so maybe he had other issues.

I'd felt uncomfortable "meeting" Crystal, afraid she'd make a comment about our previous conversation, but instead she surprised me with a huge hug while saying, "It'll be so nice to have some new energy around here. I'm thrilled it all worked out." She then nudged Kegan. "Glad you came to your senses, boss."

He said calmly, "Me too," then introduced me to at least a dozen staff members. I tried to get all their names, but only managed to remember Dorothy, the short round woman with white hair who'd given me a thumbs-up during my camping out. She smiled at me but looked unimpressed with Crystal's blather, and I didn't blame her.

Kegan walked me to the door after the introductions, and told me we'd need to hire at least a few people for Magma but for now Isaac and I would share the staff. I considered asking if I could choose not to have Crystal, but decided to try to let us start over. Since she'd been around so long, she could be a powerful ally if I let her.

Once I'd finished my sandwich and tea, I had the outline of a menu. I'd centered it around cinnamon, since I knew it better than most other spices, but I had other ideas if Kegan preferred a little more variety.

I'd ordered Kegan's sandwich already, so I picked it up from Mildred, along with a coffee. She congratulated herself again on getting me a job, then said, "And I suppose your sitting out there didn't hurt either."

Smiling at her concession, I returned to Steel to find Kegan's office door closed. Not wanting to interrupt him, I left his lunch on the bench outside his door and wandered around the restaurant, getting a feel for the place and noting how much better it looked already.

Someone jabbed fingers into my sides and I jumped and spun around.

"You changed his mind?"

Did my promise not to speak to Jimmy still apply? I wished it did but suspected it didn't. "Guess so."

He shook his head. "Hard to believe." He leaned closer, his face shifting into an expression he obviously thought was sexy. "What did you promise him?"

I swallowed against my annoyance. "To work hard."

He laughed. "Yeah, right. What did you really—"

"Mary?"

I swung around to see Kegan standing in his office doorway. "This my lunch?"

I nodded, and noticed that Jimmy took a step back from me.

"Could you come talk to me while I eat?"

With great pleasure.

Once we were in his office with the door shut, he said, "He bothering you?"

I shook my head, not wanting to get him involved in something so stupid. "It's fine."

He studied me, then said, "Okay. If you say so."

I knew he wouldn't ask again. I'd have to deal with Jimmy and his innuendos by myself.

Kegan unwrapped his sandwich. "I have news."

I pushed Jimmy from my mind. "Oh?"

"Everything's booked."

I blinked. "Everything? For the tasting?"

"Tastings," he said. "One this weekend, then two each weekend until December twelfth."

I felt my mouth fall open but couldn't gather the strength to close it. *This* weekend?

"You said you needed two days, right? So it's Sunday evening."

My thoughts were running in all directions at once. I had to organize people whose names I couldn't even remember to prepare a menu I hadn't finalized with ingredients from suppliers I didn't know in a kitchen I'd never seen. In two days.

Kegan took a bite from his sandwich and chewed in silence, seemingly unconcerned.

By the time he swallowed, I'd managed to get myself at least slightly under control. Yes, it would be chaotic. But it would also be a great way to prove that I could handle this job. Prove it to him, and to myself. I cleared my throat. "I'm surprised it all came together so fast."

He smiled. "I told you I have contacts."

True, but... "Where will it be?"

He explained, and I sat in awe. In the time I'd spent putting together a menu *outline*, he had booked a newly-opened and desperate-for-business banquet hall for Sunday and then for Friday and Saturday nights, and had also made a deal with a nearby comedy club to send a different comedian to entertain each tasting session's audience. As if that weren't enough, he'd had his web site updated to feature the tastings, with a prominent note that all profits would go to a local domestic violence hotline.

I shook my head. "That's incredible. You're a machine."

He gave me an unexpectedly sad smile. "That's probably true."

Surprised by his reaction, I said, "Why the domestic violence charity?"

He shrugged. "Their office is around the corner and it seems like a good cause."

For sure. I'd been fortunate that Charles had only disapproved of everything I did. If he'd been more aggressive I could have been calling such a hotline myself. "Any more advertising other than the web site?"

"The Toronto Times' food editor is sending someone to interview me in about an hour. Photographer too." He tugged at his shirt collar. "Guess I should have worn a tie today."

I smiled. "You'll just look casual."

"You too."

My smile fell away. "They want to interview me?"

"Chef of what will soon be the hottest restaurant in Toronto? For sure they do."

"I got *rained* on this morning. I can't—"

"Mary. You look fine. Redo that ponytail and you're good to go."

Men. But I didn't have much choice. Not enough time to go home. "I guess we won't be seeing Magma today?"

He snapped his fingers. "I knew I'd forgotten something."

He left a message for the realtor while I pulled out my ponytail elastic and combed my hair with my fingers until it felt a little less wild. Once I had my hair reassembled, I pulled the menu plan from my bag and passed it to Kegan.

He skimmed through it while I sat trying to look nonchalant, then said, "Great stuff. Now, I want every menu to be different."

I blinked. "Each session is entirely different?"

"Yup. That way, people can come more than once and not be bored."

"So I'll need... how many weeks?"

I started counting on my fingers but he was yet again there before me. "Eleven."

"Eleven different full meal plans? No repetition at all, right?"

He smiled. "You can use some of the same ingredients."

Gee, thanks.

Chapter Five

When I stepped out of the bathroom, Kegan held out a glass of water. "Tell me you didn't eat any of the food."

I accepted the glass and took a throat-soothing drink before saying, "I haven't eaten all day. I'm terrified."

"Well, that'll be why you threw up then," he said, his eyes holding more sympathy than the matter-of-fact words would suggest. "You need something to settle your stomach."

Time would help. Another hour or so, after which either this first tasting would be a huge success or I'd be fired. Right now, I wasn't sure which I wanted more. I'd never been so nervous.

"When my sister was pregnant she did well with a piece of dry toast." He held out a paper bag from the bakery down the street from the banquet hall. "Try it."

I took a tentative bite, and to my surprise it did stay down and I did feel better. Once I'd eaten it all, while he distracted me with the tale of Mildred bragging to him about her influence over him, I said, "Thanks, that helped. I think I'll be all right now."

Since Friday, my life had been a whirlwind, whipping me from the newspaper interview where I'd tried to look calm and confident and supremely competent but had felt like a babbling idiot, to the rapid-fire delivery of most of the ingredients I needed and a massive grocery shopping trip for the ones I couldn't get from Kegan's suppliers, to marshaling a staff I'd had to make wear name tags front and back so I wouldn't have to keep saying, "Hey, you. No, not you, him."

But we'd done it.

I hoped.

Every item on the menu contained at least a hint of cinnamon. I'd varied the amounts so people wouldn't be overwhelmed, ending the meal with my cinnamon peaches and the chai ice cream I'd spent most of Saturday figuring out how to make in the vast quantities we needed.

My taste tests said everything met my standards, but the crowd's opinion mattered more.

And it *was* a crowd. Kegan had, in two days, sold two hundred tickets. He seemed casual about it but I was stunned at his networking skills and at how many people he knew.

Not just regular people, either: my fellow chef Isaac was electrified at the news of two particular attendees. "The most recent Hogs captains! Think I can get their autographs?"

Kegan smiled. "They need to leave right afterward, but I'll bring you over when the comedian's done, so sure."

Isaac, grinning, returned to chopping cucumbers with far more energy than he'd had before. He didn't seem to mind following my directions for the tasting; in fact he'd seemed relieved when Kegan told the staff about the event and informed them I'd be in sole command of the kitchen.

"The Hogs are a hockey team," Crystal told me, her tone just missing patronizing.

She'd used that tone on me frequently in the last few days and I'd had pretty much enough of it. "Oh, I know," I said, mimicking her sound, "but thanks for making sure."

Kegan coughed. "I'll let you guys work." He smiled at me and left the kitchen.

I supervised the salad assembly and tried to ignore Crystal, who seemed to have a comment for everything I did. I couldn't, though: her voice grabbed hold of my eardrums and wouldn't let go.

"So *brave* of you to add cinnamon to the croutons, Mary. I've never tried flavored croutons myself, but brash used to make all different kinds."

She'd put such a reverent tone on the word 'brash' that I could almost see it written in the air in fancy Olde-English-style lettering, but I didn't understand the sentence.

The wait staff arrived for the salads, and we didn't have time to talk again until they'd all left, but then I said, hoping that giving Crystal the attention she obviously craved might make her stop treating me like a moron, "What does brash mean?"

She stared at me like I'd asked her how to boil water. "You've never heard of it? It's a restaurant. The best in New York, maybe in North America."

"I see." I made sure not to sound sarcastic when I added, "And you worked there?"

She narrowed her eyes but apparently decided I was sincere because she nodded and smiled. "Such a lovely place. Steel's great, of course, but I've never seen another kitchen like that."

And off she went, extolling the virtues of Brash's kitchen while doing no work at all in her current one. I glanced around, half-listening, to make sure we were still on track and realized the staff was divided by their reaction to her.

Three or four people, the youngest and least experienced ones, were nodding and smiling at a story they'd clearly heard many times before, but the rest, including Isaac and my thumbs-up supporter Dorothy, were working away with their stiff backs to Crystal and her fans.

Not good. Did Kegan know about this? Forming a cohesive team wouldn't be easy.

Crystal seemed to be approaching the end of that particular story, so I let her finish then said, "It does sound great. And you were the chef there?"

Someone gave a cough that sounded more like a stifled laugh, and Crystal spun round looking for the culprit. Her followers looked too, and the others stiffened even more and kept their eyes down on their work.

"What's wrong?" I said to Crystal, willing my voice to sound innocently puzzled.

"You didn't hear that?"

"Hear what? Oh, no, is the fridge acting up again?" It had been making an odd squealy-grunty noise until Kegan had the banquet hall manager call in a repairer, a noise which sounded nothing like a cough, or laugh, but I couldn't think of anything else to say to distract Crystal.

"No." She cast another look around then turned back to me. "I guess it was nothing."

Nobody relaxed; her tone made it clear she knew better.

She sighed and gave me a sad face. "No, I wasn't the chef. It's so hard for a woman to get those sorts of jobs. But I'll make it some day, although it won't be at Brash. After my divorce ten years ago I swore I'd never live in the States again."

It hit me that Crystal might have been expecting to be offered my job. She was being so nice to me, though, that I doubted it. Also, Kegan had implied only Isaac and I had any significant training. "You're trained as a chef, then?"

"Twenty years of experience is my training." She smiled. "Way better than some silly degree or diploma with only a few years' experience."

Kegan walked in then, which was good because I had no idea how to respond. Had she *meant* to say her experience was better than my education and experience? That she was a better chef? I couldn't believe she had; her tone and expression held no malice.

"Five minutes until the main course needs to go out, folks."

I lost interest in Crystal as panic ripped through me. Fighting the urge to flee, I made myself say, "Sure thing. We're ready."

He gave my shoulder a brief squeeze. "Attagirl."

He left, and I stood frozen for a few frantic heart beats before pulling myself together and directing the staff to make the final adjustments to the food.

When I turned around to show two of Crystal's friends how much rice to dish out, I heard Isaac say, his voice almost as shaky as I felt, "I'm not sure that's right, Crystal."

I turned around to see Crystal about to pour the pot of cumin-cinnamon sauce for the chicken into the vat of black beans. "No!" I hurried to her side and took the pot from her. "That's for the chicken. Isaac's right."

To my surprise, Crystal turned on Isaac and snarled, "Have some guts next time if you're going to stop me doing something. I could have dumped it in there and it would have been all your fault." She put on a sneer and mocked him with, "Um, I'm not sure... um..."

Isaac's face paled. I'd never been much good at confrontation, but I couldn't let her talk to him that way. Though I was afraid she'd turn that awful tone on me, I said, "Crystal, come on. We have to work together not blame each other."

She turned apologetic eyes on me and they filled with tears. "I know, I'm just so upset. I nearly messed everything up. I'm sorry, I guess I didn't understand."

In the face of such obvious misery, I had to say, "That's okay. No harm done. The beans get only the lightest shake of... here, let me." My definition of a light shake of cinnamon might not be the same as hers, and we couldn't afford a single screw-up.

Crystal stepped aside, still looking upset, and I got the beans ready for their debut.

Once I'd checked everything, we all worked together to get the chicken and rice and beans arranged on plates and appropriately sauced. It should have been fun, serving my first meal as Kegan's chef, but the near-disaster and Crystal's vicious reaction to the still pale and silent Isaac increased the tension in the kitchen to unbearable levels.

The worst thing? Nobody but me seemed surprised by the tone she'd used. Clearly blowups like that were all too frequent occurrences.

When a table's worth of plates were complete, the servers whisked them away immediately. Once they'd all gone out, Crystal and her crowd began fawning over me and congratulating me on our success, but I just smiled and set them to cleaning up. I couldn't celebrate yet. I was too nervous.

What if Kegan's guests rejected my food?

To put it mildly, they didn't. The wait staff came back with rave reviews of every dish, and when Kegan brought the staff out at the end of the night and introduced me as the chef the crowd's cheers and applause brought tears to my eyes and made me grin. Kegan's obvious pride and pleasure made me grin even more.

I couldn't spend too much time enjoying my triumph, though; Monday morning we set to work on the plans for the coming weekend. I centered Friday's menu around garlic, since it was Friday the thirteenth and Kegan had chosen a comedian who pretended to be a vampire, and Saturday's around sage. I was rapidly going through all my favorite recipes, and would soon have to dig deeper to find new dishes to prepare. The thought of the challenge ahead excited me. Frightened me a little, too, but mostly I relished it.

Isaac and I had lunch together on Monday as Kegan had suggested, sitting in a corner of Steel with sandwiches and sharing our favorite recipes and cookbooks. I'd wondered before whether he didn't want to work with me but one-on-one we had a great time debating changes to the recipes and finding ways we could line up both restaurants' menus, and when Kegan came by to tell me it was almost three o'clock I couldn't believe it. "We've spent half the afternoon at this?"

"And I'd let you spend the rest of it, but we need to leave soon." Kegan had arranged for his interior designer and the contractor for Magma to meet us at the first potential site at three.

I packed up my cookbooks and said to Isaac, "Thanks so much. You've got amazing ideas. We have to do this again."

"I'm free tomorrow if you want."

"You're on."

Kegan smiled at us both then escorted me to his car while I tried not to limp too much. Sitting too long still really bothered my right leg.

Once we were settled in the sleek dark blue sedan, Kegan turned down the stereo, which to my amusement was playing a Meat Loaf song though I'd never have thought he'd be into that sort of music, and pulled onto the road. "I guess it went well with Isaac."

I nodded. "He really knows his food. I think we can make both menus incredible."

"Great. And he takes you seriously, right?"

I glanced over, surprised. Had he heard Crystal that morning telling me, "If you get stuck at all, feel free to ask. I'm sure I can help you through any little difficulties you might have," in her sweet tone that was almost but not quite blatantly offensive? I'd said, "I'll keep that in mind," and then gone off with Isaac. I hadn't seen Kegan around, but I already knew he was stealthy when he wanted to be. "Yes, he does. Seems to, anyhow."

"Good. You more than proved yourself Sunday night."

I felt like he'd wrapped a warm blanket around me. "Thank you."

"What are the plans for this weekend?"

Once I'd walked him through each dish, he said, "That's great. This whole situation isn't at all what I'd planned but I think having the tastings is a good thing for Magma. You get tons of chances to try new dishes, and then we can make adjustments for the real menu."

We? I didn't want Kegan making changes to the dishes themselves, but I doubted he planned to be that involved since he hadn't changed any of them so far. Figuring he meant "we" as in "everyone on staff", I said, "For sure."

We arrived at the first site to find four men waiting for us. Kegan did quick introductions. "Gentlemen, Mary is Magma's chef."

Despite how many times he'd introduced me that way on the weekend, it still gave me a shiver of delight to hear him say it. Magma's chef.

I smiled, and he went on. "Mary, this is my lawyer Max and my real estate agent Kurt. John here is the owner of Franklin Contracting, and Lou's the interior designer who made Steel so gorgeous."

Everyone shook hands with me, and Lou said, "I had help with that, of course," with his eyes firmly fixed on Kegan's face.

To my surprise, Kegan's neck turned red. "Absolutely." He paused. "How is she?"

47

"She's great. A full designer now, specializing in retail. She won't be here."

Kegan's flush moved up onto his ears. "Understandable, since this isn't a retail outlet."

Lou gave a slow nod, then turned to me and smiled. "Well, let's go look at your two possible new homes, shall we?"

I smiled back, trying to hide my confusion. Who was *she* and why did the mere mention of her make Kegan blush?

And why did I care?

I didn't, of course, so I said, "Absolutely," and the five of us headed into the restaurant.

The poor space had been a "Bucky the Bunny" children's restaurant, decorated in sickly sweet pastels like an Easter egg factory had exploded, and it still reeked of cheap French fries. I tried to look past all that, though, to the bare bones, and what I saw I wasn't sure I liked. The restaurant was smaller than Steel, which I knew was Kegan's intention so that Magma would be gloriously intimate. That was all right, but the main dining area had several awkward angles to its walls, the kitchen was barely half the size of Steel's, and the ceilings seemed to be crushing down on me.

Once we'd seen everything, Kegan walked us down the street to his other option. I looked up at the sign proclaiming it "Wong's Oriental Buffet" and wondered why the former owner hadn't specialized in a particular cuisine. When we got inside, I further wondered if the former owner had any idea that "Oriental" encompassed many cuisines and countries. Everything remotely Asian had been all wedged in together: red and gold paint and wallpaper adorned with dragons and origami and vaguely Chinese-looking symbols.

"Mary, you look like how I felt when I first came in here."

I turned to see Kegan smiling at me. "How's that?"

"Confused about what culture this is supposed to be?"

The other men and I laughed and I said, "Completely. What is it?"

Kegan's smile widened. "Asian cuisine as interpreted by one Luigi de Luca."

John said, "An Italian guy?"

"Yup. I guess he ran lots of different restaurants in Italy but when he got here he thought there were too many Italian places already so he decided, and I quote, 'People eat that Chinese food, right? Thought I could sell tons of it.'"

We all laughed, and Lou said, "He'd have done better if it actually *had* been Chinese. I ate here once and the food was terrible."

The color scheme had to go immediately, but I felt at home in the space despite that. As we wandered around I could see myself here, much more than at the first one, cooking in the antiquated but spacious kitchen or coming out to see patrons in the high-ceilinged dining room. Every part of the place felt right.

After we'd finished the tour, Kegan said, "Well?"

John had noted some areas that weren't in great condition but thought they could be repaired fairly easily. "I have to say, though, I think the first place is a better buy."

My heart sank, and sank further when the lawyer agreed and gave a bunch of reasons why. I didn't have any reasons why not. I just knew it didn't feel right to me.

Kegan nodded. "Lou, they clearly both need your help, but what do you think?"

"I can work with either. I do think this one's easier for me, since the dining room is more of a regular shape, but the other has more options for creating private corners and I know you want those."

Another nod, and Kegan turned to face me. His eyes searched my face and I saw them warm. "You like this one, don't you?"

I nodded.

"Why?"

Feeling awkward with all the professionals watching me, I said, "The first one was weirdly shaped and had those low ceilings. This one..." I shook my head. "I'm sorry, I don't know how to say it. It just feels right."

His focus hadn't moved from my face. "I know. I felt the same way when I saw Steel for the first time."

"You did?"

He shot me a wink, which sent an unexpected ripple of energy down my spine, then turned to the men. "Gentlemen, this is Magma. Make it happen, okay? I want to open by Valentine's Day."

Delight flooded me, but even as they gave way with good grace and confirmed that February should be fine I had to say to Kegan, "Are you sure?"

"Are *you* sure?"

I looked around, and my mouth pulled into a grin I couldn't hold back. Not a single doubt in my mind.

"I'll take that as a yes. I was leaning this way anyhow, and if you like it that much then I'm convinced I'm right. *We're* right. Max, I know Luigi's away until Thursday night, but set up a meeting with him for Friday around eleven and do all that law stuff fast so these guys can get Magma whipped into shape, okay?"

Max laughed. "Law stuff. If I didn't know you were a lawyer I wouldn't believe it."

I looked up at Kegan, startled, and he said, "I did all the schooling, with this guy in fact, but never took the bar exam, so legally I'm not a lawyer. But I could be."

"You could also stab yourself in the eye, but you don't want to do that either, right?"

Kegan grinned at Max. "Exactly."

Wondering why Kegan would spend the time and money to go through law school when I knew he'd always wanted to own a restaurant, I realized that Max might present the perfect opportunity for me to handle a certain unpleasant task I'd been putting off for months. "Max? Can I ask you a question?"

"How are you?"

I sat across from Kegan and realized he truly wanted to know. How sweet. "I'm okay, thanks. It was weird, but it had to be done."

Indeed it did. I'd asked Max to recommend a divorce lawyer, then called the Linda he'd suggested on the way back to Steel from the new Magma site and made an appointment for Thursday after lunch. I hadn't wanted to wait even those few days, but it had given me time to email Charles so he'd know I planned to file. I hadn't expected him to mind and sure enough within a few hours he'd sent back, "Go ahead."

I'd spent an hour with Linda, who bore a startling resemblance to Ally McBeal right down to the too-short skirt, and while I hadn't much enjoyed discussing my marriage's demise I'd also found it surprisingly cathartic. Getting it all out in the open made it so clear to me that Charles and I had been doomed from the day I'd given up my dreams of the culinary academy for him. I'd resented him and he'd expected my sacrifices to continue and none of that was a solid foundation for a marriage.

Since we had no children and didn't own any property, and I didn't want spousal support, Linda said there shouldn't be any complications. Charles would be served with the papers shortly and would have thirty days to demand different terms, although I couldn't imagine what terms

50

he'd change: insist on *giving* me money? Then I'd pay Linda to file the final paperwork in January after we'd been separated a year and a few weeks later I'd be divorced.

I'd never wanted to be a divorcée, but it was better than staying married to Charles, and I felt lighter and more relaxed now that the wheels were in motion.

Kegan smiled at me. "I'm glad it wasn't too bad. Now, Lou's sent over a bunch of paint samples for Magma. Want to take a look?"

I pushed the divorce stuff from my mind. "Absolutely." I dragged my chair around to his side of the desk.

He spread out easily fifty paint sample cards, all in deep smoky grays and silvers. "What do you think?"

Running my eyes over them, I said, "They're pretty dark, aren't they?"

He tipped his head from side to side. "Yeah, but I think it'll work with my idea."

On Monday, Kegan had driven me back to Steel, where we'd worked for a few more hours, then surprised me by suggesting we go out for dinner to celebrate Magma's acquisition. We spent most of the meal discussing potential Magma redesigns, and he'd eventually come up with a dormant volcano theme. "Probably. I didn't realize you wanted it to be that dark."

"Close your eyes."

I obeyed, and he said, "Picture the place. Don't imagine all those dragons though."

I giggled. "No worries. They're too ugly."

"Exactly. Okay. So the walls and ceiling and floor are dark and light-absorbing. The lights are pretty low too, so it almost looks smoky. And then around the walls instead of a baseboard we have a single row of tiles that look like they're red-hot metal. Like lava trying to break through. That's the only hint of heat in the place. And your food provides the real heat."

His words drew the picture behind my closed eyelids. I could see it, and I loved it, especially the last part. When he stopped talking, I kept my eyes shut for another few seconds so I could admire the view, then opened them. "Gorgeous."

He grinned. "I'm pretty proud of it, I have to say. Lou thinks it'll work, too, which is saying something. He was leaning toward a Middle Eastern spice market kind of color combo, all reds and ambers, but I like this better."

"Me too. Way less predictable."

He smiled, and we examined and discarded paint samples until his phone rang. "Hey, Carolyn. Really? Damn. I guess we can't play then?"

He listened to the caller, but I felt his eyes on me and looked up from the samples.

To the phone, he said, "Well, maybe I do. Hold on." He covered the phone and said, "Do you swim?"

I nodded. "I was a lifeguard in high school and I swam a few times a week before moving here."

"Are you free tonight?"

"Other than working on some recipes, yes."

He smiled. "Then maybe I can borrow you. My underwater hockey team needs a—"

"Your *what*?"

The smile widened. "That's exactly what I said when I first heard about it. It's fun, though. And we need another woman tonight or we'll have to forfeit the game. Want to play?"

"I might be terrible, though. I haven't gone swimming in a while."

"At the risk of sounding offensive, we just need a female body. Even if you're bad at it."

"Now why would you think that might be offensive?"

He chuckled. "You in or what?"

Hanging out in a swimsuit with my boss had never been high on my list of things to do. But underwater hockey? I *had* to check it out. "Sure. I'll need to go home to get my suit, though." And to shave my legs, which were more than a little overdue. When nobody's seeing them, it's easier to let them go.

"No problem." He uncovered the phone. "Carolyn, I've got us a former lifeguard. My new chef. See you tonight."

He ended the call and said, "Back to the paint."

I laughed. "How can I think about colors when I'm still trying to puzzle out how underwater hockey works?"

"You'll find out tonight. It's pretty simple, really."

I shook my head. "Sounds insane."

"Well, that too."

We worked through the samples until we'd narrowed it down to three, then he said, "How's about you go home for that bathing suit? Towel too. The pool doesn't supply them. We can grab a quick sandwich from Mildred for dinner before we go."

I shook my finger at him. "As long as it's an hour before we swim."

He laughed. "Yes, Miss Lifeguard."

Jimmy caught me at Steel's front door. "I haven't seen you in a while."

No, because I'd been avoiding him. He creeped me out. "I've been busy."

He laughed. "I bet. I still can't imagine what you did to change his mind."

"Nothing." I hitched my bag up onto my shoulder, wishing we weren't alone. "I need to get going."

He shifted slightly, blocking my exit. "Any guy who gets whipped that easily, well, I can't respect him."

"Whipped?" As soon as the word came out of my mouth I realized what he meant, and my face blazed with embarrassment. "He is *not*—"

"Pussy-whipped, I mean." Jimmy made a revolting whip-crack sound and hand gesture. "He doesn't have the balls to stand up to you."

Feeling even worse now that he'd oh-so-helpfully spelled it out, I said, "I have to go."

He laughed. "Not denying it, eh?" He moved closer. "You must be something else in bed. I can't think of anything else that would have changed his mind."

So many disgusting concepts at once. That I'd have sex to get a job, that Kegan would have accepted that deal if I'd offered, that I couldn't get a job on my non-sexual merits, that this troglodyte felt he had the right to talk to me like this...

And that I didn't know how to stop him.

I wanted to slap his face, but decades of "be a good girl" training meant I couldn't do it. I felt my hand twitch at my side but I couldn't bring it up. "I have to go," I said again, hating how weak my voice sounded.

"Not that I blame him," he said, moving in even closer. "I'd bang you too."

Lovely. And still I couldn't do anything.

But when he caught my hip and tried to pull me toward him, I had had enough. I stepped back and said, "Don't touch me."

Not remotely deterred, he moved in again. This time I stepped back two paces. "I mean it."

He laughed. "Afraid your pussy-whipped boss won't like it?"

"*I* don't like it."

My words came out much stronger than either of us seemed to have expected. There was a cool stillness to them, no frantic sound or shrillness, and it stopped us both for a moment. Then I ruined it by adding, "And I said I have to go," in what really had to be called a whine.

I'd lost my momentary control of the situation and Jimmy knew it. He grabbed my wrist and pulled me toward him despite my resistance. "I don't get whipped. I take charge. Chicks like that. You'd like it too. Better than whatever your whipped boss does."

I jerked at my arm but couldn't free myself. "I told you, I have to—"

"Take your hand off her or I'll rip it off."

My stomach twisted with horror and embarrassment and I couldn't look at Kegan.

Jimmy turned toward him, though, no doubt recognizing the barely restrained fury in his voice, and I managed to get my arm free as he said, "I was just—"

"I don't give a damn what you were just. I've talked to you before, about her *and* about the rest of my staff. Get out and don't come back. You no longer work here."

Jimmy laughed, surprising me. "We'll see."

"No, we won't. Go."

"I'll go," he said easily. "For now." As he passed, he leaned toward me but I jerked away. He chuckled and left.

I shut my eyes and longed to disappear. Bad enough that Jimmy had been harassing me, but for Kegan to see it? For my *boss* to have to step in to rescue like that? I'd never felt so humiliated.

"Mary."

I forced myself to look at him, and shivered at the sight. The blue of his eyes seemed electrified, lit up by his anger. I didn't ever want to see that rage directed at me.

"He didn't hurt you, did he?"

I shook my head. "He just wouldn't let me leave."

"You'll never see him again. I won't have him working here. Utter jackass."

I couldn't argue with that assessment.

Kegan took a deep breath and his eyes cooled a fraction. "I'm assuming you didn't want him talking to you like that?"

"God, no. I tried to stop him, but..." I shrugged helplessly. "He wouldn't listen."

He shook his head. "Wouldn't listen to Crystal either. She came in a minute ago and told me she had to slap him last night. Yeah, I'm done with him. No more."

"I'm sorry."

He frowned at me. "Why, because my contractor hired a jackass? Hardly your fault."

No, but it had escalated because I hadn't been able to stop him. I should have slapped him like Crystal did. When I didn't answer, he said, "Go home and get your stuff. I'll go talk to his boss."

I nodded, not sure what to say, and he held the door open for me. I left, and heard him calling, "Danny!" as I went.

Chapter Six

When I came back to Steel with my bathing suit and towel, Kegan seemed off, not angry any more but cool and distracted. I hoped Danny had agreed to get rid of Jimmy, but Kegan didn't volunteer any information and I was afraid to ask. He loosened up a bit when we visited Mildred's, and even smiled when I insisted on buying his dinner, but we barely spoke in his car afterwards.

Carolyn met us at the door to the pool and didn't seem surprised by Kegan's distance.

"Busy day for him, I guess?" She escorted me into the change room and pointed toward an empty locker.

I nodded. I doubted Kegan would want the details spread, so I said, "It's a lot of work coordinating the contractors."

"We can always tell how his day's been. He's quiet when he gets here if it's been rough. After that awful fire I'm surprised he's talking at all."

We politely turned our backs to each other as we got into our bathing suits, and I said, "He's so committed to Steel, and I know he hates how it is right now." A thought struck me. "Now that I think about it, I'm surprised we're here. I guess I'd have expected him to skip the game tonight to get more work done."

"Ask him about his exercise schedule some time." Carolyn moved to the mirror to pull her hair into a ponytail and stuff it under her bathing cap. I didn't have one, but I'd braided my hair to keep it under control, so with any luck I wouldn't leave the pool filter clogged with stray long brown hairs. "He never misses a workout. He's convinced they make him better able to handle the long hours at work."

When we walked into the pool area, I spotted Kegan in dark green swim trunks standing with the rest of the team and realized that regardless of what his workouts did for his restaurant they had certainly done wonders for his physique. I'd known he was lean, but...

56

His stomach was taut and sleekly rippled, his strong chest bore the perfect amount of dark hair, and his arms and legs were muscular without being cartoonish. Sweet mercy, what a man.

Walking everywhere and being too broke to overeat since I'd moved to Toronto had taken away the five extra pounds I'd carried around for ages, but even so I found myself wanting to suck in my stomach.

Carolyn said quietly, "Some guys are born never to wear a shirt, don't you think?"

I laughed, and she grinned at me. I wondered if she'd ever dated Kegan. She seemed to know a lot about him.

When we reached the others, Kegan introduced me to everyone as "Mary, my star new chef". I blushed but smiled at him, and was relieved to see him smile back. He couldn't be too mad at me.

We and the opponents all slipped into the pool and swam about for a few minutes to warm up, and I was glad to see I hadn't lost my swimming form. My right leg did complain a bit as I kicked my way around the pool, but since I hadn't swum for ages it probably wasn't a surprise, and it loosened up in moments. Before the warm-up time was over, Kegan and Carolyn took me to the shallow end to teach me the basics of the game.

Carolyn demonstrated, dropping beneath the surface of the water and patrolling the bottom of the pool like a stingray, while Kegan explained. "She can only touch the puck with her stick, not her other hand. There's no intentional contact, but some people wear a thick rubber glove so they don't get too scratched up and battered by the accidental stuff. I don't bother because it makes it harder to handle the stick. Basically, you'll stay down as long as you can and push the puck toward the other goal."

"Both goals are in the shallow end, right?"

He shook his wet head, his hair turned black by the water and starting to spike up. He looked so different, much looser and more relaxed. "One is shallow, and the other is halfway to the deep end. We switch every ten minutes, and the game lasts for an hour."

"Got it. So how do you move the puck?"

Carolyn surfaced, and Kegan said, "Let's show Mary how you actually play." He settled his swim mask over his eyes and grabbed his stick and a bright orange puck from the deck, then he and Carolyn agreed on who'd be going which way and submerged. I watched, amazed, as they pushed at the puck and struggled to take it away from each other. Carolyn, with a quick swipe, got control and drove the puck far enough away that Kegan couldn't reach it, then they stood up, both laughing as they caught their breath.

"Nice one," Kegan said. "Do it again in the game."

I admired that he didn't seem to mind having been beaten. Charles had always hated it, especially if he happened to lose to a woman. Losing to me was worst of all.

"Your turn," Kegan said to me. "Grab a stick and that spare mask and let's give it a shot."

I sparred with Carolyn first while he watched, then he gave me some suggestions and we took on Carolyn. We couldn't talk, of course, but he used his free hand to point to where I should go, and we would have beaten her if another teammate hadn't joined in to help her out.

Once we had our breath back, Kegan said, "Got it?"

"I think so."

"Good. Let's win this game."

Showered and dressed and delighted with myself post-game, I left the change room to find nearly all the members of both teams clustered by the pool's front door.

"I knew it was supposed to rain but I didn't expect this," someone said as I approached.

I glanced at the street outside the door then stared. Rain slashed down, driven nearly horizontal by a clearly raging wind. I couldn't even see the other side of the road through the downpour, but I could see that the roadway itself was beginning to flood.

"Driving's going to be hell," Carolyn said. "Glad I'm taking the subway."

A few people groaned, and she grinned. To me, she said, "Nice meeting you. Maybe we'll see you again?"

"We'd better," one of the guys said, and the others agreed.

I blushed. The goal I'd scored, right at the end of the game, had broken what was going to be a tied game, and my teammates had been ecstatic. I'd been thrilled too, but had pointed out that I wouldn't have scored without Kegan's pass and Carolyn's defense of me and the puck. They'd brushed that off, both of them, and Kegan had said, "Great goal," without sounding remotely like he wanted or needed to share in the glory.

Carolyn turned to Kegan. "Bring her back next week, okay?"

"Sure, if I manage to get her home safe tonight."

She smiled and headed out with a few other subway-taking players. Before they'd gone three steps they were completely soaked, and one woman's umbrella was caught by the wind and torn from her hand. They persevered, heads bent against the torrent, and were soon gone from our sight.

"Guess I'll give it a try." The man's voice lacked any confidence, but he went out to the parking lot anyhow.

Kegan turned to me. "Mind if we wait a few minutes to see if it settles down?"

"Not at all," I said, eying the storm. "Sounds like a plan."

I had my meal plan notes for the weekend in my work bag, so we sat on a bench near the door and began to discuss them. Several other players waited a minute or two as well, but soon grew bored and decided to take their chances with the weather.

After about ten minutes, Kegan said, "If anything, it's getting worse."

I hadn't wanted to say so, but it looked that way to me too.

He turned to face me. "Where do you live?"

I winced, knowing he wouldn't like the answer. "I'm east of here. About twenty minutes, probably. I can take the subway, though."

"And then walk home from the station in this weather? I couldn't live with myself." He paused, studying me. "Look. I'm about three minutes from here and I'm east too. I will do my best to get you home, but if it's even worse than it looks... I have a guest room. Would you consider staying with me tonight?"

Waking up in the morning with my boss? Awkward. But getting us both killed to avoid a bit of awkwardness didn't seem good either. I nodded, not sure what to say.

He picked up his gym bag and got to his feet. "Well, let's hope you get to go home."

I hoped, and hoped hard, but it didn't work. After we'd gone one block, weaving past car accidents and through huge puddles, the rain pounding the windshield so hard I could barely see out, I gasped, "Please, can we go to your place instead?"

"Okay," he said, nothing more, and I glanced over to see his hands white-knuckled on the wheel.

We didn't speak again until he'd parked in the underground lot of a condo building. Then he turned to me and gave a deep sigh. "That was terrifying."

I nodded fervently. "Great job driving through it. I wouldn't have wanted to do that."

"Neither did I. Do you have a car?"

I shook my head. "Sold it so I could pay rent when I moved here."

He turned in his seat to face me, and I found myself uncomfortably aware of the intimacy of the situation. All he said, though, was, "Yet another sign of how determined you are." A smile touched his face. "There was no point in resisting hiring you, was there? It would have happened eventually."

I smiled back. "Looks like it."

We took the elevator out of the parking garage and up to the thirtieth floor of the building. The storm was impressive enough at ground level; the sight of it from Kegan's huge living room windows left me stunned. Lightning flashed, illuminating the wind-roughened Lake Ontario, and the raindrops pounding the glass were frightening in their violence.

He joined me at the windows and shook his head. "We drove through that."

"*You* did."

He smiled. "You were there too. Come check out my freezer and see what you want for dinner."

Kegan, it turned out, had frozen meals delivered every few weeks. "I eat at Steel a lot, and occasionally at other places around Toronto. But when I'm home, I just want to eat and not think about it."

"I can make something," I suggested, "so we don't use your meals."

He shook his head. "They're here to be eaten."

We sat at his dining room table and talked about the underwater hockey game until the food was ready, then we ate and talked about Magma's menus, continuing to work long after the food was gone. He didn't mention the contractors and I didn't either; he seemed so much more relaxed than before and I didn't want to remind him of the mess with Jimmy.

Eventually he bent his head forward, stretching his neck. "I think I've had enough of this chair. Want to move to the living room? I'll make coffee. Or would you rather tea?"

"Coffee's fine, if that's what you're making."

He raised his head. "I've never seen you drink coffee. Do you like it?"

Our eyes met and I had to say, "Not really."

He smiled and shook his head. "You're too nice for your own good."

That wasn't true. Was it?

Kegan rubbed his forehead. "I'm sorry, I'm tired and I shouldn't have said that. It's none of my business. But tell me, tea or coffee?"

I had trouble making myself say, "Tea, please." I *did* want it, but I knew I'd be putting him out.

He studied me, looking like he had more to say, but just said, "You got it. Go sit in the living room, it's much more comfortable."

I stood, then had to grab the table for support as my right leg rebelled.

"You okay?"

I nodded. "My leg gets sore whenever I first put weight on it. But it's fine after a minute or two."

He frowned. "How long has it been like that?"

I shrugged. "It's on and off."

It wasn't, but I didn't want to talk about it. Weird enough to be in his home without also discussing my strange leg issue.

"Good. Okay, tea in a few minutes."

A small picture frame on the living room coffee table held a child's drawing of a cat, lime green with only three legs, and it reminded me with a start of Saffron, no doubt standing impatiently at his food bowl. I found my cell phone and went into the kitchen. "I have to make a call, okay? About my cat."

He looked up from the coffee maker. "Of course."

I sank into a luxurious armchair and found Brian in my contact list. "Hey, it's Mary. Look, I need a huge favor."

"I'm not going outside. It's a mess."

"No, I need you to go in and feed Saffron."

"You're not coming home?"

I shook my head, then realized of course he couldn't see it. Kegan could, though; he'd arrived in the living room. I looked up and saw him watching me with mild curiosity. Turning my head away, I said, "No. Can't get home in the rain. Could you feed him tonight, and tomorrow morning too?"

"Where are you?"

Urgh. I didn't want to tell. But what else could I do? "My boss's house. He was driving me home, but it was closer to come here. It's too nasty out."

Brian grunted. "Spending the night with your boss?" He was jealous, I could hear it.

"Not like—" I cut myself off, mindful of Kegan's presence. "Look, just feed Saff, okay? I'm sure I'll be able to get home for his dinner tomorrow."

I expected him to push me on the staying-with-Kegan thing, but he didn't. Probably because he had something else on his mind. "I didn't get that job. Found out today. I was hoping we could talk tonight. But I guess tomorrow is soon enough."

Far too soon for me. Annoyed that he assumed I'd be willing to let him unload his issues on me yet again, I said, "I don't know if I'll have time."

"I'll come by around eight," he said, with no apparent understanding that I hadn't actually said I wanted to see him. "Have fun with your boss."

"Bye." I didn't want to dignify that with a response.

I shoved my phone into my jeans pocket, and Kegan said, "Your boyfriend's taking care of the cat?"

"He's my neighbor, not my boyfriend."

He nodded and went to fetch our drinks. He came back with a mug in each hand and said, "None of my neighbors have keys to my place."

I sipped my tea before answering, not wanting to let him see my confusion. Was *he* jealous? It almost sounded like it, but of course he couldn't be. Choosing to respond to his words and not to what I thought I sensed behind them, I said, "He's... a friend." Sort of. "And he took care of Saffron when I went to England, so he still has—"

"When were you in England?"

I blinked, surprised at his sudden intensity. "Last month. My cousin got married."

"Hmm."

Before I could ask why he cared about my travel history, he said, "Okay, let's get our plans finalized for the weekend."

We worked for another hour or so, and at about ten-thirty he said, "Looks good. I have to say, I'm impressed with how quickly you pull these plans together. You're very decisive when it comes to work."

I felt my cheeks grow warm. "Thanks. I try. The recipes I'm using now are all ones I know well. In a few weeks it'll get tougher, but I'm reading a lot of cookbooks and experimenting at home so I'll still have ideas when that happens."

"I'm sure you will. And they'll be great."

He smiled at me, and I smiled back, then he turned to look at the rain still pelting the windows. "You don't know how to build an ark, do you?"

I laughed. "Not so much."

"Then I think you do have to stay here tonight. I don't know about you but I'm beat. It's been a long day."

Now that he mentioned it... "Me too."

"I'm not meeting Luigi and Max to sign the paperwork for Magma until eleven-thirty tomorrow, so we don't have to race out first thing in the morning. Sleep in, you deserve it. Come on and I'll give you a towel and show you where everything is."

I pushed to my feet and walked toward him, trying not to wince at the renewed pain in my leg.

His eyes were intent on my face but he said nothing. Instead, he took me into the guest room and showed me the ensuite bathroom's cupboard, filled with shampoo and soap and unused toothbrushes.

"Why so many?"

He smiled. "My sister's kids stay with me occasionally on weekends and they always forget their stuff. It's easier just to buy extras so I know they'll have what they need here."

I smiled back. "And it comes in handy when staff members stay over."

He laughed. "Which, of course, happens nearly every night. Need anything else?"

I had a bed, a place to hide from the rain, and no way for Brian to come bug me. "I've got everything I need."

Chapter Seven

I woke to the rich scent of fresh coffee. Pity it never tasted as good to me as it smelled. I stretched, easing out the faint stiffness in my muscles from the underwater hockey game, and glanced at the bedside clock. Nine-fifteen. Wonderful.

Knowing Kegan was lying in bed a few rooms away had for a time left me too distracted to sleep, especially when I'd found myself wondering what he was wearing. Nothing, like me since I wanted to let my clothes air out for the next day? Flannel pajamas? Boxers? That thought led me into a "boxers versus briefs" debate with myself, which I won by deciding he seemed like a boxers kind of man. But once I stopped mentally dressing and undressing him and drifted off to sleep I was out for the night.

Awake now, I headed to the bathroom but stopped when I saw a piece of paper on the carpet, one corner still caught under the bedroom door.

Dear Mary,

Feel free to take a shower or bath or whatever you'd like. It's eight o'clock now and I'm going downstairs to the gym. I'll be back and ready to find some breakfast at around ten. If you're hungry before then, get whatever you want from the kitchen.

Good news - the ark is no longer required.

Kegan

I pushed back the bedroom curtains and realized he was right. The roads far below my window were still wet, and the remnants of car accidents lingered, but the sky was a fresh cloudless blue.

After my shower I dressed in of course the same clothes I'd worn the day before. No other options. I braided my damp hair then gave myself a light layer of makeup and headed out to find us something good for breakfast.

As I left the bedroom, the condo's front door opened and Kegan appeared. His hair was wet with sweat, the upper chest and underarms of his light grey t-shirt darkened with it too. His cheeks glowed and he looked vibrantly alive.

And sexier than hell.

He grinned, more relaxed than I'd ever seen him. "Good morning. How'd you sleep?"

"Fine, thanks," I managed through a throat gone dry. I'd thought he was good-looking before, but now? "You?"

"Once I got used to the rain beating down my windows, not bad. Did it bother you?"

No, I was too busy wondering whether you wear boxers to bed. "No, it was fine."

He grinned again. "Good stuff. Let me go shower. I must smell like a foot. And then we can eat."

"Sounds good. See you in a bit."

He started toward his bedroom, then looked back. "Any chance you could make scrambled eggs? I haven't had them for ages."

"Sure."

"See, Nora's kids never make me breakfast. Much nicer having you stay over."

I set to work and willed myself to stop fantasizing about joining him in the shower. That body, naked and wet, entwining with mine... sliding my soapy hands over his slick skin... tumbling out of the shower and into his bed together...

It wasn't until I completely smushed an egg while trying to crack it that I managed to make myself focus on what I was doing instead of what I suddenly wanted to be doing. With my boss. The man who could make all my career dreams come true.

He looked nothing like Charles. Charles and Brian, frankly, looked a lot alike, blond and lanky. That had always been my type. But I'd never met anyone quite like Kegan.

I had the eggs nearly done, and had made some other food to round out the meal, when he reappeared wearing jeans and a black t-shirt, a hint of that post-workout glow still lighting up his face and eyes.

"You made pancakes. You're amazing. And do I smell bacon?"

I nodded. "Found it in the freezer. Hope that's okay."

He pulled a mug from the cupboard. "As long as you didn't add cinnamon to it, sure."

I stared at the pan.

"Oh," he said. "Look, I was—"

"Kidding? Yeah, me too."

We laughed, then he helped me dish out the food and we settled at the table.

My new awareness of him hadn't gone away, and at first I was uncomfortable. He, clearly, didn't see me any differently, and as we chatted about Steel and Magma I managed to push the rest of it aside. I had wanted this career since high school, and now nothing stood in my way but me. I would not sabotage myself.

When we'd finished our leisurely meal, I stood to clear the table and again had to grab its edge to keep myself upright.

He jumped up and caught my arm. "Sit down."

With his support, I eased into my chair, gasping at the pain, even stronger than usual.

"You said it happened occasionally."

I looked into his concerned eyes. "I know, but really it's whenever I've been sitting for too long. I don't know, maybe I hurt it on the flight from England."

"Did you trip and fall, or bump into something?"

I shook my head. "But we were waiting to take off for a good hour or two so it was pretty cramped. I probably gave it a kink or something."

"A kink's lasted a month?" He shook his head. "I need you to do something for me."

I blinked, confused at the change of topic. "Of course."

We hadn't changed topics. "Go to the doctor. Today. I don't think this is right."

"I can't, we have the tasting tonight and—"

"And the plans are set. You've made most of the food already, and all the cookies, right?"

Garlic chocolate chip cookies. Even Kegan had doubted me, but they'd been so good I'd had to make an extra batch after the staff descended on them. "Yes, but..."

The intensity of the concern in his eyes silenced me. "Mary, look. I have a bad feeling about this. Please, get it checked out. I'd come with you but I have that big meeting. But call me when you're done. Okay?"

The pain still hadn't subsided. "Okay."

Chapter Eight

I couldn't call him. I was crying too hard. So I sent a text.

`You were right. I have a blood clot. I have`
`to stay home for two weeks. I'm so sorry.`
`Please don't fire me.`

Writing the last part made me cry even harder, and the taxi driver stared at me via the rear-view mirror. "You okay?"

I nodded. What else could I do? Tell him the walk-in clinic's doctor had sent me to the hospital where I'd had a two-hour wait that left my leg so tender even the ultrasound thing sliding over it caused me pain? Then go on, to say how the technician had casually said she'd get the doctor to check me out? Explain how I'd mentally scolded myself and Kegan for making a fuss over nothing, then how shocked I'd been when the doctor asked, "How did you get in here?" and squeezed his eyes closed in horror when I'd said, bewildered, that I'd walked in?

The doctor's reaction had hit me like a tidal wave: I was truly in danger.

I couldn't tell a taxi driver that. I couldn't tell anyone else either.

Kegan? He was my boss. A smart one, apparently, since he'd somehow known my leg was worse than I thought, but still my boss. I couldn't dump all my personal stuff on him.

Unless there was money or attention in it for Brian, he wouldn't care. Another wave of tears hit: I'd have to listen to his job woes now since I was stuck in the apartment. I'd listen to his problems and he wouldn't give a damn about mine.

I had no friends in Toronto, and all my friends back home had been *our* friends, the wives and girlfriends of Charles's buddies. I'd contacted a few after I left but they'd clearly been uncomfortable with me and I hadn't tried again.

I could call my mother. I could also slam my fingers in the taxi's door. I didn't want to do either. They'd probably be equally helpful.

She would certainly want me to go home. She rarely called me "since I know you're so busy", but I felt guilty when I hadn't talked to her for too long. Our calls always ended the same way: "Why don't you come home? You don't even have to see poor Charles if you don't want to, but come home. It's better for you here." It wasn't. Not even close.

I certainly couldn't call Charles either. He'd either refuse my call entirely or he'd pull the "let Daddy take care of you" act I'd grown to hate over our years together. He'd never thought I was competent either.

Kegan did, though.

Bizarre. The closest thing I had to a friend was the boss I'd met not even two weeks ago.

The taxi pulled up to my building and I swiped the tears from my cheeks and paid the driver, tipping him extra because he'd had to listen to me cry, then walked gingerly up the stairs to my apartment wondering if one of these steps would be the one to jar the clot loose.

The hospital doctor had been clear: if I had shortness of breath or pain in my chest, a piece of the clot might have moved into my lung causing a pulmonary embolism and I'd need to get it checked right away. He'd also said that the heparin shot I'd been given along with the little pills of a drug whose name I'd already forgotten would begin to thin my blood to make that less likely to happen.

Begin. Less likely. The uncertainty didn't make me feel any better. I unlocked my door and collapsed onto the couch, elevating my leg as I'd been told to do whenever I could to stop the blood pooling in it, and burst into tears. I was sobbing so hard I couldn't hear anything else, but Saffron, on the floor next to me studying me with confusion, did, and his meow alerted me. I raised myself enough to see Brian standing nearby.

"I heard you through the door. What's wrong?"

I sat up a bit more. "I..." The tears choked me again.

"Oh, shit. You lost your job?"

Of course he'd think of that first. "No. Not yet, anyhow. I have a blood clot in my leg."

His eyebrows went up, and for the first time I saw actual concern for me in his face. "Are you okay?"

I scrubbed the tears from my face. "I don't know. I have to get shots every day for a week, at the hospital, and then take pills for at least six months. And I had to order these crazy expensive support stockings, and a MedicAlert bracelet, and if I get cut I'll bleed forever." I gave a choked laugh. "Other than that, I guess I'm fine."

He settled to the floor next to me. "I'm sorry. What a mess, huh?"

I nodded, then my cell phone beeped and we both jumped. I pulled it from my pocket.

```
You're too good to fire. Take all the time
you need. I would come see you but I can't
tonight. Can I send a taxi with some things for
you?
```

Relief made my tears rise again. I hadn't really thought he'd fire me, but...

I took a deep breath to calm myself then sent a reply.

```
Of course you can't see me. You have to
handle the tasting. Call me if you have
questions. And you don't have to send anything.
I'm okay.
```

I collapsed back against the couch. "He's not going to fire me."

"Glad to hear it." He paused, then said, "Um, about my job? The one I didn't get?"

I waited.

He at least had the decency to sound awkward. "Can we talk while you rest? I do need it."

Yeah, and I needed someone to tell me I'd be okay, maybe even give me a hug and let me cry. Clearly that someone wasn't going to be him. "Brian, I can't. I'm still freaking out."

"It might take your mind off it."

Maybe. But I still didn't want to. I wavered, though, and was about to give in when my phone rang.

"I wish I could come over. You shouldn't have to be alone."

Urgh. "I'm not."

"Ah," Kegan said. "The neighbor."

"Yeah."

There was a brief pause, then he said, "Okay. But how can I help?"

"How did you know it was probably a clot?"

He sighed. "God, I so wanted to be wrong. Mildred's daughter Tanisha had one back in March after a long flight. Your symptoms matched what Mildred described."

I sighed too. "Well, I'm glad you told me to go. Who knows what would have..."

Tears rose again and a sob escaped me.

"Everything's going to be fine now." Kegan's voice, the certainty and sympathy in it, soothed me. I couldn't help comparing his concern and support to that of Brian, who was playing with his cell phone and didn't look up even when I started crying. "You were smart and you got it checked and you'll be okay."

"I can't work for two weeks," I whispered.

"Damn right you can't. If you show up here I'll send you home."

"But what will you do?"

"We'll follow your plans for tonight and tomorrow, and maybe I'll come see you early next week to talk about the weekend. *If* you think you're ready."

"I will be."

"If," he repeated. "Now, tell me the truth. What can I do to make this easier?"

I sighed. "I have enough food here for me and the cat so that's okay. I have the pills, and all I have to do is go to the hospital once a day until next Thursday for blood tests and heparin shots." He couldn't drive me there daily; I wouldn't even suggest it. "I'll be okay. I might get bored, but otherwise I'll be fine."

"Are you sure?"

It wasn't flippant; he was truly asking and truly ready to help me. Despite it all, I found myself smiling. "I am. Thank you so much."

"Take care, okay? And don't worry about the tastings. Your plans are foolproof. I'll be sending that taxi over in about an hour. Don't bother telling me not to, you know how I feel about that stuff."

Feeling warmed by his insistence on sending the taxi and curious about what he'd send, I thanked him again and we ended the call.

Brian finished whatever he was doing on his phone. "So, ready to talk?"

I so wasn't. I had no doubt he'd been an idiot at that interview, showing off the behavior that had lost him his last two jobs, and now he wanted me to help him pin the blame on everyone but himself. Kegan, on the other hand, had not only taken time during what I knew was an insanely busy day to call me but was buying me things to make my time at home better. Sure, Kegan had more money than Brian would ever see, but he also worked like a dog.

Brian worked more like Saffron.

I pushed myself to my feet and limped to the door. "No. You need to go."

"Mary, please."

"I said no."

But it didn't matter what I said. We went back and forth, and eventually I said, "Fine, but not today. I really need to rest. Come back tomorrow afternoon."

"If you can do it sooner, let me know. Anything I can do for you before I go?"

Since he already had one foot in the hallway, I doubted his sincerity. "Nope."

He bailed out, and I returned to the couch and cuddled Saffron, trying to get my head around what had happened, until someone buzzed up from the lobby.

"Mary? I'm Antonio. Got a delivery for you."

I let him in and he soon appeared at my door, lugging a clearly heavy cardboard box. He set it down on my hall floor and turned to go. "See you later, Mary."

I fumbled for my wallet. "Hang on a second."

He looked back. "Don't worry about it." He gave me a grin. "Kegan tipped me already."

I grinned back. Kegan had style, you had to give him that.

He also, apparently, had listened during our casual chats between work sessions: the box held cookbooks and other books along with CDs and DVDs, all perfectly suiting my interests. Only one cookbook was already in my collection, impressive given the size of said collection, and the music and movies were all new to me.

The last book came gift-wrapped, and I cried again when I removed the paper to reveal the one academy cookbook I didn't own, the one I hadn't been able to afford. I could afford it now, but I hadn't had time to go buy it. He'd remembered my mentioning it at my interview, despite Steel's devastation and his own stress. His sweetness overwhelmed me.

As if all of that weren't enough, he'd tucked two other things inside the book: a gift card to Amazon.ca, with a note saying I could buy anything else I wanted online and have it delivered, and ten taxi vouchers with another note informing me Antonio or one of his drivers would take me to the hospital or anywhere else I needed to go. "Except for work," he wrote. "He knows not to bring you here. Don't make me kick you out."

I laughed through my tears. He'd thought of everything. I'd have the best convalescence possible, thanks to him.

But it didn't quite turn out that way.

At two o'clock on Wednesday I headed downstairs to meet Antonio feeling more excited than a hospital visit deserved. I hadn't spoken with anyone since he'd dropped me off the day before, and I knew he'd have more good stories or jokes for me.

Except he didn't, because he wasn't there.

I stopped like I'd run into a wall and stared.

Kegan grinned. "Long time no see."

Indeed it was, and it had seemed even longer, both when I'd been alone and when I'd had the company I'd been stupid enough to call. "Why are you here?" As the words left my mouth I realized how they might sound so went on with, "Not that I mind, of course."

He opened the car door for me. "I gave Antonio the afternoon off. I wanted to make sure you're all right." As I moved toward the car, he added, "Besides, I need menu ideas from you for Friday and Saturday," and winked at me.

I stumbled. I'd kind of forgotten how attractive he was. His frequent text messages and phone calls to check on me had made sure I remembered his kindness and compassion, but the visual made all the difference. The sparks that wink sent through me made my feet forget how to walk.

He caught my arm to keep me upright, and I said, "Thanks. The curb attacked me, I guess. I have menu plans upstairs."

"You've been working?"

It was that or kill my mother, I thought, and then decided to say it.

He laughed and helped me into the car. "Antonio told me she'd come to visit."

I rolled my eyes. "Like how bubonic plague comes to visit."

He closed the door then went around to his side. We pulled onto the road and he said, "Antonio said you weren't exactly getting along on Monday. Don't take this the wrong way, but after that call I overheard outside Steel I'm surprised you called her."

"Me too." I sighed. "A momentary weakness. I had a rough weekend."

He looked at me then refocused on the road. "I'm sorry to hear that. And you didn't call me because..."

Because I didn't want to drag my boss any further into my personal problems. "It's no big deal. I just wasn't very happy on Saturday." I cleared my throat. "Look, tell me how the tastings went. And how's everything else? Did you get the deal done for the Magma site?"

"Fine, fine, and I did. Why weren't you happy? Other than the obvious, I mean?"

I sighed. "The hospital was crazy busy and I had to wait for ages for my blood test and shot, so my leg hurt even more. Then I was at home all alone. Even the cat was asleep and didn't want to be bothered with me. I read and watched movies, thanks to you, but eventually I just needed to talk to someone. It was either my parents or Charles. My husband. Ex-husband."

Kegan nodded. "Your parents were probably a better choice."

True, but only just. "I thought so too, but my mother came to take care of me, and once she realized the clot wasn't going to kill me she went back to telling me how I've screwed up my life."

It had started out subtle, with suggestions that I'd be more comfortable at home with her and Dad, but had soon escalated to how lonely "poor Charles" was. She insisted he now understood I wanted a career too. "If you give him another chance everything will be different."

She didn't know that I *had* given him another chance.

We'd met in early February to talk about our marriage, and he'd opened the discussion by saying he'd thought about it and I could go to culinary school. Shocked, I'd said, "How can we afford it? The academy costs—", and he'd jumped in with, "Oh, not there. It's way too expensive. But we can find something else. So, will you come home?"

We used *my* savings to pay for *his* expensive education and now he wanted to fob me off with a cheap school? I didn't jump at this offer, needless to say, and in fact I ended our discussion right there. Our only contact since had been my email to say I'd be starting the divorce process. We would never get back together.

I hadn't told my mother any of that, because it was none of her business. But she kept pushing me, and on Monday night, driven to the edge, I'd snapped, "And if I go 'home' and nothing's changed, I'm trapped all over again," and she'd snapped back that Charles hadn't trapped me, I'd trapped myself by thinking I could have everything I wanted in life. When I said, "I can, if he's not around," she stormed out with one final crack at me.

I didn't dump all that on Kegan; instead I said, "She thinks she knows best, and I disagree, and eventually she said, 'You'll outgrow all this and come back to Charles someday, if you're lucky enough that he'll take you back' and stomped off to the train station."

73

Kegan shook his head. "Ah, the old 'you'll regret it and won't be able to go back' ploy. Must be in the parental handbook because mine love it too. Anyhow, I'm sorry she gave you a hard time, especially now. You need to rest and let your leg heal. Is the neighbor any help?"

"Not so much." He'd arrived on Saturday before Mom showed up, ready to talk at me, but instead we'd immediately argued over the box Kegan had sent. Brian insisted he was trying to force me to work, but I knew Kegan knew me well enough already to know I *would* be working and he'd sent me things to make it easier. I'd finally said, "Well, he's not making me listen to all his problems so I prefer him to you at this point," and Brian stalked away.

I'd felt bad, though, and on Monday after Mom left I'd been so desperate to be told I wasn't an evil person for driving both my mom and Brian away that I'd actually picked up the phone to call Charles. I'd only dialed two digits, though, before realizing how much I'd regret making the call. Instead, I'd curled up in a ball, a lopsided ball since I kept my poor leg elevated on the back of the couch, and cried myself to sleep.

We stopped for a red light and Kegan turned to face me. "Well, I'm sorry you've been alone so much. Things have been crazy at work with the arrangements for Magma, but if you don't have plans, I'd love to hang out with you."

A warm fuzzy feeling shimmering through me at this, I said, "*You* don't have other plans?"

He shook his head. "I'm meeting with Lou tomorrow to get him going on Magma's dining room, and when you come back we can talk to him about the kitchen. My only other task is figuring out the weekend's tastings, and I need to hang out with my chef for that."

I smiled, hoping it hid my disappointment. He wanted to "hang out" on a purely business level. I shouldn't have expected anything else, of course, but his support over my clot had briefly made me think of having more with him.

I wouldn't have anything, though, with anyone, until after January sixth, when Charles and I would have been separated a year and we could get divorced and I could move on.

"So, what do you say?"

"Sounds good."

And it was. He waited with me at the hospital for nearly three hours without complaint so I could get my shot then drove me to the medical supply store to pick up my support stockings.

They were an experience: I'd never expected to need lessons to put on tights, but the ankles on the things were barely the size of a baby's wrist so they weren't easy to get on. The technician watched me struggling to pull them up wearing the nubby rubber gloves she'd provided. "Always put them on with the gloves, okay? You can't rip them with a nail or ring that way."

"Got it," I panted. "Will this get any easier?"

She smiled. "Give it a few days and you'll be a pro."

Once I'd finally crammed myself into the stockings, I put my jeans back on and went out to pay the bill, grimacing as six hundred bucks for three pairs of tights hit my credit card.

Kegan didn't speak until we were back in the car. "Need another advance?"

I shook my head. "I'll be okay. Thanks, though, I appreciate it. And the time you're spending with me today, and the gifts, and—"

"Stop, you'll make me blush. I'm glad to help. Oh, and submit the bill to the insurance company right away, okay? They take a month or so to pay out. It'll only be eighty percent, I think, but better than nothing."

Definitely. We rode in silence, as I tried not to fidget at the tights' unfamiliar restrictiveness, then I said, to distract myself, "And everything's okay at Steel?"

"Yup."

I waited, but he didn't elaborate. "The repairs are going all right? And all the food was okay on the weekend? And—"

"Mary. Define 'sick leave' for me."

"Stuck at home worrying?"

He laughed. "No worrying. I don't want you stressing over it."

"I'm more stressed not knowing."

"And I'm telling you everything's under control."

His sincerity calmed me, and I felt even better when he added, "If you're up to it, I *would* like to discuss this weekend with you. But only if you can handle it."

"I can."

"Want me to take you out for dinner?"

Before I could respond, he said what I was thinking. "No, wait, your leg's supposed to be elevated. Plan B. We could get sandwiches from Mildred and then do our menu work at one of our apartments so you can put it up."

"Great plan." Anything that didn't involve me at home alone was a great plan.

Mildred's coffee shop was only minutes away, and she was touchingly delighted to see me and worried about me. "Another blood clot, you poor girls."

"Is your daughter doing all right?"

She nodded. "She's been off the warfarin pills a few months now. Her leg swells a bit if she stands too long but otherwise she's fine." Her eyes brightened. "Do you have an email address, honey? I'll give it to her so she can send you a note."

Not sure why Tanisha would want to do such a thing, I nonetheless wrote my address on the notepad she held out.

"She needs a friend like you, needs to learn how to work to her potential." She laughed. "And maybe you need one like her, to stop you working occasionally."

"Don't stop her working," Kegan said in mock alarm. "I need her."

She frowned at him, and I didn't think it was mock. "Don't push her too hard."

"He's not," I said awkwardly. "I want to work."

She patted my head. "I'm sure you do. Teach Tanisha how to want it, okay?"

I doubted Tanisha would want a friend, if we even ended up being friends, forcing her to work, but I smiled anyhow.

Back in the car, with the sandwiches and the cookies Mildred had insisted we take, Kegan said, "So, my place or yours?"

Mine was a disaster, and Brian showing up would be an even bigger disaster, but my menu notes were there. "How about a quick stop at mine and then yours?"

After we drove the twenty-odd minutes to my apartment, chatting about the past and future tastings, he came upstairs with me, and I found to my surprise and delight that the support stockings made my leg much happier taking its first steps after sitting down for a while.

"They should help, for the price," Kegan said as I unlocked my front door.

"So true. Sorry about the mess."

"I hear your cleaning lady has a blood clot, so no worries."

I smiled at him. "You always know what to say."

He gave a grunt of laughter. "Hardly. I'm famous for saying the wrong thing."

"Not to me."

Those deep blue eyes warmed. "Glad to hear it. Need help getting your things?"

I didn't, so he stayed at the front door, which was good since the hall and kitchen were the least messy. I gathered my notes and my warfarin pills and returned to the door to find him down on one knee patting Saff who was weaving back and forth and rubbing against him.

Kegan looked up at my arrival. "What's his name? He's cute."

"He's Saffron, and he's shedding all over you."

Indeed, Kegan's black dress pants had gone orange and shaggy in spots.

He laughed. "If that's the worst thing that happens to me today I'm doing pretty well."

I shook my head. "You have the best attitude."

His face turned solemn. "I didn't always. I've been working on it."

He took a breath to go on, and panic swept me as Brian's front door opened.

Brian looked at Kegan, on one knee in front of me. "What the hell's this?"

Kegan rose in a smooth motion. "You must be Mary's neighbor. I'm her new boss." He held out his hand.

Brian, clearly feeling out of his depth, shook it, then turned to me. "How're you feeling?"

I shrugged. "Better."

"Good." Obviously wanting to get Kegan on his side, Brian told him, "She was bitchy on the weekend. Watch yourself."

Kegan said coolly, "She's got a life-threatening health condition and apparently nobody to help her. I'd be bitchy too." Without waiting for a response he turned to me. "Ready to go?"

I nodded and he moved forward, making Brian back out of my apartment. I locked the door and followed him to the stairwell, leaving Brian behind.

Halfway down the stairs, Kegan stopped. "Sorry. He's your neighbor and I shouldn't be a jerk to him since it'll come back on you. Want me to go apologize?"

I looked at him and realized he would. He'd go back up there and apologize for being snarky. Brian wouldn't, in a million years, apologize for calling me bitchy. I shook my head. "I think he deserved it."

"Oh, so do I." He smiled at me. "But if it'd make your life easier, I'd apologize."

I smiled back. "Let's just go eat our sandwiches."
He squeezed my arm. "Got it."

Chapter Nine

I didn't quite stay home for the recommended two weeks. My doctor at the walk-in clinic listened to my pleas of needing to get back to work before I went insane and let me return two Mondays after my diagnosis.

I'd been working throughout, of course, but not on my feet as I'd be at Steel and Magma. After our Wednesday hospital visit and menu planning session, Kegan and I had spent time together daily, working on tastings and designing Magma's menu. He'd even asked me for suggestions for Steel's, which I'd provided although I'd been afraid Isaac might take umbrage.

The team had pulled off the four tastings I'd missed, making me both happy and uncomfortable although Kegan insisted they wouldn't have been able to without my behind-the-scenes work.

He also insisted on sending Antonio to bring me to work my first day back so I wouldn't have to negotiate the subway, and though my leg truly felt better I gave in because I was a little afraid myself. The doctor assured me my warfarin levels were good and I shouldn't have any further trouble with the clot, but the MedicAlert bracelet around my wrist constantly reminded me of the risks of my condition.

I took extra care with my makeup and smoothed my hair into an elegant twist for my first day back, feeling the need for a little confidence, and Antonio whistled when I walked up to him. "Nice, Miss Mary."

"If you call me that one more time..."

He laughed. "At least I'm not singing the song any more."

That bloody 'Miss Mary Mack' skipping song, bane of my childhood. "True. But only because I punched you."

He rubbed his arm as if it still hurt. "Trust me, I remember. But I have to say, you do look good. Sleek."

I'd been going for cool and powerful, but I'd take sleek. "Thanks."

When he let me out at Steel, I didn't feel any of those things. I felt nearly as nervous as I had for my interview. My clot had made the team work so much harder. Would they be angry? Unkind? Not in front of Kegan, I wouldn't expect, but secretly? Even if they didn't show it, would they resent me?

In fact, they seemed delighted to have me back and it touched me so much I had to blink back tears. Dorothy squealed and grabbed me in a hug, and even Crystal smiled and said, "I'm so sorry you've been sick. But now that you're back and we don't have to worry about—"

Kegan cut her off. "Don't dump too much on her right away. Can you all go take care of the laundry delivery?"

Crystal didn't seem to mind his interruption; she gave him a simpering smile and said, "Of course, boss. Come on, you slackers."

They followed her away, her followers looking amused and the rest not at all impressed at being called slackers, especially by her.

I turned to Kegan, but before I could ask why he'd silenced Crystal, ask what he was hiding, he pulled open his office door and said, "Come see what I've done."

I saw it at once. A new desk faced his, with a footstool tucked beneath it and shelves mounted on the wall beside it. The rolling chair and small filing cabinet completed the addition.

"Like it? Now you have a place for your cookbooks, and you can sit and raise your leg at least a bit whenever it gets uncomfortable. No need to worry about where you can take a rest. We'll do the same thing at Magma."

Crystal had told me during my first weekend on staff that Kegan considered his office private space so I shouldn't expect to spend much time there. That he'd do this for me, on top of everything else...

Before I quite knew what I was doing I'd thrown my arms around his neck. "Thank you. So much."

"You're welcome." He drew me closer. "I hope it helps."

Sweet mercy, his embrace felt good. Nobody had held me since Brian back in February, and this blew that away. Kegan and I fit together like we'd been created to. The urge to bury my face in his well-muscled chest and hold onto him forever swept me, but instead I squeezed him tighter then made myself let go. "It does. I'll be okay."

He patted my back and stepped away. "I have no doubt that you will. Now. Ready to talk menus for this weekend?"

Since hugging him again, feeling his body against mine and breathing in that gloriously sexy cologne, wasn't on the agenda, I agreed, and he sat at his desk and I sat at mine and we worked through ideas and my notes and plans until lunch time.

"Let me take you to the café. Mildred will be thrilled."

She was, and also happy I'd be having dinner with her daughter that night. "You're welcome to come here."

Tanisha had made it clear we wouldn't, saying in her last email, "We won't get a second to talk if she's there. I love Mom, but she just can't shut her mouth."

I smiled at Mildred. "She has some restaurant she wants to try, but maybe we'll come here for dessert or coffee."

"Sounds good." She turned on Kegan. "Listen, you. Take great care of this lady, you hear me?"

"He doesn't have to—"

"I'll do my best." He smiled at me.

"Don't work her too hard. Especially don't try to—"

"Mildred. We have to go."

She blinked twice. "All right. I know when to shut up."

"You don't," he said with affection. "And we all know it. See you later."

She reached across the counter and cuffed him gently across the top of the head. "Get out of here before I throw you out."

We all laughed and Kegan and I left. Partway along the sidewalk toward Steel, my curiosity got the better of me. "There's something you haven't told me, isn't there?"

"Lots of things."

I stopped. "Like what?"

He turned to face me. "Like what I had for breakfast, and what color my socks are, and—"

I rolled my eyes. "Mildred obviously knows something I don't know, and you shushed Crystal when she started to talk, and Dorothy was so excited to see me, and..." I frowned, realizing who I hadn't seen. "Where's Isaac?"

He grimaced. "I didn't want to do this on your first day back. Thanks a lot, Mildred. Let's go to my office."

I followed him in, nervous. Once we were seated, he said, "I had to fire him."

"Why?"

"He showed up an hour late on Friday, and—"

"Which Friday?"

"The day you were diagnosed. And yes, I fired him and didn't tell you," he said as I took a breath to complain. "But I didn't want you worrying. We did fine without him."

I didn't like the secrecy but I had to admit, if only to myself, that I *would* have worried and probably insisted on coming in and I really had needed to let my leg recover. "So you were short me *and* him? The others must have worked so hard."

He nodded. "I thanked them all, don't worry."

Good, but I made a mental note to thank them myself. The tastings would have been ruined if they hadn't stepped up to the challenge.

"Anyhow, Isaac insisted the schedule said he needed to be in at four. We checked and it didn't, but I let it go. Anyone can make a mistake. But then he was two hours late on Saturday."

"Same excuse?"

He grunted a chuckle. "No, he said I'd texted him to say I didn't need him until five. Even claimed he'd written back and I'd written back to *that*. None of which happened, of course."

"Wow," I breathed. "How did he think he'd get away with it?"

He shrugged. "I let him work because we needed him, but I confronted him afterwards. He was absolutely insistent, even begged me to pull out my phone and check. I got it out of my coat pocket since he wouldn't let it go, and of course there were no messages to or from him. None on his phone either. Then he just stood there and stared at me. I had no choice. A mistake is one thing but he looked me in the eye and lied and I can't accept that."

"I can't believe he'd do that. It's crazy."

"Crystal suggested he was high or drunk. I guess it's possible."

I nodded, then realized something. "Now Steel has no chef."

"That's what Mildred meant. She's afraid I'll try to get you to do both jobs." He gave me a smile. "So. Want to do both jobs? For a much higher salary, of course."

Chef of *two* major restaurants? "I'm honored, but how would it work? And why not hire someone? Or promote someone maybe?"

"Here's how I see it working. You'd revamp Steel's menu, and of course finish designing Magma's. I still need you at Magma monitoring its reno, but you can do menu work there. Magma's going to be a lot smaller than Steel so you probably don't need a sous-chef there but you certainly do at Steel. Even at Magma we'd make sure there's someone good working for you, so you'd be a bit less hands-on but still in charge. And as for hiring someone new..." He shook his head. "I will if

I have to, but this doesn't feel like the right time to bring in a new person. I'd rather have you."

I hadn't even been with him a month. It felt a lot longer though, with all the time we'd spent working together, and apparently it did to him too. I loved that he thought so much of me, but had to say, "You wouldn't rather promote someone?"

He tipped his head to one side. "Would you prefer that?"

"No," I said at once, afraid he'd take back the offer, and he grinned. I grinned too. "I'd love to take them both on. But wouldn't promoting someone be easier?"

He drummed his fingers on the desk then seemed to make a decision. "Here's the thing, and I'm trusting you to keep this to yourself."

"Of course."

"Nobody else is capable of it. Dorothy's the closest, I think, but she doesn't have the vision. She's fabulous when she's told what to do but she couldn't come up with anything when we needed a replacement for one of your dishes because the ingredients weren't available."

I remembered that. Kegan had phoned me looking for a substitute, and I'd changed a few ingredients in one of my favorite recipes and he'd said the patrons loved it. So, not Dorothy. I hated it but made myself say, "Crystal?"

He rubbed a hand across his forehead. "She expects it, I'm sure. She was basically the old chef's second-in-command until Isaac came along. But Dorothy at least tried to come up with something else. Crystal actually suggested canceling the tasting. No, I couldn't trust Crystal at Magma when I'm here. Or the other way around."

But he did trust me. Happiness filled me.

"Plus, I think the staff would be happier with you. I know Crystal annoys them."

I thought back to the environment at that first tasting. "It's more than annoyance, I think. She really gets under their skins, and she was pretty rude to Isaac too."

"So there's another reason, like we needed one, not to put her in charge instead of you."

I wanted to say more, to make him understand exactly how toxic Crystal was, but he'd moved on. "So you'll be in charge of both kitchens, at least until after Valentine's Day when Magma will be open too. If we can continue after that, great. If it ends up being too much, which it might, I'll hire someone else for one place and you can keep the other."

"I'd want to keep Magma."

"Not Steel?"

His face suggested I'd said his baby was ugly, and in a way I had. "I love this one too," I said, realizing that I did. "But Magma, with the spices... it's just so me. If I had to choose one, I'd want to stay there."

"Got it." His face cleared; it seemed I hadn't offended him. "Well, maybe it won't come to that. Given how hard you work, it probably won't. So, are you ready to run *both* my kitchens?"

Crystal would be furious. "I am."

We didn't announce my promotion that day because Kegan had to go meet with his bankers. Instead, he let the staff go home early since there wasn't much for them to do and I worked in silent bliss at the desk he'd so kindly provided then went to meet Tanisha.

I recognized her right away. A little heavier than her mother, but with the same friendly face and big grin. I joined her at her table and we shook hands.

"How's the leg?"

I grimaced. "Tedious."

She laughed. "Exactly. A nagging pain in the butt. Doesn't hurt any more, right?"

It still complained if I stood too long, but nothing like the pain I'd faced before. "Yup. Now it's just the annoyance of the stockings."

"I hear ya. Like stuffing ten pounds of mud into a five-pound bag."

We laughed, and she waved over the waiter and said to me, "You can have one drink. No more, or your blood'll be so thin you'll dissolve. I, on the other hand, am finally off the pills and can drink anything that's not nailed down."

I watched, amused, as she grilled the waiter on our drink options. Once we'd ordered a nectarine concoction for her and an extra-spicy Bloody Mary for me, she said, "You know why Mom wanted us to get together, right?"

I shook my head. "I did wonder. It was nice and everything, but..."

Tanisha snorted. "You are supposed to make me grow up and I'm supposed to make you *lighten* up."

"She said something like that, but I thought she was joking."

"Nope, she meant it. Hear the words of Mildred, the great interferer. 'Mary works too much, and she won't have time to find friends working

84

for Kegan. You, my darling impossible girl, flit around like a distracted butterfly. You could learn from her.'"

"And you still agreed to meet me? I sound like a nightmare."

She laughed. "My little workaholic nightmare. To be honest, I might not have bothered if it weren't for your blood clot. I know it's scary."

Unexpectedly, my throat tightened with tears. I took a sip of my water and nodded.

She reached out and patted my hand. "I didn't know anyone who'd had a clot. The doctors and nurses are so busy and they can't let you talk it all out. I'd have liked having someone who could."

I took a deep breath to calm myself. "Yeah. It's like... being a ticking time bomb."

She put her hand over her heart. "You're brilliant. That's exactly how I felt." The hand dropped away. "Don't you dare tell her, but my mom's right about my side. I do need someone with a little work ethic in my life."

"Have you met your mother?"

She chuckled. "Yeah, but she's composed entirely of work ethic. It's intimidating. Plus, what thirty-three-year-old wants to get life lessons from her mother?"

I sighed, remembering my mother's desperate attempts to convince me I should stay with Charles. "None. And no thirty-four-year-old either."

She held out her water glass and I clinked mine against it. "To learning our own lessons," she said, and I echoed it.

"All right, Mary, so what lessons do you have to learn?"

"Apparently not to work so hard. But what else is there to do?"

She laughed. "How much time have you got? I do everything *but* work."

"What do you do?"

"Read, nap, walk around the city—"

"No, I meant, what work do you do?"

"I'm a grad student in psychology."

I blinked, and she said, "Don't tell me, you didn't expect the black chick to be a PhD candidate."

The sudden annoyance, mixed with a sad weariness, in her voice startled me. "I didn't mean that. It's just, your mother made it sound like you don't work at all."

She looked down at the table, then back at me. "Sorry. I get a lot of 'Wow, *good* for you for getting a degree' kind of comments," she said, doing a great impression of how my mother might have spoken to a black woman whose mother owned a coffee shop, "and I forget sometimes that not everyone's like that. Sorry, Mary."

"It's okay. That must suck. But why does Mildred act like you lie on the couch eating candy all day?"

"Because I kind of do?"

"If I'd known grad school was that easy, I'd have gone myself."

She laughed. "It's not usually. Only when you get stuck."

"Ah."

"Yeah. I was working with an advisor I loved, but he left and I haven't been able to figure out what to do since."

"When did he go?"

"Two years ago."

Ouch.

She gave me a grim smile. "Yeah. I have less than two years to finish this degree or they'll kick me out. But anyhow, enough about me. How'd you end up here? Mom says you're new to the area."

I wanted to encourage her to figure out what she needed to do for her degree and then get it done, but her expression made it clear she wasn't interested in hearing that so I didn't try. "I moved to Toronto in January but I've only been in her neighborhood since November when I applied to work at Steel."

She nodded, then flashed me her mother's bright smile. "Mom adores that Kegan guy. I think she hoped I'd hook up with him but he's not my type. From what I hear, though, he can be a slave driver."

I started to defend Kegan but she said, "Actually, that's not fair. He's focused as hell and doesn't let anything get in his way. And not everyone can work like that."

"Can't argue with that. Any of it."

"And you're enough like him that you can work with him?"

I crossed fingers on both my hands. "So far so good."

"I know Mom offered to hire you. Do you know she meant it?"

I shook my head. "She just wanted to make Kegan hire me."

"She *did* want that, but she'd have been even happier if you'd gone to work for her instead." Her laugh was bitter. "Since her lazy only daughter won't do it."

"If you're doing a PhD, you're hardly lazy."

She turned her hand palm-up on the table then let it topple over. "Not really doing the degree at the moment. Not really doing anything."

Before I could respond, she said, "No, forget it. No more about me. I have to know: did you really sit on Kegan's steps in the rain for days?"

I let her change the subject. "Nope. His flower box."

She shook her head, grinning, and we chatted for ages about clots and my work and our interests, but throughout I could see sadness and a deep frustration in her eyes.

Chapter Ten

Crystal hadn't moved a muscle since Kegan's announcement that I'd be chef of both Steel and Magma. Dorothy had hugged me so hard I'd had to gasp for air and the majority of the others looked happy too, but Crystal's followers stood shocked and Crystal herself didn't seem able to do anything but stare. It unnerved me, so I tried not to pay attention and instead focused on the ones who were responding to me with smiles and congratulations.

"Well, back to work, folks," Kegan said once they settled down. "We have two tastings this weekend and that food ain't going to make itself."

Crystal turned her head jerkily, as if her neck joints had rusted, to look at him. He looked back calmly, then said, "Mary has the plans ready, so I'll get out of the way and let her do her job." He gave me a good-natured slap on the shoulder and went into his office.

I gave them a brief overview of the weekend then said, "And before we get started I'd like to buy you all a drink from Mildred to thank you for working so hard when I couldn't be here."

Crystal just shook her head when I asked what she wanted, but the others smiled and gave me their orders, even her friends defrosting a little toward me. Before I left, I stuck my head into Kegan's office to offer him a drink; he was on the phone but nodded when I mouthed, "Coffee?"

"I'll help you carry them if you like," Dorothy said as I headed toward the front door.

Drinks for eleven people would be tough to transport. "I'd love the help, actually. Thanks."

She smiled and we started off, but I stopped after a few steps. "I don't have my purse. I'll grab some money and meet you there."

I slipped into the office and pulled four twenties from my purse, unable to hold back a smile at how quickly I'd gone from counting every penny to being able to buy treats for my staff (my staff!), then caught up with Dorothy near the café.

"You still don't have your purse."

I showed her the money in my hand. "More than enough here."

She studied me, looking uncomfortable. "Can I make a suggestion?"

"Always."

More studying, even more uncomfortable. "Don't leave your purse there."

I blinked. "Why not? It's safe, isn't it? It's in Kegan's office at my desk."

She seemed to be considering this. "Yes, it's there all right."

This non-answer threw me. "Look, I don't understand. Tell me what you mean."

She swallowed hard, and my heart skipped a beat as I recognized she was truly afraid.

"It's okay, Dorothy. If you have something to tell me, do it. I won't get mad or anything."

She sighed. "I know you won't."

I held open Mildred's door, and Dorothy stopped on the threshold. "I... don't leave your things unattended. Okay? Please."

Confused, I said, "I won't," and her face relaxed.

Mildred came out from behind the counter and grabbed Dorothy and me in one big hug. "My favorite girls."

An older lady standing at the counter said, "Hey, I'm right here."

Mildred laughed. "You're my favorite too, don't worry." To me, she said, "Dinner went well last night?"

I nodded. "Your daughter's great. I hope she had fun too."

"Sure she did. How could she not? She got to meet you." She grinned at me, then turned to Dorothy. "You doing okay, sweetheart?"

Dorothy gave a quick sharp nod.

Mildred's face softened and she patted Dorothy's arm. "It'll be okay. If you need me to—"

"No!"

I blinked at Dorothy's sharpness, but Mildred just said, "All right, honey, I won't. Come over and talk to me whenever you want, okay?"

Dorothy hugged Mildred again. I tried to put the pieces together, Dorothy's delight at my promotion and her nervousness over Steel's security and her insistence that Mildred didn't need to do whatever she'd been suggesting, but couldn't make them fit.

I hoped I wasn't the problem. I didn't think so, but I couldn't help worrying.

Mildred made our drinks and we carried them back in silence. I wanted to quiz Dorothy but I couldn't find a way to word it and she didn't volunteer anything.

As I held Steel's door open for her, she looked up at me and said, "I'm really glad you're here," then scooted past me into the restaurant. She sounded sincere, and my tension eased. It didn't vanish, though. If I wasn't the problem, what was?

Crystal met me at the kitchen doorway. "I changed my mind, Mary. It was so nice of you to offer us drinks that it surprised me. But I'd love an iced cappuccino." She smiled sweetly. "If you don't mind going again, that is."

I smiled back, pleased she seemed over her grumpiness. "I wouldn't mind, but I don't need to. Dorothy suggested we get you one and it turns out she was right." I plucked the frosty cup from the tray and held it out to her.

She took the cup, blinking, and I had a nasty thought. Had she deliberately said no to make me go back? I couldn't believe that. Why would she? But if she had, it hadn't worked. Because of Dorothy.

"Thanks." Crystal sounded like it choked her. She cleared her throat and turned to Dorothy. "And thank *you*. How thoughtful of you."

Dorothy paled, but raised her chin and said, "You're welcome."

"Damn it!"

We all jumped and turned toward Kegan's closed door. How loudly had he yelled to have been so clearly heard?

Crystal said, "Better leave him alone. He doesn't like to talk when he's angry."

"Good to know, thanks." I made sure I didn't sound sarcastic. I *did* want to know how best to handle my boss, and Crystal had been around longer so theoretically should have some information. So far, though, she'd told me he wouldn't hire me and he hated having people in his office and she'd been wrong on both, so maybe not the best source of Kegan-related insight.

Still, I didn't want to interrupt him, so I set his coffee on the bench outside his door then wrote "Coffee's out here" in big letters on a paper towel and propped it up in his window. That accomplished, I said, "All right. Let's get started. Here are the recipes."

I walked through them, assigning jobs and describing my expectations, finishing with, "Friday's dessert is the trickiest part.

Pineapple mint sherbet can't be left to freeze too long or you can't add the egg whites to make it fluffy, and in the quantities we need 'too long' is hard to define. I'll be handling that one myself. Any questions?"

There weren't, so I set my staff to work on the steel tables Kegan had rented so we could do at least some preparation here rather than at the banquet hall. Once they began their tasks, I stood watching, amazed.

For the first tasting, I'd been so incredibly freaked out and we'd been in such a rush that the prep had flown by. Now, though, I had time to savor it, and I loved seeing these people turning my thoughts and dreams and ideas into delicious reality.

After a few moments spent studying the scene, I decided I'd better get to work myself, but before I'd taken two steps toward the huge fridge, temporarily installed in the middle of the room while the kitchen walls were repaired, that held the mint leaves I needed to start chopping, Kegan said, "Mary, can I see you a minute?"

I turned to see him standing in the doorway of his office. The coffee cup I'd left on his bench and my sign were gone, and he looked under control despite his earlier outburst. "Of course."

He closed the door behind us then pulled down his window blinds. He'd never done that before, and nervousness flooded me. I settled at my desk facing his, resting my legs on the footstool he'd provided, and waited. And worried. Was he angry with me? Why?

Once he'd returned to his chair, he studied me then said, "You know what, it's okay. Never mind. Tell me, how're things going out there?"

I blinked. "Great. I explained the recipes and everyone's working."

"Good stuff."

We sat in a stiff awkward silence until I made myself say, "What's going on?"

"Nothing. Everything's fine."

The words came as if by rote, and a chill slid down my spine. "Do you not like my menus? Or how I divided up the work?"

He frowned, showing the first real sign of life since we'd entered his office. "Why on earth would you assume you're the problem?"

"Because you called me in here but now you won't tell me what's wrong. And you just said there *was* no problem."

He shook his head slowly. "You're about the only thing going right these days. Trust me, I have no problems with you at all."

Delight tried to fill me, but I was still too worried to let it in.

He fiddled with a pen, while my nerves frayed, then dropped the pen and said in a rush, "You've noticed the contractors aren't here, I assume?"

I nodded. I had noticed, but since nobody had commented on it I'd figured everyone else knew where they'd gone and why and I'd felt strange asking my staff to fill me in.

He rubbed his forehead. "They quit."

My mouth fell open. Quitting made no sense. Danny's firm specialized in restaurants, and making Steel gorgeous again would have been a great addition to its resume. "Why?"

He studied me again, then straightened in his chair and seemed to withdraw at the same time. "No reason. But now I need to find a replacement firm and I'm having trouble. And if I can't find one in a week or so..." He took a sip of coffee. "Steel won't reopen until January."

My heart skipped a beat. "We'd miss New Years Eve?" A huge night for any restaurant, and Kegan had already told me about last year's elegant dining and dancing event he'd planned to make an annual tradition.

He nodded. "And Christmas."

I licked my lips, afraid to push him but sure I needed to know. "Can't you convince them to come back?"

He gave his head one sharp shake. "Not a chance. Look, the staff knows about the contractors, of course, but not about the delay, and I want to keep it that way until they have to know. I don't want them stressing. I don't want *you* stressing either, which is why I wasn't going to tell you, but I had to tell someone. I'm going nuts here."

Touched, I said, "I'm honored you picked me."

"I know you haven't been around long, but I trust you. You share my obsession with this place. And Magma."

I smiled, because it was true, then my smile faded. "But you don't trust me enough to tell me why the contractors quit."

"It's not that. You don't need to know why."

"Do the others know?" I jerked my head toward his office door. "Crystal and everyone?"

"Don't. You don't want to know."

"That doesn't answer my question." I swung my legs off the footstool and pushed my chair back. "I think they do, so I'll go find out. Excuse me."

"Okay, fine." He sighed. "But remember later that I didn't want to tell you."

When I went back out to the kitchen my hands did all the right things, squeezing oranges and chopping pineapple and mint, and I kept my staff on track and answered their questions, but his words echoed in my head over and over and I couldn't think of anything else.

My perverted nemesis Jimmy turned out to be the brother-in-law of Danny, who had explained to Kegan, apparently with huge sympathy for Kegan and frustration with Jimmy, that his wife wouldn't let him fire Jimmy or even leave him off jobs. If Kegan insisted Jimmy couldn't be in Steel any longer, then Danny and his workers couldn't be either.

And Kegan had stood firm, and now he had no contractors.

Because of me. If I'd been stronger, Kegan wouldn't have needed to jump in to save me.

Steel's delay was my fault.

I'd said exactly that to Kegan and he'd said immediately, "No, it's Jimmy's fault. And Danny's too for letting him get away with it."

But it wasn't entirely their fault. I knew it, and I felt certain he did too.

At the end of our talk, he'd said, "I still have a few leads on contractors but it's not looking good. Franklin's officially signed on to do Magma but he can't start until December fourteenth, which of course means Steel won't be done by the fifteenth. Or any time in December." He sighed. "And using him wouldn't do Magma's schedule any favors either."

"I really am sorry."

"Stop saying that. If Jimmy hadn't been an ass, none of this would have happened. It is not your fault. Got it?"

I'd said, "Okay," because I knew he wanted me to, but I didn't mean it. And I couldn't stop blaming myself.

I worked in the kitchen for an hour or so, fending off Crystal's constant hinted questioning about what we'd discussed behind Kegan's closed office blinds, then let myself escape to Mildred's for a sandwich. Returning with a fresh tea and a coffee for Kegan, I was nearly bowled over by two small children racing for Steel's front door.

"I'm sorry," the woman with them said. "My kids have no manners. Are you okay?"

I nodded. "The restaurant's closed, though."

She smiled. "That's okay. They're coming to see their uncle."

The girl, a bit larger than her brother, reached the door first and flung it open, shrieking, "Uncle Kegan!"

When the woman, who I realized must be Kegan's sister, and I walked in, we found Kegan in the foyer with the boy clinging to his back making what I assumed were pterodactyl noises and the girl prancing around showing off a truly strange dance routine. He looked up at our arrival, grinning. "Nora, your children are crazy."

"You say that every time we see you."

"It's always true." He walked over, still bearing the boy, to give her a hug. He whispered something to her and she said, "Surviving," and he squeezed her a little harder then let her go.

"Nora, this is my new chef Mary. Mary, my sister Nora, and her kids, who rumor says are crazy, Lola and Rudy."

Lola grabbed Kegan around the legs. "I'm not crazy, *you* are."

He rubbed his knuckles against the top of her head. "Takes one to know one."

"Then you *are* crazy! If I'm crazy, and I know one, you're the one!"

She burst into giggles and he said, "You're too smart for me. Let's go see if Mildred can spare you a cookie."

Rudy began scrambling to get down, and Kegan swung him to the ground. "Mary, want to come along?"

He was ridiculously cute with the kids so I did, but I wondered if Nora would rather be alone with her brother for at least part of their visit. Then I had a brainwave. "Want me to take them instead? I have a coffee for you here, and if Nora likes tea she can have this one and I'll go get another one and cookies too."

Kegan turned to Nora, eyebrows raised, and waited.

She hesitated, and he said, "Or Mary and I can wrangle the brats and you can sit here and get five minutes of solitude."

Her face lit up. "That one." She turned to me. "It's not that I don't trust you or anything, it's just—"

"You just met me. No reason *to* trust me. It's okay."

We smiled at each other, and she said, "Thanks. I'm sorry, I shouldn't be such a—"

"Normally protective mother?" Kegan said. "Yeah, you're a nightmare."

She rolled her eyes, then to my surprise grabbed him in a firm hug. He hugged her back, even tighter, until Rudy said, "This dinosaur's hungry!"

"Doubt it," Nora said, releasing Kegan, "since you stuffed yourself at lunch." To me, she said, "Are you sure you don't mind me stealing your tea?"

I shook my head. "Plenty more where that came from."

She smiled, and Kegan and I headed out with the kids.

"How old are you?"

"Lola, you can't just ask people that."

"Why not? I'm eight and I don't mind saying it. Why is it bad to ask?"

She was adorable. Long brown hair like Nora's and her uncle's deep blue eyes. Nora had them too, but hers looked tired and a little sad.

"Lola, some people don't like it, but I don't mind. Lots of people ask me how old I am." I gave Kegan an innocent smile. "Sometimes even at job interviews when they shouldn't."

He winked at me, and I said, "I'm thirty-four, Lola."

She considered this. "You are... um... twenty-six years older than me." She stopped in her tracks. "Wow. You're old."

Kegan and I burst out laughing. When we'd got ourselves under control, he said, "And now you know why some people don't like to be asked, Lola. Because some crazy little girl will tell them they're old. Do you know how old I am?"

She shook her head.

"I'm twenty-eight years older than you."

Her eyes widened. "You're even older than her."

"Her name is Mary."

"You're even older than Mary."

"Gotta love the shock in her voice," I said. "Like it's hard to believe it's possible."

He patted my arm consolingly. "Well, you *are* pretty old."

"*You're* old. I'm a spring chicken."

"I'll remember that comment when salary review time rolls around."

I laughed. "You won't. You'll be senile by then."

"I'll write it down. And then you'll be sorry."

I punched his shoulder. "Will not."

Lola stopped again and glared at me, her blue eyes sparking with anger and fear. "Don't hurt him!"

I stared at her, surprised. "I didn't."

"You did, I saw it. No hurting."

I crouched to talk to her but she scrambled away from me toward Kegan.

95

He crouched too and wrapped his arms around her. "Mary didn't hurt me, Lola. She wouldn't hurt anybody. She was just playing. Like how I gave you a nougie in the restaurant?" He gently knuckled the top of her head again. "It's okay, if both people know you're playing. And I knew Mary wasn't trying to hurt me."

"It's not good to hurt people," she said, staring at the ground.

Kegan's eyes closed and he squeezed her tighter, smoothing his hand over her hair. He held her in silence for a moment, then cleared his throat. "No. It isn't. You were right to stand up for me. I'm glad you did. But everything is fine. Okay?"

She thought about this, then nodded. "Okay."

He released her and straightened up. I stayed down. "Lola, I'm sorry. I didn't mean to do anything to scare you. I like you."

"You do?"

I nodded. "You're a great dancer."

Stretching the truth a bit, but the way her eyes lit up and the last of the fear left her face made it worthwhile. She hurried a few paces ahead so she could walk backward and dance for us. Rudy went too, singing a tuneless song to accompany her, and I straightened up and murmured, "I'm so sorry." I had no idea what had happened, but I'd caused it for sure.

Kegan gave my arm a squeeze. "It's not your fault. She'll be fine."

She seemed to be, dancing away with no worries and not much rhythm either. "I hope so. Nora seems nice. Have you guys always been so close?" My distant relationship with my brothers was nothing like the warmth between Kegan and Nora.

He shook his head. "Only since the summer. And she is nice. Works incredibly hard too, taking care of them and working full-time."

"Their father's not around?"

"He divorced Nora a few years ago. She'd been with another guy for the last two years, but he left in July."

"Ah." Poor Nora. Poor kids.

"Yeah. The kids liked him, loved him really, until... he left, and they're confused and sad. I spend most of my spare time, what there is of it, with them so it's not all on Nora, but I can't make up for him."

There'd been no mention of Kegan having a girlfriend, not even from gossipy Crystal. Was this why? Not enough time, with his work schedule and Nora's kids? "I bet you come pretty close."

He wrapped an arm around my shoulders and pulled me against him for a moment. "I appreciate that. You have no idea how much."

Chapter Eleven

"Amazing food, Mary. Yet again."

I blushed and smiled as the rest of the group agreed.

The pretty blonde of about my height who'd spoken patted the flat stomach of the tall and clearly athletic man next to her. "I've never seen you eat so much, Forrest. Good thing you exercise."

"He doesn't exercise, he just plays hockey," Kegan said, earning himself a headlock from Forrest.

Ignoring his struggles to get free, I said, "I'm glad you liked it."

She smiled. "I loved it." She held out her hand to me. "I'm Tess."

We shook hands, and Forrest released Kegan and said, "Sorry, I should let him make introductions instead of beating him up."

"Yeah, you big bully." Kegan made a show of straightening his rumpled dress shirt. "You all know Mary, my savior."

I protested but he said, "You are. Please. Who else could have made these tastings so perfect?"

"Who else could put up with you?" Tess said, grinning.

We all laughed and Kegan said, "Yeah, that too. Okay, Mary, you've met Tess, massage therapist and artist extraordinaire. She makes the coolest miniature scenes, and I'm hoping if I'm really nice she'll make me one someday."

She chuckled. "I've only ever given one away," she said, casting a meaningful glance at Forrest, "and I'll certainly never sell them again, so don't hold your breath."

Kegan puffed out his cheeks then let them deflate. "Fine, be that way. This jerk here is Tess's boyfriend and the captain of the Toronto Hogs, who I'm told will win the Cup again this year, Forrest."

Forrest smiled and shook my hand, his hazel eyes warm and friendly, then Kegan introduced me to tall blond Magnus, the Hogs' former captain, and his blonde girlfriend, a painter named Pam. Her hair was long and Tess's was short, but otherwise...

My eyes went back and forth between the two women and Tess laughed. "Yup, we're twins. I warned her not to date a hockey player but she doesn't listen."

Pam grinned. "Magnus doesn't play any more, so I'm safe."

"Or so you think," Magnus said. "*I* think we're in the way. Want to go out for coffee?"

The banquet hall's workers had indeed finished with the other tables and were now hovering waiting for us to leave. Forrest and Tess agreed to coffee at once, and Kegan said, "Sure, why not? You in, Mary?"

I wasn't sure Magnus had meant to include me in the invitation. "Oh, no, I'm okay. You guys go have fun."

"You don't want to come?" Tess said. "You're more than welcome." The others nodded.

I glanced at Kegan, who said, "If you don't, I'll just go on and on about how great you are. Wouldn't it be nicer to be there to hear it?"

We smiled at each other, and Pam said, "Plus, if you don't come Tess and I are outnumbered. Don't make us suffer with these three."

Magnus poked her, and I said, "Well, I'd hate to have that on my conscience."

The others had come in one car, so Kegan and I followed in his after making sure our staff members weren't forgetting to take any of our supplies back to Steel. At first we'd been able to leave materials at the banquet hall, but the success of Magma's tastings meant the place was now booked solid so the kitchen was no longer all ours.

We made it safely through the gently falling snow and found the others easily in the nearly empty Griffin Café. Forrest and Magnus had attracted the attention of the few patrons and were signing autographs while Tess and Pam looked on, smiling. Kegan said, "Take a seat, Mary, and I'll get you a tea. And a footstool too?"

My leg burned and had swollen up after the long hours on my feet preparing for the tasting, so I nodded then sank gratefully into my chair and put my foot up on the spare chair he dragged over. I smiled up at him. "Thank you."

He smiled back and headed to the counter.

Tess turned away from her boyfriend and studied me with concern. "DVT?"

I blinked. "Yeah. How'd you know?"

"What's DVT?"

"Deep vein thrombosis. Blood clot."

Pam said, "Ah. That stinks."

I nodded. "It's usually not too bad but I've been standing a lot today." I turned to Tess. "How did you know?"

"Massage isn't a DVT treatment but we're taught to recognize it."

Pam glanced over at Forrest. When she saw he'd finished with his autographs and was listening, she nudged me, her eyes sparkling with a devilish glint. "She spends her days, and nights, rubbing a whole team of sexy young muscly hockey players. Nice work if you can get it, eh?"

Forrest laughed, clearly not bothered. "Remember, I had her first. Then she picked up Magnus and eventually took on the other guys too."

Kegan returned. "Out of context, that's an interesting statement."

"Talking about Tess's work with the team," Forrest said as Kegan handed me my tea and settled into his chair with his coffee. "She massaged me first."

I mouthed "Thank you" at Kegan, not wanting to interrupt, and he smiled.

"And fell for you, fell for my *client*." Tess pressed the back of her hand to her forehead in a mock swoon. "I'm an ethical disaster."

"Nobody's perfect." Forrest grinned at her then turned his attention to Kegan. "So, what's up with Steel? You're reopening soon, right?"

I flinched, fighting back tears for the third time that day.

After Kegan had warned me a week ago that Steel might not open on time we hadn't discussed it again, and my faith in him was such that I'd assumed he'd find a solution. So when he called me into the office after lunch and told me we'd definitely miss New Year's Eve, I just stared at him, too shocked to respond. Then I saw the depth of his pain in his eyes and stumbled forward without meaning to and wrapped my arms around him.

The way he clung to me made my throat tighten but I held him close and willed myself not to cry. I wanted and needed to comfort him, and if I cried it would be the other way around.

Eventually he said, without letting go of me, "Thank you. I'll be okay."

I squeezed him harder. "For sure you will."

He stood taller in my arms and his hand smoothed over my back. "But will *you* be okay? I know you hate this too."

Tears almost escaped then, stirred up by his sweetness in being concerned about me in the midst of his own worries, but I managed to control them. I couldn't speak, though, so I nodded against his chest.

"We need to tell the staff."

I nodded again.

He tightened his arms around me. "In a minute."

Holding him and being held by him felt too good to stop, so I wound my arms more closely around his neck and we stood together, drawing strength from each other, for quite a while before he gently set me away from him. "Ready?"

I looked up into his eyes and saw the pain still there but being replaced by resolve. I raised my chin and made myself smile. "Lead on, boss."

He did, and told the staff with me standing close at his side. I'd held myself together, but my tears had risen again at the staff's genuine shock and sadness, then risen still higher when Crystal's faux-sympathetic "Oh, if only you hadn't had to get rid of the contractors" had made me feel even worse for Kegan.

Now those tears were back with a vengeance as he grimaced and said, "It should have been next Tuesday, but it got pushed back into January. Contractor difficulties."

Forrest and Magnus and Pam commiserated with him, but Tess didn't speak, and I looked up to see her watching me fighting to get myself under control. Our eyes met and she gave me a small nod, like a salute, and an understanding smile. "That must be hard for you, both of you. It's not fun when you can't work when you want to."

My tears took over, and I mumbled, "Excuse me," and fled to the bathroom.

Alone, I calmed myself quickly, although the pain didn't subside. I had been blocked from the work I longed to do, and Kegan had opened the door for me to make it happen. Now he was blocked, because of me. And I couldn't open that door. I'd been the one to shut it.

Tess walked in. "Hey. You okay?"

I nodded. "Sorry. The whole thing's just a mess."

She joined me at the counter and smiled at me in the mirror. "I know. He told us."

I turned to stare at her. "He did?"

She nodded. "He said the contractor's employee was an ass to all the women in Steel, so he told the guy's boss not to bring him in any more and the contracting firm quit."

Her eyes were steady on my face, and I knew Kegan had said more. "He said it's my fault, right?"

"No, he said *you* say it's your fault. He doesn't remotely think it is."

I rubbed my forehead. "The other women slapped Jimmy or made him go away. I'm the one who let him act like an ass. If I'd defended myself, Kegan wouldn't have had to step in."

"But if the guy hadn't *been* an ass, then there'd have been nothing for Kegan to do."

"Yeah, but..." I sighed.

"But you still feel like it's your fault."

I nodded, and she patted my shoulder. "I understand. But you need to know he doesn't blame you at all."

I believed her, and it helped. "Okay." I sighed again. "I'll try to stop feeling guilty."

She grinned at me. "Good, because even now he's happier than I've ever seen him."

Warmth blossomed deep in my chest. "Really?"

She nodded. "He dated my friend Jen for a month or so two years ago, and he was uptight and controlling and barely listened to anything she said. I've seen him with quite a few girlfriends since then and he was the same until this summer."

When Nora's relationship broke up? Or was the timing a coincidence? I didn't have time to wonder about it because Tess was still talking.

"After that, he hasn't had a girlfriend but he's been calmer and more open to other people's opinions, but with you he's even more open. He *listens* to you, doesn't he?"

I thought of everything he'd given me the day my clot was diagnosed, how perfectly his gifts suited me. "He does. I didn't know it was new."

"It is." She laughed. "I'll have to tell Jen, she'll think it's hilarious he's finally listening."

It was surprisingly hard to ask, "Is she still interested in him?"

"Nope. She's engaged to a great guy now. He's actually the reason they broke up. Kegan thought she was bringing a new boyfriend to Steel and refused to listen when she said he was her—" She cut off and stared at me.

"Her what?"

"Her *contractor*. I never even thought. Maybe Don could work on Steel!"

Excitement flooded me. "And it could still open on time. Can you call him?"

101

She nodded, caught my arm, and pulled me with her out of the bathroom.

We garbled out the story together at the table, and Kegan said, "Hey, it's worth a try." He cleared his throat. "How is Jen, anyhow?"

"Pining over you," Tess said with no expression in her voice.

Kegan froze, and she burst out laughing. "Sorry, but no. She's engaged and blissful."

"Good," he said, clearly pleased. "She deserves to be."

As Tess pulled out her phone and began punching in a text message, I settled into my chair again and Kegan said, "Where's that leg?"

"Attached to me?"

He poked my arm. "The chair's available if you want to put it up again. If you think it's okay, though, then ignore me."

I shot a glance at Tess, who returned a wink. He definitely wasn't controlling me. "I think I will put it up, actually. Thanks."

Tess put away her phone. "Now we wait. Don's pretty busy, but you never know, right? Maybe he'll be able to help."

"Could be," Kegan said doubtfully, then rallied. "But even if he can't, we'll be fine. Mary's planning Magma's menu and revamping Steel's, and there's all the design work and stuff to do for Magma. It'll be January before we know it. And once both places are open, everything will be great."

I loved how he was so able to pull himself up and get back into believing in himself. It took me ages to do that and sometimes I couldn't do it at all.

"Do you have different contractors for the two places?"

Kegan shook his head. "The guys for Magma can't start until mid-December but they've agreed to work overtime after that to get both places in order."

"Begged them, did you?" Magnus said. "Or threatened them?"

He chuckled. "Doubled their hourly rate."

We all laughed, and I realized he would never beg, or threaten, to get what he wanted. So not his style.

"So then everything will be fine, right?" Pam gave him a smile. "A bit late, sure, but no harm done."

I swallowed hard as he said, "Well, I had to cancel a bunch of New Years' Eve reservations. I'd left them before, promised people I'd be open by then in fact, so some of them were... unimpressed."

He'd asked me to leave the office while he made the calls and I'd been all too ready to go, but the exhaustion and sadness on his face when he let me back in made it clear they'd been agonizing for him. The worst was the building inspector, who'd informed Kegan he'd be keeping an extra-close eye on the renovations.

"Don't tell the others," Kegan had said when he told me. "That guy used to be on my side. Didn't let anything big slip, of course, but we got away with minor infractions. We won't now."

Busy pondering, I missed Tess asking me something. "Sorry. Pardon?"

"You work her too hard, Kegan." She shook her finger at him. "Let the poor girl rest."

"She was at home with a blood clot and still working. I doubt I could stop her."

Tess grinned. "Probably true. So, Mary, what's your story?"

Feeling awkward, I briefly explained how I'd cooked for my family growing up and decided to make it a career. When I'd finished, she said, "Well, you do it beautifully. We can't come to any of the other tastings, unfortunately. Stupid hockey schedule. But I can't wait to see Steel when it reopens and Magma when it opens."

Me either.

Chapter Twelve

"You're sure you want to do this?"

I nodded, trying to look sure. I was nearly sure. I'd asked my doctor, and once I'd explained how underwater hockey worked he'd said I'd be fine to play provided nobody kicked me, since bruises would take ages to heal. I hadn't sustained any serious damage in my first game so I wasn't too worried. "Besides, you need me to play or you'll forfeit."

"I'd rather forfeit than see you get hurt. If you're not sure, we'll leave right now."

His obvious sincerity surprised me a little. Not that I'd have expected him to *want* me to be injured, but he was so clearly worried that he'd let me quit, embarrassing him in front of his teammates, if I wanted to.

Which I didn't. "I'll wear the rubber gloves on both hands so I don't get scratched, but otherwise I don't think anything will go wrong."

"Still don't want me to tell them?"

I shook my head. Having everyone afraid to bump into me underwater would make the game a lot less enjoyable for all involved. "I'll be fine."

He still hesitated.

"Kegan, I *want* to play. It was so fun last time. Let's go win again, and then we'll have two things to celebrate today."

His face relaxed and he grinned at me. "How shocked did I look when I came in?"

I opened my eyes and mouth wide, pressing my hands to my cheeks for good measure.

He laughed. "You're just lucky I didn't see your reaction. Weren't you surprised too?"

"Totally. But thrilled, of course."

Seeing John Franklin and his workers march in four days early to get started on Steel had been wonderful, but I'd been even happier at Kegan's delight when he returned from a meeting.

"I knew Franklin was a good guy, but I never expected him to have his crew work overtime on the previous job, on his dime, to get to Steel faster. Gotta admire that sort of commitment."

"Definitely."

He chuckled. "Of course, now I'm the one paying overtime so they can finish both Steel and Magma quickly."

I smiled, then noticed everyone else was in the pool. "We'd better get in or we'll be paying overtime here."

"Can't have that." He grabbed a pair of gloves from the deck and helped me pull them on.

We joined his team in the water, and I noticed the woman who'd helped teach me to play the first week studying us. I smiled, feeling faintly uncomfortable at her scrutiny and struggling to remember her name, and she came over and said, "Nice to see you again."

"You too."

"You told me to bring her back, Carolyn. I always do what I'm told."

Thanks, Kegan. We laughed, and she said, "I don't think so. But good for you for doing it this time."

After a few minutes' warm-up, the other team's captain called for attention and we figured out who'd be starting on which side of the pool. Then she said, "Okay, ready to go?"

She got a chorus of agreements and one "First, you should know something."

I turned to Kegan, shocked. Would he really tell after I'd specifically told him not to?

Everyone else turned to him too, and for the first time I saw my boss flustered. "I... you should know that when my new restaurant opens in February you're all invited to come check it out. Have a drink on me."

Both teams cheered and headed to their side of the pool, and I raised my eyebrows at Kegan.

"I didn't say it," he muttered.

"You were going to."

He nodded, then cut me off as I started to protest. "I know. I shouldn't even have started. But I didn't tell them. That's got to count for something, right?"

"Yeah, at least a hundred bucks in free drinks."

He winced. "Once I opened my mouth, I had to say something."

I shook my head, but had to smile. I knew he thought they should know, and the controlling guy Tess said he'd been would certainly have told regardless of what I wanted. Kegan was working hard not to be that guy any more. "Yeah, you did. And I forgive you for starting. Thanks for not finishing."

He gave my arm a gentle squeeze. "You're welcome. And thank you. Let's go play."

Since I hadn't bothered with gloves for my first game it took me a while to get used to handling my stick with the thick rubber in the way, but I still had fun. We didn't win, but nobody seemed particularly upset.

Afterward, one of our guys said, "Mary, you'll keep playing with us, right?" Several others, both men and women, chimed in with their agreement.

I glanced at Kegan, whose smile didn't tell me whether he wanted me to play or not. "I'd like to, but it depends on my work schedule."

The guy nudged Kegan. "Give her Thursdays off or get the towel flicking of a lifetime."

Kegan held up his hands as if defending himself, laughing, and they left the pool area. I noticed, though, that he hadn't committed.

In the change room, someone said, "Seriously, if you're available we would love to have you play."

I smiled. "And I'd love to do it. We'll see what happens when both restaurants are open. I might not have time to breathe, never mind play."

"I suspect he'll give you whatever time off you want."

Carolyn's tone was sweet but something dark and heavy lurked beneath it. I looked up from my lock, confused. "I doubt it. Why would he?"

She didn't speak for a moment. When she did, she sounded tired. "I don't know. I'm sorry."

She took her clothes and towel into a cubicle on the other side of the change room and I stood bewildered.

"Ignore her," the first woman said softly. "She wanted to date Kegan a while back and he didn't feel the same."

I surprised myself by feeling possessive of Kegan. "She asked him out?"

She shook her head. "Not directly, but she hinted, and he made it clear he only had time to work. She's just miffed you got in there when she couldn't."

Confusion swept me again. "I'm not 'in there'. She knows that. He's my boss."

She smiled. "None of my bosses have ever looked at me like he looks at you." With a chuckle, she added, "Of course, mine didn't look like him, so I wouldn't have *wanted* them looking at me."

I didn't know what to say. I hadn't noticed him looking at me any differently than he always had.

"And I don't think mine would have helped me put on a pair of gloves. But maybe Kegan's different, as a boss."

She said 'boss' but her tone said 'boyfriend', and I responded to that. "We're not dating. Not even close."

"Oh, you might not be dating. Yet. But I think you're close."

Chapter Thirteen

The morning of December fifteenth dawned cold and sharp, the sky a washed-out icy grey. It suited my mood. When I reached Steel and saw Kegan in black pants and a black sweater, I wasn't surprised. I wore black and dark blue. Bright colors didn't feel right.

Other than the contractors, we were the only ones at Steel that day. The last Magma tasting had been a few days before; since we couldn't do any more because the banquet hall was now booked solid, we didn't need our kitchen staff until the new year. Kegan hadn't wanted to lay them off, though, in case he lost them to another restaurant, so he did the same thing he'd done weeks ago with the wait staff: paid them in full until the start of January when they'd come back to help get Steel ready to open.

But today, we weren't open anywhere, and we weren't open with each other either. Magma's newly refinished floors were still drying so the contractors were all at Steel, and their noise made it hard to talk. That seemed to suit Kegan fine; he'd barely said hello to me before burying himself in his work.

I spent the morning wishing I could make him feel better and flipping through cookbooks for menu inspiration, and he worked his way through a stack of paperwork without looking up. I thought maybe we'd go to lunch together but when noon rolled around he said, "I'm not really hungry, I must admit. Take as long as you want, okay?"

Because there was no need to hurry. Guilt and sadness choked me and I nodded and left.

Despite being rushed off her feet Mildred grinned at me and accepted my request to make Kegan an extra-special sandwich. I had to at least bring him back some food. Even if he didn't eat it, he needed the option. I wanted to do something else for him but couldn't think of anything. Nothing I could do would make Steel open today and that was all he wanted.

When I got back to my desk, I found a note saying he'd gone for a walk. He'd obviously waited until I left to take off so he could be alone. It was far too similar to how Charles had handled our last New Years' Eve together for my liking and I threw myself even harder into my cookbook research to avoid thinking about my marriage. It didn't work, though, and eventually I pushed the books aside.

My lawyer had called on Monday, and as I'd expected Charles hadn't contested the divorce. My mother kept in constant contact with him, of course, and I got far more than I needed to know about how "poor Charles" was doing, but he hadn't reached out to me even once. Didn't he wonder about me, maybe even miss me?

Did I miss him?

We weren't divorced yet, but I had to admit I didn't. We hadn't had much of a marriage for a long time and if I'd met him today for the first time we wouldn't have had anything in common. I'd changed a lot since moving to Toronto and I knew he wouldn't like much if any of who I'd become.

Kegan walked in and I jerked a cookbook back toward me.

"Don't feel guilty for taking a break." He returned to his desk. "I just did, after all. And thanks for this." He held up the sandwich and smiled at me. "Although it's not a surprise. Mildred told me I couldn't buy one because *you* bought one for me."

I blushed. "You were right before, she does have a big mouth."

"Told you." He studied me, his eyes warm. "Thank you again."

I smiled, glad I could bring at least a little happiness into his day. "You're more than welcome."

He opened the sandwich and we got back to work, pausing only for a trip to Mildred's together at around three. At six, he pushed away his papers and sighed. "Should be open now."

My heart melted at the sadness in his voice. "I'm so sorry."

His eyes roamed my face. "I know. I knew today would suck, and it did, but you made it better."

I managed to smile instead of cry, but it was close.

"I don't think I told you before, but the date was kind of symbolic. Steel opened on September fifteenth two years ago, so reopening today would have been great."

I nodded. If only Tess's friend's fiancé had been able to help out. He'd toured the place with Kegan and said frankly, "I wish I could, but this job really needs restaurant specialists. I don't want to do it wrong."

109

Kegan had been impressed with his honesty and promised to hire him when he renovated his condo.

We sat in silence until a thought struck me. "I know John Franklin said January twenty-third, but isn't there some way we can be ready for the fifteenth?"

He drummed his fingers on the table. "He was gunning for the thirty-first at the beginning and I talked him down to the twenty-third, but..."

He picked up his phone, and his side of the call showed that John was pleased with Steel's progress and cautiously optimistic about the fifteenth. Kegan then promised a ten-thousand-dollar bonus if we made it, which seemed to strengthen John's optimism considerably, and Kegan was grinning when he put the phone down. "That's great, Mary. I had today set in my head and figured it didn't much matter when we opened if it had to be January. So January fifteenth for Steel and February fourteenth for Magma."

"Not February fifteenth?"

He shook his head. "I know it's cheesy, but people will remember it. Spicy stuff on Valentine's Day and all that."

Even though I knew he didn't know his teammates thought we were dating, I felt embarrassed discussing 'spicy stuff' with him. Mercifully, he didn't say anything else but, "We'll open for dinner only that day, so the first full day will be the fifteenth."

I smiled. "Perfect. All fifteenths, all the time."

He smiled back, and it set my heart pounding. Since last week when Carolyn and the other woman had suggested we were, or would be, together, I'd been paying more attention to his behavior with me and I was beginning to see what they meant. We had a connection I didn't think had been there before, something electric between us when our eyes met. It scared me, but I liked it.

I liked it even more when he said, "Can I take you out for dinner tonight?"

Our other dinners had been work sessions. This one? It felt like a date. He picked a place we hadn't been before, all hushed lighting and private tables and unobtrusive wait staff, and we didn't talk about work even once.

We talked about each other.

We spent ages at our cozy table without a single dull moment. He told me how he'd been driven to open Steel when he did, in only six weeks, because his best friend had died of a heart attack and it had made it so clear to him that he needed to live his life. He made me laugh until tears ran down my face with his stories of how terrible he'd been in his first underwater hockey games. And he confirmed the whole "Kegan's changed since the summer" thing.

"Nora and her... boyfriend split up in July. I don't think I was ever as big a jerk as he was, is, but I saw a lot of myself in him. The controlling stuff, the way he doesn't even acknowledge that anyone else might have a viewpoint, how driven he is to succeed on his terms and how little he cares about other people. And I didn't want to be him any more."

"You were never him."

"You didn't know me back then."

We'd exchanged several hand touches during dinner, and now I put my hand over his. "Doesn't matter. There's no way you didn't care about people. I might give you the controlling stuff. *Might.* But with how awesome you were to me over the blood clot? No way you haven't always had at least some of that."

He turned his hand over and gave mine a firm squeeze. "I hope so. I don't like thinking of all the people I've pushed around. Maybe it's not quite as bad as I think."

I tightened my grip on his hand. "Can't be. Tess still likes you."

His eyebrows went up, and I wished I'd refused the one glass of wine I'd had. With that plus the anti-coagulant drugs and the feel of his warm hand in mine, I was flying high and I hadn't thought through my comment. "Sorry, never mind."

"She told you about Jen, I assume?"

I had to nod. "That's how she got to remembering she's engaged to a contractor."

Kegan rubbed his forehead with the hand not holding mine. "Jen's probably the worst example. But I've been a pain in the ass to a lot of women."

"Not to Tess. Not to me. Or Dorothy. Or Mildred. Your sister obviously adores you."

"Five women don't hate me. How many are on the planet again?"

"Six."

We laughed.

"Five out of six women don't hate me. I'll take it." He gave my hand another squeeze and released it. "But in all seriousness, I don't want to be that guy any more. It's hard, though. I want things done right."

My hand felt cold and lonely. "Of course you do. Especially with your restaurants."

He shook his finger at me. "Don't mention them. I don't want to talk work tonight."

We smiled at each other and warmth flooded me, nearly making up for not holding his hand any more. I couldn't deny it: I was falling for him. I knew better, but I couldn't help myself.

"But I do want to talk you. What's the deal with your neighbor?"

His eyes were intent on my face, and realizing the answer mattered to him made me glad I could say, "No deal at all. We've only spoken a few times since my clot."

"Was there ever a deal?"

His voice had gone softer and a little rough, and it sent shivers through me. Was he falling for me too? Knowing if I told him I didn't want to discuss it he'd let it go, but also knowing he wanted to know and I didn't want to lie to him, I said, "Yes. Once. Both of us drunk and depressed on Valentine's Day. Dumb thing to do."

His eyes held no judgment, only sympathy. "It happens."

"Yeah, but it shouldn't when you're married."

"True. How long until you're not married any more?"

"I walked out on January sixth, so we can get divorced next month. And we will."

"No chance of a reconciliation?"

"I can't imagine how. We've barely talked since. He talks to my mother but not to me."

"Better her than you, I guess."

I gave a grunt of a laugh. "Definitely. They always got along better than he and I did. Or than she and I do, for that matter."

He shook his head. "Why did he not want you to have a career?"

I sighed. "I don't know. I don't think he really knew. His parents split up when he was young and he had this... vision of what a marriage should be that just wasn't realistic. He wanted the white picket fence and all that, and we actually *had* that fence installed when we started renting our house but it wasn't enough."

"And part of the vision was you at home, I guess."

I nodded, and he shook his head again. "I wouldn't be able to be involved with a woman who didn't have a career, or at least something she was passionate about, even a hobby like reading. I've never dated someone who wasn't driven in some way."

I'd left Charles, moved from my hometown, and sold the car I loved to get ahead in my career. That counted as driven, didn't it?

Our eyes met, and Kegan's slow smile suggested it did.

We moved into less intimate topics of discussion, and soon I knew more about Kegan than I'd ever known about a boss and still longed to know more.

Our conversation wasn't all about him, either. Not even close. We talked about my childhood and my best and worst working experiences and what I'd thought of the movies and music he'd sent me when my clot was diagnosed. We talked about the underwater hockey team and he touched me by saying he'd love me to join but hadn't wanted to put me on the spot to commit when that guy had brought it up. And we talked about Tanisha and my growing friendship with her.

We saw each other at least once a week but I still hadn't done what I knew Mildred wanted and gotten her back to school.

"Do you know why she stopped in the first place?"

I did; she'd told me a week ago after a few glasses of wine for her and half of one for me. She'd been saying how much she'd liked her professor, and then said, "One night of sex with the wrong person and everything falls apart." But she'd seemed shocked at herself for telling me and changed the subject, and I doubted she'd want Kegan to know, so I just said, "I think it was a personality conflict with her professor."

He grimaced. "It's too bad. She's smart, and Mildred would so love it if she got her life back together."

I nodded. While I wouldn't tell him what she'd said, I could and did say, "It doesn't seem like enough to make her put her whole degree on hold. But I guess it is, to her."

He smiled at me. "If anyone can get her going again, it'll be you. Look how you motivated me to open Magma."

"You wanted to. I just helped you see it."

"Nobody else saw it, though. You listened to both my words and what I didn't say."

He did too, throughout the evening. Really listened. No other man had ever listened to me like that, not just waiting for his turn to talk but really thinking about what I said and letting it guide what he said back. I felt like I mattered to him.

Inevitably, though, the night drew to a close. He drove me home and walked me up to my apartment, and as we reached my floor I wondered if he'd try to kiss me and wondered further if I wanted him to. I did like him, no doubt about that. But I loved my job. And making out with my boss was a great way to end up with no job and no make-out partner.

I unlocked my door and turned to face him. "Thank you so much. I had a great time."

He smiled. "There's nobody else I'd rather have been with today, and tonight." Then he reached out and brushed his fingers slowly over my hair and down onto my cheek.

I caught my breath at the feel of it, the way my skin blazed under his touch and tingled after he moved on.

His hand moved even slower, even more deliciously, his eyes following its path along my face. When he reached my chin, he let his fingers rest for a moment, their warmth pouring into me, then drew them back. "I'll see you tomorrow morning, okay?"

"I'll be there," I managed through the sensations dancing through me. I'd had sex that was less enjoyable than Kegan's single touch.

We stood looking into each other's eyes, then he said, "Good night, Mary," and turned to head for the stairs.

"Good night," I said softly, relief and disappointment battling inside me. Though I knew we shouldn't kiss, disappointment won. I felt sure he'd be a spectacular kisser, but I wanted to know exactly how spectacular.

He looked back and winked at me before vanishing into the stairwell.

I smiled, though I knew he couldn't see it, then my smile vanished and adrenaline flooded me in a dizzy rush as Brian opened his door.

He said, "Dating your boss now? Saw him mauling you," in a too-loud voice, and I realized he was drunk.

Kegan hadn't *mauled* me. But Brian must have been watching us through his peephole. Anger ripped through me. "No, I'm not. And it's none of your business anyhow."

I tried to pull my door closed but he got his foot into the gap before I could.

"Then why'd he bring you home at eleven o'clock?"

Was it really that late? We *had* been at the restaurant a long time. "We were working. That's what you do with your boss."

"We used to be friends. And then you got that job and now you don't have time for me."

"You don't want to be friends, you just want money. Or to dump your problems on me."

"That's not true. I feed Saffron. I help you out."

I didn't want him here, ruining what had been a glorious evening. "You're right. I'm sorry. I need to go to sleep, Brian."

His foot slid back an inch but not enough for me to close the door. "I need to talk. If I don't get a job soon, or get three hundred dollars some other way, I'll lose my apartment."

Even as part of me thought, "Which would stop you bugging me," the rest said, "I don't want that to happen."

"Then please. I can't figure it out on my own. Help me."

I sighed. "Will you actually listen and do something to help yourself?"

"Of course. I promise."

I let him in, although my every instinct screamed not to, and spent the next two hours listening to him whining and rejecting my possible solutions. He didn't even ask about my leg.

When I fell asleep on the couch in the middle of his sentence, he woke me up and asked me to lend him the three hundred dollars he needed. Half-asleep and dopey, I agreed before I realized what I'd done then couldn't figure out how to back out. He did leave when I gave him the check, though, so I managed to convince myself it was worth it.

Once he finally left, I went to bed without washing my face. Even now, when I concentrated I could still feel Kegan's caress. I didn't want to lose it.

I woke up the next morning disgusted with myself. Partly for what I'd given Brian, but mostly for how I'd replayed Kegan's touch over and over as I fell asleep. Yes, I had feelings for him, and yes, that caress had woken parts of me that had been dormant a long time, but he was my *boss*. My career dreams had been dormant a lot longer than my libido, and I would not sacrifice the former for the latter. No way.

That resolved, I took a shower and dressed to spend the day at Magma, then checked my email over breakfast in case Kegan had any instructions for me. We didn't have Internet access at Magma yet since the office was still being renovated.

Nothing from him, but to my surprise I had one from Charles. The surprise turned to shock as I saw the subject line: I want you back.

I stared at the screen as if I could somehow make the email vanish, the toast I'd eaten turning to concrete in my stomach. No. *Please*, no. Why would he send such a thing? Had my mother put him up to it? If she had, still he'd been weak and stupid enough to send it. If she hadn't, if he really did want me to come back to him...

My hands shook so hard I couldn't keep the mouse pointer positioned over the email, but with a spastic jerk I managed to get it there and click to open the message. Then I shut my eyes. I couldn't face it.

The depth of my revulsion stunned me. I couldn't think of anything worse than going back to Charles. Marrying Jimmy felt like it'd be a step up, maybe even two steps. And yet only a year ago I'd thought Charles and I would stay together forever.

True. But I hadn't thought we'd live happily ever after. I just hadn't thought I'd find the nerve to leave, and I hadn't had the final trigger to *make* me leave.

I had nerve now. I had faced down Kegan and won the job of my dreams. I'd made it through the blood clot mostly on my own. And while I hadn't been able to make Jimmy permanently back off, I *had* found the strength to clearly tell him I didn't like his actions, even if only once. I was tougher than I'd ever thought. Maybe I always had been.

I opened my eyes and read the email.

> Need electronics? I need you back. Much-
> loved former customer, come again and buy
> computer, phone, even television, all at
> great prices. Click link to buy.

I'd never been happier to realize someone's email had been hacked. My relief was so overwhelming that I burst into giggles and then full-on laughter. I did feel a tiny bit of sympathy for Charles, but mostly a great deal of "serves you right" since he'd always been so dismissive of people "too stupid to keep their accounts safe". *Takes one to know one, buddy.*

That thought made me think of Kegan and Lola, and my laughter died down. I'd have been surprised if Kegan had for some reason sent me an "I want you back" email, or if either of my exes had, but I wouldn't have been freaked out. And I hadn't just been freaked out. I'd been disgusted, revolted.

I'd known I didn't want to get back together with Charles. Now I knew I couldn't. My body was repelled by the mere thought.

Chapter Fourteen

I waited outside Kegan's closed condo door, smiling as I heard Rudy shriek, "Mary's here!"

The door flew open, and I stepped in past the clearly over-excited boy.

"Give me one second, Mary," Kegan called from the living room. "Just beating Lola at car racing, then I'll come say hi."

"You're not beating me!"

I set my bag of gifts on the hall chair. Kegan and I hadn't discussed exchanging Christmas presents but I'd wanted to get him something to thank him for all he'd done for me, and then I'd felt strange about not bringing gifts for the kids too. I shucked off my snow-dampened coat and my boots, while Rudy stood watching me intently. The instant my second foot came free of its boot he said, "Will you make cookies for us?", speaking so fast the words were almost unintelligible.

"I... sure, if your uncle has the ingredients."

Lola whooped in triumph and Kegan appeared. "Thanks for coming. I need all the help I can get with these two."

"I hear I'm making cookies."

He turned to Rudy. "You asked her already? What did I say?"

"To wait until she had her coat and boots off."

I burst out laughing. "He did. Just."

Kegan shook his head, grinning. "Rudy, I meant to let her get inside and relax first."

Rudy pouted, and I said, "It's okay. I like making cookies."

"Chocolate chip!" Lola joined the party in the hall.

"If there are chips here."

"Trust me, we could outfit a bakery. I took these weasels grocery shopping this afternoon. Cost me two hours and at least a year off my life, but I can't imagine there's anything cookie-related we don't have. Or any kind of junk food or candy."

I smiled at him. "It's nice of you to give your sister a break."

"It's her main Christmas present. And she better appreciate it."

"Mommy has a party at work tonight, and then tomorrow she's buying our presents!"

"On Christmas Eve? She's brave."

"We picked up your present today," Rudy said.

Kegan had bought me something? How sweet of him. I didn't have time to dwell on it, though, because Lola was viciously shushing her brother. "Don't tell!"

"I wasn't going to, I was just saying we—"

Not wanting to see a war erupt, I said, "Well, I have presents for you guys too."

"Can we open them now?"

I looked at Kegan.

He smiled. "*If* you're good, you can open them after dinner. Go play with the PlayStation for a while."

They went off in silence, obviously trying to be on their best behavior, and Kegan said, "That should buy us at least a little peace."

I smiled, then laughed with him when Lola screeched at Rudy for taking her controller. "You did say a *little* peace."

"Microscopic peace. Anything interesting at Magma today?"

No, just tediousness. I liked John Franklin but he did have a tendency to patronize me. I'd so far tried to get him to put shelves, electrical outlets, and the telephone jacks exactly where I wanted them and he'd always had reasons why his choices were better. I hadn't quite been able to make him do it my way because my only reason was "because I said so". I'd be able to work around everything, though, so we'd be fine. "Nope. Oh, the bathroom walls are finished. That shimmery paint looks amazing."

He grinned. "Better than the one coat did?"

"Totally."

I'd expressed my concerns about the slightly scruffy nature of the paint after a single coat during dinner the night before. We'd had lunch or dinner or at least a long coffee break together every day since the fifteenth. Ostensibly they were working sessions, but in reality we spent a few minutes discussing work and then just enjoyed each other's company. No further caresses, but the way he looked at me felt nearly as good.

I'd decided several times that I couldn't risk my career by imagining a relationship with Kegan, and I'd meant it each time, but I found myself imagining it anyhow. We got along so well outside of work, and ninety-five percent of the time at work too.

That other five, though... When I'd first started working with him I thought we'd always be on the same page but at times now we didn't even seem to speak the same language.

I'd known he would be keeping an eye on my work, he'd warned me of that himself, but I hadn't expected the degree to which he'd interfere with my plans. Time and again he called himself on his own control issues, and then the next day he'd be right back telling me I should garnish a dish with three mint leaves instead of just two.

I knew he needed that level of control: a huge part of why Steel had been so successful was Kegan's focus and attention. But I couldn't help being annoyed when he got in my way even though he always apologized.

"I'll go see it next week, after Christmas. Assuming I survive tonight and tomorrow with the monsters."

"So what's the plan?" I'd been surprised when Kegan asked me to hang out with them, but also pleased. I'd seen the kids a few times at Steel and we got along well, and I certainly didn't mind spending more time with Kegan. Besides, it got me out of the apartment and away from Brian's annoying visits. Still no job, still no money, and still no gumption to fix his life.

"I ordered pizza already, and—"

"I'd have made us dinner."

"I know, which is why I ordered pizza. So you wouldn't have to."

I smiled at him. "But I still have to make cookies."

He grinned. "You can tell them you won't, but I can't guarantee your safety after. And then I figured we could watch one of the eight hundred movies they made me rent and play some video games."

"Good plan."

We went into the living room, Kegan carrying my bag of gifts, and sat on the love seat together to watch the kids play. He dragged over an ottoman so I could put my leg up, and we chatted about nothing in between cheering on the kids. Being so domestic with him felt good. Too good, in fact, since I knew we shouldn't consider getting together, and I found myself half-disappointed and half-relieved when the pizza arrived and we had to focus on feeding Rudy and Lola.

Once everyone had eaten enough, Rudy said, "Cookie time?"

Lola shook her head. "Present time!"

Rudy jumped on the bandwagon. "Can we?"

Kegan looked at me. "Would you say they've been good?"

Our eyes caught and held and a shiver rippled down my spine at the connection between us. I took a deep breath, pushing it away. Hardly the right time or place. "Oh, I think so."

The kids cheered and scattered. Rudy found my bag and pulled out two presents, and Lola gave me a small silver-wrapped box. "You should go first, I guess. You're the guest."

"Good for you, Lola." Kegan reached out and ruffled her hair, and she scrambled up into his lap. "Go for it, Mary."

I pulled off the wrapping and opened the box to reveal a sleek silver keychain with "Property of Magma" engraved on the back and a big black-enameled letter M on the front. "You guys, it's gorgeous. Thank you." I'd once admired Kegan's silver keychain engraved with Steel's opening date and bemoaned my plain keyring, and he must have remembered. That made the gift even nicer.

The kids beamed, and Kegan said, "To clarify, *you're* the property of Magma too, not just the keys. So don't assume you're getting away any time soon."

I echoed his joking tone. "You can't get rid of me now."

Our gazes locked again, and when he said, "Good," his eyes told me he meant it, and meant it for more than work.

"Yeah," I murmured, and knew my eyes were telling him the same thing. The electricity crackling between us sent shocks sizzling through my body and made my heart pound and—

"My turn?" Rudy said.

Kegan's mouth pulled into a wry smile. "World's best chaperone."

I smiled back, sparks still dancing through me, and Rudy said, "What's a shaparamone?"

"A crazy but cute kid." Kegan swept Rudy up from the floor where he'd been lying, plopped him onto the love seat between us, and picked up his large lumpy gift from the coffee table. "Here you go, Rudes. Looks like skis."

I laughed, and Rudy said, "It does not." He shredded the paper then crowed, "So cool! A pterodactyl!" He gave the plush toy a squeeze and shrieked with delight as it roared.

"Nora is going to cut you into tiny pieces," Kegan said to me over the repeated roaring. "And I think I'll help."

"It's got removable batteries."

He laughed. "Then maybe not such tiny pieces."

Rudy was eventually persuaded to give the pterodactyl a break and Lola opened her present. Kegan had told me that he'd bought the kids a PlayStation in the summer, so I'd hoped she'd like the Dancing Queen game, but I hadn't expected her to scream and throw herself out of her chair and into my lap.

"My friend Ella has this and she loves it and I wanted it and you're so cool and this is the best Christmas ever!" She flung her arms around me. "Thank you thank you thank you!"

I hugged her back. "You're very welcome. I hope it's fun."

"It's *so* fun!"

Kegan said, "Should we try it out?"

Lola slipped off my lap and began scrambling to undo the game's wrapping then thrust it at me. "Can you open it? I want to play!"

"I will, but there's something else in that bag, I think. Someone doesn't have a present."

Rudy found the bag and gave Kegan his gift. He unwrapped it, while I watched his hands moving over the package and tried not to imagine them moving over my body, then looked at me. "You're amazing. How did you get this?"

I smiled. I'd spent ages hunting for the perfect present for Kegan, then happened to be nearby when a woman returned a strap for a men's Vivana watch. Kegan had mentioned his needed a new strap but said they were next to impossible to find. The clerk had been stunned that one was coming back, but after asking the woman three times if she was sure she'd accepted the return, and I'd stepped up immediately and bought the strap.

I told him the story while I peeled the plastic from Lola's game, and when I finished he said, "But how did you know I needed one?"

"You said something about it once."

He shook his head slowly, his eyes fixed on mine. "And you remembered from that?"

"How did *you* know I didn't have a keychain?"

He smiled. So did I. We didn't need to say anything more.

I tore my eyes from him with an effort and popped Lola's game into the PlayStation, then arranged my keys on their new ring while Kegan replaced his watch strap and Lola danced her little heart out accompanied by frequent roars from the pterodactyl.

When my keychain was complete I said, "Time to make cookies?"

"You don't have to."

I laughed and looked pointedly at the kids, who'd both stopped what they were doing when I spoke and were watching me hopefully. "I think I might have to. Not that I mind anyhow."

At first I was working alone, but soon Rudy and then Lola came to 'help', which mostly involved stealing chocolate chips. It became a game; I'd pretend to be busy with something else and then throw a hissy fit whenever I saw them with their hands in the bag. They shrieked with laughter every time, making me laugh too. Kegan sat at the kitchen table and helped the kids by pointing out when I might be too focused to notice them. It certainly wasn't my most efficient baking session ever but was probably the most enjoyable.

Once the cookies were done and cool enough to eat, we returned to the living room and stuffed ourselves while watching a movie. At first the kids sat in armchairs, leaving Kegan and me on the love seat, but before long Rudy crawled into Kegan's lap then Lola surprised me by giving me the same treatment. I looked over at Kegan, and he smiled and gave me a thumbs-up.

When the movie finished, I saw Rudy yawning and said, though I longed not to, "I should probably get going."

Kegan glanced at his watch. "Yeah, I guess it's bedtime for these two."

Rudy whimpered, and Lola said, "I want to stay up all night."

Kegan laughed. "Your mother would not be impressed. No, Mary's right. We'll say good night to her and then I'll get you guys tucked in."

Lola turned to face me and wrapped her arms around my neck. "Can't you stay?"

Touched that she wanted me to, I hugged her and felt bad having to say, "No, I really can't. I need to go home and feed my cat, and you guys need to get a good night's sleep."

"Plus you and Rudy have the spare room so there's nowhere for her to sleep."

Lola looked down at the love seat, then pouted, apparently having decided it was indeed too small to be a bed. Her face cleared, though, and she said to Kegan, "She can sleep with you."

"Yeah! Let her sleep with you, and then tomorrow she can make us pancakes."

I felt my face growing warm at the thought of sleeping with him, or better yet staying awake in bed with him, and struggled to control it. I had to laugh, though, when I realized Kegan was blushing too.

"Out of the mouths of babes," he said, smiling at me. "Look, guys, that won't work."

"Why not?"

He leaned toward Lola and me as if about to impart a secret, then whispered, "I snore" and gave a huge fake one. Lola burst out laughing and pushed him away, and I said, "Well, that settles it then. I can't stay if you snore."

He rapped himself lightly on the forehead. "Don't *tell* her, you fool. When will I learn? Okay, guys, let me call for the taxi and then we'll say goodbye to Mary."

Once Antonio had been called and had promised to have a driver there in ten minutes, I watched Lola do one more dance routine then made myself get ready to go. I put my coat and boots on and waved my keychain at the three of them. "I love this. Thank you so much."

"You're very welcome. Merry Christmas."

I looked into his eyes and the noise of the kids' Christmas greetings seemed to fade away. "Merry Christmas," I said softly.

He smiled, then it widened into an evil grin. "Enjoy your time with your parents."

"Same to you," I said sweetly, conscious that his parents were the kids' grandparents. He'd told me they disapproved of his restaurants, which I couldn't understand even though I knew they'd wanted him to become a lawyer.

"Hug!"

I laughed. "Yes, sir."

I knelt to give Rudy the commanded hug, then had to hug the pterodactyl too.

Lola threw her arms around me and said, "Bye, Mary."

"Bye."

I released Lola then pushed up to my feet and looked at Kegan. We hadn't hugged since the day we'd learned Steel would be delayed, and I missed the feel of his body against mine.

Maybe he did too; he smiled and opened his arms to me.

I didn't even consider not hugging him. He pulled me close as I wound my arms around his neck, and I shut my eyes and relaxed into his embrace. He smelled delicious, a combination of that rich sexy cologne and the cookie crumbs Rudy had left on his sweater, and having him hold me felt even better. Our other hugs had been during times of crisis or great emotion; this was a hug for its own sake and I never wanted it to end.

"Thank you for tonight," he said softly, his breath ruffling my hair and sending a wave of heat through me.

"You're so welcome. I had fun."

"Me too."

He squeezed me even tighter then released me. "Well, have a great Christmas. Let me know when you're back and we can have dinner."

"Us too?"

Kegan smiled at Rudy. "No, we have to talk about work. Boring stuff." He turned the smile on me, his eyes intent on my face. "Nothing we'd need a chaperone for, right?"

Definitely not.

Chapter Fifteen

I sipped the ginger ale I'd brought with me as a pale imitation of champagne and watched the candlelight flicker on my desk's polished top. Funny how I felt more comfortable in Kegan's office at Steel than I did at home. But then, this was where I'd been spending nearly all my waking hours.

Since December twenty-sixth, when I'd escaped my parents' place to come back to Toronto, Kegan and I had seen each other daily, spending hours at Steel and Magma and then talking and laughing together late into the night. When we weren't together I knew that starting a relationship with him could be disastrous, but when I was enjoying his company it seemed like the best idea I'd ever had.

Maybe it wouldn't be all that disastrous. He still interfered in my plans more than I would like, but while we'd had a few blowups over his interference they resolved quickly and we were still friends afterward.

After one of our worst arguments, over whether the cinnamon on a cheesecake should be sprinkled evenly or be given a swirled pattern, I'd complained to Tanisha, and she'd surprised me by booking us a trip the next day to a gorgeous spa about an hour outside of Toronto, saying it would both calm my nerves and give Kegan a chance to miss me.

"He'll be nicer to you after," she'd said with a Mildred-like grin, and she'd been right. I'd come back peaceful and more able to shrug off Kegan's obsessiveness, and he'd been gratifyingly happy to see me and appreciative of my work. If only I'd known about the spa before Christmas, I would have gone there and relaxed myself before seeing my parents.

I didn't want to think about Christmas, or my mother, or Charles. I reached for my ginger ale again, then jumped and knocked it over as I heard Steel's front door open. I got the bottle upright before too much poured out, but confusion filled me. I'd locked that door behind me, and nobody else but Kegan had a key. It couldn't be him, though; he'd gone to a New Years' Eve wedding, and it was only eleven so he'd still be there.

Or not.

He arrived in the office in a swirl of icy air and stared at me, his eyes nearly as tired and sad as they'd been the day we met. "Why are you here? Should be out having fun." On the last word he tossed his coat at its hook, missing by a long shot.

I went over and hung it up, relieved he was my intruder but still confused. "I'm *here* having fun. And what about you? What happened to the wedding?"

He shook his head and ripped the tie from the collar of his shirt. "Everyone laughing and having a great time, and me like the cloud of doom." He dropped the tie onto his desk and loosened his collar. "I had to get away. Even Antonio, when he drove me over here, was happier than I am. And the poor bastard's driving drunks all over the city."

I didn't have to ask him why he wasn't happy. I felt it too. "We'll be open soon."

He sat on the edge of his desk and rubbed a hand over his mouth. "I know. But if I hadn't screwed up, we'd be open right now."

My stomach twisted and I couldn't look at him. I fled to the kitchen to grab paper towel for the ginger ale all over my desk and called back, "You mean if *I* hadn't screwed up," then took my time returning, not wanting to see his agreement on his face.

As I walked back into the office, he said, "No, I said it right. I've had a few drinks but I know what happened. I didn't talk to Danny about alternatives, about ways we could work together to keep Jimmy away from you. I just demanded he obey me, and of course he didn't."

I didn't think he'd noticed his "keep Jimmy away from you", but I had. I wasn't the only one Jimmy had harassed, but maybe Kegan hadn't minded so much with the others? I bent over my desk, soaking up the mess. "But if I hadn't—"

"Mary. We could do this all next year and probably all the year after that, but what's the point? Maybe you could have stood up for yourself more, and I definitely shouldn't have been such an ass, but we can't do anything about it now. Can we agree we both screwed up?"

His eyes looked so sad I couldn't agree to anything that wouldn't cheer them. "Nope. But I'm willing to agree Jimmy's an ass."

He smiled at me, and his eyes did brighten a fraction. "Works for me. Have we got coffee? Mildred's closed and I'm desperate for one."

Glad I could help, I got the coffee maker running and returned to the office a few minutes later with a mug for him and tea for me.

He took a long sip. "Great, thanks. If I never get Steel opened again, or Magma for that matter, you've got a future with Mildred."

I sat at my desk and gave him a mock glare. "You're not getting rid of me that easily."

"Thank God."

"Seriously, we will open both of them, and by the end of February we'll have more customers than we know what to do with."

He tipped his head to the side and studied me. "I love that."

"What?"

"The way you say *we*."

I smiled but didn't know what to say.

"So, why *are* you here?"

I shrugged. "Nothing to do."

"Could have gone to see your parents."

My shudder wasn't entirely faked, and he laughed. He knew I'd stayed exactly as long as I'd had to and no more at Christmas; he and I had talked for ages on the twenty-seventh about how infuriating I'd found my mother's "poor Charles" comments.

"Do you think she really invited him over for dinner?"

"Oh, I don't know." I'd left right after she told me her plans. "But I wouldn't put it past her. And I so don't want to see him."

"Only a week and then you'll never have to."

I nodded. I'd be a divorcée. Not something I'd ever wanted, but far better than still being with Charles.

We sat in silence, then he said, "This isn't right. We need champagne."

I held up my nearly empty ginger ale bottle. "Want some?"

"No, I do not. One can't celebrate New Years' without champagne."

"Can't one?"

"No, one cannot."

He headed down the hall to the wine room, fortunately undamaged by the fire, returning in moments with a bottle and two glasses. He poured us each half a glass. "There. You can have two like that."

I smiled, touched he remembered I couldn't have more than one drink.

He raised his glass. "To next year."

I echoed it, and we clinked glasses. As I was about to drink, he added, "Because this year sucked ass," and I burst out laughing.

He rescued the glass from my shaking hand. "Well, didn't it? Leaving your husband, the fire, the blood clot."

I calmed myself enough to say, "I guess so. But I got to work with you, and we're on the brink of great things. So it was an amazing year too."

He studied me, his eyes full of emotion and something much hungrier, and for a heart-leaping second I thought he might kiss me. Instead, he handed me back my glass and said, "Let's drink to that instead. To great things."

Again I echoed him, though my voice shook a bit, and this time we drank without issues.

The candlelight and the champagne made our office intimate and cozy, and soon we were talking as we never had before. He pulled his chair over to my desk so I could keep my leg elevated on my footstool, and we sat close together and opened our souls to each other.

"I heard you talking to your neighbor the day Steel was supposed to open."

I stared at him. "After you left me at my apartment?"

He nodded. "I got onto the stairs and had to tie my shoe. I heard him, so I waited until I heard you invite him in."

He'd heard me trying to shut Brian down and then giving in to him. And he'd heard Brian say he was mauling me. How embarrassing. "You never said anything."

"When, then? No. I knew you could handle it."

The certainty in his voice felt good, even though I hadn't handled it the way I'd wanted to. Kegan believed in me. "Then why'd you stay?"

He put his hand over mine. "In case you needed backup. *Not* because I thought you would, but in case the guy was a jerk. I didn't want you to want help and not be able to get it."

I covered his hand with my other one. "Thank you. I hate letting him dump all his problems on me, but I can't say no."

"You will," he said calmly. "When you've had enough."

I looked into his eyes, impossibly gorgeous by candlelight. "Everyone says you've changed since the summer. It sounds like the old you would have stormed up the stairs and stopped me letting Brian in. Is it really just Nora's ex that made you change?"

Pain filled those eyes. "Oh, it was him. But..." He swallowed hard.

I tightened my grip on his hand. "I'm sorry, you don't have to—"

"He hit her."

My heart skipped a beat. "Nora?"

"At first just her." He gave an awful laugh, and I squeezed his hand. "As if it's okay to hit her. But that's how she said it. 'It wasn't so bad when he was just hitting me.'"

It *was* so bad, of course. But... Lola the dancing girl. Rudy the pterodactyl. God. "The kids?"

"Lola. Just her, although Rudy was probably the next target. She wasn't badly hurt, thankfully, but some nasty bruises. She was terrified, of course. They all were."

I shook my head, sickened. Nora's sad eyes. Lola's fear that my joking punch on the arm had hurt Kegan. How tenderly he'd calmed her and how tightly he'd hugged her. Horrible that they'd all gone through that.

"Nora left that night, brought the kids to Steel and then back to my place. She cried for hours once they'd gone to sleep, told me so many things I didn't know about him and their relationship, and I just kept thinking, "Okay, I've never hit anyone, but how he bossed her around and controlled her? That's all like me.' And I promised myself I'd change."

My eyes filled with tears. Blinking them away, I said, "You're amazing."

"Hardly. I'm just trying to do the best I can." Then, surprisingly, he chuckled. "Sounds like a cheesy movie line."

"A little." I smiled. "Doesn't mean it's not true. Also doesn't mean you're not amazing."

He refilled our glasses, carefully making sure mine was only half full, and I said, "So he's gone for good now?"

"I would have cheerfully torn him to pieces myself, and I'm not sure I don't mean that literally, but Nora just never wanted to see him or hear about him again."

I nodded. "I can imagine."

"She got a new phone number and email address and all that, and the three of them stayed with me for a month or so, never left the condo, and with all the security at my building he couldn't get to them. He's moved on, and rumor has it he treats his new girlfriend just as badly." He shook his head. "Thank God he's not the kids' father and Nora never married him. My mother used to be so upset that she was 'living in sin' with him, but at least poor Nora didn't have to go through a divorce."

I sighed.

"Sorry."

"It's true, though. It'll be over soon, but it still stinks."

"Of course. Nobody gets married expecting to divorce."

I put a good dent in my champagne before saying, "I did."

Kegan's eyebrows went up, and I qualified it with, "Well, more or less. I knew it wasn't working out before we got married, and I didn't think it'd be much better after. But..."

"Why marry him then?"

"I did love him. Or thought I did, anyhow. Plus it got me out of my parents' house, and he swore blind that after he finished his degree I could go to culinary school. Of course, once that happened he was used to having me at home all the time."

"And conveniently forgot about his promise, I assume."

"Said he'd agreed we could discuss it."

"'I said no, Mary' is not a discussion."

I feigned shock. "I didn't know you were hiding outside our window. Yeah, that's pretty much how it went down. We can't afford it, you don't need to go, once we have kids you won't need a job..."

"So that's why you left, I guess."

"Kind of. The final straw was last New Year's Eve, actually. I'd been taking over for the chef at a local restaurant who was off on maternity leave. I sometimes ended up staying late when I got caught up in stuff, and even if we had no plans Charles hated it. On New Year's, we did have plans to go to his friend's place, and I promised to be home by seven. When I got there, though, he'd already gone, leaving me a nasty note about my lateness and how inconsiderate I was."

Kegan waited, clearly knowing there was more.

"I got home at six-forty-five," I said, and he winced. "He never meant to wait for me. Didn't even care if I was there. He just assumed I'd be a jerk. I sat home all night, trying to think of one good reason to stay married. I couldn't find a single one, so I got myself organized over the next few days and left on January sixth."

"Good for you."

I finished my champagne and it fueled my words. "You want to talk controlling? You've got nothing on him. I never wear nail polish on my fingernails because of cooking, but I used to like wearing red on my toenails. He nagged and bitched about how much he hated the look of it, and so I eventually gave it up. The first thing I bought myself in Toronto was red nail polish, but I did two toes and felt so awful I couldn't do any more. All I could hear was his voice telling me it was trashy."

"You're wearing it now, right? Show me your feet."

I laughed. "You can't see them, they're in the tights! And no, I'm not." I sobered. "I threw the stuff out. I wish I could do it, but..." I shrugged.

He rubbed my shoulder. "I had a girlfriend, a patron here actually, who insisted I looked best in black. No big deal at first, but over time she took over my wardrobe and before I knew it I was some pathetic thirty-something goth dude."

I laughed, and he smiled. "Without the black eyeliner, of course. Trust me, I get why you don't wear the nail polish. But I wear colors again, and you'll have red toenails someday too."

I rested my elbow on the desk and my chin on my hand. "I hope you're right."

He took my other hand. "I know I am." He shook his head. "Are all relationships disasters, do you think?"

"I can't believe that. I used to have a friend, before she moved away, whose husband bought her a dozen red roses every New Year's Eve, one for each amazing month he wanted to have with her in the new year. And they did have amazing months, from what I could tell."

"So there's one good one."

"That's enough to keep the hope alive, right?"

He smiled at me. "I think so."

We sat looking at each other, then Kegan said, "So Charles is just going to let you go?"

"Looks like it. He hasn't contested the divorce or anything."

He squeezed my hand. "Does that bother you?"

"Honestly? Maybe it should but it doesn't. I guess on some level I want him to be upset I'm gone, but then I'm not upset to *be* gone."

"No?"

I shook my head and told him about the 'I want you back' email and my reaction, then said, "And it's good anyhow, because I shouldn't be in a relationship right now." True, but I wanted to. With him. Hoping he'd make sure it didn't happen, I added, "I've wanted this career forever and now I have it and I don't want to risk it."

He nodded slowly. "No doubt. I've had too many relationships that threaten this place. Patrons and... other people. I shouldn't do that again."

Something inside me whimpered at his words, but I made myself say, "So we'll both be single then. It can be our New Year's resolution."

"Yup." He drained the rest of his champagne. "We'd be crazy to do anything else."

"Yup. Crazy."

Our eyes met.

Insanity, and desire, swept through me.

He leaned forward and stroked my cheek without breaking our eye contact. "Speaking of crazy, Charles must be certifiable. Not to mention blind."

I swayed toward him involuntarily as my body erupted with heat and hunger at his touch. "Thank you," I managed, loving his words but afraid the champagne and his previous drinks were doing the talking.

He took a breath to speak, but was interrupted by a ragged chorus outside of "Ten! Nine!"

We both glanced at our watches. Sure enough, nearly midnight. Time for kissing.

I looked at him, and my heart skipped a beat at the new purpose and passion in his eyes. He said softly, "Seven, six," along with the chanters as he stood and extended his hand to me.

Even without the champagne in my blood, I'd have been tingling everywhere. With it, I could barely think. I wanted his kiss, no question. I'd wanted it for a long time. But what about our resolution?

Oh, who ever keeps those things anyhow?

I stood too, taking his hand as I did, and murmured, "Three," certainty filling me and my lips curving into a smile to answer his growing one. *Crazy or not, here we come.*

He supplied the "two" as he squeezed my hand and drew me closer.

We said "one" in unison. My heart raced.

He took my face in both hands, his warm skin against mine sending shivers through me, and said softly, "Happy New Year, Mary."

"Happy New Year," I breathed, and he kissed me as the crowd outside cheered.

I'd thought he'd be spectacular. I hadn't known the half of it. Kegan kissed like he did everything: thorough and powerful and with exquisite attention to detail. Never, never had a kiss felt this good. I wrapped my arms around his waist and held on, losing myself in the moment and the feel of his strong sleek body against me.

His kisses changed constantly. Passionate hunger gave way to teasing me with the lightest possible contact gave way to slow sweet exploration gave way to hunger again. Always different but always amazing. Kissing was supposed to be fun, and Kegan made it more fun than a million amusement parks.

Until he stopped.

During a deep hard kiss I moaned against his mouth, lost in sensation and unable to control myself. He jerked me closer and kissed me even harder for a few glorious seconds, then broke the kiss and set me away from him. "I should go."

I longed to beg him to stay but instead I managed to say "Okay" despite my breathlessness. I didn't beg because I knew he meant it. He wasn't playing, I could see it in his eyes. He wasn't flirting, didn't want me to try to make him stay. He was leaving.

"I don't want to, trust me, but I should. So I will."

And he did. He paused at the door to say, "I'll see you on the second. Happy New Year," and he was gone before I could say a word.

I sank into my chair, overwhelmed, before my desire-weakened knees gave way. I'd wondered how he'd kiss, how we'd be together, but I could never have imagined anything like that. Why had he left like that? I'd been pressed tightly enough against him to know he'd wanted me, and I'd clearly wanted him. More than that, though, we'd *connected*. Couldn't we have kissed for even a minute or two longer?

I glanced at my watch, then stared at it. Twenty after twelve. We'd been locked in each other's arms for that long?

He was incredible. He was also my boss. What the hell would happen when I saw him on January second?

Chapter Sixteen

Kegan and I didn't talk at all on January first. I spent the day giving my apartment a good cleaning and the evening hanging out with Tanisha. At first I was distracted by thoughts of Kegan, but Tanisha's New Years' resolution put paid to that.

"I want to be honest with people about who I am."

"That's cool. Sounds like a good plan."

She pressed her lips together and sat silent.

"Not a good plan?"

"Terrifying plan."

She brushed some cat fur from her jeans and I realized her hands were shaking. "What exactly do you want to be honest about?"

When she didn't speak, I said, "Would you rather not talk about it?"

She shook her head. "I have to. It's killing me not to. Everyone thinks I'm a..." Clearly searching for words, she looked at Saffron, curled up on my lap purring and shedding orange fur all over my polar-bear-print lounging pants. "People assume I'm a cat, and I'm really a polar bear. I can't go through life as the wrong animal. Not any more."

"How are polar bears different?"

She took a deep breath and sighed it out, then raised her chin and said, "I... they're lesbians. At least, this one is."

I couldn't say the wrong thing, it would destroy her. I had a strong feeling she hadn't come out to many people. But I didn't know the right thing. I had nothing against gay people but I had never knowingly talked to one until I came to Toronto. "You're a lesbian polar bear."

She nodded, her eyes searching my face.

My mind flitted from word to word then I caught sight of her iPhone on my coffee table and knew what to say. "I bet there's an app for that."

She burst out laughing. "No doubt."

I laughed with her, then she sobered. "Are you okay with it, with me?"

"Of course! I'm of the cat persuasion myself but there's nothing wrong with polar bears. Did you really think I wouldn't be okay?"

She sighed. "No. Do me a favor?"

"Sure." Unless it involved switching to the polar bear team. I would so miss kissing Kegan. Assuming he wanted to kiss me again.

"Can you tell my mother for me?"

I'd almost rather switch teams.

She laughed. "I know. I can't figure out how to tell her either."

"Maybe leave the polar bear thing out of it," I suggested, smiling. "But it'll be okay, right? She loves you."

"I know. But it's all so complicated. And with the grad school stuff..."

She trailed off, and I found myself confused. "Have you always known you're a polar bear?"

"I should practice saying it. Have I always known I'm gay? Yeah. Since high school. I did date a few boys but only because I felt like I had to."

"But you said you slept with your professor and that's why he left."

She rubbed her hand over her mouth. "No, I said I was stupid and had sex with someone I shouldn't have. Not him. His wife."

Ah. "I guess he caught you."

"I wish. No, it was the biggest jerk in the department. He'd asked me out three times and didn't like that I wouldn't go. The wife and I were in my office, after hours, when nobody was ever around, and he barged in to try yet again to convince me. Then he told the entire department why I wouldn't. And who I'd been with."

I sighed. "Dear God." No wonder she didn't feel able to show her face at the school.

"Yeah. I never saw my prof again. He quit his job and he and the wife moved away. I got an anonymous letter in my mailbox a few days later saying that they'd had an open relationship for years, on her side anyhow, but that she'd promised never to sleep with one of his students. Once she broke that rule, he did what he'd said he'd do and moved them to another town even though it probably screwed up his career."

"Who knew all that? To send the letter, I mean?"

She gave me a sad smile. "It was in his handwriting. She seduced me, and he knew it. Not that I resisted. But anyhow, I got tons of other notes, calling me a slut and a whore and other charming words, especially the one that rhymes with trigger, and I couldn't stay there."

135

"They called you... *that* word?"

"It's the easiest insult to throw at a black person. He was hugely popular and everyone knew he left because of me, and... and now I have two years to go and nobody wants to supervise my research and I can't stand being in the place anyhow. So I pay my tuition fees so I can at least tell myself I could go back and I work at the grocery store and try not to hate myself too much. But it's not working."

I shook my head. "I'm so sorry. What a mess."

"I know. So... how do I fix it?"

I didn't have a clue.

"All right, then, how do I tell my mother?"

"Do you need to?"

"I think so. It's weird knowing she doesn't know such a fundamental thing about me."

"Okay. Do you want to tell her the whole thing? The bit with the wife and all that?"

She gave a mock shudder. "No way. But I *do* need to explain why I can't finish my degree."

"You *can* finish it."

She shook her head but I went on. "Not there. I can see that. But isn't there anywhere else you can do the degree, and the research you want to do?"

"Yeah. British Columbia. And I doubt she wants her only child to move across the country."

"Yikes."

We spent the evening hunting for a solution, while also watching TV and eating pizza, but didn't get far. At ten o'clock she said, "I'd better head out. I have work tomorrow."

"Yeah, I do too." And I had *no* idea how it would go so I should probably get some sleep.

Once she'd put on her boots and coat I reached out to hug her, as we'd been doing since our first few get-togethers.

She froze for an instant then squeezed me tight. "I was afraid you wouldn't want to."

I leaned back to look at her. "Why? Is it contagious or something?"

She laughed. "No more than your straightness is."

"There you go." I hugged her again.

"You're awesome, Mary."

I hoped Kegan agreed.

On my way to Steel the next morning, after a restless night of puzzling over Tanisha's dilemma and wondering about me and Kegan, I remembered that the rest of the staff would be there. Since we had an inspector visit on Monday he'd brought everyone in for the weekend to get the place ready. I couldn't decide if having them all there would make seeing Kegan easier or more difficult.

What would he say to me?

Would he tell me he'd drunk too much on New Year's and hadn't meant to kiss me? I didn't want to hear that.

Maybe he *had* meant to, and would ask me out. If he did, it might be crazy but I wanted to go for it. I liked him, and his kisses, too much not to. But what would happen at work? Thus far, I'd been able to shrug it off when he became excessively controlling, but if I were romantically involved with him would that be impossible?

The only thing I knew for sure: I didn't want Crystal to know anything. I thought Dorothy would be happy if I dated Kegan, and the rest of the staff probably wouldn't care, but Crystal certainly wouldn't like it and she'd be sure to let me know.

When I walked into Steel, Crystal was all smiles but they felt thin and fake. Dorothy's greeting, on the other hand, was too cheerful to be made up. She hugged me hard. "Happy New Year, Mary. Do anything special?"

It would have been a lot easier to answer if Kegan hadn't been lounging against the wall a few feet away. I kept my eyes on her instead of letting them roam to him. "No, not really. You?"

She'd spent the night babysitting her two young grandsons, and she didn't stop sharing stories of their antics, which sounded more exhausting than cute, until Kegan said, "Okay, folks, let's get to work. Happy New Year, by the way. I hope you all had good holidays, because we'll be working hard from now until mid-February."

"Party pooper." Crystal took a step closer to him so she could lean in and bump her shoulder against his.

Dorothy had told me before Christmas that Crystal had tried to get a relationship going with Kegan not long after Steel opened and had been politely but firmly shut down. Even knowing he wasn't interested, I didn't enjoy seeing her touch him and act like she owned him.

He moved away, heading toward the huge front windows. "Yup. That's my job. To start, we need to wash the windows and put the curtains back up. The glass in the front door needs to be cleaned too."

"Why now? Why not right before we reopen?"

"We'll redo it then. But the inspector will have less to complain about if it's perfectly clean. The less he sees, the better for us."

Crystal didn't look convinced, but I was since I knew that the inspector wasn't impressed with Kegan and the New Year's Eve cancellations. "What do you want me to do?"

Kegan turned to me. "Something sitting down would be better for your leg, right?"

I shook my head. "I'm fine to stand."

Our eyes met for the first time that day and a memory jolted between us. Me standing. In his arms on New Year's Eve. Kissing him. Heat flashed through me, and I saw it blaze in his eyes and knew he could also see it in mine.

He looked down at his clipboard and cleared his throat. "The bar is covered in dust. Could you get rid of all that, and maybe wash the glasses if they need it?"

"Of course."

"I'll help you, Mary."

Fear flickered through me. Something in Crystal's tone told me she'd seen my connection with Kegan. What would she say to me?

He must have thought the same thing. "No, that's okay. I need you on the windows." Once everyone had tasks, he said, "And I'll be cleaning out the wine room."

We all set to work. The bar area was indeed filthy, but seeing the lovely granite countertop gradually emerge was satisfying. The others chatted a bit, between Crystal's complaints about how much she hated washing windows, but I was too far away to join in and frankly didn't want to.

I couldn't stop thinking of Kegan and our potential relationship. The alcohol might have fueled the fire between us, but it was clearly still there sober. I so wished I knew what he wanted, how he felt.

After about an hour Crystal stepped outside to answer a phone call, after first looking at her phone and proclaiming, "I simply *must* take this. It could be about Brash," even though nobody had tried to stop her. The door had barely closed behind her when Dorothy reached me.

"My New Year's resolution was for Crystal to find another job. Let's hope that's really what this call's about."

I laughed. "She does rave about that Brash place a lot. Maybe they do want her back."

Dorothy shook her head and leaned closer. "They didn't want her the first time."

"But I thought she was a big part of the place. The way she talks—"

"I happened to be in New York last year and went to Brash. When I mentioned her name the server burst out laughing and said she'd lasted three weeks before they fired her for picking a fight with the head chef."

Crystal returned before I could respond, shaking snow off her bleached hair and saying, "*Interesting* call, that," to nobody in particular.

Dorothy muttered, "We all know she's full of it," and returned to her work.

Surprising that Dorothy would have told everyone about Crystal's misrepresentation of her career. But then, Crystal was frequently nasty to her so maybe she'd felt justified.

Only three weeks. Did Kegan know?

Thinking of him wiped Crystal's situation from my mind, and I cleaned and daydreamed about my boss's mouth on mine until noon when a man knocked on the door.

Crystal called, "We're closed."

He shook his head and held up a cardboard florist box. "Delivery."

She unlocked the door and reached for the box, but he said, "Mary?"

"That's me." I came forward and Crystal backed up, although I could feel her hovering behind me as I accepted the flowers and relocked the door.

Everyone was clearly ready for a break so they crowded around as I set the box on the now-clean bar. A movement in the hall caught my eye, and I looked up to see Kegan, standing apart from the others, watching me.

My heart began to pound. Charles didn't know where I worked, and he wouldn't have sent me flowers anyhow. Brian had no reason to either, and he would only have done it if I'd given him the money; I'd had to lend him another twenty bucks "so I can buy my mother a Christmas present". Annoyance at myself snapped through me but I pushed it away, not wanting Brian to taint this. It had to be Kegan.

I untied the ribbon holding the box closed, then lifted the lid and stared at the contents.

A dozen perfect red roses. Twelve. With one finger, I brushed the nearest's cool velvety-damp outer petals, hardly believing what I was seeing.

"There's a card." Crystal reached into the box and pulled it out.

I plucked it from her hand before she could open it. "Thank you."

"Who're they from?" Dorothy was nearly as excited as she'd been about her grandchildren. "A nice man, I hope."

Feeling Kegan's eyes on me, I read the card silently, holding it close enough that Crystal couldn't see it.

"It's not original, but I mean it. One for every amazing month I want to spend with you this year."

I read and reread the card, my face pulling into a smile I couldn't hold back and my body flooding with a warm rush of happiness. He hadn't been that drunk if he remembered the roses my friend had received every year from her husband, and he'd sent them so he must want to be with me. My delight proved to me that I wanted to be with him too. We'd make it work somehow.

"Look at that grin." Dorothy elbowed me. "He *is* a nice man, right? And you said you didn't do anything special on New Year's."

I slipped the card into my pocket and elbowed her back, so excited I wanted to dance. "I can't give up all my secrets, you know. But yes, he's a very nice man."

"Good. You deserve one." She looked to Kegan. "Can I help Mary get them in water?"

"Of course."

I turned to face him, longing to thank him but knowing I could hardly do that in front of everyone. "Want to see them in their box first?"

He laughed. "Roses in their natural habitat? Sure."

He stood close beside me, looking down at them, then touched the same one I had. "Soft. And gorgeous. But Dorothy's right, you should get them out of there." He didn't look at me. Probably good; I might have thrown myself on him if our eyes had met again.

The giddy Dorothy and I took the box to the kitchen. Once there, though, she sobered at once. "Keep them in the office and take them home tonight where they'll be safe."

I wouldn't have left them at work anyhow, but her insistence that I shouldn't surprised me. I frowned, but before I could speak she said, "Please. Just trust me."

I leaned in and lowered my voice. "You know things you're not telling me."

She swallowed hard and nodded.

"You can trust me."

"I know." She jumped as another worker came in for a fresh bucket of water. We didn't speak until he left, then she said, "You can trust me too. I can't tell you now."

I didn't like it, but there wasn't much I could do. "Tell me when you can."

"I will."

We finished arranging the roses then stood looking at them. "They really are gorgeous, Mary. He *must* be a nice man."

If I wanted her to trust me, I'd have to trust her. And I did, so I turned to face her, looking directly into her eyes, then flicked my gaze to Kegan's office door and back at her.

Her eyes widened and a grin lit up her face. She mouthed, "Kegan?"

I nodded, grinning too, and she grabbed me in a hug. "Good girl," she whispered. "You two will be great together."

"I hope so," I whispered back.

She released me and took a breath to ask what would no doubt be the first of a barrage of questions about my relationship with Kegan. Questions I didn't even know the answers to yet.

Before she could start, though, the man himself appeared in the kitchen doorway. "Nearly done? I'm finalizing an order for candles and need to know if you want anything special for Magma."

I was afraid Dorothy would make it clear I'd told her, but she was a better actress than I'd have expected. "We're finished, I think. I'll go back to my napkin folding. Mary, you're right to take the roses home tonight. I *will* miss them, but you should get to enjoy them every morning. And maybe even with the man who provided them?"

She gave me a sweet smile and disappeared down the hall.

Kegan took the heavy glass vase for me and I followed him into the office. He set the vase down on my desk then closed the door, and the window blinds, and returned to my side. We stood looking at each other for a long moment before he said, "So."

"So."

We were standing almost where we'd been on New Year's, and I wanted to kiss him again more than anything.

So I did. I slid my arms around his neck, said, "Thank you so much, they're gorgeous," and kissed him on the mouth.

In broad daylight, no candlelight or champagne, with our staff roaming the restaurant just outside the office door, the kiss was easily the equal of anything we'd shared on New Year's, maybe even better.

Shorter, of course, but deep and sweet and strong, and the way his eyes glowed when it ended sent shivers down my spine.

"I left on New Year's," he said, holding me close, "because we'd both been drinking and I didn't want anything to happen that you'd regret later."

"Or that you'd regret?"

He shook his head and brushed his lips over mine. "I meant it, with the roses. I've known for a while but New Year's made it definite. I like you, and I want to see where it goes."

Tingling at his words and his light but delicious kiss, I said, "I want that too, but—"

"But you're still married."

I blinked. I hadn't even thought of that. "Legally, I guess I am, but I haven't felt married in a long time. I was thinking about work. This career means so much to me, and like we said on New Year's I don't want to risk it. But I *do* like you, and..." I shrugged helplessly.

He gave me a squeeze. "I feel the same way. But I honestly think we'll be okay. We're both professionals, and most of the plans are set anyhow. If we get on each other's nerves, we can reconsider, but I don't think it'll happen."

I wanted him to be right. "I hope not."

He smoothed a hand over my hair. "If you want to, of course. If you don't want to date me, if New Year's was a mistake, let me know."

I smiled. "If I thought it was a mistake, would I have kissed you here?"

His fingers curved around the back of my neck and he drew me closer. "Good point." He kissed me again. "Mary, will you have dinner with me tonight? Our first real date?"

Oh, definitely.

Chapter Seventeen

I waited with the rest of the staff but couldn't find it in me to relax and chat like they were. The inspector had spent two full hours that afternoon examining every inch of Steel, and he and Kegan had been locked in the office for a good forty minutes. What could they possibly be discussing?

The contractors had done an amazing job, and we seemed to be well on track to being ready for January fifteenth, but had the inspector spotted something that would prevent the opening? Kegan had his heart set on it, and I didn't want to see the sadness and disappointment he'd feel if it didn't happen.

I still had reservations about falling for my boss but I was doing it all the same. After a blissful dinner out for our first real date, we'd spent an even more blissful half hour kissing goodbye in my apartment. Before he left we made plans to go out for breakfast, and ended up spending the entire weekend together, alternating between work and kissing with perhaps a little more time devoted to the latter. Sunday night we went out for dinner and to a movie with Tess and Forrest, who had fun teasing us every chance they got about the foolishness of hooking up with someone from work.

I adored kissing Kegan, but also loved just being with him. Every moment we spent together made me happy and I could tell he felt the same way. I didn't want to lose the glow, and if the inspector—

Footsteps in the hallway, and my heart kicked against my ribs as the men appeared. Kegan looked tired but not upset, and the inspector seemed calm. Kegan shook hands with him and locked the door behind him, then dropped onto a barstool and looked at us all, ending with his eyes on me. "I'm glad that's over."

"Are we still going to open on time?"

He smiled at me. "Absolutely."

My shoulders released tension I hadn't realized they were holding and I grinned at him.

He grinned back, but it faded and he again looked around at the others. "But we have a ton of work to do. Most of it, frankly, is little and picky, but if it's not done when he comes back next Wednesday then he'll stop the opening. So let's make sure that can't happen."

After assigning everyone a job he left the list of tasks on the bar so we could pick up new ones when we needed them. Crystal, in the corner with her buddies replacing light bulbs, muttered about how this wasn't the work she'd been hired to do and how at Brash she'd never have been forced into it, but everyone but her friends ignored her. It wasn't the work any of us wanted, not even Kegan, but he was right there taking on the biggest jobs and not seeming to notice as his pale gray shirt and black dress pants got steadily dirtier.

He and I kept our interactions thoroughly professional, since we'd agreed that the staff didn't need to know about our fledgling relationship. I had admitted that I'd told Dorothy, not wanting any lies between us, but he said, "She's no problem," then blushed adorably and confessed that Crystal had been after him at one point. "I doubt she cares now, but why tell her? There's no need for her to know about us. Not yet anyhow."

A little part of me wanted him to want to tell the world we were together, but mostly I knew keeping quiet was smart. Our romance was great so far, but it wasn't even a week old.

Still, Crystal seemed to sense it. Her mutterings dropped off whenever I was nearby, and I felt her eyes on me whenever I spoke to Kegan.

Knowing how vicious she could be, remembering how she growled at Isaac, made me nervous but I did my best to act normal. It was tough, though, and when Kegan went to his office to request some estimates for the work we couldn't do on our own I felt myself relax.

Maybe too much.

Carrying a bucket of water with both hands, I stepped around a pile of dirt on the floor and dragged my arm along the wall. Pain flashed through me, and I set down the bucket and pulled open my ripped cardigan sleeve to see my anti-coagulated blood pouring from a cut that stretched nearly the length of my upper arm.

Gripping my arm to try to stop the bleeding, I slid down the wall to sit on the floor. The wound didn't hurt that much, really, but the sight of the flood made my knees weak.

Dorothy, up on a ladder replacing a light bulb Crystal had claimed was too tightly installed for her to remove, nearly fell rushing to my side. "Mary, what happened?"

"I cut myself. I think there was something on the wall."

She helped me out of the cardigan then grabbed a stack of clean napkins from the top of the bar and handed me one.

I wrapped it tightly around my arm but quickly soaked through it.

She gave me another. "Push harder."

I squeezed with all my might despite the extra pain it caused, but when we peeked beneath the makeshift bandage after a few seconds Dorothy shook her head. "It's not slowing at all." She turned toward the office and called, "Kegan? Mary's hurt."

He was there in an instant, crouched down before me. "What happened?"

I shook my head. "It looks worse than it is. I bumped into a nail or something and it won't stop bleeding."

"I'll call an ambulance."

"No, don't. It's really just a big scratch."

"But with the anti-coagulants... at least call your doctor, okay?"

He waited until I agreed before fetching my phone from the office, then found the number in my contact list, dialed, and held the phone to my ear for me.

Once I'd finished talking to the nurse on duty, I said, "Okay, you can hang up," and Kegan closed my phone and said, "Well?"

Embarrassed at now being surrounded by the curious staff along with Dorothy and Kegan, I looked down at the bloody mess of napkins on my arm. "I'm supposed to keep it elevated and apply pressure. If it doesn't stop in thirty minutes, or if I feel sick or dizzy, I have to go to the hospital. Otherwise, I'll be okay."

"If you feel bad at all, you'll tell me, right?"

I nodded. I did feel freaked out, of course, but not like I'd lost too much blood.

Kegan brought over a chair so I could put my arm up on it, then checked the wall until he found the half-attached drywall staple I'd cut myself on. He pulled it from the wall and threw it with force into the pile of dirt I'd dodged to avoid before returning to my side and taking a seat next to me on the floor. "How is it?"

I eased the napkins back. "Not good."

He re-wrapped my arm firmly but gently, then piled a few more cloths on top and closed his hand tightly around the bandage.

"You don't have to—"

"I want to." He rubbed the underside of my arm with his thumb.

The contact sent shivers through me despite the pain and the situation, and I let myself lean into him.

He returned the favor, then looked up. "Back to work, guys. I'll stay with her."

Crystal, eyes narrowed, stared at me for a moment before heading off. Dorothy studied me too, but her motivation was clearly concern.

Once they'd all left us alone, Kegan said, "I'm going to kill that contractor."

I shook my head. "It was an accident. I just didn't see it."

"There aren't supposed to be accidents here."

"Kegan. I'll be fine. If I weren't on the anti-coagulants it would be no big deal."

"But you are, and it's a big deal to me." He leaned closer. "Don't want my new girlfriend getting hurt at work."

A warm glow spread through me. I hadn't been anyone's girlfriend in a long time. "Well, I don't want my new boyfriend upset about it, so we're even."

He winked at me. "Indeed we are."

Twenty-nine minutes after I'd been cut, the bleeding didn't resume when we tentatively peeled back the bandages, and I breathed a sigh of relief. "So didn't want to go to the hospital."

"I know. Remember how long we waited when I took you for your shot?"

"Forever."

"At least." He gathered up the blood-soaked napkins. "Think I'll throw these out. They might wash clean, but..."

"I doubt the inspector would be thrilled if he found out."

He smiled. "Definitely not." He stuffed the napkins, and my ruined sweater too after checking with me, into a garbage bag then held his hand out to me. "Ready to get off the floor?"

I nodded and he eased me upright and into the chair. Once we knew I wouldn't pass out, he helped me get to my feet. "Feeling okay?"

"Yeah. Thirsty but otherwise fine."

"I'll get you a drink. Water?"

"That'd be perfect."

He gave my shoulder a squeeze and headed off.

The instant he was out of sight, Crystal was at my side. "What's the deal with you guys?"

Determined to brazen it out, I said, "I don't know what you're talking about."

Dorothy came to my defense. "Crystal, come on. She was cut, bleeding like crazy. Of course he wanted to make sure she was okay."

"By sitting with her for half an hour while the rest of us worked?"

"They worked while we were off for nearly three weeks. Off with full pay. I think we're even."

Crystal's eyebrows went up and she took a step closer to Dorothy, who took half a step back but then held her ground. Kegan returned, though, before Crystal could say another word.

"Nice of you to check on Mary," he said to both women. "I'll take over now."

He handed me the water and crouched beside me. Crystal turned and stalked away while Dorothy hovered nearby.

As I drank, he said quietly, "Dorothy, it's okay."

She turned so her back was to the others. "Crystal's angry."

He nodded. "I know. It'll be all right."

She gave me a sad smile and left.

My boyfriend and I sat in silence for a minute or so, then I said, "I think I'm okay now." I put down the glass and got to my feet, and sure enough I felt fine, if a bit tired.

"Good."

"So I'll get back to work."

"The hell you will."

"Come on. I'm fine. Everyone else is working, so I should too."

He checked his watch then said to the group, "Okay, guys, it's nearly five. Let's call it a day, but please be here by eight tomorrow."

I looked up at him, trying to hold back a smile.

"What? Should I make them stay longer so you can work?"

I laughed. "You're impossible."

"Thank you. Now sit down and rest. Or better yet go to our office and get your stuff."

Our office. I liked the sound of that. I headed towards it but took a detour into the bathroom to wash the dried blood from my arm, carefully avoiding the cut itself so I wouldn't start it bleeding again.

When I came out, Kegan was waiting for me. "Everyone's gone. You still okay?"

I nodded. "Just figured I should clean up."

He pulled me into his arms. "I wanted to hug you before," he said into my hair, "but I couldn't."

"I know. It's okay." It sure felt good now, though.

He tipped my face up and gave me the sweetest kiss imaginable. "Don't get hurt again, please."

I squeezed him tight, warmed by both his body and his concern for me. "I'll do my best."

"Good stuff." He cleared his throat. "I... you know I'm going to Niagara Falls this weekend. Like I did before Steel opened the first time."

I nodded. He'd put it on the calendar after the re-opening was set for January fifteenth.

"I called the hotel today, and I can get a second room." He touched my cheek. "Would you like to go with me?"

A weekend away. With the sexiest man I'd ever known.

Two days after my divorce papers would be filed with the court.

I'd be single, nearly.

Nearly. Not quite.

"I'm not suggesting... I'm not expecting anything. I just want to spend that kind of time with you. You wouldn't... owe me anything."

His awkwardness made it clear what he was trying to say, and I cuddled into him. I'd never have thought he'd expect sex in return for the trip, but I liked that he felt the need to spell it out. "I've never seen the Falls, you know."

He squeezed me. "Then you have to come. I'll show you around. If you want to, that is."

"I want to," I said into his shirt.

He leaned back and kissed me again. "I'll make the arrangements."

"Sounds good."

We went into the office for our coats then headed for the front door. But as we reached the dining area, Crystal, recognizable by her bleached hair, skittered out of the restaurant without looking back.

We looked at each other, both aware she'd left then returned to spy on us.

I sank into a dining room chair. "That's not good."

He sat next to me. "So she knows. Big deal. Who cares what she thinks?"

"Um, a lot of the staff?"

"Oh, they do not. They know she's full of hot air. All that stuff about Brash, when they all know she didn't even last a month."

I stared at him. "*You* know that?"

"I checked her references. Of course I know."

"Then why do you let her go on and on about it?"

He shrugged. "Doesn't hurt me any. I just ignore it."

"But it hurts the staff."

He put his arm around me. "Yeah, it's annoying, but it doesn't hurt them. Every team has one blowhard, and she's ours."

I attempted to explain how horrible she'd been to Isaac, and how toxic the environment became when she let loose, but I couldn't find the words and he wasn't listening anyhow.

"I know she's a pain. But she works hard and we need her. There are always arguments in a kitchen when everyone's working toward a deadline. Trust me. I pay attention whenever I'm in there and I know it's fine. Now stop worrying and come here."

His certainty calmed me, since he'd known the staff much longer than I had, and I let him pull me in and kiss me until Crystal was the furthest thing from my mind.

Chapter Eighteen

Wednesday January sixth. The anniversary of my leaving Charles, and time to sign the final paperwork for my divorce. In a few weeks I'd get an envelope in the mail and my marriage would be over.

I knew I wanted that. Dating Kegan made it even clearer how weak and sad my relationship with Charles had been. But it still felt icky. I'd been married to him for six years, after all.

Before I left for my ten o'clock appointment, Kegan called me into our office. "Take your time, okay? Get a coffee, go shopping, do whatever you want. Whatever will make you happy."

I smiled and hugged him. "Thanks." I didn't kiss him; it felt wrong to do that on my way to the lawyer.

He cuddled me close then let me go without trying to kiss me. "I hope it works out."

"Me too."

It did, with almost indecent ease. I signed my name multiple times, paid the lawyer another three hundred dollars, and walked out nearly single.

Kegan had said I should do whatever I want. But what *did* I want?

I could get a pedicure. Vibrant red toenails, like Charles had hated. But I didn't have the gloves with me to put my support tights back on. Besides, did I want to spend money to essentially stick my tongue out at Charles?

No. I wanted to be at work. I wanted to be with Kegan.

I went back to Steel, pausing only to pick up cookies from Mildred to treat the staff. They'd been working so hard to get Steel up and running, and while Kegan had told them he appreciated it I thought they might like a tangible sign of how much *I* appreciated it too.

When she gave me the cookies, I said on a whim, "Mildred, what's wrong with Dorothy?"

She folded her arms. "Not a chance. If she wants to tell you anything, it's up to her. I don't share people's secrets. Not the big ones, anyhow."

I sighed. "She won't tell me. I just want to help her."

She patted my arm. "You are. By being there."

"You think so?"

"I know so. Now get back there, and I expect to see you and your man for lunch."

Somehow she'd known we were dating even before I told her or Tanisha. I'd asked her how and she'd just smiled and said, "It's been written all over you both for ages, honey."

"I'll try. He's busy."

"He's got to eat."

"Yes, mommy."

She laughed and shooed me out of the café.

I passed out the cookies, to the staff's delight. Kegan joined us in the dining room, and said quietly to me, "Everything okay?"

I nodded, and he squeezed my arm, avoiding the healing cut. "Good stuff. Left some papers on your desk. Take a look, would you?"

He settled into a chair with his cookie and I went to my desk. There were indeed papers. There was also a small gift bag. It looked more interesting, so I opened it first.

Inside, a card rested atop crumpled tissue paper.

Mary,

You only have to listen to your own voice from now on. I hope you enjoy these, whenever you're ready.

Kegan

Confused, I pulled away the tissue paper, then stared down into the bag feeling tears and laughter struggling to escape me at once.

I drew out the bottles one by one. Ten different shades of red nail polish.

Laughter won over the tears, and I sat at my desk facing the line of bottles and giggled. Who else but Kegan could make a gift of nail polish so sweet?

"Paperwork amuses you that much?"

I looked up and smiled at him. "You know it's not that. Thank you."

He bent and kissed me. "You are so welcome. Did you even look at the papers?"

"Easy, boss. I was about to."

The first few pages were invoices for the food for Steel's opening, which I'd check against the deliveries when they arrived next week. The last sheet, though, was the confirmation notice from the hotel in Niagara Falls. I held that one up. "Thanks for booking this. How much do I owe you?"

He ran a hand over my hair. "You owe me showing up and having an amazing relaxing weekend. That's it."

"I can afford to pay my share," I said, but then I looked up into his eyes and saw clearly how much he wanted to give me this. I smiled at him. "But I won't. I'll show up and have an amazing relaxing weekend."

He smiled back. "Perfect."

"On one condition."

He raised his eyebrows.

"You have to have a great weekend too."

"Oh, all right."

I laughed and he kissed me on the forehead. "I will, because you'll be there."

We grinned at each other, then he cleared his throat. "I think we should tell the staff we're both going."

I grimaced, and he said, "I know. But if we keep our relationship a secret they'll wonder why when they find out. Nobody's commented, so Crystal might not have told them we're together, but I think we should. Then there's nothing for them to gossip about."

I suspected Crystal would find something, if she hadn't already, but I had to agree with him that secrecy wouldn't do us any favors. "Are you telling or am I?"

"I am." He held out his hand to help me up. "And you'll be beside me."

That's what we did. I stood with him as he reminded the staff he'd be in Niagara for the weekend and told them I would be going with him. He didn't explicitly say we were dating, but the message definitely got through.

Crystal and her friends looked like they were contemplating which kitchen knife to throw at me first. The rest of the staff seemed amused but not otherwise bothered, and Dorothy was clearly delighted.

"Any questions?"

There weren't, so he said, "All right, then." He cocked his head and I heard his phone ringing in the office. "I'll get that, and then Mary and I are going out for lunch and you guys can take a break too. Oh, Mary, the new menu inserts are here. Can you put them into their covers?"

"Of course."

He left, and I took only one step toward the box of inserts before Crystal was in front of me, her main minion Dave behind her. "You and Kegan."

I put my shoulders back and said, "Yes?"

"You're dating. Not just making out in the hallway."

I ignored her words and snarky tone, and Dave's suppressed snickers. "Yes, we're dating. Nothing will change around here, though, and—"

"I give it two weeks, tops. You won't keep him."

I stared at her, surprised she'd be so blatantly rude. She'd never been like that with me before.

"Why not?" Dorothy said from behind me, making me jump. "He obviously cares about her, and you feel the same, right, Mary?"

Before I could respond, Crystal said, "Have you slept with him yet?"

Shock flooded me, and I didn't even try to hide it. "That's so not your business."

She laughed. "That means no. Kegan's had a *lot* of girlfriends here and some of them liked to talk. Trust me, you're nowhere near wild enough to keep him interested."

Thursday night after underwater hockey, I should have been packing for the Niagara trip but instead sat staring at the bottles of nail polish lined up on my dresser. They *were* a sweet gift, but they'd come to represent a lot more in my mind.

Sex. With Kegan.

He said he wasn't expecting me to sleep with him in Niagara, and I knew he meant it. But I wanted to, physically at least. Though we hadn't gone further than kissing, the passion behind those kisses had left me breathless and hungry for more.

I could probably have more on the weekend. If I wanted to.

In a few weeks I'd be officially divorced but at the moment I was technically still married. Maybe I *should* have felt bad about considering sleeping with Kegan before my divorce came through, but I didn't. I was no longer married in any way that mattered. My worries lay elsewhere.

Would I be good enough for Kegan?

Crystal had obviously been trying to upset me with her words, but what had upset me more was how Dorothy deflated. Her reaction made it all too clear that Kegan's exes *had* revealed how he was in bed; while Crystal might have been exaggerating a touch, she wasn't lying.

I'd slept with two guys before Charles, and neither of them had wanted anything more exotic than a garter belt and heels. Charles hadn't even wanted that: he'd hated that I had more experience than he did and when I'd tentatively suggested a little lingerie might spice things up he'd been so upset I thought we needed spicing up I'd never been able to mention it again. Sex with him had ended up basically a chore, as routine as washing the kitchen floor and nowhere near as satisfying when it was done.

So far Kegan seemed happy with my kisses, if his eagerness to kiss me meant anything. Would I please him, though, if we slept together on the weekend? Or would he be expecting me to be an expert at things I'd never even heard of and be disappointed with my performance?

I turned a nail polish bottle around in my hand, wondering. I'd bought my first garter belt and stockings in years for this trip, along with a sexy lace nightgown and three new bra and panty sets and a sleek skirt and pretty top and high heels for the fancy restaurants we'd no doubt visit. Plus a box of condoms, just in case. Would all that be enough?

I set the nail polish bottle down, then my shoulders relaxed as I spotted the roses he'd given me, now hanging upside down to dry so I could keep them forever. He'd given them to me because he liked me, and right from the beginning he'd insisted he wanted me to be myself with him. Well, "myself" wasn't kinky, and I didn't know how to fake it even if I thought he wanted me to. I briefly considered looking online for inspiration but the thought of all the truly overwhelming material I'd find with a search for "kinky sex" put an end to that.

So I wouldn't fake it. I would be myself.

But myself with red toenails.

When the thought slipped into my mind I knew it was exactly what I needed. A private boost of confidence and sexiness. Not kinky, no, but knowing I'd done my toenails as I loved doing would make it easier to do other things if I wanted. Or not do them if that felt right.

I scanned the bottles then picked the one that seemed to be calling me. When I realized the color was called "Reddy" I figured it was a sign. I was ready to do this.

Taking my time, I painted each toenail, every stroke of the brush pushing Charles a little further back and giving me a little more space to be myself.

When all ten nails were done, I stretched out my legs and admired my handiwork. Even with only one coat, my feet looked elegant and sexy at once. I smiled down at them. I would stand on those two feet, decorated as I liked, and make my own decisions on how my relationship with Kegan would progress.

Between coats of nail polish, I packed for the trip, making sure I had comfortable clothes for sightseeing and my new skirt and top and shoes. And of course, my new lingerie and the condoms.

It would have to be enough. It was the best I could do.

Chapter Nineteen

The hotel clerk looked confused. "There's a note in your file saying that's what you wanted. I can try to find a different room, but we're pretty booked."

"Please do try."

He began typing, and Kegan said into my ear, "I'm sorry. I definitely did not ask for that."

That was obvious by his reaction when the clerk said it. "It's okay. Really."

"You can keep your side locked."

I frowned at him. "Do you honestly think I'm afraid you'll sneak in on me in the middle of the night? I know you better than that. Adjoining rooms are fine."

Which was good, because the clerk couldn't do anything about it.

In the elevator, Kegan said, "I asked for our rooms to be on the same floor so it'd be easier for us to meet up for breakfast or whatever. I guess they misunderstood."

I slipped my arm around his waist. "I swear to you, I'm fine with it. Stop worrying."

He kissed my temple. "Sorry. You're supposed to be relaxing."

"So are you," I said, snuggling closer to him.

When I opened the door to my room, I gasped at the view. The Falls were incredible from this height, and I could hear the roaring of the water even with the windows closed.

"Pretty, huh?"

I turned and grinned at him. He was standing in my open doorway. "Just a bit."

"Hungry?"

I considered. "Yes, actually."

"The main restaurant here is great, and you'll be able to see the Falls from our table. How's about I call and get us a reservation?"

"Sounds good."

He went to his room, and I began unpacking my things, stashing the condoms in the bedside table and making sure that the other sexier items weren't anywhere he could see them if he happened to come in. I was nearly done when my cell phone rang.

"The earliest they can get us in is eight tonight. Is that okay?"

I glanced at the alarm clock by my bed. It wasn't even seven yet. "I might run down to the coffee shop and get a little snack, but sure. I'd like to see the restaurant."

"Good enough. I'll make the reservation, and then I'll go to the coffee shop with you if that's okay."

"Kegan."

"Yes?"

I smiled. "Anything that involves me getting to spend time with you is okay."

I could tell he was smiling too when he said, "Glad to hear it."

As we shared a muffin, which we both agreed wasn't remotely as good as the ones Mildred made, he said, "Anything interesting at Magma today? I wish I could get over there more often."

I was glad he hadn't been there that day to hear my pathetic conversation, if it even deserved that name, with John Franklin. I'd requested shelves near the sinks for spare dish towels, so the staff would have no excuse not to replace them frequently. John had taken notes a few days ago on where I wanted the shelves, and I'd been pleased with myself for making my desires so clear, which was why I was so shocked to come in and find he'd put the shelves on the other side of the room.

"Yeah, I know you wanted them over there but the studs weren't in the right place. It wouldn't have worked out."

To my shame, I hadn't done anything but mumble, "I understand." I didn't understand, especially not why he hadn't even given me the chance to put the shelves somewhere more useful than where he'd chosen, but he was moving on to instruct his staff in something and I hadn't found the nerve to make him continue talking to me.

So, my shelves were misplaced but at least Kegan hadn't seen me do nothing about it.

We talked about Magma for a few minutes then fell into a comfortable silence. Eventually I broke it, since I'd been wondering about something. "Why did you decide to come here before Steel opened the first time?"

He shrugged. "Needed a break. The prep work was exhausting, and I knew I'd need to go full-tilt once Steel opened, so I figured a weekend away would get me in a good frame of mind."

"Makes sense."

His eyes, suddenly intense, searched my face. "Plus, I had another reason. I wasn't going to tell you but now I want to."

Unnerved by his changed demeanor, I said, "Okay. What's the reason?"

"I was... romantically involved, let's say, with someone who was part of Steel at the time. It ended a few weeks before the opening and I came here at least partly to get her off my mind."

"Did it work?"

He gave me a half-smile. "No. But being busy with Steel did. And I realized here that I'd been a fool to risk Steel for her."

"That New Year's resolution, it was about her, right?"

"Partly, but I dated a lot in the first six months or so, trying to forget her, and like a moron I dated patrons too. The resolution was more about staying away from them and from any other woman who has influence on my work. I won't risk my restaurants again."

I stared at him.

He laughed. "Don't look at me like that. You're different. You'd never ask me to give up Steel or Magma. You know it'd be like cutting off my arm."

"True, but..." I leaned closer. "Do you really think we can date without causing problems at Magma and Steel?"

He stroked my cheek and I shivered. He smiled. "Yes, ma'am, I do. You get me, and I like to think I get you. We'll be fine."

Loving his definite tone, I smiled back, then a dreadful thought hit me. "The one you were involved with... it wasn't Crystal, was it?"

He burst out laughing and I joined him, relieved, and we went on to chat about anything but work. After ten minutes or so he said, "I think I'll go shower and get ready for dinner. I'll pick you up a few minutes before eight." I agreed, and we went back to our rooms. He gave me a hug at my door then left me.

I walked into my room, then stopped. It smelled different. It smelled like...

Like the vase of red roses now adorning the desk.

My mouth pulling into a smile though there was nobody to see it, I picked up the card. The smile widened and my eyes prickled with tears as I read, "One for each month doesn't seem quite enough. Thank you. For everything."

I sat on the bed still holding the card, grinning, then jumped as I heard the sound of rushing water from his room. He was in the shower, no doubt. Wet and naked.

My mind wandered deliciously for a few moments. Knowing I might be able to walk right through into his room and join him was exquisite torture.

But some of my thoughts weren't quite so exquisite.

More and more, I felt like I *had* to sleep with him. Not because he expected it, but because the situation demanded it. A fancy dinner at a lovely restaurant, no doubt by candlelight, with the Falls as backdrop, then up to our adjoining rooms. After that, how would I say, "Well, have a good night," and close the door on him?

I took a quick shower while trying and failing to answer that question, then got ready while still grappling with it, blow-drying my hair so I could leave it down for once and doing my makeup and easing on my garter belt and stockings instead of my thick support tights. My silky skirt wouldn't look right with them, and a few hours tight-free wouldn't hurt me, especially since we'd be sitting.

But I'd become used to wearing them, and the sheer stockings felt so different. Everything felt different. I was dressing to sleep with Kegan and I so wasn't sure I wanted to. But I wasn't sure I didn't, so I wore the sexy new bra and panties and garter belt and stockings and hoped to hell I'd know what I wanted when the time arrived.

His knock on my door scared me so badly I jumped and knocked over my foundation bottle. I picked it up and wiped up the little bit that had spilled while calling, "I'll be right there."

"Take your time."

I didn't, of course. I straightened the pale blue top I'd bought, making sure the fluttery hem lay properly across my hips, and put on my simple silver necklace and earrings with shaking hands. Then I studied myself in the mirror. I was ready. As ready as I'd ever be.

I slipped on my new heels, found my room's key card, and opened the door.

Kegan gave a low whistle. "You look amazing."

"You're one to talk," I said, then coughed to try to hide the tremor in my voice. He always looked great, but he'd obviously made more effort than usual. I'd seen his black suit before, but not the dark blue shirt that made his eyes glow, and he was stunning.

His expression said he felt the same about me. He slid his hand around the back of my neck, under my hair, and kissed me slow and sweet.

My nervousness faded as my rising desire took over.

Far too soon, he drew back, his mouth curving into a smile. "You are gorgeous, and I'm happy you're here, and we're going to have a great weekend. No pressure. Got it?"

My throat tightened. He just *knew* me, somehow. How had he realized I was feeling like I had to put out? I believed him, though, and I wouldn't sleep with him unless it felt completely right. I reached up and kissed him again. "Got it. And thank you for the roses. They smell terrific."

He pressed his face to my neck and breathed deeply. "That makes two of you."

I imitated him, and the rich sexy scent of his cologne weakened my knees. "Three of us."

"Good. No stinkers allowed." He took my hand, then tugged my door card out of my grasp and slid it into his jacket pocket. "Why do women's clothes never have pockets?" He took my hand again and we headed down the hall toward the elevator.

"So we have to buy purses."

"Ah. Anything for accessories."

I giggled and he squeezed my hand, and for the next three hours we sat at an isolated corner table in the gorgeous restaurant and ate incredible food and laughed and talked and watched the Falls, illuminated for the night by bright lights of every color imaginable.

Once we'd finished eating Kegan pulled his chair around beside mine and wrapped an arm around my shoulders. We sat close together and watched the lights playing on the water while finishing our coffee and tea. I had never had a more perfect evening.

In the elevator on the way back to our rooms, though, my heart began pounding again. I had to decide. Now. I still didn't know. I did want him, but something felt wrong.

At my door, he put both hands, one holding my door card, on my shoulders. "That was amazing. Thank you so much."

"I should be thanking you."

He gave a small laugh and shook his head. "Without you, I wouldn't be opening Magma, wouldn't have survived Steel's renovations nearly as well, and would certainly not have had as good a time tonight." He gave my shoulder a squeeze. "I haven't had a girlfriend since the summer and the mess with Nora. I needed someone like you. No, I needed you. I'm so glad I found you."

I threw my arms around his waist and burrowed into him. "I'm so glad too."

We held each other close for a long moment, then he tipped my chin up and kissed me, his mouth moving gently and sweetly over mine. Then he said softly, "Good night."

There'd been passion in that kiss too, and predictable parts of me were screaming, "Go for it! Sleep with him!" But I wanted every part of me ready for our first time and I wasn't there yet, so I took a deep breath, said, "Good night," and took my door card from his hand.

He kissed my forehead. "Sleep well. Breakfast at ten tomorrow? Or later?"

I smiled, proud of myself for not caving in and relieved that he'd handled it the way I'd expected, without being offended or upset. "Or earlier?"

"Nine?"

"Perfect."

We studied each other for one last moment, then I went into my rose-scented room and left him standing in the hall.

Chapter Twenty

"You're sure you don't mind?"

He shook his head. "It'll only take a minute, and you can't enjoy the Falls if you're cold."

I'd debated whether to wear a sweater under my coat and decided against it, which turned out to be a mistake. We'd spent the morning inside, losing forty dollars a few quarters at a time to various slot machines at the casino by our hotel, but after lunch we'd gone out to walk beside the ice-laden Falls and despite Kegan's arm around me I'd had to admit I was freezing.

When we reached my room, I stepped inside and held the door for Kegan but he said, "I'll wait out here."

The hallway was bustling with people. "No, you won't. Get in there."

We had a brief staring contest, and he gave in. "If you're sure."

"Definitely."

I let the door close behind him, said, "I'll be right back," and went further into the room. I dropped my coat on the freshly made bed and tried on the three cardigans I'd brought, then put on the one that fit the best over my long-sleeved top, picked up my coat, and turned to leave.

Kegan stood studying the "in case of fire" instructions screwed to my wall like he'd been looking for them all his life.

My chest squeezed as I realized he was deliberately not watching me. He hadn't moved an inch from the front door either. He was doing everything he could to give me my space, to make sure I didn't feel pressured into sleeping with him.

I didn't feel pressured. Not by him, and not by myself. I felt touched by his consideration, and relaxed, and *ready*. I dropped my coat on a chair then walked to him, certainty growing with each step, and kissed him full on the mouth.

After a startled instant he dropped his coat and wrapped his arms around me and kissed me back, and I pressed myself against him and gave in to what I knew for sure I wanted.

When kissing wasn't enough any more I took a step backward, drawing him with me toward the bed.

He broke the kiss then, his hungry eyes locked to mine, and said softly, "You're sure?"

In answer, I kissed him even harder. With my doubts gone, all that lay between us was pure raw passion, and I realized we'd been restraining ourselves before, in all our kisses. No more, though. I gave him everything I had and he gave it right back.

We reached the bed and tumbled onto it, still kissing. His hands moving over my arms and sides, my hands clutching at his strong shoulders and back, our panting and gasps... glorious.

I yanked off his sweater, taking his t-shirt with it, and tossed them both onto the floor, and he rolled onto his back and pulled me to kneel straddling him. "It's too bad, you know," he said, his voice teasing.

Nothing seemed bad to me at the moment. I'd thought his body looked good at the pool, but nothing beat the view from only a foot or two away, not to mention knowing I could both look and touch. "What is?"

"You put that sweater on and now it's coming off. All that work for nothing."

I laughed and ran my palms over his exposed sleek abs and up to his chest, shivering as the crisp hair there made my skin tingle. "It's coming off, is it?"

He sat up and pressed his torso to mine. "Oh, I think so. Don't you?" He nipped at my neck and I moaned as pleasure shot through me.

"Yes," I managed. "Please."

Instead, he moved to my mouth and kissed me long and deep, and I locked my arms around him and abandoned myself to his kisses until he tugged at my sweater sleeve. "Are you sure you want this off?"

"Why wouldn't I?"

"Well, you were cold before."

I couldn't imagine ever being cold again. "I'm not now, for some reason."

He freed me from my sweater and top then traced along the upper edge of my bra's cups with his tongue until I whimpered and undid my bra myself, desperate for more.

The bra joined our other clothes on the floor and his mouth found my nipple and I arched against him and began fumbling with the button on his jeans. I had to have him. Now.

He caught my hands. "Mary, listen."

My racing heart skipped a beat. "Oh, God, you don't want to."

He gave me an evil grin. "Yeah, right. Sit down a little more and say that again."

Relieved, I sank down onto him and ground against his erection, surprising myself at my forwardness, and he groaned. The contact and his reaction sent an electric shock ripping through me, making me shudder.

"I want you. Trust me. I... look, I meant it that you didn't have to."

"I know. I want to." I tried to free my hands but he wouldn't let go.

"I'm getting that idea. Listen, though, okay?"

My hands and mouth ached to touch and kiss him, but I nodded.

"I didn't think you had to and I wasn't expecting this to happen. But I thought I should... in case you did... I didn't want us to..." He shook his head. "I'm being an idiot, so I'll just say it. I have condoms next door."

So sweet, being afraid I'd think he'd expected me to surrender, but I had to grin. "Good for you. Check the bedside table drawer." I joined him in laughing when he found the condoms I'd brought. "Great minds think alike, I guess."

"Or horny ones."

"Those too."

"Now, you were trying to undo something a minute ago," he said, guiding my hand back to his jeans' button. "Don't let me interfere."

He did, though; his mouth on me made it next to impossible to keep focused on the button. I kept going back to it, though, and at last I had his jeans unbuttoned and unzipped. I scrambled off the bed and pulled them down then went for his boxer shorts, wanting to see exactly what was tenting them to such an amazing degree.

He sat up and gently pushed my hands away. "My turn." He drew me to stand before him so he could kiss my breasts while spending a gloriously long time undoing my jeans.

When the jeans hit the floor, I said, "Oh, crud. Forgot about these."

He pinged my tights' waistband. "Can I get them off you?"

"It's a bit of a science, and it's so not sexy. Like pulling plastic wrap off a cucumber."

He laughed. "Spoken like a true chef. Well, take 'em off then."

I got my fingers into the waistband and pushed the tights down to my knees, careful to leave my black lace panties on since I wanted him to remove those. Then I forced each leg down to the arch of my foot and pulled on the toes to get the tights completely off. "Sorry. Like I said, it's not sexy." I dropped the tights on the floor.

"Oh, I don't know." He glanced at them. "They look pretty sexy now. Get back here."

I did, and he pinned me to the bed and kissed me until I was begging him to take me.

"Got another date later? We have all the time in the world. And I want to see something."

He slid down my body and stood at the end of the bed looking at me.

At my feet.

He gave a low laugh. "You did your toenails. I love it."

I pushed up on my elbows and looked at him, so gorgeous with his hair mussed and his eyes full of amusement and passion. "Seemed like a good idea."

"Did I ever mention I think red toenails are sexy?"

"You did not."

"Probably because it never occurred to me before." He kissed the inside of my ankle. "But now I do." His mouth moved upward and his hand caressed my other calf. "Very much."

Shivering with desire and anticipation, I spread my legs as he gently pushed them apart. Was he going to... Charles had never wanted to put his mouth... oh, please...

"The only thing sexier," he continued, sliding further up both legs, "is black lace underwear." His lips found my knee and his hand stroked onto my thigh. "When it's on the floor, I mean."

He moved higher, then higher still, and then my underwear hit the floor and pleasure took me over.

A long time and two incredible orgasms later, I lay with my head on Kegan's chest and his arms close around me. The room was silent and beginning to grow dark, and I'd never felt so peaceful, so still.

His hand moved slowly, lazily, over my hair, and eventually he said, his voice low and dreamy, "I've made a decision."

"What's that?"

"I'm never leaving this bed."

I tightened my arm around him. "Good call. But what about food?"

"That's why you're here. I brought my own chef."

We laughed, and he kissed my head and said, "We'll order room service."

"Sounds good."

I burrowed in closer and he cuddled me against him, and we didn't speak again for a long time, until he said, "Do you want to get up and go see the Falls?"

"I thought you never wanted to get out of bed."

"But this is your first time here."

I pushed up on my elbow so I could see him. "This was *our* first time."

"And second, I'd say," he said, his eyes dancing.

He'd alternated between driving me wild with his fingers and mouth and driving himself into me in every position I'd ever tried and a few new but amazing ones, and I'd loved every moment.

I understood what his exes had meant; I didn't think 'kinky' was the right word but he had an adventurous nature in bed that I'd never experienced before, always changing things up and switching positions. But he'd awakened a corresponding side of me I hadn't known existed and by the end I'd been asking for even more variety.

He'd provided it beyond my wildest dreams, satisfied me completely, but just thinking about it made me want him all over again. "I saw the Falls already. Doubt they've changed. And they say third time's the charm."

He grinned. "I'm just a man, Mary. I have limits." But he pulled me close and kissed me and I felt him growing hard against me, and the third time was indeed the charm.

And the fourth wasn't bad either.

Chapter Twenty-One

Roller coasters have fewer ups and downs than my relationship with Kegan the week of Steel's opening.

We had sex a few more times in Niagara but did manage to get our clothes on too, and savored another amazing restaurant dinner, wonderful chats about nothing in particular, and the excitement of winning fifty bucks from a slot machine. Every moment with him felt better than the one before.

On the way home he seemed quiet, and I was about to ask why when he sighed and said, "I wish we didn't have to leave."

I did too. "But then we wouldn't see Steel open."

"True. But I don't want to see us bickering over it."

I rubbed his hand on the steering wheel. "We won't. We're all relaxed now so everything'll be fine."

He smiled at me before returning his attention to the road. "I do feel pretty mellow, I must admit, so you might be right."

On Monday, it looked like I *was* right. Back at work we still had our newfound bond, and though we didn't agree on every aspect of the final details for Steel's opening we weren't far off and we didn't argue.

Tuesday, though, tempers began to flare all over the restaurant as Wednesday's final inspection neared, and Kegan and I weren't immune. We'd worked until nearly midnight on Monday, barely finding time for a few short kisses never mind anything more. I'd never seen him like this, attacking a deadline, and I understood better why others had called him impossible and a hard-ass. Even remembering his sculpted rear end didn't make it easier to deal with his barked orders, although he reserved most of those for the other staff.

Wednesday morning was pandemonium from seven o'clock until the inspector's arrival at eleven. Kegan even snapped at me once, although he quickly apologized, and he ordered me and the others around constantly as his stress built.

Once the inspector, obviously reluctantly, had admitted we'd fixed everything he'd noted the previous visit and approved Steel to open, Kegan's relief was so great that he hugged me even before the inspector left and then bought lunch for the entire staff to celebrate.

I was delighted for him, of course, and also thrilled to see him relax over his pizza, but when the food was gone his relaxation vanished too. The inspector might have been satisfied but Kegan wasn't. He wanted perfection, and he was going to get it regardless of what it did to his staff. Or his girlfriend.

"Crystal's telling everyone it's exactly like when Steel opened the first time," Dorothy muttered to me after I'd walked away from yet another confrontation Wednesday afternoon, this one over how far apart to place the mini quiches on their platters. "He'll be better by Friday night."

"I might have murdered him by then."

She grinned. "No, you won't. One of *us* might have, but not you."

I had to laugh. "Okay, fine. But I'll have wanted to."

"Oh, no doubt. Crystal says it'll be amazing. Once the first guests arrive, he'll be a different man."

Back to the one I'd fallen for, with any luck.

Crystal hadn't said any of this to me: we hadn't spoken since she informed me I wouldn't be good enough in bed for Kegan. She'd looked furious on Monday, though, no doubt recognizing the new intimacy between us, and since then she'd avoided me. Instead, unfortunately, she'd been taking out her frustration on Dorothy, criticizing everything she did in that oh-so-sweet tone. I'd tried to stay near so she'd control herself, but I felt sure she was slinging even ruder comments at Dorothy whenever she could. "You doing okay?"

"Oh, sure."

I raised my eyebrows, and she said, "I'm used to it."

"Doesn't mean it's okay."

She patted my arm. "Just keep your eyes open." She scanned the room, clearly checking that Crystal and her pack of followers weren't near. "They stop talking to each other when I'm around. I think they're up to something."

If they did anything to sabotage the opening, it would devastate Kegan, and even though he was making me crazy I wouldn't be able to bear that. "If you hear anything definitive..."

She nodded. "For sure."

Kegan shouted, "Mary! Where the hell are you?"

I rolled my eyes. "Probably wants me to add a molecule of something. Or take one out."

"Hope he wants you to add it, that's easier," she said, smiling, and I returned to the kitchen feeling outraged at his interference and not bothering to hide it any more.

We dealt with that oh-so-vital issue, whether the basil leaves garnishing the garlic-cheese toasts should be stem in or stem out, and what seemed like a hundred even more pathetic ones over the rest of that day and into Thursday. On several occasions he locked himself in the office for a bit, returning calmer, but the peace didn't last more than a few minutes and I started to wish he'd stop trying. His swinging between rationality and ridiculousness was more annoying than just dealing with his obsession would have been.

Thursday night, we had to skip underwater hockey. I suggested he play to relax himself while I finished the preparations but he looked surprised and said, "I can't make you do all the work."

I insisted I wouldn't mind, and for probably the first time in my life that I'd said, "Oh, I don't mind" I truly *didn't* mind, but he stayed and drove me and Dorothy and the rest of the staff except Crystal insane. Crystal had left right on time, claiming a friend's father had died and she had to attend the funeral. I had my doubts, but I didn't mind much because the restaurant felt calmer without her. Even her circle of cronies seemed more relaxed.

Everyone else left at eleven, but Kegan and I stayed, working through the endless list of tiny last-minute details. At least, I did; he fiddled with the napkins and silverware and tablecloths until I finally said, "For the love of God, go home. I'll finish up."

When he turned to me, the fear and pain in his eyes shocked away my irritation. "What's wrong?"

He swallowed hard. "My parents are coming tomorrow. They haven't seen Steel since a week after it opened. Couldn't be bothered. It has to be perfect."

My throat tightened. I hadn't invited my parents, since I knew they wouldn't want to make the three-hour drive each way. But his lived right in Toronto and never came to Steel? I went to him and wrapped my arms around him, not sure what to say.

He held me close and pressed his cheek against mine. "I know I'm being an ass, and I hate it. But I can't help it. I'm trying, swear to God I am, but it just happens. I'm so sorry."

I squeezed him tighter. "The opening will be all right. Better than that. It'll be amazing."

"If it is, it's because of you."

"It will be, and it's because of all of us. Especially you."

He pulled me even closer. "It's you. I couldn't do it without you. Not like this."

"You'd have another chef," I began, but he shook his head.

"You were right at the beginning, we're meant to work together. You don't deserve any of how I'm acting, and I know it. I hate how I am and I want to be better. For you."

I reached up and took his face in my hands, my heart melting at the determination in his eyes. "You are already incredible. And I know you're working on the ordering me around thing. We'll get there."

He smiled, then kissed me deep and sweet and slow as we hadn't had time to for days.

I wound my arms around his neck and kissed him back, instantly hungry for him.

After a delicious while, he murmured against my mouth, "Your place or mine?"

I shivered and pulled him closer. "How about here? Our office?"

"I like the way you think. Still have that condom in your purse?"

He'd stuffed one in there as we packed up before leaving the hotel, joking that it was good to be prepared. "I do. Want to go make sure?"

We stumbled back to the office, kissing all the way, and wiped out the stress and frustration of the week in glorious work-inappropriate behavior on his desk.

Chapter Twenty-Two

But wiping out our stress and frustration permanently wasn't in the cards. Though we both went home relaxed and satisfied, by the next afternoon his tension had risen to dizzying heights again and mine wasn't far behind.

He wanted everything perfect, of course, but so did I. This was my chance to impress all of his patrons and friends. The success of Steel's grand re-opening was to a significant degree on my shoulders and I wanted it to be spectacular.

At last, it was time. Kegan had decided to make the night an open house rather than a seated meal to allow more people to attend, so we had buffet tables laden with a huge variety of nibbles from both restaurants' menus. Champagne glasses and bottles stood ready, with lots more champagne chilling in the wine room, and every table bore a white rose and a lit candle. Steel glowed in the candlelight, the refinished golden hardwood and freshly painted teal walls bouncing the light around the dining room, and my heart glowed too as I looked at Kegan.

About ten minutes before we opened, he'd changed into a suit and the dark blue shirt and tie he'd worn in Niagara Falls, and he'd laughed when I came out of the bathroom in black pants and the top I'd bought for our trip. "Great minds think alike," he said, and his grin told me he remembered my saying that to him about the condoms we'd both brought to the hotel.

"Indeed they do."

We smiled at each other and stole a quick but hungry kiss, and he said softly, "See you in the office afterward? I brought the condom this time."

I kissed him again in response, and we'd headed off to handle the last-minute details, but now I stood near the front door watching Kegan once again briefing the wait staff and tried to put aside my nerves and relax into joy and delight that Steel had come together for him.

Tess and Forrest were the first guests to arrive, and their obvious happiness for Kegan made tears fill my eyes.

"Looks great." Forrest slapped Kegan on the back. "You done good, man."

Tess hugged the grinning Kegan. "He's right, you did. You and Mary." She turned to look for me, then hugged me too. "Congrats," she whispered to me, and I squeezed her tight.

When we released each other, she said to Kegan, "Jen wanted to come but I wasn't sure..." She glanced at me and back at him. "Would you rather she didn't?"

I knew the story of Jen now, knew about the immediate attraction between her and Kegan and what he termed his insanity in treating her like someone he could control. I also knew he saw her as almost a symbol of the other women he'd pushed around. He'd told me more than once he wished he could apologize to her.

Kegan's eyes met mine, and I winked.

He winked back, then said to Tess, "I'd be happy to see her."

She grinned and pulled out her phone, then stepped to the side of the entranceway as at least ten people walked in. "I'll let her know. Carry on, good sir."

He did just that. I'd seen him chatting with people at the tastings and been impressed with his easy relaxed style, but here at Steel he was utterly in his element and many a politician couldn't have pretended more friendliness.

Kegan wasn't pretending, though; he was clearly honestly delighted to see each guest. Past patrons and his friends congratulated him and he beamed as he accepted their kind words. The ecstatic Mildred hugged us both at once, nearly crushing us, while Tanisha stood laughing. Other restaurant owners and various food reviewers came in looking coolly professional but soon mellowed as Kegan spoke with them. Everyone got at least a few words from him, and he left them all smiling.

He'd asked me to stay in the dining room as much as I could so people could chat with me about the food, and I gradually became more comfortable going up to strangers and asking how they were connected to Steel. Most raved about the food and the renovations and how excited they were that Steel was open again, so I enjoyed talking to them, but I didn't expect the older man who said, without looking up from the platter of food he was inspecting, "My son owns the place."

His brusque manner, so unlike Kegan, startled me. "Oh! You're Kegan's dad?" I hadn't seen Kegan speaking to him yet. The man, and a woman I'd lost track of in the crowd, had slipped in while he was busy at the other side of the room. "I'll go get him for you."

He raised his silvered head. Kegan's deep blue eyes in a stiff cold face. "That's all right. He doesn't have time."

"Of course he does," I said, surprised yet again. "He's been so excited that you were coming." Well, terrified, but I couldn't imagine saying that would do Kegan any favors.

"He has?"

I turned to see the woman giving me a shy smile. "Definitely," I said firmly. "I'm Mary, his new chef here and for Magma. May I get you some champagne and show you around?"

Her smile widened a fraction. "Mary. My grandchildren mentioned you. Apparently you gave Lola a dancing game? It was all she talked about for days."

I smiled back. "I'm glad it made her happy." I hailed a passing waiter and got them each a glass of champagne.

"Won't you join us?"

I shook my head. "Thank you, but I'm working."

Kegan's father took a deep drink then set his glass aside. "Good quality, at least. We raised him to always want the best. That's why I don't understand why he decided to—"

"Gregory, please. Not now."

"You feel the same."

Kegan's mother took a deep breath. "I said not now."

Her voice shook even with the extra air, and the shock in his eyes suggested she never stood up to him. He turned his back on us both to study a painting on the wall.

She gave me a tremulous smile. "I'm sorry, Mary. We just had big dreams for our son."

I didn't know what to say. Wasn't all he'd accomplished good enough?

Apparently not; she leaned closer and said, "He was supposed to be a lawyer. Even went to law school. But then he opens this place instead, and his dad's never quite been the same."

I was all too afraid he *was* the same, still as controlling and diminishing as he'd been throughout the lives of Kegan and Nora and their younger brother Thomas.

I knew full well that Kegan hadn't wanted to be a lawyer, and I also knew he'd repeatedly told his parents the same thing. But he'd ended up in law school anyhow, unable to escape the pressure any other way. Nora had 'escaped' via a series of increasingly disastrous relationships, Thomas by playing professional hockey in Germany. From what Kegan had told me, the other two had become passive, particularly in their personal lives; Kegan alone had taken on his dad's worst traits, which he was now struggling to leave behind.

"I think Kegan's doing an amazing job," I said firmly. "This place is wonderful, and Magma will be incredible, and it's all thanks to him."

I felt a hand on my shoulder and Kegan said, "Thanks to you too, of course. Mom, this is Mary, my chef and—"

His father turned to us. "She introduced herself already." He cleared his throat. "Good champagne."

Their eyes met, and I hoped Kegan heard the attempt at support in his dad's voice.

He seemed to; he said, "Thank you. I learned to pick it from you."

They shared an awkward smile, then Kegan added, "And as for Mary's introduction, unless she told you she's also my girlfriend it wasn't quite complete."

His mother smiled at me again. "You didn't mention that part. You're managing to put up with him all right?"

I looked into Kegan's eyes. "He's not that bad."

He winked at me and gave his mother a hug, and we chatted for a minute or two about the restaurant and the food. His mother at least seemed to be willing to tolerate Kegan's career choice though she clearly didn't like it. His father stood silent throughout, not even nodding or smiling. It was like having a rain cloud hovering at the edge of your picnic, not yet ruining your fun but promising to do so at any moment.

Nora came up to us with her kids and a tall blond man, who she introduced as a friend from work named Jack. Once we'd all shaken hands, Lola and Rudy demanded and got hugs from Kegan and me and then from their grandparents. Kegan's dad lightened up somewhat in the face of the kids' excitement at being out at night, but I was still glad when Dorothy sent me a text message to call me to the kitchen and I could make my excuses and head back.

Fortunately, nothing was wrong except a brief panic about where I'd stored the spare basil leaves, so I stayed there a few minutes to keep an eye on things and then returned to the dining room.

All of Kegan's relatives seemed to have left, and I hoped his dad hadn't upset him. I couldn't see Kegan at first amidst all the people but then spotted him walking over to two women and a tense-looking man hovering near the front door.

Before he reached them, he turned back and scanned the crowd, and when our eyes met he beckoned me over. He didn't move until I joined him, then took my hand and led me to the newcomers without a word. I could feel his stress, though, pouring into me through his tight grip on my hand, and I grew more nervous with every step.

When we reached the group, the man and the blonde woman moved closer to their companion, a pretty woman about my age with short dark highlighted hair who appeared to be about six months pregnant, as if protecting her. She stepped forward though, ignoring them. She glanced down, apparently noting Kegan's hand holding mine, then she looked up at him and said, "I'm so sorry about the fire."

"Thank you." He held her gaze for a long moment. "And thank you for coming tonight."

Her cheeks pinkened. "I wanted to."

"Well, you made it happen the first time so I'm glad you're here now." He turned to me. "Candice works for Sapphire Interior Design, and she helped design this place. Picked out the colors and the tiles, and did an amazing job." He looked back at her. "I didn't change anything this time around, since it was gorgeous just the way it was."

She started to respond but he cut her off. "I'm sorry—" He cleared his throat. "I'm sorry it all got destroyed."

His first "sorry" sounded heart-felt and passionate, very different from his second, and I saw the man and the blonde woman both stiffen while Candice murmured, "Thank you. That means a lot."

I didn't understand everyone's reaction but I didn't want any confrontations to ruin Steel's opening so I smiled at Candice and made my voice cheerful. "But at least everything's back to how it should be now. I haven't seen you at Magma. Too busy with other projects?"

Her blush deepened but her voice stayed calm. "I'm actually a full designer now, and I specialize in retail design. I know about Magma, of course, from Lou, but I'm not involved."

Kegan had been involved with a woman related to Steel right before it opened. When I'd met Lou he'd said something about a woman who was now a retail designer and the mere mention of her had made Kegan blush. Was this Candice the one? Their awkwardness, and the coldness of her guards, said she might be. Certainly there was more between these two than a brief working relationship, but I wasn't at all sure I wanted the details. "Well, Lou is doing an amazing job. I can't wait to see Magma finished."

"I'll tell him you said that." She paused, and I said, "I'm Mary."

Kegan shook his head. "I'm useless. Mary, this is Candice, and her friend Larissa." He straightened his back and turned away from the unsmiling Larissa, who'd barely acknowledged his introduction, to the man. "And you must be Candice's husband Ian."

Ian nodded, his jaw set.

I briefly expected Kegan to release my hand so he could shake Ian's, but it was probably obvious to him, as it was to me, that Ian didn't want to do any such thing. Instead, Kegan drew me a little closer. "Mary's my chef and motivational speaker and general lifesaver."

I rolled my eyes but squeezed his hand, and Candice smiled at me. "The food is great."

"Thank you. We worked hard."

We stood in an uncomfortable silence for a moment. Ian and Larissa were so clearly dead set against Kegan that I couldn't think of anything else to say. Candice rubbed her stomach, as I'd seen so many pregnant women do, and though I was afraid she might not actually be pregnant I took a chance and said, "Everything okay in there?"

She laughed, and even Larissa and Ian smiled. "Eleven weeks to go. I already feel huge."

"Well, you look great," Kegan said, with a jovial-uncle tone in his voice. "Got names picked out?"

Candice looked up at her husband and I saw his face soften as she smiled at him. "We're keeping them secret until the baby's born. Just between us. Not even Larissa knows."

Ian wrapped an arm around her and rubbed her lower back, seeming more relaxed. "Not that she hasn't asked a million times."

Kegan smiled at Larissa. "My sister wouldn't tell me the names she picked for her kids either. Made me crazy."

Their eyes met and held, then she smiled too, reluctantly from what I could tell. "It's frustrating, no question. But it's kind of cute too."

"Absolutely. It's a nice way to bond, I bet, keeping it secret." He turned to me. "I'm thinking Hepzibah or Felix. What do you think?"

176

I raised my eyebrows and said, "In this case, great minds do not think alike."

We all chuckled, but he slipped his arm around my waist and I leaned into him. The words "great minds" would make me think of Kegan and that hotel room for the rest of my life, no question, and he obviously felt the same way. I loved that we had a private joke already.

"And how long have you been together?" Larissa said to me.

"Since New Years' Eve. So not long."

"But we've been here for endless hours so it feels longer."

I turned toward Kegan with a mock frown. "I'm not sure how to take that."

He laughed. "It was a compliment. Said badly, I admit, but meant in a nice way."

Larissa took a breath to say something but Candice jumped in with, "We can't monopolize you two all night. We'll wander around and see what's changed."

"Please do," Kegan said. "If you have questions about anything, or suggestions for how I could do it better, let me know. Especially suggestions. I'm pretty happy with the place at the moment but I'm open to advice."

Larissa gave a cough that sounded like a snort and Candice blushed.

I looked up at Kegan, who looked so sad I couldn't bear it. "I know, that's what's great about you," I said to him, pretending I hadn't noticed anything. "I've never met a man who listens like you do." I caught his hand, resting on my waist, and gave it a squeeze. "Well, I'd better go make sure the food's behaving itself. Nice to meet you all."

They smiled at me, and as I left I heard Kegan say, "Again, thanks for coming," and then felt him following me back to the kitchen. I didn't look behind me but I knew he was there.

He caught up to me in the hall and drew me into our dark office and into his arms. "Sorry. I couldn't face them alone. Candice is... she was..."

I wrapped my arms around his neck. "The resolution."

"Yup." He shook his head. "God, I was such an *ass* to her. Seeing her brings it all back. I wanted to apologize but I couldn't do it in front of them and they'd have killed me if I tried to see her alone."

His sadness hurt me, and I wanted to soothe him. "She seems to be doing well now."

He nodded. "Which is good. I just wish I hadn't screwed her around first. Twice. Pushing her around before Steel opened and years before that when—"

My heart breaking, I pressed two fingers to his lips. "Kegan, don't. Don't torture yourself. You made mistakes. Who hasn't? But you're doing everything you can to change and it's amazing. And you *did* apologize tonight and I think she understood. Plus she came here, which must mean she'd already forgiven you. Now you have to forgive yourself."

He squeezed me tight for a long moment then bent his head and kissed me softly. "You're the best."

I smiled up at him. "No, that's you."

"It's you." He kissed me again. "For telling them I listen now, and for meaning it." Another kiss. "And for putting up with me when I don't listen." Another. "And for being amazing. And sweet. And sexy. And..."

He stopped talking and kissed me in silence with unusual tenderness, and I kissed him back and did my best to tell him that I'd meant every word I'd said.

Chapter Twenty-Three

By the end of Steel's open house, we were booked solid for the next three weeks and also for Valentine's Day. Kegan's delight was obvious, and I was thrilled for him even though I was utterly exhausted.

At least, I thought I'd reached 'utter'; I soon learned I could be even more tired. My days post-opening quickly fell into a routine. I started at Steel, ensuring everything was right for lunch, then spent hours at Magma making sure the renovations were going well and also planning my menus.

I had multiple menus on the go: I needed Magma's regular menu, plus one for the special fourteen-dollar Valentine's Day dinner that would be Magma's unofficial opening, and another for February first, "Magma Night", when we would turn Steel into Magma to give our invited guests a taste of the final menu. Coordinating all the similar but slightly different dishes felt next to impossible.

Every day I returned to Steel at around five o'clock to supervise dinner preparations and make any necessary arrangements for upcoming days. Kegan handled staffing, which suited me fine, but I'd gradually taken over more and more of the food ordering since I knew exactly what I wanted, and keeping on top of it all wasn't easy.

I loved what I was doing, no question, but I was steadily more desperate for a day off, or even a few hours. Kegan had suggested we go to Niagara again for the weekend before Magma's opening, but we'd eventually had to accept that with Steel open we simply didn't have time. We'd settled on going for one night, the Thursday before Valentine's Day, and I was looking forward to it as I'd never looked forward to a vacation before.

With any luck, Kegan and I would be able to relax and really connect with each other, because while we spent hours near each other we hadn't shared more than a kiss or two. We got along so much better when we had time to decompress away from the restaurants, and I had the chance to see him as my boyfriend instead of just my boss.

My increasingly aggravating boss. Though I knew he was trying not to, he was still ordering me around at work, more and more each day as he became busier with Steel and more focused on Magma where before I'd had nearly free rein, and I hated it.

The Friday before Magma Night, I returned to Steel delighted with myself for finally standing up to John Franklin and insisting he move the towel shelves, which still bothered me, to the sink area like I'd originally wanted.

John had again explained it would take too long, but I stayed calm and said, "I need them there. We need to make that happen. This simply doesn't work for me."

He blinked. "I didn't think it mattered that much to you. Yes, I can move them."

I took a breath to suggest leaving the old ones and adding new rather than moving them, but before I could he said, "Actually, you can probably always use more shelving, right?"

"Definitely."

"All right, so I'll leave those and put new ones over the sink." He frowned. "I *am* sorry, Mary. I really didn't think you minded the new location. I'll get it done the way you want."

And indeed, by the time I left for Steel he had the first shelf up and it looked great.

As my taxi carried me away from Magma, I thought back to our earlier shelving-related conversation and realized he was right. I hadn't been clear enough. But today I had, and every time I saw those shelves I'd know I'd stood up for myself and made them happen.

I marched into Steel, still smiling and proud of myself, to find Kegan rifling through my desk drawers. "Hey there," I said, instantly annoyed. "Can I help you?"

He looked up, not seeming remotely apologetic. "Nope, I've got it."

I pulled back on my chair, rolling it and him out of my way. "What are you looking for?"

"The order you placed yesterday, the poultry one. The guy's claiming we ordered three hundred Cornish hens." He reached for my files again but I cut in front of him.

"I didn't do that. Give me a second." I flipped through the folders and quickly found what I wanted. "See? Thirty."

He took the paper from my hand. "Thank God. I had no idea where we'd stash them all."

"I can deal with—"

But he was gone, off to chastise the supplier I'd been working with since November. I dropped into my vacated chair and shook my head though there was nobody there to see me. It made me feel better. He swore blind that he trusted me, that he knew I could handle things, but at every tiny provocation he took over. I wanted to be in charge of the things that were my responsibility, but it so wasn't happening.

I checked on the kitchen and found everything in order save the freezer the staff had messed up while trying to find a storage spot for the unexpected Cornish hens. I rearranged that, spent a few minutes monitoring the night's preparation, then went back to the office to give my menus a bit more attention.

Kegan stood and held out his arms to me. "Come here. I'm sorry. Yet again. I should just record myself apologizing, save my breath."

I let him pull me close, but had to say, "Or you could stop taking over and then you wouldn't need to apologize."

"I love that you still think I could do that even though I'm a total failure so far."

Surprised at his suddenly sharp tone, I pushed back so I could see him, and my heart skipped a beat at the frustration in his eyes. "You're not remotely a failure. I know you're trying."

"Yeah, I'm very trying."

"That's not what I—"

He kissed me, cutting off my words, then said, "Look, my lovely lady, I think you should take the night off. Get some rest."

"What? I can't. You need me here tonight."

"Actually, I need you desperately over the weekend and on Monday. I do need you today but I can make do without you better now than then, and you need a break."

"So do you."

He touched my temple at the edge of my eye. "You need it more."

I flinched away. I'd hoped he hadn't noticed my eye twitching with tension and tiredness. No such luck.

"Look, when Magma opens and you're working at both places, you won't be here every night at dinner. We should get used to that now."

I took a breath to argue, then gave in as another wave of fatigue hit me. He was right, I *did* need time off, and he had everything under control. Besides, Crystal was off work for the day, having apparently had yet another friend's parent die, and I much preferred leaving Steel when I knew she wasn't there to wreak havoc. "Okay. But when will you get your rest?"

"I'll leave at nine tomorrow night."

"Yeah, right."

He laughed and shook his head. "You know me too well. Nine-thirty. Ten at the latest. But I will go before we close. Good enough?"

"I suppose."

He smiled, then kissed me, lightly at first then with a deep hunger. "Sunday night let's both leave early," he murmured against my mouth.

I shivered and said, "Definitely." We hadn't had time for sex since our frantic encounter on the office floor after Steel's reopening, and I missed it desperately.

His arms tightened around me. "Get your rest. You'll need it."

I giggled. "Glad to hear it."

We gave each other another quick squeeze and a brief kiss, then I headed out into the cold dark night. Only seven o'clock but it was dark enough to be midnight. I'd feel more cheerful and have more energy once spring arrived and the days got longer.

Assuming I survived that long.

I reached my building and climbed the stairs to my apartment slowly, making yet another mental note to make sure my next place had an elevator. I was now on a month-to-month lease; I hadn't wanted to renew for another full year when I wasn't sure what would happen with me and Kegan. He'd already hinted about my moving in with him, but I was afraid of what would happen if we broke up. Bad enough that he was my boss as well as my boyfriend, but if he were also my landlord and I lost my home as well as my job...

I grimaced and pushed the thoughts away. We weren't breaking up. We argued occasionally. So did most couples. We'd be fine. End of discussion.

I changed into my favorite fuzzy pants and sweatshirt and had barely had time to feed Saffron and collapse on the couch with a book when a knock at my door sent dread through me.

Brian. I hadn't seen him for a few weeks, but he'd left several moping messages on my voice mail, first telling me he'd found a job, although not one he liked naturally, and then saying how much he missed our 'friendship'. Far more likely he wanted to have sex again, which of course I wouldn't do, or wanted to dump on me, which I so didn't want to let him do.

Screwing up my face into hideous expressions to release my frustration, I forced myself off the couch and toward the front door. I was nearly there when a thought struck me.

He wanted to see me, but I didn't have to see him.

I went back to the couch and sat perched on the edge, wondering if that was actually true. Would I be able to ignore him until he went away? Or would it ruin my entire evening?

He kept knocking, no doubt having heard my arrival, and I gave up. Maybe I didn't have to see him, but he didn't have to leave me alone either, and that was what I wanted. The fastest way to get it was to see him and give him what he wanted.

I yanked open my door. "What?"

He blinked.

Rage, at myself and at him, filled me. I shouldn't have given in and he shouldn't have kept harassing me. "It must be important or you wouldn't keep knocking, so what do you want?"

He sighed, his whole body radiating dejection. "I had a bad day. I really need to talk."

Oh, no. No no no. My precious evening off, wasted listening to Brian whine? "I can't."

He deflated further. "Got a date with *him*?"

I considered lying but didn't want to. "No. It's my night off, my only one for ages, and I need to relax."

"We can relax together, can't we?"

I doubted it. "I truly need to be alone tonight. I'm sorry."

His head tilted a bit to the side, like he was listening to a foreign language and trying to pick out a few words. "But I need to talk. I'm probably going to get fired."

Joy flared through me. Without a job he'd have to move out. Immediately after the delight, though, came guilt. What kind of monster would be happy about Brian losing his job and home? The guilt said, "Fine, but not here," and forced me into the hall and into his apartment.

Of course, once I was in I couldn't get out, and I sat on the couch trying to be sympathetic and biting my tongue not to point out all the ways he'd brought his misfortune on himself. Brian was clearly the worst kind of employee, passive-aggressive and unwilling to give even an ounce more than he had to, and my sympathies were entirely with his boss and not with him.

He wasn't listening to me, though. As he droned on and I attempted to interject a few hints that his behavior might be part of the problem, I realized that he was simply ignoring everything that didn't fit into his own view. He was perfect and his boss was a jerk, all of his bosses had been jerks by some amazing coincidence, and nothing I said would change his opinion.

He didn't want his opinion changed anyhow. He didn't want my help either. He wanted me to say it wasn't his fault, to agree his boss was a jerk and console him at his bad luck. He wanted to feel like a victim, like someone who'd been hard done by, instead of being forced to see himself as the cause of all his problems.

Charles had been much the same way, insisting that if only I stopped trying to have a career everything would be fine. I'd believed that, at least to a degree, but now it hit me hard: if I *had* given up on the career, it wouldn't have fixed our marriage. Some other problem would have popped up, because the real problem was that he wanted the kind of wife I didn't want to be. We saw the world differently and nothing would ever change that.

Kegan, though. We saw things exactly the same way, were both committed and driven and determined. True, that caused us conflict far too often, but it also meant we understood each other on a level I'd never known before.

I remembered his words at New Year's, his statement that when I was ready I would stop letting Brian suck the life and money and energy out of me, and I felt a calm sweep over me. I was ready. Now.

"Brian," I said, interrupting him mid-sentence, "I have to go."

"But I still haven't told you the rest of it."

I stood up. "Here's the thing. You won't do anything. You'll tell me all about it and then ignore whatever I say. I can't do that any more. Especially not now."

He sat frozen, staring at me.

I took a breath to explain it all, how I wanted my time back and didn't want to listen to him complain any more and needed to take care of myself, but then realized it wouldn't matter. All that mattered was that I was putting an end to this. "I am going home. If you make plans to change things and want to talk to me about those, I'd be happy to help you out. But until then..."

I couldn't get the last words out. I'd never been this forceful in my life, and though I knew I needed to, it still felt wrong. I could almost hear my mother telling me I should be more helpful and give poor Brian what he wanted.

I shook my head. No. I was taking care of myself for once, giving myself what I wanted and needed. I took a deep breath and finished my sentence. "Until then, don't talk to me."

I turned and headed for the door, and had my hand on the knob when he said, "But I don't know how to fix it on my own."

Without looking back, I said, "Time to learn. Be a grown-up," and left his apartment.

It wasn't quite that easy, of course. Once I got home, I realized he'd come over in a few minutes at the most to try to change my mind, so I grabbed my purse and a book and slipped out of the apartment, closing the door quietly behind me, then took off for the Starbucks down the street.

I'd wanted to be home in my fuzzy pants relaxing on the couch, but I refused to let Brian and his text messages, which started even before I reached Starbucks, ruin my precious night off. I set the phone silent so I wouldn't hear the messages come in and spent several hours enjoying a caramel apple drink I hadn't tried before and reading the book I'd brought and a cooking magazine I picked up on the way. It wasn't what I'd planned, but it was good. Occasional bursts of guilt did hit me, but mostly I knew I'd done what I needed to do.

Having had a bit of a rest was invaluable, because the weekend was insane. The last-minute work for Magma Night combined with Steel's fully-booked reservation list meant Kegan and I were ridiculously busy. Brian kept sending messages, but I honestly had no time to answer even if I'd wanted to, and they gradually tapered off. I suspected I'd hear from him again but for now I was glad of the reprieve.

Partway through the dinner rush, I was in the kitchen checking to make sure everything was on track when a waitress came in, shaking her head. "You'll love this one, guys. He wants the roast chicken, but with ketchup and mustard on the side. Bizarre, huh?"

The others agreed, but I couldn't speak. It couldn't be... could it? I cleared my throat. "What does he look like?"

She turned to me, surprised. "Tallish, blond, skinny. Kind of cute, actually."

It was. Why was he here? He'd never been the fine dining type.

"You know him?"

I nodded. "I think it's my ex-husband."

She grimaced, and Dorothy patted me on the shoulder and said, "Stay in here with us until he's gone. You don't want to see him."

No, I didn't. But I also didn't want to hide. I'd spent so long being afraid of what he thought of me, and I didn't want to do it any more. "What table is he at?"

The waitress told me, and I left despite Dorothy's well-meant insistence that I shouldn't.

Once I'd made sure that my hair was still sleekly braided and I didn't need to freshen the rich red lipstick I'd started wearing after Niagara Falls to match my toenails, which Kegan loved on me and I knew Charles would hate, I took a deep breath and headed into the dining room.

I was stopped twice on the way to Charles' table, by people who'd attended Steel's re-opening and were happy to see me again, and by the time I neared his side he was already staring at me in shock, his salad fork held forgotten in his hand. "What are *you* doing here?"

I pulled up all my nerve and gave him a smile, though my heart was racing. "I work here. I'm the chef. Your turn."

His eyes flicked to his dinner companion, and I turned to look at her too. I'd never seen her before, thankfully; how awkward if he'd been with someone I knew. She wore no makeup and had her brown hair loose at her shoulders, just as Charles liked, and I realized he'd essentially found a new version of me. The old me. The me that didn't exist any more.

Realizing I was truly my own person now calmed me, and I held out my hand to the woman, delighted to see it wasn't shaking. "I'm Mary. You may have heard of me?"

She nodded and glanced at Charles before shaking my hand. Like a lightning bolt, a memory snapped through me. I'd been out for dinner with him when his work buddies showed up, and I'd extended my hand before the buddies offered theirs. Charles had been furious later, saying I'd made them look rude by not waiting until they offered. Had this poor thing had the same experience with him?

Charles set down his fork and wrapped his arm around the woman's shoulders. "This is Lois. My girlfriend. We've been together since the summer."

His eyes dared me to comment, but I didn't care about his love life, didn't care that he'd obviously been dating long before even the first

186

paperwork for our divorce. What did surprise me, though, was something else. "I assume my mother knows that."

He frowned. "Of course. She's met Lois several times."

I shook my head in disbelief, and his frown deepened. "She's never mentioned it?"

"No. She's always telling me how 'poor Charles' is all alone."

Our eyes met and we shared a reluctant smile. For all his flaws, Charles had at least been a great buffer between me and my infuriating mother.

His smile faded, though, and he said, "She knows you work here?"

I nodded. "I even showed her the web site at Christmas."

He took a breath and let it out in a sigh. "Well, you should probably get back to work."

It was clearly a dismissal but I didn't leave. "Why did you ask that?"

"No reason. Look, we don't have long for dinner before we need to get to a show, so..."

"So answer my question and I'll leave you alone," I said calmly, and he blinked. The Mary he'd known would have felt guilty about interrupting their dinner, embarrassed to be seen by his new woman, and devastated that she so closely resembled me. That Mary had never been able to challenge him.

Now he had no power over me, and I felt only a faint amusement that he was stuck in the same rut and pity for Lois who'd probably find herself giving up her dreams for him.

Our eyes met again, with no smile this time, and when I didn't look away he sighed again. "Your mother told us to come here. Said she'd heard it was great and we should check it out."

My eyes widened. "She did? When?"

"A few days ago, when I said we were coming to Toronto for..." His ears turned red. "Well, to celebrate the divorce."

The not-yet-finalized divorce. So classy, Charles. "She sent you here to see me."

"Apparently."

Lois shifted in her chair, and I felt bad for her. "My mother only sees what she wants to see," I said to her, "and she's convinced we were perfect together. Not even close."

"We were fine until you wanted—"

"Don't even bother." I raised my chin. "Unless you're going to finish that sentence with 'wanted to have a career and I wouldn't let you', don't bother. It's all moot now anyhow."

Charles shook his head. "Don't pout, Mary. It's pathetic."

I hadn't pouted and he knew it, and all the times I'd apologized for pouting or whining when I'd *known* I wasn't rushed back to me. A surge of anger hit me but I fought it off. He wasn't worthy of my energy. "Whatever you say."

A faint frown crossed his face, and I knew I'd surprised and confused him by not defending myself. I knew, and I liked it.

The waitress arrived with their meals and said to me, "Kegan wants to see you when you have a moment." She gave me a conspiratorial grin and added, "I always swore I'd never date my boss, but I don't blame you. I'd have gone for that too."

I felt sure she and Dorothy had cooked up this unnecessary comment to make sure Charles knew I was dating Kegan, but in all honesty I wouldn't have bothered telling him. I didn't need to care about his opinion any more. I smiled, though, knowing she meant well. "Tell him I'll be right there."

She turned toward the kitchen and gave a thumbs-up, then headed on with her tray. I joined Charles and Lois in looking where she had, to see my tall sexy boss leaning against the wall, and I heard Lois's tiny gasp as Kegan smiled at me and returned my nod. When I looked back at Charles, he said, "You're dating your boss? Already?"

I nodded, knowing he meant it as a shot and refusing to accept it. He couldn't zing me if I didn't let him. "Yup, already. Why wait? He's amazing."

"Yeah," Lois murmured, studying Kegan, then jumped when Charles snapped, "What?"

She flushed. "I just meant, I know this place burned. Must have been a lot of work."

To help her out, I said before Charles could speak, "Definitely. But now everything's perfect. And we're opening another restaurant on Valentine's Day. Way better present than some box of chocolates."

Lois gave me the tiniest of smiles, almost more of a flicker, and I smiled first at her then at Charles, who didn't smile back. "Well, you made a good choice coming here. Best food in Toronto. At least until Magma opens. And look, I'll tell my mother to smarten up."

He laughed. "Yeah, right. You look different but you haven't changed that much."

I looked back at Kegan, still lounging in the doorway. Undoubtedly he'd been told Charles was in the restaurant and he was there because of it. Not taking over, not expecting me to fail, but there as a silent supporter should I need assistance. He believed in me. He'd believed in me from the start.

My lips curved into a smile, and I said to Charles while looking at Kegan, "Yes, I have. And I'm finally ready."

Chapter Twenty-Four

I didn't even consider confronting my mother that weekend. Way too much to do before Magma Night. I'd worked so hard to get the menu in shape, and this would be its first real test, and I couldn't let even one tiny detail be less than perfect.

I was so focused on the food once the guests began arriving that night that it took me a while to notice how strangely my staff was acting. Dorothy was sticking to Crystal like a burr, and Crystal seemed delighted to be at work, not her usual grouchy self. The other workers were split: Crystal's friends were happy and those who didn't like her were silent and withdrawn.

Crystal must have heard Kegan and me fighting earlier that day. The more we bickered, which was more frequently by the day, the happier she was. She'd even told me on the weekend, in her best faux-sympathetic tone, how sorry she was that our relationship was obviously coming apart. I'd told her she was wrong and walked away, but I wasn't sure she was.

I hated arguing with him, and not just because it pleased Crystal, but we could barely discuss work now without some sort of confrontation. He was more relaxed about Magma, although only just, but anything involving Steel left us battling. Weirdly, far from backing off as I proved myself capable, he'd become steadily more controlling. I couldn't understand it, and I knew it didn't bode well for us.

He was in the dining room entertaining the patrons, including Tess and Forrest who'd insisted on being among the first to try Magma's cuisine, so at first I thought I could relax a bit. I even managed to grab a quick bathroom break without wondering whether he'd change anything in my absence, a rare treat. Once I came back and the wait staff came in with orders, though, the tension in the kitchen began to climb and I had no idea why.

Figuring I should free myself to wander around and try to find the source of the stress, I said, "Dorothy, could you please stir this sauce for me?"

I almost didn't realize she'd refused, so sure was I she'd be her usual helpful self, but the gasps from the other staff made it clear. I turned to her again in shock. "Did you say no?"

She nodded, her face white. "I'm too busy."

"Doing what, exactly?"

"Yeah," Crystal said, her tone icy. "Doing what?"

Dorothy's terrified eyes begged me silently to trust her, and to save her, and so I said, "Sorry, I shouldn't have asked you. I know you're taking care of the steaks. Angie, will you—"

"Yes," Angie said fervently, grabbing the spoon from my hand.

Activity resumed, and I stood in the doorway and wondered what the hell had happened and what I should do about it. Dorothy had never once refused to do anything I asked, and she certainly hadn't wanted to this time.

I thought it through, knowing I needed to understand. She hadn't been willing to focus on the sauce, which needed constant attention so it wouldn't boil, so she must have felt she had to watch something else instead.

Someone.

Nervousness turned my body weak even before I consciously made the connection.

Crystal. It had to be her.

I took several long deep breaths. Well, Dorothy had managed to warn me, which had no doubt been her intent in refusing so publicly, and I would heed that warning.

I kept focused on the food, of course, but also did my best to monitor Crystal and her buddies. The first few meals went out without incident, exactly as we'd planned, and Kegan came in shortly afterward, delighted to report the diners loved them.

I gave him a smile, hoping it hid my stress, and thanked him for letting me know, then let him leave even though I longed to take him aside and tell him what had happened. I had no proof, no evidence, and I'd only be upsetting him for nothing.

I kept my eyes on Crystal as much as I could without being obvious, since she would either do whatever she'd planned herself or signal someone else to do it, and soon realized I could spy on her most effectively by working near the windows with my back to her and watching her reflection in the glass.

That was how I saw her look up, glance about to check for observers, and dust something from her pocket over the steak on the nearest plate.

My mouth fell open, both at what she'd done and how close I'd come to not seeing.

A waitress reached for that plate and the one next to it and I snapped, "Leave it."

Everyone looked up, and adrenaline flooded through me making my words tumble from me before I thought them through. "Crystal, what did you just do?"

We locked eyes, and the innocence in hers stunned me. I had *seen* it and yet I almost didn't believe it. Her "what do you mean?" was pitch-perfect, surprised and a bit confused, and I wondered how many things she'd gotten away with by using that tone.

Not this thing, though. "You put something on that plate."

Dorothy, who'd been standing next to me, slipped from the kitchen but I didn't look away from Crystal, who looked completely horrified. "Of course I didn't. Why would you say that?"

"I saw you."

"There was nothing to see. I don't understand." No snarl in her voice, only confusion.

"I saw you," I repeated. God, I hoped I had. I was sure I had, but her shock seemed genuine. If she really hadn't done anything, we'd never be able to work together again.

"What's going on?"

"She hates me, Kegan." Crystal dissolved into tears. "She's hated me since she got here and now she's accusing me of tampering with the food," she whimpered.

He looked at me, his face expressionless, but I could see horror growing in his eyes. He knew, as well as I did, that she was capable of it, and he also knew I'd never have accused her without a good reason. "Tell me what happened."

"She has something in her pocket and she sprinkled it on that plate." I pointed, and he glanced at the waitress. "Table six, right?"

She nodded, clearly afraid she'd somehow be drawn into this.

"Forrest and Tess." He turned on Crystal. "You're trying to hurt my *friends*?"

Her eyes widened and this shock had a depth and reality to it that the other had lacked. I'd thought the first was real but now I knew the difference, and I also knew I hadn't accused her unfairly. She wiped away her tears, smudging her makeup dramatically onto her cheeks. "I don't know who the plate's for! And I didn't do anything anyhow."

"Turn out your pockets then."

She blinked at him. "What?"

"If you did nothing," he said, the rage beneath his calm tone twisting my stomach into nervous knots even though it wasn't directed at me, "then you have nothing to hide. If you did, well... turn out your pockets."

Crystal shifted beneath his gaze but didn't respond.

"Pockets. Now." His tone brooked no argument.

They stood staring at each other while the rest of us watched in a silence so tense I could barely make myself breathe. I had just enough time to think of those old movies with two gunfighters in a standoff before Crystal shot her mouth off.

She threw her head back, fire blazing in her eyes. "God, you're pathetic, pathetic and useless and stupid," she said, her snarl suddenly in full effect. "If you'd believe your bitch of a bedmate, who you obviously only promoted because she'd put out, over me, you and your shitty restaurants don't deserve me anyhow. I quit."

Kegan stared at her as if wondering who she was. He'd told me he paid attention whenever he was in the kitchen, but Crystal had clearly been smart enough not to let her vicious side show. The rest of us knew this tone all too well, but I felt sure he'd never heard it, and I found no satisfaction in watching him realize he'd utterly underestimated the damage she'd been doing to his staff for years. My heart hurt for him.

He recovered fast, though. He didn't dignify her crack at me with a response, which suited me fine since he *did* say, "I'll accept your resignation, of course. Right after you show me your pockets. Or I call the police. Whichever you'd like."

Her face paled. "The police?"

"You tried to poison one of my guests. I suspect the police would be interested."

"It's not poison," she growled at him. "It's a joke. It'd just make them sick for a few days."

"And they'd blame the food," I said, my hands closing into fists. "How *dare* you?"

193

She took a breath to answer but Kegan didn't let her. "You can't quit, you are fired. Get out, and if I see you again I *will* call the cops."

She grabbed her coat and purse and stormed out the kitchen's back door and Kegan turned on the rest of the staff. "Anyone else got secrets in their pockets?"

They shook their heads frantically. He studied them each in turn, paying special attention to Crystal's minions, then refocused on her closest friend Dave. "Do I need to worry about you?"

Dave blinked, apparently not having realized Kegan knew he'd allied himself with Crystal. "No. Seriously. She was bragging about it but I thought it was like with Brash, all talk. I really didn't think she would—"

"You have one more chance. The rest of you, watch him. If he so much as sticks his hand near his pocket you tell me, or Mary. Right away. Got it?"

They all nodded.

"Redo that plate. I'll go make sure she doesn't sneak back in." He stalked away.

Dorothy lost control. "I'm so sorry, Mary," she sobbed, her tears real where Crystal's had been manufactured for the occasion. "I was watching but I missed it."

"You knew she'd try something?"

She nodded sadly, and so did several others. She took a deep breath and let it out, and once she'd calmed herself a bit she said, "I knew she was plotting something, and she was actually bragging about it a few minutes before she did it."

When I'd left the kitchen to use the bathroom. So brazen of her.

"But I couldn't figure out how to tell you. Not without her maybe being even more subtle." Her tears rose again.

I squeezed her shoulder. "You let me know and that made all the difference." I looked around at my stunned staff. "Well, she's gone now, so let's not give her any more of our time and energy. We have things to do."

They all nodded, and we set to work replacing the tainted food and sending out the other meals. Crystal's departure changed a lot of my planned duty schedules and revising them on the fly meant I didn't have time to rehash the whole mess, but when I went out to meet Kegan in the dining room after he sent a waiter to fetch me the tension in his face and shoulders told me he'd rehashed more than enough for both of us.

"We're getting compliments," he said when I reached him at Tess and Forrest's table, "and I figured you should be here for them."

Forrest grinned at me. "That steak was amazing. I've never tasted anything like it. There's a secret ingredient, isn't there?"

The steak. Oh, Forrest, there was so nearly one you wouldn't want. I made myself grin. "Maybe. I'll never tell. That's what 'secret' means."

He laughed, and Tess smiled at me. "Thanks for taking a second to come out here. I'm sure you're crazy busy."

I nodded. "It's been quite the night."

"Yes, I'm sure," she said, and I realized she knew something had happened. How, I didn't know, unless she too had picked up on Kegan's stress. Certainly he wouldn't have told her.

I looked up at him, noting a muscle jumping in his jaw, then slipped my arm through his. "But it's great too. Thanks, of course, to this lovely man. He's done so much to make this place a success." He hadn't stopped Crystal, though, and I felt sure he was furious at himself for that and for letting her poison the staff for so long. So I added, "No better boss, no better boyfriend, ever," and squeezed his arm.

He looked down at me and smiled, a small smile but at least I'd coaxed one from him.

"Well, I kind of like *my* boyfriend, but I see your point." Tess winked at me. To Kegan she said, "Tonight has been absolutely perfect. I'm sure there have been little glitches behind the scenes, but don't let them get to you. It's incredible."

I leaned against him. "See, told you."

His smile was a little bigger this time. My gratitude toward Tess was immense.

Once the guests had all left and Steel was spotless, Kegan returned to the kitchen. "Mary, Dorothy, can you go buy coffees from Mildred for everyone?"

Dorothy said, "We can make some here if you'd like. Less expensive."

I suspected he wanted us out of the way more than he wanted drinks, and sure enough he said, "No, you guys deserve a treat for how well you worked tonight." He pulled his wallet from his pocket and handed it to me.

Dorothy and I gathered the group's orders, a significant number since "everyone" included all the wait staff, and left the restaurant. She didn't speak to me as we walked, but her posture said it all.

"Dorothy, you're not blaming yourself, I hope."

She gave me a sad smile. "Kind of."

"Well, don't. As your chef I'm ordering you not to."

I smiled at her, and her answering smile was a little brighter. "I'll do my best."

Once Mildred had finished her good-hearted scolding for wanting so many coffees only minutes before her ten o'clock closing, she said, "Night went well over there, I hope?"

"It had its moments, let's say." I adored Mildred, but her ability to keep a secret was next to zero and I knew Kegan wouldn't want the details broadcast. "We survived, though."

"Wonderful." She turned to Dorothy and frowned. "You look upset, honey. Is it still..."

She trailed off, and Dorothy said, "No, she got fired tonight so that'll be the end of it."

Pieces fell into place with a near-audible clang in my mind. "You've been warning me about Crystal all along. Not leaving my wallet around, taking those roses home with me... you've been afraid she'd do something to me."

Mildred shook her head. "Not the sharpest knife in the drawer, are you?"

I rolled my eyes at her. "Hey, she seemed to like me when I first started working there. Why would I assume she was out to get me?" I turned to Dorothy. "Why *was* she?"

"She did act like she liked you," Dorothy said, "but I think she thought sucking up to you would get her the chef position she wanted."

"How, exactly?"

"She expected to be made Steel's chef when the old one got fired for starting that fire. Isaac being promoted was a slap, but once he was gone she bragged about how she'd get Steel for sure, especially since Kegan would think you two got along great. Then he gave you *both* restaurants when you'd just been hired. She got Dave and a few of the other young ones worked up about how it wasn't fair, and convinced them that if they got rid of you she'd be made the chef and she'd make sure they got the easiest jobs in the kitchen."

I shook my head. It seemed so high-school, so petty. "Tell me the truth, do you think Dave and her other friends are dangerous?"

I appreciated that she paused, giving my question serious thought. At last she said, "No. They're followers. If they like who they're working for, they'll be fine."

196

"But they don't like me."

"Actually, I don't think that's true. Crystal talked big and they listened. When you left the kitchen near the end tonight Angie gave Dave a hard time for going along with Crystal and he said he has nothing against you, that he doesn't even know you."

"Which is true." I sighed. "Think I can get him to like me?"

She smiled. "Of course. It'll be fine."

"Well, and who wouldn't like you, honey?" Mildred set down the last two trays of drinks to pat me on the head. "Now take these and get your butt out of here so I can go home."

We laughed and Dorothy and I carted the trays back to Steel, where Kegan stood by the bar with the staff sitting before him in the dining area. Once we'd passed out the drinks and settled at a table, he said, "All right, folks, thank you for that. I really appreciate your honesty. See you tomorrow."

They left, and Dorothy and I looked at each other, confused. Once only the three of us remained, I said, "I'm assuming something happened while we were gone?"

He nodded. "I asked for what they don't like about working here. Got quite the list." He tapped the notepad next to him.

"Like what?"

Carrying the notepad, he left the bar and sat beside me. "The first person to speak said I can be a little overbearing, and that got the others going." He flashed us a wry smile. "Did you know I'm not always the easiest person to work with?"

Dorothy chuckled, and I put my hand over his, so impressed he'd open himself to his staff's criticism like that. "I think I might have heard that somewhere."

He freed his hand and wrapped his arm around me. "No doubt. Well, they'd all heard it too. They did understand why I get like that, but they'd rather I didn't. Other than that, mostly little things. Kitchen floors are too hard so their feet get sore, not enough pens for the wait staff, stuff like that. I'll fix them all, though, however I can. It should help with their morale."

"Anyone mention Crystal?"

He shook his head. "So I did. Dave swears he just got caught up in what she said and wasn't thinking. I took him aside before we all started talking to ask if he can work for you and he says he can. If he's any trouble, let me know. The others all say they have no problem working for you, here or at Magma."

"Sounds like it went well."

Dorothy said, "It does, but why did you have us leave?"

His arm tightened, stiffened, around me, and I realized he'd had a reason and didn't want to share it with her. So I said, "Well, we both think this place is perfect, so there's no point getting our feedback. Right?"

She grinned. "That's right. I do agree with the hard floor thing, though. My legs ache every night."

"Well, go home and put them up." Kegan smiled at her. "And thank you. I understand from the others you've been keeping an eye on Crystal."

She blushed. "It didn't work. I wasn't the one who saw her."

"You were, indirectly," I said. "I figured out that you were worried about her and it made me watch her."

Kegan dropped his arm from my shoulders and leaned toward her. "Why didn't you tell me what she'd planned?"

His voice was gentle, but tears filled her eyes anyhow. "I was scared. And I didn't have any proof she was trying to sabotage Mary so I couldn't do anything. I didn't want her against me. She made people's lives miserable."

"She can't do it any more," he said. "Thanks in big part to you."

She smiled through the tears. "And Mary. Do you need me any more tonight?"

"Go home," Kegan said, smiling at her, and on impulse I got up and hugged her.

She hugged me hard and whispered, "It'll be great working with you without her around."

"Ditto."

We grinned at each other and she left. Once the door closed behind her, Kegan got up and locked it then slumped back into his chair. "God, what a night."

"Yeah."

He shook his head. "You tried to warn me about her and I didn't listen. I had no idea it was that bad. I should have known she'd only show her best behavior around me."

"Until she didn't."

He grimaced. "That comment about you pissed me off but I figured there was no point letting her debate it with me." He looked at me. "You're not upset I didn't confront her on it, are you?"

My heart melted at the concern in his eyes, and I reached out and gave his hand a squeeze. "Of course not. Who knows what she'd have said next if you'd given her the chance?"

"That's what I thought too."

We sat in silence until I said, "So what else did you discuss with the staff?"

He looked at me.

"Dorothy's right, you didn't need to send us away to find out what they didn't like."

He shifted his chair closer to mine and put his arm around me again, cuddling me closer than before. "I wanted to know what they really thought about you, and her, and I didn't want either of you to hear it."

"Us? I'm their supervisor, so I get me. But why her?"

"I wanted to know if they thought she could be your sous-chef."

"That'd be a promotion for her, yes? I totally think she could do it."

He kissed my hair. "And they did too. But I don't want to do that just yet. I think we should see whether there's anyone with a little more training and more initiative. Dorothy's great when she knows what to do but she's not a real go-getter."

I had to admit this was true. "So you're going to interview some people?"

"Actually, I thought maybe you should."

I raised my eyebrows. I'd never have expected him to give up something as vital as staff recruitment, not even to me.

"The menu went over so well tonight that it shouldn't need much of your time over the next two weeks before Magma opens. That'd be more than enough time to hire someone else, or to promote Dorothy if that's what you think we should do."

Still not sure I could have heard him right, I said, "So it's up to me?"

He nodded. "I know you can do it. Besides, you'll be working with the person, more than I will anyhow. So let's post the job tonight so we can start getting applications right away."

We spent about fifteen minutes in our office reviewing what Crystal ought to have been doing, in the process realizing how little she actually *had* been doing other than griping and bragging, then wrote it up and posted it on Kegan's usual job-ad sites.

"There," he said once it was online. "If you need help deciding let me know, but otherwise I'll meet whoever it is once you've done the hiring."

I couldn't believe he was trusting me with this. It felt like a great sign. "Yes, sir. Will do."

He laughed and wrapped his arms around me. "I like the sound of that. What else can I command you to do?"

I kissed him.

"I didn't command that."

"You were thinking it."

"What am I thinking now?"

I widened my eyes and let my mouth fall open. "You dirty man!"

"You *are* reading my mind," he said, pulling me closer. "So let's do it already."

We did. Twice.

Chapter Twenty-Five

I had no time at Steel or Magma the next day to even glance at the steadily rising stack of applications for Crystal's job, so I hauled all the faxes and hand-delivered resumes home to go through them there.

I'd just barely made myself a tea to drink while I worked when someone knocked on my door. Tanisha had mentioned she might be in my neighborhood, so I opened the door without checking the peephole.

Big mistake.

Brian said, "Can I come in? I need to talk to you."

Hadn't I made myself clear enough for him on Friday?

Apparently not, since he took my momentary shocked silence for a yes and walked into my apartment.

"Brian, no. I don't want to talk."

"But I made a plan."

I hadn't expected that. "You did? For what?"

He dropped onto my couch. "For getting a decent job."

I took a seat on the couch's opposite end. "Really? Well, good for you." I couldn't help thinking it was good for me too, good for me for having made myself tell him the truth though I'd felt bad. Now he'd taken the first steps toward changing his life. "So? What's the plan?"

He glanced at the stack of applications on my coffee table. "You're doing the hiring now?"

"This time, yes. We're seeing if it works out. Come on, out with the plan!"

"It's pretty simple, really, and actually it just got easier. I was going to apply and have you tell your boss to hire me, but now we don't have to worry about that step."

I pressed my fingers to my temples, wondering if my sudden headache meant my brain was trying to escape this idiot. "So, your plan is that I give you a job? When you've never worked at a restaurant before?"

"It's perfect. You'd be nice to me since we're friends, and I wouldn't have to worry about getting fired for some stupid reason, and then we'd get to hang out all the time."

The first two parts of that sentence were bad enough but the third... one person's "get to" is another's "I'd rather live with Crystal". I stared at him, trying to decide where to start.

"What? You don't like it?"

Sure, let's start there. "No, I don't. For starters, we're not friends. For another thing—"

"Of course we are. We talk, we—"

"*You* talk. You know nothing about me, and you don't care either."

"I do," he said, looking like I'd kicked his puppy. "Why would you say I don't care?"

"How's my leg doing?"

He blinked. "How should I know?"

I shook my head and couldn't hold back a humorless chuckle. "Exactly. You should know because you would have *asked* me about it if we were really friends, if you cared at all. I listen to all your problems and you don't pay any attention to mine. You've never asked about my leg, not once. And when I tried to talk to you, right after it happened, you didn't even let me. It's all Brian all the time with you, and I don't want that any more."

"Oh, so it's supposed to be all about you instead?"

I stared at him, trying to figure out how he'd gotten that from what I said. "I..." What was the point? He would never get it. "Fine, whatever, it's all about me. Which is why you need to go. Because *I* won't be hiring you and *I* will tell Kegan not to either and *I* have work to do."

He shook his head. "I thought I'd given you enough time to get over your pissy mood on Friday but I guess not. I'll come find you later."

I couldn't help it. I burst out laughing.

"What's so funny?"

I managed to pull myself together. "Do you actually speak English? Because you don't seem to get what I'm saying. I am not in a pissy mood. I am simply not willing to be your free therapist and bank machine any more. Don't come find me later. Don't come find me in a month, or a year, or a decade. I am done with this. I am done with *you*. You are on your own."

He stared, then to my surprise said, "Okay."

"Really?"

"I'm not completely useless, you know. I'll be fine." He stood and headed to the door.

I watched in complete confusion. He'd actually heard me? It sure seemed like it. But then why did he sound so calm and unconcerned? He didn't seem offended at all.

He left without a word, and I sat stunned on the couch for a bit then turned to Saffron. "I think we're free, baby."

Saff opened one eye and gave me a huge sigh then went back to sleep, and I picked up the first resume and began to read. I'd nearly reached the bottom of the page when my cell phone signaled a text message.

`Sorry, I shouldn't have come with such a lame plan. I'll bring a better one once I have it.`

I rubbed my temples as the headache surged again. Seriously? What was it going to take to convince him to back off? I'd made it simple enough that Rudy or Lola could have understood it, so why didn't Brian get it?

I felt like I'd run into a brick wall as understanding smashed into me. He *did* get it. He knew I didn't want to do this any more.

He also didn't care.

My feelings and opinions were completely irrelevant to him. He'd decided how things were going to be and I would fall into line.

Or so he thought.

Another brick wall. So *everyone* thought. Charles, my mother, Jimmy, Crystal, even John Franklin the contractor... they all assumed they could do what they wanted with and to me. I'd told John otherwise, though, and he had moved those shelves. I had won there.

I felt the faintest glow of achievement and pride over that, and encouraged it to grow and brighten until I was full of such energy and drive I felt like I might explode. I'd done it once, I could do it again. I'd made a start with Brian today, and I would do the same with my mother. Tomorrow. One confrontation a day was sufficient.

Other than the confrontations with Kegan, of course. Far more than one a day there.

But those were different. Yes, we bickered and disagreed, and yes, I did want him to back off on his interference with my work. Most definitely. But he never acted like I shouldn't have my own opinions. He respected me, even when he disagreed. He did listen to me.

I picked up my phone to respond to Brian, and after giving it some thought sent:

`No.`

Really, what else needed to be said?

Brian didn't contact me again that night, but I knew he would. I also knew how I'd handle it: I would be like a non-stick pan and let his greasy aggravating behavior slide right off me. I couldn't change him, but I could change myself and how I responded to him. That would be a huge step in the right direction.

I reviewed fifty resumes that night, and not a single one was even a tiny step in the right direction. Crystal had obviously mobilized her friends to send us garbage applications. The ones from names like Donald Duck and Edward Cullen were easy to weed out, but some were so close to real that I couldn't discount them. I had to go through each one individually, searching for clues to its truthfulness.

When I told Kegan about it the next morning he posted a revised version of the job ad under a new name, which did stem the tide of spam but also brought a new deluge of resumes. I wanted to do the hiring, because it was so amazing that he was letting me do it, but the whole mess was making me crazy. Combined with how close Magma was to opening, I had so much to do I barely had time to breathe.

On Thursday night, after leaving Steel "early" at eleven, I was again on the couch working through the applications when my phone rang.

Ding dong, the witch is dead!

The thought, "I wish she were dead," flashed through my mind and then guilt and horror exploded through me. How could I possibly think that about my own mother?

"Mary, when are you coming home? Poor Charles needs you."

I rubbed my eyes. This was *not* the time I'd have chosen for this, but maybe that was for the best. Less time to prepare meant less time to get myself freaked out. "Mom, you know he has a girlfriend."

She didn't act shocked, and she didn't ask me how I knew. She just said, "Oh, that won't last. He's meant to be with you."

I opened my mouth to ask where she got that from, then closed it. How could she be so delusional? I'd intended to make her admit that Charles and I weren't meant to be together, but now I couldn't imagine she'd ever do that. But I could insist we never discuss him again. Not quite as good, but certainly better than how things were now.

Before I could figure out what to say, though, she said, "So, he's coming over this weekend and I think you should too. It's time to patch this silly thing up."

I brought back my memory of making John change the shelves and again let it swell within me. When I felt alive and energized, I said, "No, it isn't. And it never will be."

"Oh, Mary, honestly. So Charles made a few mistakes. He's still your husband."

I thought of Kegan agonizing over whatever he'd done to Candice and Jen. Charles hadn't spent a millisecond agonizing over me. "He's not, Mom. The divorce papers are filed."

"So you get remarried."

"Mom. Please listen." She tried to cut me off but I said, "No, listen," and kept going over her protests. "Charles and I will never get back together. He has a girlfriend, and I have a boyfriend, and I wouldn't want him back even if we were both single. We won't remarry, we won't get back together, and I hope never to see him again. It is over. And if you talk about it again, I will hang up the phone."

She didn't say anything. I didn't either, for the first time. Usually when she went silent I filled the gap with my own words and ended up saying more than I'd intended, offering something I hadn't wanted to give. Not this time, though. I held my silence, though the urge to apologize was almost unbearable, and in the end she cracked first.

"That city isn't good for you. You're not yourself. Come home."

"Mom. I am home. I live here now. I'm more myself now than I've ever been. And I love it."

Another silence. I waited this one out more easily than the first.

She sighed. "Oh, Mary. You were so much better with Charles. I just think—"

But I didn't hear what she thought, because I said, "I'm sorry, Mom, but I told you. Goodbye," and pressed the "End Call" button.

The guilt that rushed me made what had come before seem like a pleasant tickle, but I grabbed Saffron and hugged him to me and managed to get through it. Yes, I hung up on my mother. But I gave her fair warning. And while I felt terrible, I'd never felt so free either.

And I felt terrible about that too.

While I was still thrilled Kegan had passed the hiring duty on to me, I devoutly hoped I'd never have to do it again. He didn't overtly pressure me to hurry up, but he did ask me at least once a day how it was going, and by Friday afternoon I'd had enough.

"No different from how it was before lunch. I've called twenty people and seven of them turn out to be actual applicants. Two of those have other jobs already and one says he can only work weekends because he's in jail during the week, which doesn't sound promising. I still have nearly sixty applications to go through and they're still coming in."

He held out his hands in a "calm down" gesture, but I was beyond being calmed.

"Brian keeps texting and coming over to show me his non-existent job plans, and though I keep ignoring him and leaving when he shows up he won't quit. And my mother is convinced I belong with Charles and I hung up on her on Wednesday and she hasn't called back which I think means I'm a huge bitch. Maybe even huger because I'm glad she hasn't called. And—"

I pulled in a breath to continue.

Pain ripped through my chest, like a sharp skewer driven through my breastbone.

I gasped at the shock of it, losing what little air I'd managed to catch.

Kegan caught my shoulders. "What is it?"

I took a tiny breath and winced, then put my hands over the middle of my chest, trying to somehow ease the continuing pain. "It hurts. When I breathe."

He gripped my shoulder with one hand and dialed three digits on my desk phone with the other. "I need an ambulance. My girlfriend's on anti-coagulants for a blood clot and she's getting pain when she breathes. I think she might have a pulmonary embolism."

Chapter Twenty-Six

"You don't need to be embarrassed."

I moved closer to him, disturbing Saffron, who meowed in protest before resettling on my lap. "Well, I am. And how did you know the right terminology? You called it a pulmonary embolism on the phone. Not that it is one."

"I did some research online after you were diagnosed so I'd know what to watch for."

I put Saff on the floor and snuggled up to Kegan. "That's so sweet."

He kissed my forehead. "Don't be embarrassed, seriously. I'd rather go there and have them say it's not the clot than keep you at work and find out later it is."

"Yeah." The ambulance workers had said the same thing but I still felt like an idiot. "I had no idea stress could do that."

"Me either." He cuddled me closer and I let myself relax against him as he said, "I didn't even know we have joints along the middle of our ribs."

"Yeah. Weird." The emergency room doctor had diagnosed my pain as a stress-related inflammation of those joints combined with not enough sleep and a side dish of dehydration, and prescribed painkillers, lots of water, and a relaxing weekend. Kegan had bought the first for me on the way back to my place, kept pressing the second on me, and was pushing hard for the third.

"You're officially off this weekend."

"I'm not. What about the hiring? And Magma? And Steel, for that matter."

"You won't be ready to handle any of that if you're getting chest pain all the time."

"It was once."

"It was the first time," he corrected. "It'll happen again if you don't take care of it." He brushed his fingers over my hair. "I don't want you in pain."

"Me either, obviously. But I have to be there."

Kegan eased me off his shoulder and held me away so he could look at me, and I realized I'd never seen his eyes so soft and warm. He tipped my chin up and kissed me just as warmly. "I love that about you, how you don't give up. And you're not. You are regrouping before the battle starts again next week."

I widened my eyes. "It'll be a battle?"

He grinned. "Figure of speech. Look, you've booked interviews for next week, right?"

I nodded. "Monday right after lunch. Six interviews."

"So you'll take this weekend off, and then you'll be ready for them. With any luck, one of those six will be perfect and you won't need to go through any more applications. And maybe you should stay at my place to keep Brian away from you."

I'd given Kegan the story in the taxi back to Steel from the hospital, how Brian was still bothering me despite my absolute refusal to engage with him. I'd repeated, "No. Go home," so many times that I'd had a dream in which it was all I could say, but he still kept calling and coming over. "Yeah, maybe. Can Saffron stay over too?"

He bent and looked deep into the cat's green eyes. "Do you promise not to shed?"

Saffron stared back unblinking.

"I'll take that as a yes."

I laughed. "I wouldn't."

Kegan pulled me close again. "You know, you *are* having some success with Brian." He held up a hand to stop my protest. "I know he's still trying, but you've sent him away every time. You didn't give in even once. That's progress, right?"

"Yeah. I guess it is." I might not be able to teach Brian new tricks but apparently I could learn them myself.

"So reward yourself with a weekend off."

I sighed. "I really can't."

"I'm your boss. I say you can. So you can."

I wavered. I did want a break, and I knew I needed it, but...

"Do it for me if you won't do it for you. I need to know you're okay."

I snuggled into him, my heart melting. "You are the sweetest thing ever."

His phone rang but he didn't reach for it. "No, that would be you. You'll get some rest, right?"

"Answer your phone."

I could hear the smile in his voice when he said, "Not until you promise."

The chest pain had frightened me badly. "I promise."

He gave me a quick kiss and pulled the phone from his pocket. "Hey, Tess. What's up?" He listened for a moment, running his hand over my hair, then said, "Yeah, she's here too. Want me to put it on speakerphone?"

Apparently she did.

"Hi, Tess," I said once he had it working. "How are you?"

"I'm great. You guys?"

I looked at Kegan, touched my breastbone, and gave my head a quick shake. I was fine, so why bother discussing my brush with medical science?

He smiled and wrapped his arm around me. "We're great too. Forrest's good, I hope?"

"I'm perfect."

Kegan laughed. "Not what I hear, man, but if you say so."

"I do. Look, what are you doing Monday?"

"Working. Probably me at Steel and Mary at Magma, but we have no real plans yet."

"Well, we do," Tess said, her voice full of excitement, "and now you do too. Will you come to our wedding at five o'clock?"

"This coming Monday?"

She laughed. "I know it's really soon, but we've been planning it for a few hours now. Does that help?"

I giggled, caught up in her obvious delight. "Sure, why not? Why so soon, though?"

"He asked me this morning, and I want to marry him before he changes his mind."

We laughed, and Forrest said, "No, that's why *I* want it to be so soon. Seriously, though, we don't want the media to find out, and we're both happy to do it this way."

Charles had wanted the big white wedding. I'd wanted something much closer to what Tess and Forrest were doing. No prizes for guessing what I had. "That sounds amazing. Can we help at all?"

"Um, yeah," Forrest said. "We were hoping you'd cater it. At Magma."

I sat up straight and stared at Kegan, who said, "I wish you could see her face, guys. I think you gave her a heart attack. How many people are you expecting?"

"Twenty, max. It'll probably be eighteen. Including you two, of course."

I relaxed back against Kegan. "Okay, I can handle twenty. I was envisioning two hundred or something. The dining room at Magma doesn't have any ceiling lights yet, though. I can try to rush the contractors but they're waiting on some special plaster."

"No problem," Tess said. "I want lots of candles and no lights anyhow."

"Perfect. And what do you want to serve?"

"We liked everything you had on Monday at Steel," Forrest said. "But it's all up to you and Tess. It's her day. Whatever makes her happy, okay?"

Kegan cleared his throat. "You got it." I wondered if he too had been touched by the love in Forrest's voice, the love that had brought tears to my eyes. I'd never heard such emotion from a man. I burrowed into Kegan, blinking, and he stroked his hand over my head again.

"Any chance you guys could come over to discuss it?"

We could, so we ended the call and I gathered a few favorite cookbooks to show Tess and we headed out. On the way, I stopped to pick up my mail. The usual bills and flyers and a catalog for the previous occupant of my apartment...

And an official-looking envelope from the Family Court of Ontario.

I opened it right there by the mailboxes, and sure enough it held my divorce papers. They were dated February first, so thirty-one days from then I'd be a single woman. I didn't know why the additional delay: maybe to make sure the paperwork reached Charles before the effective date? Although, since he'd been with Lois since the summer the effective date clearly didn't matter to him. Truthfully, the effective date had been the day I walked out.

I handed the papers to Kegan and he flipped through them then handed them back. "I'm not sure what to say."

I sighed. "Me either."

"Can I say you're gorgeous?"

I leaned against him. "Yes, please."

He put his arm around me. "Well, you are. And sweet and sexy and one hell of a chef. Now let's go put a wedding reception together in three days."

I laughed. "Think it's possible?"

"Absolutely, if you're involved. But are you okay with being involved?"

I stared at him. "Why wouldn't I be?"

"You need your rest."

I shook my head. "It'll be fun. Tess isn't demanding, and we'll come up with something great. I love menu planning." I grinned at him. "Anything for a break from reading résumés."

He kissed my cheek. "Good stuff. And my gift to you both is staying out of your way."

I kissed his cheek too, then his mouth. "Sounds good."

It *was* good. Wonderful, actually. After we chatted with Forrest and Tess for a bit, Kegan said, "We should let the ladies work," and took Forrest out for a few drinks to celebrate while Tess and I sat on the black leather couch in their lovely apartment, with vibrant paintings by her sister Pam and other artists adorning the walls and Tess's amazingly detailed miniature scenes on shelves, and began figuring out what to serve.

I only got a few hours sleep each night, since planning even a small wedding in a weekend was an incredible amount of work, but I enjoyed every moment. I didn't have to do any of the stuff I'd started to dread at Steel and Magma, the staff management and coordinating contractors and all that. I only had to put together a menu, make all the food with the help of the kitchen staff, and come up with little touches to make it even better. Exactly what I loved doing.

Kegan didn't interfere even once, and he didn't complain that I spent next to no time in his restaurants over the weekend. He did fret a little about how hard I was working, but seemed to understand that I was enjoying it.

Saffron took to Kegan's condo like he'd lived there all his life, and every night when I came in the two of them were curled up together on the love seat awaiting my arrival. My two adorable boys. We kept the cat out of the bedroom, since he wasn't remotely abiding by the no-shedding promise Kegan insisted he'd made, but I spent three nights in a row in there with Kegan and I loved it. We'd spent the night together a few times since Niagara but never night after night like this. We had breakfast together each morning before I rushed off to see Tess, and drifting into sleep in his arms was bliss. Despite all the work I was doing, the weekend felt more like a vacation.

By Monday mid-morning we had everything ready for the wedding. Kegan suggested I take the rest of the day off to relax before the festivities, but I reminded him of the interviews.

"I can do them for you."

I shook my head. "It's my job to find the right person."

"I know, but you could use a break."

When I still refused, he said, "Well, what if I sit in? You can run the interviews but I'll be able to give you my perspective afterward."

I wasn't sure, since he might well steamroller me, but I decided that two heads were indeed better than one, especially one filled with wedding thoughts, although I did add, "I want to be in charge."

He kissed me. "No question."

That was in fact how it went down: Kegan sat next to me in the office as I interviewed the six people who'd seemed like the best of the applicants. He introduced himself and me but then let me take over and run each interview.

By the fourth interview, I was feeling frustrated, and by the sixth I barely managed to wait until the candidate had left before erupting.

"They're so clueless! What rock are these people crawling out from under?"

He shook his head. "One where they know nothing of kitchens, apparently. None of them is good enough."

"Not even close." I sighed. "I'll have to go through the applications again and find someone better. There must be someone."

"For sure. But not now. We need to get ready for the wedding."

We sat in a semi-circle in the candlelit Magma with Tess and Forrest and their officiant standing in front of us.

When I'd asked Tess what she was going to wear, she'd given me a dreamy smile and said, "We decided to go with what we wore the first time we went out for dinner. It wasn't supposed to be a date, but in hindsight..." With a laugh, she'd added, "We actually went to Steel. First time I met Kegan."

She'd told me her mother was horrified she'd be wearing a black dress to her own wedding, but the soft pink shawl she wore over her shoulders, a perfect match to the roses in her bouquet, brightened it up. It was her expression, though, that really made the outfit. I could barely look away from her. Her love for Forrest shone from her, and I knew she'd have married him any time, anywhere, in old dirty jeans if she had to.

Forrest looked much the same. He'd been touchingly nervous, and cute in a dark suit and deep blue shirt, while waiting with Magnus for Tess and her bridesmaids Jen and Pam to arrive, but when his bride walked into the dining room he'd lit up in a way that was hard for me to look at. Charles had never looked at me like that, like I was his whole world. Nobody had.

They moved through their vows, and Kegan held my hand resting on his knee, releasing me only when I needed to wipe my eyes as Forrest repeated, "I, Forrest, take you, Tess" with almost unbearable emotion in his voice. I reached for my purse beneath my chair, but Kegan held out a tissue from his pocket before I could get to it.

I turned to look at him with a watery smile, and he smiled back.

Then both our smiles faded and we held each other's gazes, and for the first time in my life I felt that unbreakable connection I could see between Tess and Forrest.

Kegan and I hadn't talked about our relationship's future, but we said a million words looking into each other's eyes in the seconds before Forrest said, "As long as we both shall live."

Without breaking our eye contact, Kegan wrapped his arm around me and drew me against his side, and the warmth and tenderness in his touch and his eyes swelled my heart until I couldn't hold back my tears any more.

He brushed one from my cheek, then tightened his arm around me and faced forward again to watch our friends get married.

I rested my head on his shoulder and dabbed at my eyes, overwhelmed by the sudden bond between us. Nothing had ever felt like that before, sacred and joyful and awe-inspiring, and I knew for certain that we were right for each other, felt the truth of it ringing through every part of me. We had to make it work somehow.

Kegan had told me Tess and Forrest's history, how he had lost a fiancée to a car accident before meeting Tess and how great they'd been for each other. They were so much stronger together than they could ever have been apart, and I now knew I wanted that for Kegan and me. I wanted us to be each other's best supporters, best friends, best everything.

Tess said her vows, making me cry even more, and I wasn't the only one unable to hold back tears. They were gorgeous together, and we all seemed to know we were in the presence of something real and important. When the officiant said, "I now pronounce you husband and wife," and Forrest took Tess's face in both hands and looked deep into her tear-filled eyes before moving in to give her a sweet and gentle kiss, nobody cheered like at most other weddings I'd been to. The moment felt too special for that.

We did cheer, though, when they raised their clasped hands into the air, grinning so hard their faces must have hurt, and from then on they were buried in hugs and congratulations until Forrest called for attention.

"Everyone needs to be introduced, okay? You're all here because you're our favorite people." He laughed and nudged an older man. "Or because you pay our salaries."

The man roared with laughter, and Forrest said, "You probably all know the Hogs' general manager, Filmore. I assume he has a first name but I don't know it."

As we all clapped, Filmore said, "Boss, to you," then slapped Forrest on the back.

The introductions continued, with Kegan and me at the end.

"This strange man, Kegan, is the owner of this gorgeous place, and Steel too." Forrest joined the others in clapping for him. I clapped so hard my hands hurt and Kegan winked at me.

"And the wonderful lady with him, who for some reason puts up with him," Tess said, giggling as she avoided a mock swing from Kegan, "is Mary, and she's the one who put together the amazing food we're about to eat."

I got a huge round of applause too, which made me blush. Kegan kept clapping after the others were done, until I caught his hands to make him quit. We grinned at each other, then I headed to the kitchen to supervise the last-second preparations while Kegan encouraged everyone to find their spot at one of the four tables.

There were no final preparations: Dorothy and two Steel staffers had been holding down the fort in my absence, and every last job was done to perfection. I looked around then said, "Well, clearly I'm not needed here so I'll just leave."

They all laughed. I had noticed, since Crystal's departure, that everyone was far more relaxed. I hadn't truly realized how much strain she was putting on the staff. Things would be better now that she was gone, and probably better for Kegan and me too.

Dorothy said, "Oh, come on, we need you. You did all the planning and lots of the prep work."

"We're a great team. Now you keep working while I go have fun."

They laughed again and I left. Kegan met me at the door and escorted me to our table. We were sitting with Pam and Magnus and Jen and her fiancé Don, both of whom I'd met at Steel's open house when they showed up later in the evening. Kegan had taken her aside there, and had told me afterwards he'd apologized for his behavior and she'd accepted it. I'd been so impressed and touched that he'd do that, and now I was especially glad because it meant there was no awkwardness between them. She was hilarious, and Don was a great straight man for her jokes.

Once the salads had been eaten and the main course was arriving, Tess and Forrest went around to each table to say hello and thank us for coming.

"Show me that ring." At Jen's command, Tess held out her left hand, now adorned with a sleek platinum band matching her emerald engagement ring. "Awesome. I love platinum."

"The emerald's lovely too," I said, and Tess tilted her hand so I could get a better look. "I love non-traditional engagement rings."

"Did you have one?"

I grimaced. "I wanted an opal, but he said you're not engaged without a diamond, so that's what I got." I'd left it, and the wedding band which was also totally not my style, behind when I walked out.

"Opals are stunning." Pam nudged Magnus. "Are you listening? I said they're stunning."

He chuckled. "I'll remember."

The rest of the wedding dinner went by in a flash of laughter and fun. Everyone was so clearly delighted for Tess and Forrest, and most people knew at least a few other people, so conversation was lively and entertaining, often spanning multiple tables. Eventually, though, Filmore said, "Well, some of us have to fly to New York tonight. Forrest, do not miss your plane tomorrow morning, got it? We need you tomorrow night."

"I'll be there," Forrest said, and they gave each other a rough hug.

Filmore gave Tess a much gentler one and said, "Sorry I can't give him more than a night off."

She laughed. "When you marry a hockey player you know what you're getting into. Besides, don't you remember how grouchy he gets when he can't play? I don't *want* him taking time off."

Filmore's departure began the party's breakup. I received tons of compliments on the food, which had in fact worked out beautifully, and Kegan went to the kitchen to supervise the staff so I could stay out front and receive those compliments.

Forrest and Tess were the last to leave, and Tess hugged me so hard I felt my ribs creaking. "Thank you so much. It was perfect."

I squeezed her tight. "I'm so glad. It was great working with you."

She released me then snapped her fingers at Forrest. "Hand it over."

He laughed, reaching into his pocket. "And it begins. No more niceness, huh?"

"I don't have to be nice to you any more, we're *married*," she said, then grinned at me and gave him a quick hug and kiss before taking the envelope he'd found in his pocket and handing it to me. "Thank you so much, Mary. I'm free all day Thursday if that works."

I blinked, confused, and she laughed. "Open the envelope once I'm gone. You'll get it."

Kegan came out from the kitchen. "Well, congrats. I hope it was everything you wanted."

She smiled up at him. "Couldn't have been better."

"Did you..." He trailed off and glanced at me.

She nodded and he smiled, confusing me further.

Forrest gave me a hug while Tess hugged Kegan, then exchanged a back-slapping one with Kegan while Tess hugged me again, then the newlyweds left holding hands.

I tore open the envelope to find a note from Tess thanking me again and offering a two-hour massage as further thanks. "You knew about this?" I said to Kegan.

He nodded. "She asked if you'd like it and I said I thought you would. Thursday was my idea, so you'd be relaxed before we went to Niagara Falls."

I hugged him. "You're a sweetheart."

He held me close, one hand tangling itself in my hair, which I'd left down for the occasion. His lips against the top of my head, he said, "Takes one to know one."

I laughed, remembering his discussion with Lola on that topic, and he squeezed me tighter then said, "Let's help clear up so we can all get out of here."

His cell phone rang as he finished the sentence. He checked the screen. "Steel." He answered. "Hey. No, it's fine. Calm down, Angie, and tell me what's wrong. What? Who said that?" He rolled his eyes at me. "Yeah, I'm not surprised. Hold on one second, okay?" He covered the phone. "It's that old guy with the ridiculous toupee who complains about everything. He made her cry."

"Jerk."

"I have to talk to her. I'll help clean up as soon as I can, okay?"

I smiled at him. "Of course."

He squeezed my shoulder and headed outside, grabbing his coat on the way. "Angie, it's okay. No, really. Listen, here's what you say..."

I helped the wait staff tidy the dining room and made sure the things we'd borrowed from Steel didn't get mixed into Magma's supplies, but I stayed out of the kitchen since I figured Dorothy would let me know if she needed help and it might be a good way to see if she could handle being promoted.

Once the cleanup was done and the staff began to leave, Dorothy came out of the kitchen and headed for me with a huge grin.

I smiled at her. "You look happy. Things went well in there without Crystal, I guess?"

She hugged me hard. "Thank you so much. I know it was at least partly your idea, and it's so sweet. I'll do my best, I promise."

"Of course you will, you always do," I said, bewildered. "At what?"

She stumbled back, her eyes huge. "He didn't... he said he would... that you..."

"That I what?"

Kegan returned as I spoke, and Dorothy shot him a panicked look. He rubbed his forehead. "I didn't have a chance to tell her, Dorothy."

"Tell me what?"

He turned to face me. "I decided to promote Dorothy instead of doing more interviews."

I stared at him, shocked to the core. "*You* decided?"

The last of the wait staff made for the door at light speed. Dorothy followed and I realized how she must be feeling. "Dorothy, wait. Promoting you is a good decision. I'm not upset about that part at all. It's just, it was supposed to be *my* decision, not his."

She ducked her head, all her happiness gone, and kept walking.

I went after her and gave her a hug. "Seriously, I am thrilled for you and I'd have made the same decision myself. You're great. I guess you're my sous-chef now, right?"

She smiled, still looking upset at what she'd accidentally done but with some of her joy returning. "Can't wait."

She left, and I stood staring at the door. What could I possibly say to Kegan?

"Mary."

I turned. "I can't believe this."

He grimaced. "It happened kind of fast. I flipped through the other applications and—"

"And you were not supposed to because I was going to do that. But carry on."

"I was trying to help."

Frustration filled me. "But I didn't *ask* for any help. And 'helping' and 'promoting someone without talking to me' are hardly the same thing. So, basically you checked the applications, figured the people were useless, and decided to promote Dorothy."

He dropped into a chair, and I realized he was probably even more tired than I was. He'd kept Steel going all weekend without me. I was too angry to want to sympathize, though, and I got even angrier when he said, "I did. And you said you'd do the same thing, so it's fine."

I took a seat across the table from him and shook my head. "It is not fine. You gave me the responsibility and then took it away. Without even telling me! What if I'd contacted some other people for interviews or something? I'd have looked like an idiot."

"That didn't happen, though. We made the same decision, we just didn't make it at the same time. We agree on the outcome, so what's the problem?"

When the angry words left his mouth, his expression made it clear he regretted them, but I didn't care. "The *problem* is that I've had enough of men pretending they care what I think. You're as bad as Charles, acting like you want to listen to me but then just doing whatever you want to do anyhow. So much for all that talk about wanting to change yourself."

My turn to regret words. I so hadn't needed to add the last sentence.

His face turned cold but his eyes blazed with rage, and he pushed back his chair and stalked toward the door.

My own fury battled with my sudden realization that if he left I might lose him forever, and it lost. I couldn't let that happen.

Just as I stood and took a step to go after him, he stopped, a few steps from leaving, and slowly turned to face me. "I do want to change. You're right, I shouldn't have promoted her." He swallowed hard. "I was wrong. I did mean to help but I should have known better. Mary, I apologize. Can you forgive me?"

His obvious sincerity and the pain on his face and in his eyes made me go to him with my arms open.

He drew me in and wrapped his arms firmly around me, and I wound mine around his waist and said, "I forgive you. I don't like what you did, but I do like you." I pressed my face to his chest. "I like you a lot. And I know you're trying to change. I should never have said that. I didn't even mean it. I'm so sorry."

He kissed my hair. "I said some stupid stuff myself, so I can't judge. And I like you too. A lot."

We held each other in silence for a long moment before he said, "The wedding was beautiful, wasn't it?"

I looked up at him, and my heart skipped a beat when our eyes met. That bone-deep connection again, like during the ceremony. "It was. I've never seen anything like it."

He stroked my cheek. "I haven't either."

Were we talking about the wedding or about what had happened between us?

He kissed me then, with amazing sweetness and tenderness, and we stood in the place we'd created together and bonded on a level I'd never imagined existed.

Chapter Twenty-Seven

I nearly cancelled my massage at least three times. I could barely find time to go to the bathroom with Magma opening in less than a week; taking an afternoon off for a massage seemed far too decadent.

Kegan persuaded me, though. "You need to relax, and Tess really wants to do it. You'd hurt her feelings if you said no."

I didn't want to do that, and I was definitely tense enough to need a massage what with Magma and Steel and the unsettledness of my relationship with Kegan. We hadn't discussed what had happened between us during the wedding, but I thought about it constantly and felt sure he did too. Our embraces and kisses felt different, somehow more emotional and more distant at once. Were we trying to protect ourselves from getting hurt if everything fell apart?

I knew that might well happen. I liked him so much, but I couldn't stand him sometimes. Even knowing how badly he was trying not to push me around didn't help much any more. But I couldn't imagine not being with him either.

In the end, I left my work and my issues, and my suitcase for the Niagara Falls trip, at Steel and headed out for the massage, and when I arrived at Tess and Forrest's apartment she gave me a huge hug. "I'm so glad you're letting me do this. I can't thank you enough for the wedding but at least this is something."

I laughed. "A massage from a pro hockey team's therapist? More than just something. And it's so sweet of you to do this on your time off."

She released me and grinned at me. "You planned my wedding on *your* time off. Besides, the odds are you're less hairy than the guys so that'll be a nice change."

I pretended to look worried that she was wrong and she giggled. "Shall we find out?"

I agreed, and she led me to a softly lit dusky blue room with a massage table, a low cabinet, and a plush-looking couch. "So, bathroom's across the hall if you need it. I'll of course let you out mid-massage if you want. Take off everything but your underwear and lie facedown on the table under the sheet. Any music preferences?"

A little surprised at her sudden switch to professional but glad she wasn't embarrassed about massaging me, I said, "Something soothing, I guess."

She pushed a few buttons on the stereo sitting atop the cabinet and mellow music combined with ocean sounds filled the room. Once she'd adjusted the volume, she said, "Get yourself settled and I'll be back in a few minutes. Holler if I take too long, okay?"

I nodded, and she left. I visited the bathroom then stripped and slid under the crisp white sheet, letting my face rest in the table's head hole. I closed my eyes and breathed a deep sigh. Even being here was relaxing. How great would a two-hour massage be?

Not great. Incredible. She first gave my entire back and my arms and legs a quick treatment then went over my body again focusing on the tensest areas, leaving me so relaxed.

She worked on a particular muscle knot for quite a while, leaving whenever it became too uncomfortable for me and then returning after I'd had a break, and laughed when I groaned at its eventual release. "Feels better?"

"So much. Thank you." I had no idea how long we'd been there but I felt I had to say, "It's been so amazing. If you have stuff you need to do, I'm fine to stop."

"But I'm not. And Wayne isn't either."

I lifted my head from the table. "He's here?"

"In the corner by the window. He loves watching massages."

I looked over and smiled at the adorable grey-and-white cat curled up in a Toronto Hogs pet bed, indeed studying the proceedings with interest. "He's so cute. Why'd you name him Wayne?"

She chuckled. "Forrest did. For Wayne Gretzky, of course."

I put my head down. "Oh, of course."

"We got him when I moved in here last year. Forrest loves him. I got the impression last week that Kegan likes your cat."

I laughed. When we'd shown up for our wedding-food discussion, Kegan had been laden with Saffron's orange fur and hadn't minded at all. "It's mutual. They're buddies."

"Nice." She paused, focusing on another tense spot in my back, then said, "I've known Kegan two years now. He's a good guy. A pain in the butt sometimes, but a good guy."

"So true. Both parts."

She laughed. "I know I've said this before, but he really has changed. Jen couldn't believe how he let you handle the wedding plans. So not his style before."

I sighed.

"What does that mean?"

I told her about Dorothy's promotion, ending with, "I know he's trying to change but it just infuriated me."

"Of course it did. Stupid of him. Did he apologize?"

I nodded against the table, and she said, "Well, good. That's an improvement too. With Jen, he used to walk away when he didn't like something. She was trying to explain that Don was a contractor and not a new boyfriend and he stomped off and left her standing there. I'm glad he's not doing that any more."

I remembered him making for the door after I accused him of being like Charles. The old him would have left me there. He'd started to leave me, but he hadn't. He'd changed that much, at least.

I remembered, too, that I'd been out of my chair and heading for him when he turned back and headed for me. Even furious with each other we'd been drawn together. Didn't that mean something?

I sighed again. "If we didn't work together it'd be so much easier. But I love my job and he can hardly quit owning the restaurants. He's so good at letting me run my life personally but at work he just can't stop second-guessing me. I know why he does it but I still hate it."

"No doubt." She worked my shoulder in silence for a while then said, "Want my opinion?"

"Of course. You know him better than I do."

She laughed, obviously surprised. "Not a chance. I bet you know things he hasn't told anyone else."

The reason he'd changed during the summer. His pain over how he'd treated his past girlfriends. How desperately he'd wanted to open Magma at the beginning and how he loved Steel so much he hadn't thought he could do it.

She was right. I lay silent, thinking about that.

"But I'll give you my opinion anyhow. You are damned good for him. He needs a strong woman, and I think he's finally ready for one."

I considered this. I didn't want to but I had to ask, "You think I'm strong?"

She rubbed my shoulder, more friendly than therapeutic. "Aren't you?"

"Yeah." I smiled into the table. "I guess I am."

"Hey, sleeping beauty. How're you doing?"

I stretched and smiled up at Kegan. "Amazing. I don't think I've ever been so relaxed." After Tess finished the massage she'd suggested I rest on the couch. I'd made it there before I fell asleep, but not by much. "What time is it?"

"About six."

I blinked, trying to wake myself up. "That late? I hope Tess didn't plan to go anywhere."

He smoothed my hair back. "She's been working on her art. Says she didn't mind a bit. But we should probably get going."

"I'll get dressed."

His fingers slipped beneath the sheet I'd wrapped myself with instead of bothering to put my clothes on, then slid back and forth across my collarbones. "I like this outfit."

I gave a little whimper, unable to hold it back, at the unexpected but delicious sensations, then pouted as he withdrew his hand. "If I wear it at the hotel, will you do that again?"

He kissed my forehead. "Sounds good."

He left, and I dressed and made my way out to the living room, where Tess and Kegan sat talking about Niagara Falls. They looked up at my arrival, and Tess said, "How do you feel?"

"Like a rag doll. Thank you so much, that was exactly what I needed."

She grinned. "I'm so glad. Have a great trip."

I hugged her, and Kegan did too, then we headed down to his car and were soon on the highway. My brain was awake now but my body was still so relaxed and peaceful, and I sat watching the roads go by and enjoying my lack of tension.

Kegan slipped a hand around the back of my neck. "You look great."

I laughed. "I was face-down on the table for two hours and then fell asleep. I bet I don't."

His thumb traced circles on my skin. "You do. Relaxed and happy. And gorgeous."

I turned my head and rubbed my cheek against his hand. "Thank you. For everything."

"I'm the one who should be thanking you. I... there's something work-related I want to tell you but maybe I should do it later."

"No, now's good. Or I'll be wondering what it was."

"True. Well, I've been thinking since the Crystal thing. Specifically, thinking about Isaac."

He took his hand from my neck to navigate a tight corner and I put my hand on his knee, not wanting to lose our contact. "What about him?"

He didn't answer until the road again lay straight before us. "The whole thing with me supposedly sending him a text message not to come in. He had to have known I'd check for evidence but he had none. The way Crystal looked right at me and insisted you hated her so you were lying... she sounded exactly the same when she suggested Isaac was on drugs."

"Hmm." It made sense, unfortunately. "Dorothy said that after Isaac got fired Crystal assumed she'd get his job. Maybe she was trying to get rid of him."

"I called Isaac this afternoon."

I turned in my seat to face him. "Really? Why?"

"I wanted to know what happened."

I studied his profile as he drove. He'd called the guy he'd fired to get the truth. "And?"

He sighed. "I believe him. Crystal set him up."

"She sent the messages?"

"I think so. I don't like having my phone ring when I'm out in the dining room so I usually leave it on my desk. Everyone knows that. At the tasting, I didn't have a real desk, but I was using a table in the storage room and I left it there. Isaac left his coat in there too, like everyone did, with his phone in the pocket."

I shook my head. "So she had the opportunity to erase the sent message from your phone. I guess she took the message off his phone too?"

"Seems like it. It was so *risky*, though. That's what gets me. If I'd caught her with my phone, if she hadn't been able to get Isaac's... it could have fallen apart at any time."

I tipped my head from side to side. "Isaac's was a risk, yeah, but yours would have been easy. She could have done it any time. Maybe when you were in the bathroom or something so she'd know she had a minute. It wouldn't take long. If she hadn't been able to erase Isaac's phone, she'd probably have suggested he faked the message."

"Yeah, I guess so. Still, it's incredible."

"Definitely." I was afraid to ask but had to know. "So, are you rehiring him?"

He shook his head. "I *was* going to talk to you to see if you wanted him back."

I gave his knee a squeeze, appreciating that he hadn't just offered Isaac a job.

"He's got a job he likes, though, and he told me before I could ask. But I did tell him I'll give him a glowing reference if he ever needs one. He *was* great. I wish I hadn't let Crystal screw things up."

I sighed. "I know. But you'd never have assumed she'd go that far, risk the tasting and her own job. At least she's gone now."

"True."

"I think it's amazing that you called him. Most people wouldn't bother. Even if they'd made a mistake, they'd figure it's over so why worry about it?"

"I worry."

"No kidding."

He put his hand over mine. "I didn't used to, but I do now. I run through people in my head, trying to see if I've gone back to my old ways with them. When I have, I do whatever I can to fix it. I should have realized Isaac had always been reliable and not immediately assumed the worst. With you away with the blood clot I was already tense and his 'misbehavior' was the last straw for me. It wasn't right, though."

I rubbed his wrist with my thumb. "You really do that? Think through people and see where you might have gone wrong?"

"Yup. It's part of my weekly planning now."

The question hung in the air, and eventually I had to ask it. "Do you do that with me?"

He raised my hand to his lips and kissed my knuckles. "With you it's daily. Sometimes a few times a day when I'm truly being a jerk."

My throat tightened and I squeezed his hand. "You're not a jerk."

"Maybe not, but I sure do a great imitation of one, don't I?" We chuckled, and he went on. "You're so great at what you do, you know. I watched you on the weekend putting that wedding together. You're brilliant with food. There is no reason for me to interfere, and I know

225

that but in the heat of the moment I keep losing touch with it. I *am* trying, though."

"I know you are," I said, touched by his words.

He kissed my hand again. "I really am." He sighed. "Because I don't think we can keep going like this for much longer. Do you?"

The idea of losing him hurt deep in my chest. "I don't know."

"Me either, but unless I can loosen up for more than a day at a time it doesn't look good."

I didn't answer, but I had to agree.

Chapter Twenty-Eight

Kegan had only booked one hotel room for us, after asking me if I minded which I thought was adorable given how many nights we'd spent together while preparing for the wedding. Our room was on a lower floor than last time so the view wasn't as spectacular, but being there with him, away from everything work-related, more than made up for the lack.

Once we'd checked in we had about twenty minutes to kill before dinner at the hotel's gorgeous restaurant, and we spent a good fifteen of them kissing and fooling around. We naturally considered canceling our reservation but he insisted I deserved a nice dinner out. Once I'd made him promise we would finish what we'd started later, which wasn't exactly difficult, he took his dinner clothes into the bathroom and left me the bedroom.

I hurried to put on my new black garter belt and stockings then cover them and the matching bra and panties with a dark green dress, not wanting him to see the lingerie before its time. I'd touched up my makeup and was struggling to fasten my silver chain behind my neck when Kegan emerged. I looked at him and laughed. "I like your shirt."

He tugged at his cuff, a near-perfect match to my dress's color. "We're twins."

"I hope not. You're not quite like a brother to me."

He chuckled and moved to stand behind me. "May I?"

I gave him the ends of the necklace, but to my surprise he took it away instead of doing up its clasp, so I turned to see why.

He set the chain on the bed and pulled a small gift-wrapped box from his pocket. "I got you something. Early Valentine's Day present."

"You didn't have to do that."

He brushed my hair back from my cheek. "Open it."

Part of my brain was shrieking, "An engagement ring!" but the rest realized that rings generally didn't come in rectangular boxes like this one. It did have a jewelry feel to it, though. I undid the paper and removed the box's lid, then stared at the contents.

"Do you like them?"

I couldn't take my eyes off them. The opal pendant and matching earrings contained every color imaginable, and as I tilted the box the colors moved and danced within the stones. "How could I not? They're gorgeous. I love opals."

"I know. May I? For real this time."

I handed him the box, then turned my back to him so he could secure the delicate silver chain around my neck. "You know? How?"

The pendant settled cool and solid against my skin. "You said it at the wedding."

I leaned against him, solid too but deliciously warm and strong. "I did? When?"

He closed his arms around me. "When Tess was showing her rings."

I turned in his embrace and looked up into his eyes. "You remembered, just from that?"

"I listen to you."

I slid my arms around his neck. "Yes, you do. Thank you so much. I love them. But I didn't bring anything for you."

"You brought yourself."

My heart melted, but I did have to say, "That's kind of cheesy."

"As a million pizzas," he agreed, grinning at me. "But I do mean it. Speaking of pizza, shall we go eat?"

We did, once I'd put on my new earrings, and the dinner was as lovely as our first one there had been. Maybe even better, since I wasn't worrying about whether to sleep with him. Our waitress complimented my jewelry, which gave Kegan the cutest proud look I'd ever seen, and we laughed and ate and watched the Falls and talked about everything and nothing. Except work. We didn't touch on that even once.

We made love after dinner, and fell asleep in each other's arms, then spent the next morning losing a few bucks at the casino and finally doing the sightseeing walk my need for a sweater had prevented on our first trip.

Kegan took pictures of the Falls, and me with the Falls, then asked a little old couple to take our picture together.

I figured he'd have to explain his digital camera to them, but when he handed it over the woman said, "Oh, we have the same one. Great minds think alike."

"That they do," Kegan said, his voice full of the same laughter I was trying to contain. "How about right here? With the Falls behind us?"

We stood against the black metal restraining fence and the woman took pictures while the man directed us. "Put your arms around her, son. Now maybe one holding hands. How about a kiss?"

Kegan gave me a light kiss.

"Not like that, boy, like you mean it!"

I laughed, but Kegan took my face in both hands and in seconds I'd nearly forgotten we had an audience. His mouth was sweet and strong on mine and the tenderness and emotion in his kiss brought tears to my eyes. So good. Everything about him was so good.

Nearly everything.

"That's better," the man said, his voice full of satisfaction, and Kegan and I burst out laughing and broke apart.

"I took lots of pictures." The woman held out the camera. "I hope everything turns out."

Kegan took the camera in one hand and my hand in the other. "Thank you. Me too."

Chapter Twenty-Nine

Dorothy called me as we drove back to Toronto to inform me that the tiny cinnamon hearts I'd wanted for Valentine's Day were back-ordered. When that sparked a fifteen minute disagreement between me and Kegan over what I should use instead, I knew things were *not* turning out, and the conflict between us only got worse from there.

I'd hoped the brand-new Magma would be popular on Valentine's Day. I hadn't expected to be entirely booked up and still have people calling for reservations. Steel was booked solid too, and while Kegan and I were delighted it did mean we were insanely busy leading up to the big day.

After agonizing over where he should work on Valentine's Day, Kegan had eventually decided that he needed to be at Steel. "I don't recognize quite a few of the names on the reservation list, so I should meet those people and make sure they want to come back. I know you'll do a great job at Magma, and then we can hit the hotel afterward and talk about it."

He'd decided to book us a room at a hotel between the two restaurants for Valentine's Day and Magma's opening night so we wouldn't have to waste time commuting. "Okay, Kegan. Will do."

But we didn't.

He sent his first "did you remember to think about" text message less than fifteen minutes after I reached Magma the morning of the fourteenth, and by noon I'd received so many that I had to phone him.

"Seriously, back off. I can do this."

"I know. I just wanted to remind you of things without interrupting you with constant phone calls."

"The constant messages are no better, and I don't need reminders. Please. Quit it."

He said he would, but the peace lasted barely half an hour. His first few messages included an apology for bothering me but then he stopped adding that and just fired messages at me every few minutes.

I'd have turned the phone off, but Tanisha had decided that her and Mildred's "we're single so let's have a great Valentine's Day together" event was the right time to tell her mother she was gay, and that some of her fellow students knew and were being hard on her so she couldn't keep studying at her current school.

I wasn't at all sure about this, especially with the bullying aspect that seemed far too elementary-school, but Tanisha was doing it anyhow. She'd tell Mildred at some point that day, whenever the time felt right, and I didn't want to miss the message she'd promised to send when the deed was done. I did mute the phone, though, before the beeping of Kegan's useless messages drove me insane.

Once the first patrons arrived at six o'clock, I didn't have much time to check messages anyhow, although I did glance through them occasionally to make sure I hadn't missed anything important. I spent some time in the kitchen but mostly I stayed in the dining room to greet people and see how both the food and Magma itself were being received. Kegan would ordinarily have handled the patron contact, and would certainly be doing it tomorrow when we had our official opening, but that day I was the public face of Magma.

As I chatted with guests and accepted their compliments on the food and décor, I understood for the first time exactly how tightly Kegan was bonded to Steel. He'd been involved in every last tile and piece of hardwood and he loved them all, and I felt the same way about Magma. The place was my dream come to life, even more than it was his, and I adored it.

If only he'd have left me alone. Though I didn't answer the messages right away, and didn't bother at all when he repeated stuff he'd said earlier, fury flashed through me each time the phone vibrated in my pocket. Yet another sign he wasn't sure I could handle my job.

I handled it beautifully, me and the kitchen staff and the wait staff. Dorothy was taking care of Steel's kitchen, and Kegan and I had agreed she should keep most of our pre-existing staff so she wouldn't have to train new people so soon in her new job, so I was working with nearly all new staff but it was still wonderful.

At about eight that night, I'd settled into my office chair to grab a quick bite when Dave, who I'd brought with me to Magma because I wanted to keep an eye on him, came in with his phone in his hand and an awkward smile on his face. "Can I talk to you?"

I pushed my plate aside. "Of course."

"I have a message for you."

He flipped the phone around so I could see it.

Get Mary to answer her messages.

Oh, for the love of... "Thanks, Dave," I said. "Ignore him. Geez, he's a nightmare today."

"Why doesn't he just leave you be? He should know you can handle the place. You're doing a great job. Both here and with Steel."

I smiled, knowing he was trying to apologize for allying himself with Crystal. "Thank you." My phone buzzed and I rolled my eyes. "Could you tell him?"

He laughed. "He knows, I'm sure. He's just obsessive."

"Gee, you think?"

Dave went back to work and I checked the message, which turned out to be from Tanisha instead of Kegan.

Told Mom. She walked out. But she came back 5 minutes later with candy. Says she's proud of me. We're on the other school's website now. Hope all's well there!

I wrote back, telling her I was proud of her too and that everything was great. At the end, I added, "If you see Kegan, take his phone and break it. He's nuts."

An hour or so and seven more text messages from Kegan later, one of the waiters came into the kitchen and took me aside. "A guy's been here for nearly two hours. He keeps ordering more drinks and stuff, but it's weird and I thought you should know."

I frowned. "Thanks. That *is* weird. He's here alone?"

"Yup. Saw him on the phone a few times but he stopped talking whenever I came over."

I went out, trying to look nonchalant, and quickly spotted the man in question. "Good evening, sir. How are you enjoying Magma?"

He looked up. "It's great, thank you. You must be Mary."

I blinked. "I am. And you are?"

He beckoned me closer and said softly, "I'm working for Kegan."

I stared at him. "I don't understand."

"You'll have to talk to him about it. I'll be in here about another half an hour and then I'll patrol outside until you close."

"He hired you to watch the place? He didn't tell me anything." How could he leave me in the dark like that? Make me look like a fool?

"And I can't either. Sorry. Talk to him."

"I will," I managed through my fury and frustration, "and I'll tell your waiter it's okay."

"Thanks. Oh, and great food. You're an amazing chef. I've eaten at a lot of restaurants for work and this is by far the best. Might bring my wife next weekend." He smiled. "Have to make up for being out tonight."

"Thank you." I forced a fake smile and walked away before I exploded.

`Why did you hire security and not tell me?`

I paced the office, too angry and uptight to talk to anyone, until he wrote back.

`You figured it out, good job. I was worried Crystal might do something, so I hired him. I didn't want to bother you with it.`

But bothering me with a million ridiculous text messages, no problem there.

I slumped into my chair and rubbed my neck, trying to remember how Tess had massaged away my tension. I couldn't come close to matching what she'd done, though, and even she might not have been able to relax me at the moment.

All his talk about how smart and talented I was, and he didn't even trust me to know he'd brought in a security guard. Did he think I'd have blown the guy's cover or something? That was far more likely to happen when I didn't know what was going on.

So many messages and nothing I actually needed to know.

I got through the evening somehow, but when everything was cleaned up and I stood outside waiting for my taxi I thought of going to that hotel room and somehow not telling him off, and I just couldn't face yet another argument.

Once I was safely in my apartment I sent him a message.

`You've got the room to yourself. I'll see you tomorrow at Magma.`

It felt cold, but I couldn't find it in me to say anything else.

Chapter Thirty

I'd thought it might be better having Kegan at Magma with me the next day instead of just his aggravating text message presence, since he'd be able to see that everything was running smoothly. I was wrong. He couldn't be muted like I'd turned my phone silent, and he simply could not stop himself interfering.

The kitchen staff, who'd worked together so well the night before, were constantly confused as Kegan's instructions conflicted with mine. He didn't change anything major, but he fiddled with everything, from what tasks were done at which station ("It'll be more efficient like this") even though they were comfortable and fast the way they were working to how to swirl caramel over my chai ice cream ("Clockwise makes more sense"), and after a few hours I couldn't stand it any more. "I need to talk to you. Now."

He knew he'd screwed up. I could see it in his face. He'd also known it last night, when he'd responded to my "not going to the hotel" text message with "I understand. And I'm sorry", and he'd known it all the other times he'd interfered. The difference this time was that I didn't care to yet again hear him apologize and promise he'd do better. I'd had enough.

I didn't give him the chance: as the office door closed behind us I said, "Do you *want* me to quit?"

"Of course not." He didn't quite snap, but nearly.

"Well, it feels like it. You obviously think I'm useless, I haven't done a damned thing right all day, so maybe I should just leave you."

I'd meant to sound like I was considering quitting, but as the words came out I knew I meant them exactly as I'd said them. I couldn't be with him like this. When he treated me like a moron, I hated him. Our relationship and the work were tied together, and we wouldn't be able to succeed in the first while he supervised the second. Since he'd made it abundantly clear he'd never give up control of either restaurant...

He stood looking at me, his face solemn, and didn't speak.

"*Do* you think I'm useless?" I knew he didn't but I needed to hear it.

His eyes didn't leave mine as he shook his head. "Never have, never will."

"Then why can't you—"

"I don't know." He reached for me. "I *am* trying, and—"

I stepped back. "You know what? That's not enough any more. You keep telling me you're trying but nothing changes. I need more than words." My anger was gone, and I'd never felt more miserable. I wanted him *and* the career and I couldn't have them both. Not like this.

He nodded slowly, his jaw tight. "So are you leaving me, or the restaurants, or both?"

God, it was awful to hear it flat-out like that, especially said in such a calm, almost robotic, way. It could have sounded like he didn't care, but one look at his eyes told me that wasn't the case. He was holding his voice cool because neither of us could bear the emotions.

Was I leaving? If we both knew it wasn't working, was it time to call it quits? But with what? What did I keep and what did I give up?

In a rush, I knew I couldn't give up anything. Not yet. I cared about him and Magma far too much for that. "Neither," I said, and relief flooded me, feeling like that first sip of hot chocolate on a bitterly cold day. "I can't leave. But we have to... somehow..."

He put his hands on my shoulders and drew me toward him. I went willingly this time, and we clung to each other like we wouldn't survive otherwise. "I know." He kissed my hair and squeezed me even tighter. "We'll figure something out."

He didn't harass me or the staff for the rest of the afternoon. I almost missed it, though, because he was silent and withdrawn instead, not even able to muster up the whole of his usual charm while chatting with the patrons, and I knew he was searching for a way to make our relationship work.

And I was terribly afraid he wouldn't find one.

We survived the day, somehow. It was already clear that Magma was an amazing success, which did help. Every server came back into the kitchen with stories of how excited people were by the flavors and presentation. Kegan did too, whenever someone was especially complimentary, and I loved listening to the stories and hated the tension I could see in his face.

I hated, too, when Nora appeared at the kitchen door, with her work friend Jack, to tell me how gorgeous everything was. I didn't mind that, of course, and I was thrilled to see she and her "friend" were clearly more than friends now, since she deserved a good relationship after what she'd been through.

But when she gave me a hug and whispered, "I'm so glad you and Kegan got together. I've never seen him so happy," knowing how close we were to the end of that happiness hurt more than I could have imagined.

The only faintly bright spot in the evening was when a waitress told me Kegan needed me in the dining room and I went out to find Tess and Forrest beaming at me. I didn't look at Kegan, afraid I couldn't meet his eyes without crying.

"Just wanted to tell you everything's amazing, Mary." Tess jumped up and hugged me, and whispered into my ear, "Are you guys okay?"

My eyes filled with tears and I longed to drag her into my office and tell her everything. "Nope," I whispered back and squeezed her hard, fighting to control myself.

"I'm so proud of you," she said, then hugged me tighter and whispered, "Want to talk?"

I took a deep breath, pushing back the tears. "Yes. Please."

She patted me on the back and released me. "Hey, I didn't get a chance to see your office yet. I've seen the one at Steel but not here. Can I get a backstage tour?"

Forrest said, "Yeah, that'd be neat," but Tess said, "I need to talk to her about girl stuff. You know, *girl stuff*. So you're not invited."

He laughed. "Fine, then. I'll stay here and eat the rest of your dessert."

"You do that. Mary'll give me another one, right?"

I managed what felt like a fairly convincing smile. "For sure."

We walked away, and I didn't look back though I could feel Kegan watching me. Once we reached the office, I closed the door behind us and gave in to the tears I couldn't hold back any longer.

"Oh, Mary. He looked tense so I thought something might be wrong. Sit down and give me your hand."

I dropped into my desk chair, putting up my leg automatically, and Tess pulled over Kegan's chair and began massaging my hand. I cried for a few minutes, and she worked on my hand without speaking, and gradually her soothing touch calmed me enough that I could talk. "You're amazing at that."

She grinned. "Forrest spilled the beans and now the players all fake sore wrists just to get hand massages. But enough about those goofs. What's wrong?"

Through occasional bouts of additional tears I explained how Kegan was interfering and how much I hated it and how I couldn't see how we could work it out. When I finished, I said, "Well? What do you think?"

She switched to my other hand. "I think there has to be a way."

"Does there?"

She nodded. "You care about him, and he cares about you. There has to be something."

Her calm certainty helped, even though I couldn't see what would save Kegan and me. "But he won't give up the restaurants, and I love my job and don't want to quit, but I will shove a meat skewer into his stomach if he doesn't back off. But I don't think he *can* back off."

"Mental note, do not eat meat at Magma."

I had to laugh, but the tears rushed in again. "I so want it to work, Tess, seriously, but I can't see how." I wiped my eyes and sighed. "We're just at each other's throats all the time."

"That's what happens when you're passionate about things. And about people."

"Any way to be a bit *less* passionate?"

She shook her head. "You wouldn't be who you are then. Neither would he. There *is* a solution that won't leave you single or unemployed. You guys'll just have to find it."

"Let me know if you think of it."

She patted my hand. "I think it'll only work if you two come up with it. But if I get any brilliant ideas I'll pass them along. Now, you'd better get back to work, and I'd better get back out there before Forrest finishes my dessert and probably steals my after-dinner mint to boot."

Kegan and I stood side-by-side silently holding hands as the elevator whisked us up to our floor. We'd barely spoken for the rest of the night, but once the kitchen was clean and the dining room was reset for the next day he'd leaned in and said, "Stay at the hotel with me. Please," and I hadn't been able to refuse. I hadn't wanted to. Our time together might be nearing its end and I didn't want to miss a moment.

As our room's door closed behind us, he pulled me into his arms and held me tight.

I buried my face in his shoulder and tried not to cry. From the very first time I'd hugged him being with him had just felt right, and it still did. There had to be a way.

He kissed the top of my head, then worked his way down my face to my mouth. His kisses were different than they'd ever been, without their usual playfulness and full of a hunger that went far beyond the physical, and I kissed him back and wordlessly gave him all my emotion and pain and longing.

We kissed for a long time, our mouths and bodies pressed together, desperate for more, more connection, more bonding. If I could have somehow fused myself to him I would have, and I knew he felt the same way.

Eventually we undressed each other without a word, still kissing, knowing we needed this now more than ever. The air on my naked skin felt heavy, significant, and his every touch stirred both my body and heart almost beyond endurance.

He guided me to the bed, his mouth on mine and his hands splayed across my back, then released me so I could lie down while he reached into the bedside table drawer and retrieved a condom. I'd often helped him put them on, teasing and making a game of it, but tonight wasn't about games. He sheathed himself quickly and I pulled him atop me.

His first stroke into me was the most beautiful thing I'd ever experienced. He filled me completely and stayed deep inside, his forehead pressed against mine. We held still for a long moment, savoring how perfectly we fit together, then his mouth found mine and his hips began to move.

He'd never been into staying in one position for long, far too interested in variety, but now he held my face in both hands and kissed me and made slow sweet gorgeous love to me, and I moved with him and let sensations and emotions overpower me.

Along with those, something else was rising in me. I could almost hear a word. I felt it, sensed it, in his kisses, in the way he caressed my face, in the sadness in his eyes. But it wasn't until he groaned and buried himself in me, bringing me over the edge with him into a climax stronger and deeper and richer than I'd ever known before, and we clung together silently that I realized what he'd been saying the entire time.

One word. Goodbye.

Though he hadn't said it aloud, every cell of my body knew I was right. Tears rose like a tidal wave and I pressed my forehead to his shoulder and let them loose. I'd lost him. He'd made his choice. We were finished. I might still have a job, but I didn't have a lover any more.

And I did love him. I hadn't let myself realize it before, but now I knew, and it made me cry even harder. He was everything I'd ever wanted in a man and I loved him. And I'd lost him.

He eased out of me and rolled onto his back, drawing me with him, and I rested my head on his chest, as I had so many times before, and sobbed. I wanted to tell him I loved him, wanted to beg him to change his mind, but I didn't because he couldn't and nothing had ever hurt so much.

His hands smoothed my hair and my bare back, and we lay together without a word, the only sound in the room my crying.

Eventually it slowed, then stopped, but we still didn't speak. Nothing to say.

He held me close, his lips against my forehead and one hand stroking my hair, and though I tried to stay awake to savor this last time in his arms my exhaustion took over and I fell asleep in his embrace.

Chapter Thirty-One

When I woke the next morning, I knew I was alone even before I opened my eyes. I could feel it. He was gone.

I could so easily have dissolved into tears again, but I made myself get up and shower instead, though I had a moment of not wanting to remove his last fingerprints from my skin. Afterwards, I noticed a note on the carpet by my shoes.

We need to talk. Come see me when you feel ready.

I didn't think I'd ever feel ready, but I dressed and packed my overnight bag and left the room. I was halfway to Steel when I realized I hadn't checked at Magma to see if he was there. I knew, though, that he wouldn't be. He'd have gone to the place he felt safest.

When I walked into our office at Steel, he looked up. "Are you all right?"

Seeing him hurt so much. He looked exhausted and miserable, and for the first time since I'd known him he hadn't shaved, and I wanted to throw myself into his arms so badly I felt my muscles twitching with the effort to stay where I was. I couldn't hug him, though; we had issues to resolve. "I'm okay," I said, though I wasn't. "You?"

"About the same." He gestured to my desk. "Have a seat."

I shook my head. I felt better standing. Stronger, somehow.

"Okay." He looked into my eyes. "Last night, I decided our relationship was over."

"I know."

"I know you know. After you fell asleep, though, I realized I couldn't do it. I can't give you up. It's a cliché but you are truly the best thing that's ever happened to me."

My broken heart cracked even further and I swallowed to push back tears. "Same to you."

He sighed. "But we can't work together, can we?"

I shook my head.

"And I can't give up my career, and neither can you. I was up all night. Trying to find a way to make this work. But I can't. I think you'll have to."

I frowned. "How? And why is it up to me?"

"We can't go on like this, Mary. I want you, and I want full control of my restaurants, but I can't have both. I can't decide which I want more, which I'll resent less for making me lose the other. I need you to decide for me, for us."

I stared at him. "You want me to decide whether I lose my job or my boyfriend."

"I can't do it. So yes, I do. If you pick us, we'll find you another job. If you pick work, well, you and I will have to pull way back and be professional and nothing more."

Each choice was worse than the other. "And you'll go along with whatever I say?"

He nodded. "I'll hate it either way, I think, but yes."

I sighed. "Well, that's lots of incentive for me to make the decision. Whatever I do, you'll hate."

He rubbed his hand over his forehead. "I didn't mean it like that. I just... I love the restaurants, and..." His eyes met mine and I saw the pain in them, and the emotion. I knew before he said it, and my heart surged as he added, his voice low and rough, "And I love you."

"I love you too," I whispered.

His eyes softened, then he closed them. "God *damn* it. It should be so easy for me but I can't let go." He opened his eyes. "Look, you make the decision. Okay?"

Not remotely okay, and hearing the confusion and frustration in his voice made it even worse. We couldn't let this go much longer or we'd both be insane by the weekend. "Okay, I'll decide. I need time to think though. Could you and Dorothy take care of Magma and Steel for the day? I'll come back tomorrow."

Something flickered in his eyes, but it vanished before I could identify it. "You need that much time?"

I raised my chin, instantly furious though I didn't know why. "You can't make the decision at all. Can't I have a day to think?"

His face hardened. "Fine, if that's what you need. See you tomorrow." He grabbed a file at random from his desk and began flipping through it.

His dismissal was obvious, but I stood frozen, unable to believe he'd cut me off so completely. When he didn't look at me again, I turned and left.

Walking down the street in a haze of sadness and anger and confusion, I realized I needed to go somewhere quiet and peaceful to think. Whatever I decided would change my life, our lives, forever. I needed to listen to nobody but myself, for the first time ever.

Chapter Thirty-Two

The spa, while gorgeous and peaceful, is unfortunately not a miracle worker. Despite constantly worrying through my options, even during a eucalyptus body wrap that should have been so relaxing, by the time I wake up in the morning from my fitful sleep I still don't know.

I love Kegan, and now that I know he loves me too I can't see how I could give up on us. He's trying so hard to change himself, to be a better man, and he's made such progress since the summer. No, he's not perfect, and he does make me crazy sometimes, a lot of the time, but how could I leave him?

But I've wanted my career for so long and I love Magma more than I'd ever thought I could love a workplace, and the idea of losing it hurts too. Differently from how losing Kegan hurts, of course, but it still torments me. Would I rather cut off a hand or a foot?

I head down to the quirky but charming dining room and am soon eating delicious pancakes for breakfast. Halfway through, I remember making pancakes for Kegan when I stayed over because of the rainstorm, and my eyes fill with tears. Everything everywhere would remind me of him. How could I let him go? But—

"Can I get you anything else?"

I blink hard but the waitress obviously sees my sadness. "Oh, dear. Are you okay?"

I nod, then say, "If you had to pick between a man and a career, what would you do?"

She considers. "A good man?"

"The best."

"Good career?"

"Also the best."

She drums her fingers on my table. "That's tough. Can't have them both?"

I blink again. "We can't make it work."

More drumming, then she says, "I'd pick the career."

My heart sinks, but I suspect it would have reacted the same if she'd given the other answer. "Why?"

"There are always more men. And I think women need to be strong and stand on their own."

"Yeah. I do too."

She smiles at me. "Hope that helps a bit. Do you want more tea?"

I nod, and she fills my teapot with fresh hot water and leaves me and my teabag to stew in peace.

Stand on my own. That's what I wanted all the way along. That's why I left Charles, why I moved to Toronto where I knew nobody. I'd wanted to stand up for myself and run my life my way, and I still want that.

I have to pick the career.

I can hardly breathe through the pain in my heart but I make myself keep going. I have to. I will keep Magma. And Steel too. In time, surely Kegan and I will be able to work together. Our feelings for each other will fade, disappear.

Even as I think it, I know it's not true. We love each other. How will that go away? I don't *want* it to go away. Not even for the career of my dreams. And there aren't always more men. At least not men like Kegan.

I *could* keep the career without keeping Magma. I would miss it, of course, miss it terribly, but I had a huge influence on its creation and I'd always know that. It would always be part of me and I'd always be part of it. I could work at another restaurant and be with Kegan.

Could I, though? Or would I wind up resenting him for taking Magma from me?

I know he'll have considered all these possibilities, but I can't find any new ones, and I go around and around as I finish my breakfast, not seeing a way out. The only thing that seems remotely possible is giving everything up. Leaving Kegan, leaving Magma, and starting again.

But then I'd have nothing at all.

On the mid-morning train back to Toronto, I make my first decision: I won't lose everything. I will have either Kegan or Magma.

I have to pick my career.

Don't I?

I have to go after what I want more than anything. Have to stand on my own two feet.

As I think that thought, think of my feet and standing on them, I feel the world lurch around me like I've been picked up and thrown somewhere different. Everything's changed.

I know.

It's not logic, it's not reason, it's not even emotion... but I thought of standing on my own two feet and now I know. What I want. What I need. What I'm meant to have.

I try to make my mind review my options again but it won't. I'm absolutely certain what I want, and though what I'll lose is agonizing I'll gain so much more.

I know what I want. And I can't wait until the train reaches Toronto so I can go get it.

Chapter Thirty-Three

Though I know what I want, my heart races as I walk into Steel. A few early lunches are underway but the place is still mostly empty, and I go straight to the back and find Kegan at his desk. He still hasn't shaved, and I wonder whether he's stayed there the whole night. Love fills me, so much it hurts. Hurts more than it already did.

He watches as I close the door and the blinds behind me, and when I turn back to face him he says, "Have you decided?"

I nod.

He folds his hands on his desk. "Let's hear it."

I lick my lips, trying to figure out how to say it. "Everyone says you have to stand on your own two feet. I've wanted to do that my whole life. My marriage ended because I couldn't do it with Charles. I need to do it now."

His hand moves toward a stack of papers on his desk. "I understand."

"I doubt it," I say, and his hand stops moving. "The thing is, part of standing on your own feet is deciding where to put them, and then putting them wherever you need them to be without worrying about what you're supposed to decide."

His hand returns to his lap. "I agree with that."

"I'm supposed to pick the career. But I love you. And I want to be with you."

I know I'm doing what I need to do. I've known it from that moment on the train, when I saw myself standing, on my own two feet, and kissing him at Niagara Falls while the cute old couple took our picture. With Kegan at my side I've stood taller and stronger than ever before, and I will not let that go. I want to be with him when we're as old as that couple. Still, it's unbelievably hard to say, "So I am resigning from Magma, and Steel. And I'll find another job and—"

"I don't want that."

And you think I do? "It's my decision to make. And I've made it."

His eyes search my face. "I was mad when you left yesterday, you know."

Why is he changing the subject? And isn't he at all glad I picked us? My heart sinks; did I do the wrong thing? "I know. I was too."

"Do you know why?"

I shake my head, lost.

"I wanted you to decide right there."

"But that's not—"

"I told myself I was mad because you wanted to think, because you didn't say goodbye, because of all sorts of stupid things. But about fifteen minutes after you left I realized I'd wanted you to throw the career aside and say you wanted to be with me. I know it's utterly unfair but that's what I wanted."

I nod slowly, remembering my own sudden confusing anger. "Now that you say it, I know I wanted you to do the same thing."

"I tried to call you but you had your phone off."

"Wanted to be left alone to think."

He gives me a wry smile. "I've spent a lot of time thinking too. And the first thing I thought was that you would pick Magma over me. I was sure of it. I'd pretty much driven you to it, not to mention I know how much you love it. So the rest of my thinking was about how I could keep you *and* the restaurants. And I decided I couldn't."

I don't understand where he's going with this, and I take a breath to ask why he's rehashing what we'd already established, but he plucks the first page from the stack of papers on his desk and hands it to me.

Seeking a restaurant manager for the newly opened Magma. You will have *no* control over the food, because we have an outstanding chef already, but will handle all decisions related to staffing and day-to-day operations. The owner won't be interfering at all: you will truly be in charge.

It goes on to describe the ideal candidate's characteristics and experience, but I don't care about those. I have to make sure I understand. "You're giving up Magma?"

"I can't lose you. I love you," he says, and delight spears through me, driving away my confusion. "I was expecting you to make all the sacrifices. Give me up or give up the career you've worked so hard to get, so I can keep all my control just like I always have. And then I'd have what I've always had: not nearly enough. So I'll keep Steel, and

I'll get another chef for it, and you can have Magma with the manager handling all the administration crap. And then we can have each other."

I know I should leap on this but I can't. "But... you'll give up Magma. That's not right."

He smiles, shaking his head, and the love in his eyes takes my breath away. "Oh, Mary. You were going to give them both up for me. I can certainly give one up for you. And I will. I will remove myself completely."

"Will you really?"

"Mostly."

I have to laugh. "You're so honest." Somehow that makes it easier to believe.

"I won't lie to you. There's no point anyhow, you know what I'm like."

I smile, and he says, "But I'm changing. I want you in on the interviews and this time I will not hire someone without your approval. Once we've found the right person, I will leave Magma up to the two of you. We'll get that done in a week or so and I'll just let you run Magma until it happens. I'll stay out of it."

"We'll find someone in a week?"

He gestures to the stack of papers, easily an inch high. "These are all faxed resumes. And some of them are spectacular. Yes, we'll find someone fast. I am highly motivated."

He posted the ad already. He's serious. I finally let myself accept it. The king of the control freaks has given up his newest castle for me. Happiness floods me. "Are you?"

He leaves his desk. "Highly," he says, his eyes dancing as he moves toward me. "One might even say passionately."

I shiver as his arms slide around my waist. "Might one?"

He pulls me close. "Definitely. Of course, we did say you should make the decision. So if you'd rather quit, we can go with that."

I lock my arms around his neck, grinning. "What would you do if I said yes?"

He looks deep into my eyes, not grinning back. "I'd find a new chef. If you like your solution better than mine, I'll go with it."

I search his face and don't see even a hint of doubt. He means it. Despite the job posting he's already made, despite knowing I'd certainly end up regretting my choice, he'd go with my decision purely because it was my decision. Sweet mercy, I love this man. "No, I like yours. Trust me. I love yours. But do you really think it will work?"

He kisses the top of my head. "I will stay absent from Magma and very much present with you, and it *will* work. We will make it work. Let's face it, we'll probably still fight every so often, but I'll make sure it's rare and I promise to make it up to you every time." His arms tighten around me. "I love you."

I bury my face in his chest and squeeze him hard. "I love you too."

We hold each other in sweet silence for a long beautiful moment, then he says, "So, how late are you working tonight?"

His tone makes it clear what he's suggesting, and I laugh. "Apparently I don't have a boss any more. Maybe I won't even go in."

"Yeah, right. How late?"

"I was thinking eleven."

He tips my face up and kisses me with passion and love and joy. My heart overflowing, I kiss him back. When we break apart, he says, "Want to make it ten?" just as I say, "Maybe ten."

We laugh, and he says, 'Great minds think alike," and pulls me in to kiss me again.

Thank you.

I so appreciate your reading "Stir Until Thoroughly Confused", and I hope you enjoyed it. I would love to know what you thought, so feel free to visit my website at http://www.heatherwardell.com and send me a message. If you could post a review to your favorite book-related website as well, that would be terrific.

Also, if you would like to receive a free electronic copy of this book to go along with this paper copy, please email me at ebooks@heatherwardell.com and I'd be happy to send you a PDF file.

Turn the page to see a preview of my next book. Thanks again, and happy reading!

What's Coming Next?

My next book is currently untitled, but here's a short description and the first few pages. If you're not on my mailing list already, you can sign up at http://www.heatherwardell.com and I'll be sure to let you know when the book is available.

In this new book, twenty-eight-year-old Andrea has to rebuild her life and determine who she is after her boyfriend of fourteen years leaves her.

Chapter 1

I managed to get the apartment door open without spilling even a drop of the coffees I'd bought for Alex and me, and flush with success I called out, "Hey, babe, it's me. Come get your coffee." I couldn't help feeling disappointed that he wasn't already at the door to meet me. I'd called him from Starbucks to let him know I was on my way, and since I'd been away for two weeks I'd have expected a bit of enthusiasm for my return.

While I wasn't *expecting* this, I'd actually been thinking he might propose. We'd only talked a few times while I was away because he'd been busy with work and I'd been rushing around attending conference sessions and meeting other data analysts and promoting DataSource as a great place to work and an even better place to hire, but he'd seemed shy and a little strange on the phone and I'd thought maybe he'd changed his mind on his "no interest in getting married" stance. I hadn't expected it, but I'd hoped...

I certainly didn't expect the strange look on his face when he did appear at the door. "What's wrong?"

He shook his head. "Here, let me take those."

He relieved me of the tray, and I left my suitcases and briefcase in the hall and followed him to the living room, confused and worried.

"How was your flight?"

"Fine," I said, saving the stories of the guy who'd sat beside me after apparently rolling around in a vat of spoiled milk and the "fruit platter" snack which had turned out to be nothing but a slightly black banana to tell him later when he seemed more normal. "What's going on?"

Again he shook his head. "Just relax."

I could almost see the word "first" hanging in the air. Relax first, and then I'll tell you... what?

I'd been on the go since six that morning, with barely a relaxing moment in the fifteen hours since, so I did take a few deep breaths and relax back into the sofa. I'd never been able to rush Alex, not even when we were picking out his tux for junior prom, and I'd given up trying years ago. Whatever it was, he'd tell me when he was good and ready.

A few sips of my coffee revitalized me enough to let me take a good look around the living room. "Wow, you cleaned up. Thank you."

Instead of the cheerful "you noticed" I'd have expected, his face turned red and then pale.

I took another look around, wondering what had him so upset, and realized something. "You didn't just clean up. You got rid of a lot of stuff. Those shelves look..."

I'd been going to say they looked amazing, but on closer inspection I realized they were actually looking empty of anything that wasn't mine. Alex's collection of Stephen King novels, his Star Wars and Star Trek DVDs, even the picture frame with shots of him and his buddies on various camping trips... everything was gone.

He sighed. "I didn't want to tell you right away. I was going to let you rest first."

I stared at him. I'd known him for more than half my life and three weeks ago we'd celebrated my birthday and our "been dating half your life" anniversary on the same day. But now I felt like I didn't know him at all. I had no idea what he was going to tell me, but I felt sure it wouldn't be good.

He took a long drink of his coffee then set the cup down on the coffee table. My coffee table, from my parents' old place.

He picked up the cup again without speaking and I looked around at the other furniture, terrified of what I'd see. Sure enough, anything that could reasonably be considered 'mine' was still there, and all of his things were gone.

I turned back to him, to see him still sucking back his coffee as if his life depended on it, and I knew. I could barely breathe. I made myself say, "You're..." but couldn't get out the next word. He couldn't be. He and I had been together forever and we were staying together for another forever. That was the plan.

Apparently the plan had changed. He set his cup down on the table again, and stared down into it. "I have to leave."

No part of his voice or demeanor suggested a temporary departure, but I clung to that possibility anyhow. "For a little while? For work, or..."

He raised his face and looked at me, and his expression held something I'd never seen from him before. Pity. "Andrea. Forever."

I had a necklace in my jewelry box with those exact words engraved on it, his gift on my eighteenth birthday. He seemed to have forgotten. "But why?"

He looked at me without speaking.

I stared at him, at the face I'd seen nearly every day for fourteen years, and again felt like I didn't really know him. "Tell me," I said, in a voice that sounded nothing like mine.

He did.

Then he left.

And I didn't leave the apartment for the next three weeks.